THE LIFE OF MILLIE TORI CHILD

KATIE KYLE

For all who serve in the British Armed Forces, for their families and for my personal favourites:

Jack, Gracie, Max, Benjy, Simba & Bear

Preface

I wrote this book 7 years ago, during my last pregnancy, thinking life would never be the same again with the arrival of baby number 3 (and it hasn't been)! After completing the book, and after various rejections from agents, my lovely husband got it directly into the hands of a publisher, who asked if they could publish it. As I drank a turmeric latte in the top floor café of their flash London offices, discussing their vision for my novel, I was beyond excited, unable to believe it when they described me as an 'author'. I remember thinking that that moment alone made the many hours spent writing through the waves of morning sickness worthwhile, even if it eventually came to nothing. And, sadly for me, that's what happened. The latte was the closest I got. Covid, and maybe other factors that they did not disclose to me, led to a prolonged period of silence from the publisher, which was concluded with an apologetic rejection.

I was going to leave the book in a metaphorical drawer but I find myself, periodically, opening it to take a peek inside. After licking my wounds, encouraged by some dear lady friends to try again, I have decided to publish the book myself! My original audience, the people I was writing for in my mind's eye, were, and still are, the military wives I live amongst and our civilian friends, those remarkable creatures juggling more than perhaps they should be, their heavy loads challenging not only them but sometimes their marriages and relationships, their parenting and careers as they try to prevent any of their plates from falling to the ground.

As I have been reflecting on the options for my book, which discusses a period when British troops were in Afghanistan, life in that country has imploded for its people. For that reason, I will split any money raised by my book between The Red Cross Afghanistan Appeal, an organisation that has been working there for the past 30 years and which is now faced with trying to assist the estimated 18 million people in need of humanitarian help, and the RAF Benevolent Fund, which provides support to RAF veterans and serving personnel and their families.

Katie Kyle

October 2021

Prologue

Like many military children, I was conceived before I was planned. My father is an RAF pilot and I have sometimes wondered if this is true of all military operations. Don't get me wrong: I'm not saying the military fails to plan, just that the planning, in my short experience, sometimes happens after the event.

My parents had their baby-planning meeting whilst they were on holiday in the Lake District, not realising that my little cells were already dividing and multiplying. They had married eighteen months earlier and set up home together at an RAF station in Oxfordshire. Fresh from flying school, Dad had started his first real job as a helicopter pilot and Mum, a criminal solicitor, began to get acquainted with the locals at the police station and magistrates' court.

They had just scaled the Old Man of Coniston and were trying to navigate their way down a sheep track in gale force nine winds when Mum raised the subject of trying for a baby. Uncle Alex was there too. I expect he wished he wasn't but he suffers with vertigo and was stuck in the thick of it as Mum (his sister) and Dad (his school friend) each had him by the arm. Maybe he wished he hadn't agreed to rent a cottage with them for the week when Mum yelled over his head that she wanted to start a family and Dad advised her to quit her twenty-a-day- Marlborough Light habit first.

The holiday passed without anyone realising that I had snuck along for the ride. It was only weeks later, weary of Mum's endless complaints about weight gain and exhaustion, that I was discovered on the promptings of a colleague. After a day with the magistrates, she took her friends' advice, bought a kit and, whilst waiting for a leg wax, tried it out in the beauty salon loos. The announcement of my existence was then squealed into her mobile as she lay, legs akimbo, getting her bikini line done. With Mum still squealing, legs still akimbo, I made my entrance into the world six months later.

My arrival set the stop-clock going on the seven-week countdown to Dad's first deployment; it was then that motherhood and military life properly kicked in for my naïve, non-military Mum.

2007

Tuesday 21 August

I'm less than a day old and yet we have already been in trouble several times with the hospital staff. To start with, neither Mum nor I had a clue what we were supposed to do when we attempted the first breastfeed. Apparently, some babies shimmy half the length of the mother's body when they are placed on their belly, snuffle around for the bosom like pigs searching for truffles, then clamp onto the nipple and start suckling away. After having my cranium squeezed through Mum's pelvis, I was in no mood for that and Mum, who regarded pregnancy as her last opportunity for trashy magazines and early nights, was undoubtedly wishing she'd read a few more baby books as she unsuccessfully tried to get me to latch on.

The only person receiving any sustenance was Dad, who had spent the last twenty-four hours working his way through the contents of Mum's maternity bag, which was stuffed full of snacks to help keep up his strength. Although I have no point of reference, his greed is apparent even to me. When Mum was screaming on all fours with labour pains yesterday, demanding to be taken to the hospital, we were forced to wait whilst he busied himself warming part-baked baguettes to eat in the car.

As Dad sat on the end of the hospital bed, demolishing a cereal bar, a doctor rapped on the door.

'Time to sew you up,' she said.

Mum reached for the gas and air, her new best friend, sending herself back into another Entonox delirium. To be blunt, she showed us all up, kicking the doctor in the face, with her feet still in the stirrups, as the first stitch went in. Later on, it transpired that a jungle frieze painted around the room had, in some hallucinogenic fashion, merged into one with the hospital staff. Mum was under the impression that her own knees were the grasses of the savannah, and that the doctor was a safari hunter, with an uncontrollable giraffe, who kept appearing through the foliage to bite her. We were fast earning a reputation as the awkward ones.

All patched up, Mum was ordered to get a shower.

'No, I don't want one,' she said. 'My legs are like jelly.'

'You need to have a wash, dear,' urged the midwife. 'Having a baby is a messy business.'

As she shuffled off the bed, Mum didn't look as though she cared. Two steps later, she was a crumpled heap on the floor. An alarm started wailing overhead, signalling pandemonium as doctors and nurses piled into the room, with somebody else's aunty bringing up the rear.

'Mrs Child! Mrs Child!' roared the doctor/safari hunter, straddling Mum, their faces pressed up against one another. She appeared to be dead so I was partly relieved, only partly mortified, when she hit the doctor.

'Call off your giraffes, she said, her eyes still closed. 'I'm not having a shower.'

Much later, whilst giving Mum a flannel wash in her hospital bed, a new midwife explained that she'd suffered a major blood loss during the labour, which no one had calculated due to a handover between staff. Mum ended up on an observation ward, drifting in and out of consciousness, just alert enough to acknowledge the trio of grandparents who had come to meet me. Mum's father, an old school doctor, is happy to be known as Grandad but the grandmas are refusing to be called anything that might give away their identities as people with a grandchild.

To be fair, Bunny (that's Dad's mother) and Moomin (Mum's mother) are not your typical grandmas. Bunny is an actress whose waist-length, flame-red hair and colourful language defy the usual grandparent stereotypes. Moomin is a psychotherapist who tears around London in a Ferrari when she's not listening to other people's problems, flitting between Bond Street shopping trips and Mayfair parties.

It's strange to think that the combined DNA of this eclectic bunch has been woven together to make me.

Friday 24 August

These first few days in the hospital have not all been plain sailing. Along with the joy, there has been a certain amount of trauma, felt by us girls at least. Mum wasn't allowed to leave hospital in the usual time frame because we couldn't get the hang of the breastfeeding. Instead of using Dad's paternity leave to nest at home, we spend our days without him in a room Mum calls the Cowshed (not that fancy spa in Somerset frequented by A-list yummy mummies but a hospital pump room for lactating women). She pushes me there in my cot and straps herself up to an industrial-sized breast pump. After a while, during which time an actual cow might produce enough milk for a whole county, the net yield, at best, is a few drops of colostrum. She then transfers this precious elixir, painstakingly slowly, into a plastic syringe before easing it into my mouth, whereupon I regurgitate it.

'Never mind, lovely, just try it again,' the midwives encourage. Mum often cries at this point.

We are now on an open ward. I see Mum jealously eyeing up the other mums and babies sleeping soundly around us as she wheels me back to our corner of the room. Hungry, I proceed to wake them all up until the whole room is wailing, including Mum.

Last night, as we made our way back from the pump room, Mum's favourite midwife sneaked over with a carton of formula like someone smuggling non-organic carrot sticks into an NCT kids' party. She is one of the older midwives, a comfortable woman who has delivered over 1,000 babies. Her name is Millie.

'Don't tell anyone,' she whispered, returning with a bottle. 'I'm not allowed to give this out to breastfeeding mums but breastfeeding mums also need a rest. I'll feed her and you get some sleep.'

Mum and Dad named me 'Millie' today.

No one could ever work out why I didn't want to feed. The answer was simple. Tongue-tie but no one checked it so no one knew. Plus, we millennial babies are a discerning crowd. We want Heston, not Heinz. Organic rice cakes, not rusks. I wasn't interested in tiring myself out rooting around for colostrum and so we watched as other new mums arrived on the ward, got smiling all-clears at their paediatrician check and left with their new-borns, ready for their first foray into the big wide world, whilst we trundled back to the pump room.

Saturday 25 August

Around day five, when one of the midwives was recommending another trip to the Cowshed, Mum started sobbing and seemed unable to stop. 'I just want to go home,' she said, dabbing at her eyes with a nappy.

The midwives wouldn't hear of it because of the ongoing breastfeeding problem. They didn't know Mum's hospital bedside cabinet was chock-a-block with cartons of formula smuggled in by Dad.

'I've read about post-natal depression,' Dad hissed at the midwife. It was an unsuccessful attempt at discretion as the other new mums in our hospital bay, ears already cocked towards us, now visibly leaned into catch the conversation, all the while feeding their babies as easy as breathing. Dad didn't let that stop him, persevering in his attempt to break Mum free. 'My wife's been on anti-depressants before. She needs to come home, we'll manage somehow.'

'You'll need to pass the car seat test first,' said the midwife, pursing her lips.

I don't know if the midwives have some arrangement with the police or DVLA but the next challenge was for Dad to prove to the hospital that he knew how to use the infant car seat, still in its cellophane by Mum's bed, which had been tripping people up ever since he abandoned it there when he came to take us home three days ago. Dad might be skilled at flying crewmen and soldiers around in the back of his helicopter but this particular test seemed beyond him. We nearly spent another night at the hospital because he didn't think he needed to listen to the instore car seat safety advice when he bought the thing at Mothercare.

After much swearing and reminiscing about his childhood, when it was fine to stuff the back of the car with as many children as would fit, without belts or car seats, he somehow rammed me in and off we went, stopping at Mothercare to get the most expensive breast pump they sell.

Sunday 26 August

I quite like my new home. It's a military quarter at the RAF station where Dad works. It's not pretty- quite dilapidated, really- and the furniture is fraying and mismatched (newlywed hand-me-downs mixed with military furniture on loan) but it's cosy.

I'm not so sure about Dannatt, the enormous black Labrador who lives here. He is less than a year old and, despite not having grown into his over-sized paws, he clearly regards himself as the top dog around here, as Mum and Dad's first-born. He looks seriously cross about my arrival, skulking in corners and squeezing himself between me and Mum, a canine who's not ready to be dethroned.

Neither Mum nor Dad knows how to handle his jealousy, sometimes fussing over him, at other times yelling at him to keep away from my Moses basket, then back-tracking.

'If you make her out to be too precious, you'll just put his nose out even more,' Mum warned.

As Dad rocked me to sleep on his lap in the nursing chair, one foot raised to keep Dannatt at a distance, Dannatt seemed to get the message, walking sulkily away, but then he reappeared behind us on his back legs, trying to climb over Dad's head, nearly capsizing us backwards.

Dannatt has the measure of Mum and Dad: devoted but clueless owners who only occasionally need heeding. We may actually get on.

Monday 27 August

This morning disaster struck. Whilst making the bed, which was partially wet with spattered milk and strewn with soggy muslins, Mum flicked the corner of the duvet at the bedside table where the award-winning, essential-for-everyday-life-with-a-non-breastfeeding-baby breast pump had been left. It's now broken and there is no way of feeding me.

Dannatt slunk downstairs as Mum's hysteria mounted. Dad's (to my mind, very reasonable) suggestion that we drive to Reading to buy a new one didn't go down well.

'It will take hours to get there,' she lamented (it's a twenty-minute drive away but it does, for some reason, take us at least half a day to exit the house). 'And she's due a feed any minute now.'

It didn't occur to anyone that Dad could have gone to Reading by himself. Instead, the long pack to get us out began. Despite my views on colostrum, even I started to feel like I was going to die of hunger on the journey there. With Mum's frequent outbursts and my more restrained cries, it wasn't a happy trip. Nor was the episode in the Mothercare loos once we'd bought the new pump, with Mum feverishly trying to produce milk in one corner of the room, Dad trying to do his 'skin-on-skin' thing with me in the other corner, whilst a queue of babies in need of a nappy change cried outside.

On the way home, I noticed tears leaking out from under Mum's sunglasses. She seemed to be crying but I'm not sure why. We had the pump. (In fact, we had two pumps. Dad insisted on buying a back-up after the trauma of this morning.)

'Are you ok?' Dad asked

'Yes, I'm fine.'

She didn't seem fine. Before long the tears were sobs and then the sobs became howls. Dad pulled the car over and smacked the steering wheel.

'What? What now?' His eyes were red and he looked as though he might start crying too.

'Today's our second wedding anniversary,' she said, blowing her nose into a baby wipe.

Dad was quiet for a moment. 'Yes, you're right,' he conceded.

'Two years and not even a card.'

'But you didn't get me anything either,' he said wearily.

'I did.'

'What did you get me?'

'I gave you a child,' she said.

I could tell he wasn't going to win this one.

'If we're going down this route, I got you two breast pumps,' he exploded.

Thankfully, Mum stopped crying then and we drove the rest of the way home in silence.

Tuesday 28 August

We got the first photos of me back from Boots today whilst we were buying more nipple cream for Mum. She has been upset ever since she saw as there are hardly any of her, mainly just ones of me and Dad, generally with me in a nappy and Dad stripped to the waist, doing the skin-on-skin thing that gets the midwives so excited and Mum so annoyed. She says it's unfair that he can take off his top without revealing four stomachs like those she has acquired since having me but that's precisely why no one took photos of her at the hospital- she said she didn't want any.

There was one photo of her, though. It was taken in the final stages of labour. I may be a novice when it comes to current beauty icons but even I could tell she wasn't going to be admired as one in that picture. It might make a useful image in a medical or science journal but Dad would have been wise not to have admitted posting it on Facebook the day after I was born.

I don't think Dannatt likes raised voices as he kept out of sight for the rest of the day.

Wednesday 29 August

Mum's stitches have become infected. She has spent the past three nights running baths in between my feeds.

'You need to go back to the midwives,' said Dad.

'I can't cope with anymore poking and prodding. Can you look?'

Dad has no medical knowledge whatsoever but he agreed to a full guided tour. Half an hour later, breaking all the usual time frames when it comes to leaving the house, we were back at the hospital, packed into a small room, Dad and I with front row seats as a group of midwives poked and prodded Mum.

This scenario is becoming all too familiar for us. They certainly don't show this side of things in the adverts for nappies and formula. I think there would be fewer unplanned pregnancies if they did.

Friday 31 August

More machine-related disaster today. The washing machine malfunctioned, which would have been bad enough if it had contained a normal cycle. But it didn't; it contained my 'real nappies'.

The first thing to point out about 'real nappies' is that their name is a total misnomer. In my opinion, real nappies are the plastic ones that you buy in the supermarket, which go to landfill and which environmentalists get upset about. Admittedly, mountains of nappies that can survive a nuclear attack aren't desirable but if you've had any experience of 'real nappies', you might think they are sometimes justifiable, at least if they are the biodegradable sort.

'Real nappies' are made of fleece or some other natural fabric. Once soiled, they get slung in a massive plastic bucket, the smell of which Mum tries to mask with lavender oil. When the bucket is full, she forces them into the washing machine, the same washing machine that will then wash our tea towels, underwear, face cloths etc. Hygiene isn't often mentioned in the blurb for 'real nappies'...

Mum is a recent convert, her enthusiasm underpinning her newfound desire to be a modern Earth Mother, changing the world one nappy at a time. I am not sure the real nappy rep at the antenatal classes where they first met regarded Mum as an authentic eco-warrior.

'Do they tumble dry?' Mum asked her as she deliberated over whether to buy a set.

'If you want to quadruple their carbon footprint, you can,' the real nappy lady patiently explained.

'I thought they were made of bamboo,' said Mum, 'I don't like the idea of my baby being wrapped in carbon. Is there less carbon in the hemp ones? Do they tumble dry?'

From the outset, Dad hated the fleece nappies that Mum ended up buying. She loved them, or she did until this morning, when one of them got wedged in the washing machine door. Within minutes, the kitchen floor looked like a scene from the sewers. Dad refused to help as she pulled on her wellies over her pyjamas and set to work with her mop. Dannatt chose that moment to appear in the kitchen, walking poo water through the rest of the house as he quickly worked out that it was wisest to be where Mum was not.

Saturday 1 September

Mum and Dad forgot that Moomin and Grandad were coming for lunch today. We'd had a particularly bad night, with Mum sitting by the power socket in my room for a lot of it, hooked up to both breast pumps, Dad by her side, hunched over me with a bottle. At 6am they took me into their bed, where we all crashed out until we were woken by the sound of brakes and Dannatt barking.

According to Dad, his mother-in-law's arrival is generally heralded by the sound of car brakes. He decided she's a pedal-to-metal-sort-of-a-woman after witnessing her beat his entire squadron at the RAF's family Go Karting event last year.

As Dad opened the front door, he couldn't restrain Dannatt, who launched himself at Moomin. Dannatt is not very polite when it comes to greetings, terrifying the postman and regularly giving people a bit of a cardiovascular workout as they try to cross our threshold, but this was an especially boisterous bit of guard-dogging. He sent Moomin flying backwards onto the porch, where she valiantly teetered in her stilettos, before collapsing into Grandad behind her.

The reason for Dannatt's excitement then became apparent. Moomin was carrying two dead pheasants.

'I killed them on the way here,' she explained.

'How?' asked Dad, whilst locking Dannatt in the downstairs loo to prevent further fatalities.

'With the car. Obviously, an accident. I know you're not supposed to pick up ones you've killed yourself but it seemed a shame to leave them. I'll help you pluck them. Save you buying dinner for a few nights.'

Dad was raised as a vegetarian by Bunny, who last ate meat in 1956. She used to waitress at Cranks in the late 60s in-between acting jobs. She's still mourning the fact Dad is now a carnivore after realising, on a survival course near Milton Keynes, whilst being shown how to skin a rabbit, that vegetarianism wasn't always going to be a viable option in the RAF. But even so, he's a half-hearted meat-eater and still gets upset about offal or any meat that looks too much like the animal from which it originated. He went to the bottom of the stairs and yelled for Mum to hurry up.

'I'm sorry- I forgot you were coming,' said Mum, appearing in her dressing gown. 'I haven't really got anything in apart from tins.'

'That's fine, sweetheart. We can eat my pheasants,' said Moomin, waving her dead fowl around as Dannatt made appalling sounds in the loo.

'Fancy a beer in the mess?' Dad asked Grandad. He seemed to have forgotten it was only 11 o'clock. Grandad replied by putting his jacket back on.

I'm sure new grandparents are supposed to bring bags of food shopping, cuddly toys, a helium balloon or two and offer to clean the house whilst the new parents take a nap. Instead, our menfolk headed for the bar and Moomin disappeared into the kitchen with her roadkill.

Mum picked up my Moses basket, in which I had been abandoned on top of the tumble drier (military quarters have sparse and random electricity points, forcing people to do things like house their laundry system in the hallway) and took me upstairs to get us dressed, leaving Dannatt still howling in the loo.

Her mobile started to ring in her dressing gown pocket as she tried to get me out of a baby gro with poppers down the back. Who designs a piece of clothing like that? Clearly, someone who has never had to remove a child from one.

'Yes,' said Mum into her handset as I did front crawl on my changing mat.

'That beast is making quite a racket down here,' said Moomin. 'Do you think he'd enjoy the pheasant carcasses? They might make him simmer down a bit.'

'I'm sure he would but he'll probably choke on the bones and I don't fancy a trip to the vets this morning. Shall we just have beans on toast?'

'No, no. I've already got the meat marinating in some milk and garlic. We had it like that last week at Claridges.'

'But we're out of milk.'

'I know but I found some UHT in your cupboard.'

'That's emergency formula.'

'Well, it is a type of emergency. Hungry men to feed. Anyway, don't worry about that. Hurry up and come down- I bought the baby a dress you're going to want to wear yourself it's so gorgeous, pure silk with lace trim.'

Tuesday 4 September

I met Amy today, a remarkable woman who weaned Mum off cigarettes before I was born. She is a therapist working for a council initiative that provides expectant mums with smoking cessation sessions in their own homes. Dad says Mum swapped one addiction for another, replacing cigarettes with nicotine lozenges, but at least this new addiction is a healthier one.

Amy tickled my cheek whilst Mum blew into the nicotine breathalyser. A little green light started to flash.

'That's great news,' Amy said. 'Good job. You've managed 5 smoke-free months. What we need to work on now is reducing the number of nicotine lozenges you have each day.'

Amy didn't seem to be aware that Mum was sucking on two at the time. I can tell Mum has no desire to give up the lozenges. I've seen her inhale on the spout of a cafetiere drained of coffee just to get that ashy flavour and stand in bus queues when we're not getting a bus just to catch a few wafts of someone else's second-hand smoke. Amy may not realise it yet but she's got her work cut out here.

Monday 3 September

'I don't think I'm making enough milk for Millie,' said Mum at breakfast.

'She's doing great,' said Dad, 'you're doing great. Don't give yourself something else to worry about.'

'But that's my most important role right now. It would be like you not being sure your helicopter had enough fuel. I'd be worried if you weren't worried about that.'

'OK, good point. But what makes you think you're not producing enough.'

'There's a woman on YouTube who can squirt hers across a room.'

Dad put down his smoothie. 'That's not a good thing.'

'But I can't do that.'

'Leaving aside the fact it's weird you even know that, you don't need to be able to do that unless you're planning to feed Millie from 10 feet away. What are you girls doing today?' he asked, seemingly trying to change the subject.

'I'm making lactation tea so we need to go to Waitrose this morning to buy galactogogues. I got a recipe off Mumsnet.'

'What?'

'It's just fenugreek, blessed thistle and nettles. Waitrose don't sell nettles-'

'You reckon?!'

'- so I will have to hunt for some on Dannatt's walk. I've invited my new friend, Charlotte, to come with us.'

'Lucky Charlotte. Who is she?'

'I met her at the church coffee morning. Anyway, you boil it all up and put it in a Thermos and sip on it throughout the day.'

'It sounds more dangerous than flying my helicopter without enough fuel,' said Dad, grabbing his lunchbox and kissing her on his way out.

After sourcing the herbs, we collected an unsuspecting Charlotte for our nettle walk. I don't think she wanted to be involved in harvesting the stingers but she was the one who ended up wearing the Marigolds whilst Mum shouted instructions at her from a friendly patch of grass.

'Pinch the leaves hard to avoid getting stung,' Mum shouted, too late.

Wednesday 5 September

The phone rang midmorning. It was Dad calling from work. 'What is this in my flask? It smells like a cesspit.'

Mum scanned the kitchen. 'You must have my Mother's Milk tea,' she said. 'I'll come and swap them over. I was wondering where I'd put it.'

Dad spent a lot of time in the bathroom this evening.

Thursday 6 September

Dannatt hasn't been getting much attention since I arrived so whilst no one was watching him this morning, he gnawed a corner off one of the kitchen units. As the units were installed circa 1970, and as they have long since gone out of production, Mum can't get a replacement.

'When we move out, they'll charge us a fortune for a new door.' Mum was on the phone to her sister, my Aunty Chloe.

Aunty Chloe is married to Uncle Mark, an Army helicopter pilot. It's no coincidence that Mum and Aunty Chloe are both married to military pilots. Dad and Uncle Mark went through flying school together. Having never done any matchmaking, either before or since, Dad was convinced Chloe and Mark were soulmates and set up them up on a double date, bringing Mum along to balance out the numbers. They all fell in love over dough balls in Pizza Express and ended up, less than a year later, having a joint wedding since half their guests were the same.

After flying school, they were posted to different stations- Dad remaining in the UK and Uncle Mark being sent to Germany, where he and Aunty Chloe still live.

'And I know,' fumed Mum, 'that they'll leave this half-eaten door on for the next family who move in after us.'

'They' are the Service Housing Improvement Team, a civilian company responsible for the upkeep and repair works for military accommodation. Aunty Chloe is a good person to vent to as she has her own experience of this organisation.

'You will,' said Aunty Chloe. 'I have inherited the last occupants iron burns.'

Mum doesn't seem to like the Service Housing Improvement Team. It's a bit of a mouthful so she and Aunty Chloe just call them S.H.I.T.

Saturday 8 September

'The lactation tea has made my sweat smell of maple syrup,' said Mum.

'I really did prefer the days when we didn't discuss the flavour of your sweat,' said Dad, pushing away his pancake.

'Well, anyway, it's irrelevant because it's not actually boosted my milk supply and it's supposed to work within 72 hours so I am going to try making some lactation cookies today. They're meant to taste quite nice.'

'I'll take your word for it'.

Dad was dispatched to buy the ingredients. He rang Mum from Tesco.

'None of the shop assistant have ever heard of Brewer's Yeast. All four of us have searched the baking aisle three times.'

'Try the garden centre.'

'This can't be normal,' Dad said as he rang off.

Sunday 9 September

I made my debut appearance at church today. Mum and Dad go to the station chapel run by the padre. It's just down the hill from us, right by the entrance to the camp. We arrived, mid-hymn, to find a small crowd of people gathered there. As we barged our way in, nosily and late, Mum using the pram as a battering ram on the stiff chapel door, everyone turned towards us. The singing trailed off, with just one tuneless woman on the front row continuing in her stoic efforts to create the volume of about 10 choirs, maybe to make up for the sparse congregation.

After an awkward pause, the padre lolloped down the central aisle towards us, trying not to trip on her gown.

'I didn't recognise you with a pram!' she said, hugging Mum.

The padre is called Claire. She looks about Mum's age. 'Do you want to introduce us to our newest member?' she asked gently. When Mum didn't respond, Dad lifted me out of the pram and smiled proudly.

'This is Millie,' he said.

Then everyone came over to smile, hug and congratulate us. Charlotte and her husband were there too and came and sat with us.

Mum was very quiet throughout the service.

'Why were you so unfriendly to everyone?' Dad asked as he pushed my pram back up the hill to our quarter.

Mum didn't reply.

He asked her again over lunch.

'Today's the last day of your paternity leave,' she said, 'which means it's only four weeks until you go to Iraq.'

Dad put his hand on hers. 'It's still a whole month away.'

Mum moved her hand. Then she got up from the table, even though she hadn't eaten anything.

Dinner time followed a similar pattern.

By the end of the day, if I had been Dad, I would quite happily have agreed to go to Iraq.

Monday 10 September

After waving Dad off to work this morning, Mum put me back in my Moses' basket for a nap. It was short-lived as my nappy leaked all over my sleeping bag and Babygro, meaning I needed a full change of clothes and new bedding. By the time she had me dry, I was hungry again. I started crying for milk, which made her leak all over her clean top so she had to dress herself again too, during which time Dannatt chewed one of her best jumpers.

By mid-afternoon, we were ready to do the weekly shop that we were supposed to do this morning. During these supermarket trips, Mum always seems content to park up the trolley and let fellow shoppers cluck over me. The problem is, she doesn't follow the usual etiquette for these exchanges. As far as I can tell, when people ask after a new baby, standard procedure is to give its age, maybe its weight, smile and look proud.

Mum doesn't do this. Instead, she applies the trolley brake, props herself up on its handlebar and launches into descriptions of her sore nipples, the pros and cons of stuffing your bra with cabbage leaves, the fears she has about Dad making it through his time in Iraq and what she will do if she becomes a single mum. Old ladies' faces undergo a strange metamorphosis, changing from cheery smiles to frozen stares, then finally expressions of alarm, accompanied by some hurried excuse about running out of time in the car park.

As they scuttle away, Mum sails on down the aisles, unaware of her inappropriate behaviour, seemingly comforted by offloading her problems on the general public, now more able to decide whether to get the value bananas or fair-trade ones (shopping for her is a constant moral struggle, sometimes taking hours, with her frugality pitched strongly against her conscience).

Thursday 13 September

Mum and Dad are starting to look like they're sleep-walking through life. They are both grey-faced and Mum's eyes often water but I can't always tell whether it's through tiredness or the baby blues. It's not entirely my fault. It was the chickens that finished them off this morning.

Mum bought the chickens as her first Christmas present to Dad as a way of distracting him from the fact that he really wanted a dog, which Mum really did not want. But they didn't distract him and her second Christmas present to him was Dannatt.

Mum has recently started encompassing the hens into her Earth Mother persona, even though she didn't seem to have any environmental motives when she acquired them.

'We have our own free-range chickens,' she tells people, looking very pleased with herself. They originally christened the hens 'Sage' and 'Onion' but Mum has renamed them 'Flora' and 'Fauna.'

Most mornings, Mum or Dad get up in the early hours to stop the chickens from squawking. There's usually a row about who should do this as they belong to Dad but were bought by Mum. Dad tends to lose the argument, disappearing outside with a watering can to douse them into silence. And they wonder why the hens have stopped laying.

Around 3am, Dad came back into the bedroom fuming. 'They've got to go,' he said, punching his pillow as he climbed back into bed.

'What have they done this time?' asked Mum, yawning as she tried to get me to latch on.

'They'd escaped and were sitting on next door's Weber. Goose yelled out of his window-'

'A goose yelled at you?' she asked, rubbing sleep from her eyes.

'Of course not! Not a goose. Goose our neighbour. Stuart.'

'Yes, that makes more sense,' said Mum.

'Goose says he'll BBQ the chickens the next time they do it.'

'You'd better clip their wings again tonight, then. Stop them getting over the hedge.'

'Look, I am a pilot, not a bloody vet. I am sick of being given these farm jobs to do when I come home in the evenings. As an aviator, and as a former vegetarian, grounding birds goes against most of my ethics.'

'So will watching the neighbours eat them.'

Dad didn't reply. He was already asleep or doing a good job of pretending to be anyway.

Saturday 15 September

Dad is becoming quite an accomplished chef, according to Dad anyway. Since my arrival, he's completely taken over in the kitchen as Mum is generally feeding me during their dinner time, no matter what time they decide to eat. Today, he bought himself some chef whites, which he swaggered about in as he tried to make julienne potatoes.

Mum says in their early days together, back when she used to visit Dad at flying school, his idea of cooking was to pour boiling water onto some pot noodles and open a bag of Wotsits. She had to teach him basic things like how to boil an egg after he ruined her microwave, and how to make to make cheese on toast when he got her toaster involved in his first attempt. From his fortnight's experience, he now offers tips from his new friends 'Michel' and 'Jamie'.

'Let's swap,' said Mum, passing me over. 'I'll cook the fish, you get Millie ready for bed.'

Dad hovered by the kitchen door, studying her technique.

'I wouldn't have the pan quite so hot,' he advised, 'It's starting to catch.'

Given the stress levels in our house at the minute, be they Iraq/ sleep/ nappy/ chicken/ dog-chewing related, this was probably unwise. It may account for why Dad slept in the spare room tonight.

Tuesday 18 September

Amy came to the house today, congratulating Mum on still being smoke-free, all smiley-smiley. But then we saw a new side to her. Stern Amy.

'You're going to need to drop down from twelve lozenges a day to eight over the next two weeks.'

Those lozenges are like a pacifier for Mum, soothing her through the trickiest parts of the day. I see her popping a couple into her mouth late afternoon, when we're both tired and Dad rings to say he'll be late back. Or when everyone's leaking milk and Dannatt's not been walked. Or when anyone mentions Iraq.

'Yes, I'll try,' Mum nodded. She should have told Amy that she's currently on twenty-four a day.

Friday 21 September

This afternoon, Mum pushed me in my pram to the other side of the camp to have coffee with another new mum called Laura. They met at the midwives' weigh-in service at the med centre, chatting about mastitis and episiotomies like long lost friends, causing various uniformed men to move seats.

It made a change to go to someone else's house as we don't often venture out unless we are goings to the shops or on a dog walk. Dad has lots of friends here- colleagues and people he was at flying school with- but Mum doesn't seem to have many. I think most of her local friends are people she worked with and they are still busy working.

'Hi, lovely to see you again.' Laura held the door open for us, balancing Nichola, her baby, across her shoulder. There was a trail of sick down Laura's back but neither of the mums noticed.

'It's really kind of you to invite us over,' said Mum. 'I still don't feel as though I know many of the wives yet. I worked right up until I had Millie.' '

'Me too. Coffee?' asked Laura, holding up a cafetiere.

Mum nodded, 'Lovely, thanks. I live off it now.'

'Me too! Nichola's not a sleeper.'

'Neither's Millie.'

Maybe a caffeine-insomnia connection they haven't yet noticed…

'What were you doing before you had Nichola?' asked Mum

'I was teaching at a school in Oxford. How about you?'

'I'm a solicitor. I was working in Oxford as well.'

'Long hours then?'

'Yes. Lots of weekends too so I didn't get to know many people here on the station. I still feel a bit out of the loop.'

Laura passed Mum her coffee.

'Me too- this whole baby thing makes you feel a bit housebound. Just walking the dog takes half a day.'

'Same for us! Maybe we could walk our dogs together.'

'I'd like that.' smiled Laura.

Laura also has a black Labrador. In fact, everyone in the RAF seems to have a black Labrador; perhaps they are issued with the uniform.

'What's your dog making of it all?' asked Laura.

'Dannatt's not happy. He's currently chewing everything in sight. It seems to have got worse in this awful build-up to Will's deployment. Is your dog the same?'

'No, Shadow's been quite good. Can't complain really. When does your husband go to Iraq?'

Mum looked as though she was mentally calculating it but she ticks the days off on the kitchen calendar every morning. She must know to within a few hours.

'In about two weeks. How about your husband?'

'Rob's squadron isn't on operations. I'm so lucky.'

'Oh, yes you are,' said Mum.

'Rob shouldn't be deployed anywhere for the next two years. We're just enjoying being a little family and bonding with Nichola.'

Mum started putting my muslins and play mat back in the changing bag.

'It must be hard for you when Millie's so little. You're amazing. Do you want another coffee? Get in another before the witching hour?'

'I ought to be getting back to make dinner,' said Mum.

'Ah, ok,' said Laura, looking a bit confused.

It seemed early for dinner.

Saturday 21 September

Mum is still worrying about her milk supply. She's been reading up on Mumsnet about the idea of a 'bed day', where mum and baby stay in bed all day long, breastfeeding as much as possible.

'I think it would be good to try it tomorrow when you're here to give me a hand,' Mum told Dad last night.

Dad wasn't won over by the plan.

'Why do you need a hand staying in bed?'

'I'll need food and drinks bringing to me. And I'll need you to change Millie for me. There'll be lots more wees and poos if this works.'

'I was hoping to go for a run.'

Dad loves running. He used to run for his school and college. There are photos around the house of Mum and Dad at 5km runs and the one that has pride of place in the downstairs loo is of Dad finishing the London marathon with Mum cheering him on.

'Wouldn't we all just like to carry on as we used to but some of us have bodies that now need to make milk, not skip off into the fields, all fancy-free.'

'Why don't you try? We could put Millie in the pram and take it in in turns to push her. It would be like the old days, when we used to go on our Saturday runs with Dannatt. Maybe we could do another race together- pick a 5 or 10km for us to aim towards. It would do you good to get out.'

'I have already told you what I have planned for today. Please could you support me and Millie in this. I think I'll need a bell,' she said, looking about her as though they keep them lying about. 'Never mind, just keep your mobile on when you're downstairs so I can ring you.'

Dad looked miserable all day.

'Has it worked?' he asked wearily at bedtime.

'Not yet, I think we need to do this again tomorrow.'

'But-'

'When you can produce milk from your mammaries, you can object,' she said, switching off the light.

Sunday 23 September

Whilst trying to burp me post-marathon feed, Dad rang Uncle Alex.

'Just need a bloke to talk to about something other than boobs and bottoms.'

'Isn't that what we're meant to talk about?'

'Non-lactating boobs and nappy-free bottoms.'

'Got you. Sounds grim.'

Dad and Uncle Alex were at school together- they've known each other since they both picked Spanish for GCSE. They had been hanging out for years, spending endless weekends and holidays together, never imagining they would one day end up as brothers-in-law.

'Where's Anna?' asked Uncle Alex.

'Upstairs having a 'bed day'?'

'What?'

'Don't ask. It's meant to be a way of increasing her milk supply. Anyway, gotta go, mate, she's ringing me on my mobile.'

'Sounds like you're the one being milked,' Uncle Alex laughed.

Monday 24 September

This afternoon, Mum decided we'd combine Dannatt's walk with a visit to the hangars to see Dad taking off in his helicopter. I felt excited and a bit apprehensive; I hadn't seen Dad fly before but I had seen him drive. Behind the wheel of a car, he gazes out of the windows, looking all around, sometimes craning his neck back to watch aeroplanes flying overhead. Perhaps it's alright to do that at three thousand feet. There are presumably fewer traffic lights and speed cameras up there.

All togged up, we left the house with me in a sling on Mum's front. We walked past the other houses in our road, all pretty much the same as ours, red brick, slightly shabby, some with strange porches that look as though they were knocked up one Friday afternoon with the contents of someone's skip.

This area of the station is known as the 'Married Patch'- the place where married people live in houses provided by the military. Mum says we pay next to nothing in rent so we can't complain (and yet she frequently does). Single people in the military usually live in a room within the Mess. Apparently, the promise of a house rather than communal accommodation can make marriage seem an attractive option for military folk but I can categorically say right now, aged four weeks, that the offer of one of these houses, with only S.H.I.T. on hand to help when it goes wrong, won't ever entice me to marry.

Anyway, I digress. On the way to the hangars, we stopped at the post office. Mum couldn't decide where to leave Dannatt. There was nothing to tie him to so she eventually settled on the free-standing metal sign, advertising photocopying, on the pavement outside.

Once inside, we queued behind other women clutching parcels similar to ours. Maybe they were also sending gifts to Iraq. Even though Dad hasn't left yet, Mum thought it would be a nice surprise for him to find a parcel when he arrives, which is why we were there a fortnight before he's due to leave.

As Mum was weighing her parcel, a loud crash cut through the post office chatter, followed by a whimper, the screech of brakes and shouting. The post office emptied out onto the pavement, with the postmaster scampering around the crush of customers to investigate.

In the middle of the road, wedged beneath a car, lay his metal photocopying sign, tangled up in our dog lead, with Dannatt straining against it, trying to chase after a pretty Labradoodle. Beside the car stood the Station Commander, the person in charge of the whole station, decked out in full RAF dress uniform, his medals jostling for space on his jacket. He looked seriously unimpressed.

Dannatt must have leapt across the road as the Station Commander was driving past. His position as Station Commander means he's obliged to have a military flag waving on the bonnet of his car. On a Jaguar or a Rolls, a ceremonial flag might not look amiss but a group captain's salary doesn't usually stretch to luxury cars. This particular Station Commander drives a custard yellow Nissan Micra.

The flag hung down, bent and misshapen. I wished at that moment that I wasn't strapped to Mum's front, forced to watch as she tried to disentangle Dannatt and simultaneously apologise to the postmaster and the Station Commander, both of whom watched her in silence, not moving.

Then the postmaster found his voice. 'What made you think you could attach a massive brute like that to my sign?' He looked incredulous. 'It's made of ALUMINIUM!'

I thought I saw smoke appearing from his ears but that might have been from the audience of customers still gathered on the pavement, holding their parcels, enjoying their first-row seats at this farce, now starting to light up as they watched. You'd have thought the postmaster had made the sign himself.

'My wife made that sign at her metalworking evening class.'

Mum mumbled something about Iraq, sleepless nights, and single motherhood. Dad hasn't even gone yet- I think she's playing that card a bit early- but the Station Commander's face softened. He helped Mum bring Dannatt under control and then he wrestled the sign from under his car. As metal ground unhappily against metal, we could have done with the postmaster's wife. The Station Commander placed the sign back outside the post office, where it promptly fell face forward. Its feet had taken the brunt.

'It's all bent out of shape,' the postmaster muttered into his phone as he examined it for scuff marks. 'You'll need to bring your metal nibbler home with you tonight.'

Mum hovered unhelpfully by the sign but there didn't seem anything constructive she could add so she walked over to the Station Commander.

'I could mend your flag for you- I have a sewing kit at home.'

It's one of those free ones you get in hotels. I have seen Mum try to sew on a button- I don't think her offer was likely to help.

'Don't worry. I have a spare,' he said. 'It's Will, isn't it, your husband? He's deploying soon.'

'Yes.'

'He's a great pilot. One of the best. Hang on to that.'

'Thank you,' said Mum, looking at the pavement. 'That's kind of you.'

The crowd dispersed and we headed for our next stop- the airfield. Delayed by the post office drama, we missed seeing Dad take off. We could hear and just about see two helicopters flying away into the distance. Mum waved frantically at them.

Over dinner, she told Dad we had been down to the airfield to watch him

'I know- we were practicing hovering,' he said. 'Didn't you hear us overhead when you were outside the post office.'

Mum went a bit red and laughed. Typical- the one time he was paying attention to the road in front!

Dad didn't laugh.

Wednesday 26 September

Dad's hardly ever around at the moment. There's now about a fortnight until he leaves for Iraq and there's lots to do before then, which is why he's started coming home so late. I say a fortnight but that's a bit of a guess. His flight hasn't been confirmed yet so no one actually knows when he's going. Mum is planning a trip to Germany to see Aunty Chloe after he leaves but she's waiting until Dad knows his dates before she makes her plans.

'I can predict that as soon as I arrange my flight, your dates will change,' she said tonight, hunched over the computer, ever the pessimist/realist. 'I don't want to book it and then find out you're delayed and we could have spent more time together but the prices keep going up.'

'Just do it. It may be another week before I know when I'm going,' he shouted through from the dining room, where he was eating his dinner alone after coming in way after my bath time.

Mum didn't reply. I could only see her back from my bouncy chair. She sat still for a long time, only moving to pop the occasional nicotine lozenge. I don't think she booked anything in the end.

Dannatt's chewing is getting worse. This week alone he's destroyed the camera cover, a real nappy (clean, thankfully), one of Mum's ballet pumps and another kitchen unit.

Saturday 29 September

Parenthood, especially when combined with an impending deployment, seems to demand an infinite stream of cheerless tasks. Todays was a trip to the shops today to buy things for Dad to take to Iraq. Mum said everything in a weird sing-song voice.

'Aren't we blessed with this weather; I love September sunshine.'

Dad didn't say anything. I didn't like it.

'Aren't we lucky to get a Parent and Child parking spot at the weekend. And I've got the exact change for the parking ticket.'

Dad remained quiet as Mum tucked me into the sling.

Inside the supermarket, we went straight to the toiletry aisle, where Dad quickly lobbed in bottles of moisturiser, deodorant sprays and facial scrub. Mum stood looking at lipsticks. We'd done the weekly shop a few days before so she had nothing to buy. I'm not really sure why we came- Dad could have done this by himself- but I was glad she'd stopped her running commentary about all the things we have to be grateful about.

As Dad chucked three tubs of designer hair wax into the trolley, Mum spun round and marched over to him.

'Why do you need all this? Aren't you going to a war zone?'

'Yes, but I still need to wash.'

'Are there any women on your flight?'

Dad looked up from the shower gels.

'Yes, obviously. This is the twenty-first century.'

Mum did an about turn and stomped out of the shop.

I didn't know where we were going but a few minutes later, we were outside the church bookshop at the far end of town. We went in. Mum chose two copies of the same Bible reading notes and went over to the till to pay.

'Did you mean to get two copies of the same notes, dear?' the cashier asked.

'Yes.'

Drops of water landed on my head.

'Would you like to come and sit down for a minute?'

The cashier led us through a door of beads to a small room with a kettle on a table and two chairs.

'Shall I make us a herbal tea if you're feeding little one?'

More wet on my head. The lady handed Mum a cup.

'It's very hot, mind your little one.'

Mum took me out of the sling and cuddled me. She looked a mess. A mix of snot and Maybelline Great lash. She needs to invest in something waterproof next time Dad deploys. The lady handed her a box of tissues. Mum blew her nose noisily, trying to explain the need for two sets of the same notes.

'You can pop in anytime, dear,' she said. 'Even if you don't want to buy something.'

When we got back to the car park, Dad was standing by the car (we had the key).

'I put the hair wax back. I'll have bad hair out there every day if that helps you cope with all this,' he said, putting his arm around us and kissing Mum. 'I got you this,' he said, handing Mum one of the lipsticks she had been looking at. A bright red lipstick I know she will never wear.

'I love you so much,' she smiled and kissed him back. 'We bought you these.'

From out of her bag, she produced three pots of hair wax.

Monday 1 October

I could record the following conversation and just play it every night as Dad walks through the door. It would save us all time.

'Do you know when you're leaving?'

'No.'

'When will you know?'

'I don't know.'

Tonight, Mum asked (foolishly, to my mind) if anyone has been tasked with planning this deployment.

'You don't understand the complexities of military planning. It's mildly more complicated than planning the weekly shop or the next baby weigh-in.'

I assume Dad was planning on sleeping in the spare room tonight.

Tuesday 2 October

Today was Mum's six-week check with the GP to see how she is getting on the birth. We had to go to the RAF medical centre where we often get me weighed. The doctor looked a bit like Grandad, with silvery hair and a big fat fountain pen in his top pocket. He held the door open as Mum struggled in, carrying me in my car seat.

First, he checked me over, calling me bonny and tickling my tummy.

Then he turned to Mum: 'How have you been feeling since the birth?' he asked.

There followed a long description along the lines of her supermarket conversations to the unsuspecting supermarket Grannies.

'And how are you doing emotionally?'

Mum took a shortcut here and started to cry.

The doctor took off his glasses and sat back in his chair.

'Is your husband around to help you at the moment?'

'Yes, he's good, very hands-on, but he's deploying soon. That's the problem. I don't know how I'm going to manage by myself.'

'OK, I want you to come back and see me next week to check how you're getting on.'

Mum nodded.

'Now, I'll need to examine you.'

A female nurse was summoned to act as chaperone. Mum undressed behind a curtain, which seemed pointless, given what happened next. As the doctor examined Mum, he asked about 'married relations.'

'We aren't having any- it's too painful.'

The doctor took another look. There was a long pause. 'Your anatomy's not quite as it ought to be,' he said, not making eye contact.

'Pardon?'

The doctor looked at the floor. 'I'll draw you a diagram once you're dressed.'

The doctor left the curtained area. With her tights only half on, Mum followed him out.

'What do you mean?' she asked.

The doctor showed her a picture he had just drawn. She lunged towards him, still trying to pull up her tights. On the third lunge, she managed a proper look. Then she stopped lunging and started screaming.

The doctor tried to calm her down. 'Don't worry, this can be corrected. At least it explains why you've been experiencing discomfort.'

'What can you do?'

'You'll need to see a specialist, who will probably need to operate.'

'So I am not a proper woman?'

The doctor tried to reassure her.

'I feel so humiliated.'

Mum sat down and the doctor tapped away at his computer, not saying anything. The nurse squeezed Mum's hand.

'How long will it take to see someone?' Mum asked.

'I'm doing the referral now. They'll probably offer you an appointment in a couple of months.' He coughed a little cough. 'Before you go we need to talk about your birth control options.'

Mum appeared to have had enough at this point.

'I think we can all agree that the only silver lining to this situation is that I don't need any.'

As she carried me over to the door, the nurse hurried after us. 'Your skirt's in your knickers, petal.'

Thursday 4 October

Just before lunch, the phone rang, waking me and Mum up. We'd had a bad night and I was in her bed. It was someone from the guard room, ringing to say that Amy was waiting there. Mum hadn't signed her in so they couldn't let her through the gates to come and see us. As we live behind the wire, within the confines of the RAF camp, all visits have to be pre-arranged. Mum must have forgotten to fill in the paperwork.

'Someone will be there shortly to sign her in,' she told the guard.

Then she rang Dad's mobile. At times like this, I imagine Dad must wish he didn't work within spitting distance of home.

His mobile went to his answer machine.

'Damn, he's doing that flying exercise in Wales today.'

As she lifted me off the bed, she saw that I was lying in a puddle. She carried me into my room, where she discovered I had no clean nappies left (they were half climbing out of the bucket). She grabbed a towel and tried to make a nappy using the hair clip she that was keeping her unwashed hair up. Downstairs, she put on one of Dad's coats over her pyjamas. On the way out, she nearly fell down the outside steps as she ran to the car, skidding in her slippers.

We zoomed off to the guard room and located Amy. She didn't acknowledge us.

'I'm so sorry about this, Amy.'

'Oh. It's you,' said Amy, sounding surprised.

'Yes, it's us,' said Mum, sounding puzzled. Maybe she didn't realise what she looked like.

Thankfully, she had remembered to bring her military ID, although she still had a job persuading the guard that the person in the photo was really her. Reluctantly, he gave Amy a visitor's pass. Then Amy followed us in her car back to our house.

On our return, as we got out of the car, we were greeted by the chickens, who were strutting up and down the pavement outside our house, pooing and clucking as if this had been their natural habitat for years. They had attracted a small audience of neighbours and children. Mum mustn't have shut the gate behind us.

She tried shooing the chickens back into the garden. After it became apparent that the chickens weren't going to co-operate, Amy revealed that she grew up on a farm.

'I'll get them back in for you,' she said, disappearing through the gate. Returning with some of their feed, she tempted them back into their run.

'Sorry about that,' said Mum, leading the way back towards the house.

'Excuse me, are you the occupier of this quarter?'

We couldn't locate the voice and then a uniformed man with a clipboard appeared from behind a bush.

Mum stared at his clipboard.

'I am an officer for the Service Housing Improvement Team,' he said

'S.H.I.T,' said Mum. She looked at him warily.

'Are these crazy chickens yours?' he asked.

'Ye-es.'

'Do you have written permission from the station to keep livestock in the garden?'

'Are you really here to check up on my pets?'

This led to an argument about whether chickens are technically livestock or pets.

'They're not livestock. I'm clearly not running a farm,' Mum said. 'Domestic chickens are an improvement on the evils of battery farming. Your organisation ought to embrace them, not harangue new mums for useless bits of paper.'

I realised at that point that she mustn't have the written permission.

'Not useless, an MOD requirement,' said the S.H.I.T. officer.

'Pah,' said Mum, rudely.

The man looked at Mum's muddy slippers.

'I genuinely don't know what's going on here,' he said, shaking his head. 'You in your nightwear at 11am, chicken whisperer in tow, inexplicably armed with a breathalyser, and this frankly bizarre menagerie of dog and fowl. I feel like I have slipped into some parallel universe but, as confused as I may be, what I do know is that YOU CANNOT KEEP FARM ANIMALS OR PETS IN A MILITARY QUARTER WITHOUT AUTHORISATION!'

Mum glared at him.

'So may I please see the relevant documentation authorising you to keep the chickens?' the man said.

'They actually belong to my husband and he's currently deployed,' said Mum, folding her arms over her pyjamas.

It was therefore the wrong time for Dad to come bounding round the side of the house in his flying suit, give her a big kiss and explain his helicopter had gone 'tits up' (a term recognised throughout the RAF as meaning 'broken'- some sort of reference to the aircraft being on its back).

'We didn't make it to Wales after all,' he said.

'I didn't know we were deploying our armed forces to the Welsh Valleys,' said the man, his lips curling as he made notes on his clipboard.

I don't think Mum was deliberately lying. 'Deployed' in Mum-speak basically covers everything that Dad does for work that means he is unavailable to help her. I think other mums probably have a better understanding of military jargon. Dets, dits, fairies, flunkies, redders, riggers, potato, potartoe, tomato, tomartoe. It's all Greek to her.

It turned out that the chickens were a complete red herring- the man was there to evaluate the house to see if it needed regrading and our rent readjusting. When Mum heard this, she became extremely vocal about her views on our bathroom arrangement, which she describes as 'medieval', whilst Amy, who was late for her next appointment, tried to get her to blow into her breathalysing machine.

Even I can see that the bathroom is ancient. There are exposed pipes all the way around the bathroom walls and a deep, yellowing bath, which takes nearly half an hour to fill, forcing Mum and Dad to wake up much earlier than they would like to in order to wash in the mornings. They have to share the bathwater as there is never enough water or time to run another. They sometimes talk about fitting a shower but they've been told they'll have to remove it when they leave as the property has to be returned to the exact S.H.I.T. condition as when they arrived, even if that means to an inferior state.

Mum didn't take it well when the clipboard man said he thought the house would go up a category, thereby triggering a rise in rent.

'You can send in your objections along with your chicken application,' he advised.

Friday 5 October

Dad came home from work last night with the news that his flight to Baghdad has now been confirmed.

'I leave on Tuesday,' he said.

'Definitely?'

'Yes.'

Armed with this information, Mum booked us a flight to Germany on Wednesday, at nearly twice the original cost due to the short notice, so that we can stay with Aunty Chloe once Dad has gone. Then she rang Charlotte to see if she wanted to walk Dannatt with us.

'I need to get off the camp for a bit- do you fancy coming?' Mum asked.

We collected Charlotte on the way and drove to a nearby woodland. The constant whirring of helicopters overhead made it a poor choice of location if Mum was hoping to forget the military. It's one of Mum and Dad's favourite walks. We come here most weekends and, even in my short lifetime, it's been the scene of both handholding and rows as the post-birth closeness has given way to the Iraq tensions. It wasn't the right place to come if Mum was after some escapism.

'I am so cross about him leaving us,' she said, throwing a ball for Dannatt, 'but when I get angry with him, I feel guilty as I know he's got to go.'

'I expect that's really normal,' said Charlotte.

'Do you think it's normal to be angry?'

'I can't fully imagine it yet but I've heard other wives say similar stuff.'

'When does Matt go?'

Matt, Charlotte's husband, is a crewman on the same squadron as Dad.

'Not for a couple of months yet. It's Matt's flight that's relieving Will's so he'll go shortly before Will comes back.'

They walked in silence for a bit.

'I'm just terrified Will won't make it back to us,' Mum blurted out. 'I know I shouldn't be morbid but I find it hard not to think about.'

Charlotte put her arm around Mum.

'I feel so scared,' she continued. 'It's just one big angry, frightened mess. And it's not like I'm being fanciful. There was obviously the Iraq helicopter crash earlier this year. Those poor people who died were on Will and Matt's squadron- they were their colleagues. Sorry, I haven't said this to anyone, not even Will, and I definitely shouldn't be saying this when you're in the same situation.'

'That's why you can say it to me. I get it. And I know that you're scared and cross and it's all because of how much you love Will.'

Linking Mum's arm, Charlotte fished a tiny Bible from her coat pocket.

'Love always protects, always trusts, always hopes, always perseveres. Love never fails,' Charlotte read out.

It was growing dark when we got home but there were no lights on in the house. Mum nearly dropped me when she went into the dining room and found Dad in there, crying. I've seen Mum cry a lot in the last few weeks but this was the first time I have ever seen Dad cry. She knelt beside him and looked at the writing pad in front of him, damp and puckered, the writing smudged.

'The boss said I should write it. He sent us all home to do it,' said Dad.

'What is it?'

Mum was scanning the first few lines.

'It's a good-bye letter, in case anything happens to me.'

She handed me to Dad and stood up. After hunting on our bookshelves, she found a Bible and read out the same verses Charlotte had read to us on the walk.

'Let's have a takeaway,' she said. It always cheers him up when she says that. 'And a glass of wine.'

It was one of the cosiest evenings we have ever had together, with Dannatt snuggled up next to me in my bouncy chair, Dad sneaking him the odd prawn cracker and Mum pretending not to notice.

As she started to clear away the takeaway boxes, Dad pulled her down on to his lap and rubbed his nose against hers.

'It's ages since you've done that,' she laughed.

'I know,' he said. 'We always used to do that when we first started going out. Do you remember?'

'Yes. That seems a different lifetime now, doesn't it?'

'A decade and a whole lifetime ago. And I love you more now than I ever have done.'

'We haven't been together that long,' said Mum.

Dad blushed. 'I know but the more I think about it, and the more I worry about leaving you, the more I realise I have loved you much longer than I thought.'

'Since when?' Mum laughed.

'Since I was invited to your 18th as your brother's plus one and I asked you to dance.'

'No! What did we dance to?'

'Puff Dad's 'I'll Be Missing You.' Do you remember it? Everywhere was playing it that summer.'

He found it in his C.D. collection. 'Dance?'

She smiled at him as he put his arms around her. They hugged and shuffled about until the end of the song.

'Do you need a tissue? I've got a bit of dust in my eye,' said Dad.

'Me too,' she said.

Tuesday 9 October

Today is our own little D-day, the day we've been working up to for the last seven weeks. For the past few days, we seem to have been suspended in some sort of strange limbo, with Mum and Dad trying to enjoy their remaining time together, whilst concentrating hard on not arguing.

The tension peaked this morning as they packed for their separate trips. Even though going anywhere with me seems to involve packing up most of the house, Dad had barely filled a corner of his trunks before Mum was zipping up our wheelie bag and positioning it by the front door. The problem was that she then had nothing to do but sit and wait for him to finish his packing.

Mum's OCD tendencies mean that when she's stressed, as she seems to have been a lot lately, she washes, cleans, wipes, organises. The house was already like a new pin and there was nothing domestic left for her to do. So she turned her attention to clock-watching. Dad had promised to be packed by midday so that we could cheer ourselves up with lunch out and a walk.

His packing ground to a halt late morning as he realised that he was missing various things vital to his trip. Chief amongst these were his head torch and gas mask. Mum seems to have made a mental inventory of everything in the house, except, that is, for Dad's military stuff. When he couldn't find his torch or mask, she seemed to be as stumped as him.

She tried to help. She peered into the spare room wardrobes, which are bursting with cabbage green camouflage uniform and sandy beige desert gear, ceremonial garb, hats, boots and endless rucksacks and bags. She felt in the back of drawers stuffed with pistol holsters, dog tags, fire resistant long johns, military passes and squadron badges. She even went into the shed and started sorting through his body armour and survival kit. But she couldn't find them. Time ticked away.

Frustrated by Dad's lack of organisation, Mum started making fruitless comments about how he should have checked in advance that he had everything.

'Didn't you go through your kit list before today?' Most of the questions she asked had glaringly obvious answers. Maybe that was why Dad didn't reply.

Lunchtime came and went; Mum got me and Dannatt ready for our walk.

'Are you coming?' she called up the stairs as she attached Dannatt's lead to his collar.

'I'll be a bit longer.'

'How much longer?'

'Soon.'

Mum opened the front door, grim-faced, and we walked miserably around the fence line of the camp. In taking us out on our own, I'm not sure if she was trying to demonstrate to Dad how he had ruined their plans to spend the afternoon together or if she just needed to escape the sight of those big black trunks slowly filling up. Maybe both.

When we arrived home, Dad was pacing around manically. It looked as if we'd been burgled, with cupboards and drawers stripped bare and mounds of stuff piled high in every room. He'd found the gas mask but he couldn't find his head torch. He still had more packing to do and he was panicking. The trunks were nearly full, which meant the good-byes were imminent. Mum seemed uncharacteristically calm about the fact that her house had been ransacked.

'Would you like me to drive into Oxford and buy you a new torch whilst you finish packing?' she asked. Another question with an obvious answer.

When we got back home again, Dad was finally ready, with his trunks by the door next to our bag. The enormity of his luggage alongside our one bag only seemed to highlight the fact that he wouldn't be back next week like us- he would be gone a lot longer. Two months. Dannatt was lying on the doormat, his head sunk low on his paws.

Dinner passed almost in silence, with the odd polite comment about the salt or the need for spoons. Then we all went upstairs, me and Mum to get ready for bed and Dad to put on his uniform. Dad needed to be at the airfield for 11pm to get on a coach that would take him to Brize Norton, the RAF equivalent of Heathrow. He had already explained that he didn't want us going out at that time of night so he'd arranged to get a lift with his friend, whose wife was driving them down.

Dad tucked me up in my Moses basket by their bed. He didn't look at me when he bent down to kiss my forehead. Then he went and sat with Mum and they prayed together.

'Don't look under your pillow until after I've gone,' he said.

'Okay and don't you look in your hand luggage until you're at the airport.'

I didn't hear Dad go- I must have fallen asleep- but I did hear Mum crying in the darkness and footsteps coming up the stairs. The bedroom was pushed gently open, then Dannatt's outline appeared against the landing light. Padding into the room, he put his head over the side of my basket on the way to Mum's side of the bed, where he lay down heavily until morning.

Wednesday 10 October

It's 6am. We've just been startled from our sleep by the phone ringing. It was Dad to say the plane taking them out to Baghdad has gone 'tits' and he's being bussed back home. Mum sounded delighted and appalled.

We're meant to be leaving here in a few hours to catch our own flight to Germany. Apparently, it could be a day or two before Dad can get on another flight so Mum is now on the airline website, trying to find out if we can swap ours.

Thursday 11 October

Mum and I are in Gutersloh with Aunty Chloe and Uncle Mark. It wasn't possible to swap our flights because Mum had mitigated the rise in the cost of our airfare by buying the most basic seats. Despite her usual frugality, Mum wanted to cancel the trip and rearrange it once Dad leaves again but he wouldn't let her. He insisted we stick with our plans.

'Who knows when I'll be going? It could be tomorrow or next week. Anyway, it's my turn to be the one left behind.'

Mum was a bit of a wreck, not seeming to know what she wanted to do, so she let Dad take over.

Dad rearranged things with the kennels where Dannatt was due to go, then drove us to Luton. It all got a bit tearful when we approached passport control.

'We could have all had a few more days together. It's crazy that we were going off and leaving you by yourself.'.

'I won't be by myself, I'll have Dannatt. And that awful cuddly toy you got me.'

Mum's secret present to Dad had been a 'Biggles' teddy bear, which fell out of his rucksack, in front of his colleagues, when he was checking he had his passport at Brize.

'I'll never live that down,' he joked. 'Do you remember the last time I waved you off at an airport?' he asked, wiping her tears with the sleeve of his jumper.

She shook her head.

'It was when your friends took you skiing for your 21st and I couldn't come cos I had exams.'

'Yes, and I tried to bring a vanilla strudel back for you because they were so delicious and-'

'They ripped it up going through security and handed you back the pieces-'

'And you ate it anyway!' Mum laughed.

'I didn't want to seem ungrateful,' said Dad, taking her head in his hands and kissing her for way too long whilst I got squashed between them in my sling.

'Auf wiedersehen, gorgeous,' he said, when they came up for oxygen. 'Auf wiedersehen, little one,' he said, kissing me.

Friday 12 October

Gutersloh was the perfect place for us to come. Uncle Mark has already done three tours of Iraq so he and Aunty Chloe understand Mum's situation better than most. They are treating us like royalty, with lie-ins for Mum, all the cooking and chores taken care of and lots of commiserating about the challenges of this stage of a deployment. Without being told, they knew that she wouldn't want to see or hear anything Iraq-related. I saw them changing their computer home page so that she doesn't catch the headlines when she goes online and they never have the news on the television or radio when she's around.

The only fly in the ointment is that poor Dad is back in England, all by himself, with nothing to do but wait for his flight.

'This is harder than I expected. The house seems so empty,' he said on the phone tonight.

Saturday 13 October

'The Germans would never have allowed a situation like this to develop,' said Mum stoutly as she came off the phone with Dad, who still doesn't know when he will be leaving for Baghdad.

Her OCD has been totally won over by the Teutonic way of doing things. Here the trains run on time, everyone recycles, no one's allowed to make any noise between noon and 3pm and it's against the law to hang out washing on Sundays. Personally, I think it all seems a bit dull. I already know enough about the British to realise conversation would be limited if there were no train delays, a good refuse system that didn't attract rodents and no shouting matches over the washing line on a Sunday afternoon.

'Could Will get a posting out here?' Mum asked.

'Not easily,' said Uncle Mark. 'There aren't any RAF bases here anymore, only Army ones.'

'We love living in Germany but I'm struggling with military life. Last time Mark was sent to Iraq, his dates changed five times,' said Aunty Chloe, as if anyone needed to hear this again. Even I know this and I wasn't alive when it happened. 'I want him to leave the Army.'

Mum was admiring the undercounter compartmentalised recycling unit. 'LEAVE?' she said. She looked so sad. 'We're in this together, aren't we?'

I'll also be sad too if Uncle Mark does decide to leave the Army- it's nice having people who understand this bizarre way of life we lead.

Uncle Mark shot Aunty Chloe a look. 'Let's go shopping,' said Aunty Chloe. 'There are some lovely places in Bielefeld.'

Aunty Chloe is so stylish. She has painted nails and pretty jewellery that matches her outfits. She knew where all the fashionable shops were around the Old Market place, some nestled downside streets and tucked away beside imposing Gothic facades.

'Why don't we get you some new clothes?' she suggested, looking at Mum's maternity jeans. 'You don't need to be in those still.'

Mum didn't seem enthusiastic. Maybe the thought of taking me, the sling and all of her layers off was too exhausting. Aunty Chloe's was carrying our enormous nappy bag that was so full it didn't quite zip up. It didn't quite match the rest of her immaculate look.

As they were walking along past a fountain, sipping on coffees, Mum stopped by a bag shop.

'I love that,' said Mum, pointing to the back of the shop.

'Yes, it's quite nice if you like red leather,' said Aunty Chloe. 'Hard to match up, though.'

'No, the one with wheels,' said Mum.

'The shopping trolley?'

'Yes, the one with the swirly pattern, made of oilcloth. Very handy for spills. And it would hold a lot of stuff. You wouldn't need to carry all that around for me,' said Mum, indicating the nappy bag. 'You could just pull it behind you.'

'I'd rather be carrying this,' said Aunty Chloe, looking horrified.

'I see all the German ladies have them. Very eco,' Mum said with meaning. 'Very me.'

There was no dissuading Mum. It was one of the quickest decisions I have ever witnessed her make. She came out of the shop, yanking it over the doorway. 'It will be so useful back at home. Pop the nappy bag in it for me, would you?'

'I am not pulling it for you,' said Aunty Chloe.

'That's fine, I want to pull it myself.'

Uncle Mark gave Mum an odd look when we got back. I overheard Mum regaling Dad with it on the phone.

'I'm not having sex with you until you get rid of it,' he said.

I am not sure what that means but it didn't seem to worry Mum.

'That's not the best threat when you are about to go away for two months,' she said.

Monday 15 October

Dad rang this morning to say is finally on his way to Baghdad. Even a walk with her new shopping trolley didn't cheer Mum up.

Wednesday 17 October

By bedtime, Mum still hadn't heard from Dad to confirm whether he's arrived in Baghdad. It was a stressful evening all round. I cried for several hours. No one ate dinner until 10pm because Mum and Uncle Mark took it in turns to cuddle me whilst Aunty Chloe tried ringing Grandad.

'He's not answering but Mumsnet seems to suggest this is something called colic.'

'Is it dangerous?' Mum asked, trying to get me to feed. I just screamed.

'No, I don't think so. It's like tummy ache and it usually comes on at night-time.'

'Does it say anything else?'

'It usually lasts three hours.'

'Poor little thing but at least it's nearly over.'

'For three to four months.'

Mum looked as cranky as I felt.

Thursday 18 October

After some very tearful farewells at the airport, Aunty Chloe waved us off his morning. Moomin had offered to meet us at Luton and drive us home.

'I tried to persuade her that a taxi would be fine,' said Aunty Chloe, hugging Mum. 'I know you don't like how fast she drives.'

As Mum carried me out into Luton's Arrivals, pulling our cases, my car seat precariously perched on top of them, Moomin rushed towards us.

'Sweetheart, you look AWFUL.'

'Hi,' said Mum from inside the cocoon of designer coat and perfume that Moomin had enveloped us in.

'What the hell is that?' Moomin asked, pointing to Mum's shopping trolley. Not waiting for an answer, she continued without pausing for breath: 'Let's get you out of here. I hate this airport,' Moomin scowled. 'I don't know why people use it.'

'Cos it's cheap,' muttered Mum.

'Here we are,' announced Moomin, setting off the car alarm on a silver Range Rover Sports.

'Is that yours?' asked Mum.

'Yes, Dad said I wouldn't get a car seat in the back of the Ferrari so I've had to buy this. Ugly as sin, looks like a truck that's had a baby grand dropped on it from a great height, but needs must- it has plenty of space for a baby at least,' she said.

'So do all normal cars,' Mum whispered to me.

As we were driving along the motorway, Moomin turned around to me. 'So you've been keeping Mum awake at night, have you, you naughty girl?' she laughed.

'Yes, it's colic,' said Mum, her hand hovering near the handbrake. We were getting very close to the car in front.

'No, it's much more likely to be separation anxiety,' said Moomin, still smiling at me. I think she really does mean to help when she says stuff like this. 'We could employ some therapeutic techniques to help, now if you like?'

'Does it involve closing your eyes?'

'Yes.'

'Then no,' said Mum firmly.

I thought Mum might nod off in the car but she remained very alert.

'So when did Will arrive?' asked Moomin.

'I don't know, he's not been in touch yet.'

'What?' roared Moomin, swerving dangerously close to the central reservation. 'I thought you said he left on Sunday.'

'He did.'

'But it's Friday. That's ridiculous. No wonder you all have separation anxiety,' Moomin concluded, as though this was now official. 'Where is the person in charge of his platoon? How do we contact them?'

'It's a squadron and I don't know,' said Mum, suspiciously. 'Why?'

'Heads will roll if I have got anything to do with this. It's serendipitous that I'm dropping you home,' she said, undertaking five cars.

'It's fine, let's just leave it for now.'

'No, it's not fine and no, I won't leave it.'

Mum either didn't know or wouldn't reveal how you go about contacting the RAF big guns because she offered no help.

'Sweetheart, I don't want to be rude but I would like to express feelings of intense frustration towards you right now. You must know someone who knows something.'

Mum shrugged. Moomin wasn't to be thwarted. In the guard room, where we had to go to sign in the new car, she called for the head guard. Whilst she waited, she spied the noticeboard where the names and faces of all the high-profile people in the station are displayed.

'My daughter's husband, Flight Lieutenant Child, is currently serving in Iraq. I can't quite remember where the Station Commander lives.'

Two wholly unrelated statements but the tired guard didn't seem to notice.

'It's on the way to your daughter's quarter,' he said, pointing at the map selloptaped to the top of the counter.

'Thank you,' said Moomin triumphantly, taking her car pass.

'Please don't,' said Mum.

'Just a quiet word. I'll drop you and Millie home and then I'll pop over.'

Later on, as Mum was unpacking, Moomin reappeared.

'What happened?' Mum asked nervously.

'The Station Commander is also in Iraq and his wife's not heard from him either,' said Moomin. 'She wants me to tell her if I hear anything. I'll get Dad to ring The Times tomorrow, they must have correspondents out there.'

I saw Mum texting Grandad before she turned the light off.

Friday 19 October

There was still no news about Dad by the time Moomin screeched off this morning.

'I have a client who works in government,' she called out of her car window, tapping her nose and winking. 'I'll get her onto it. Don't worry, sweetheart. We'll track him down.'

'Thank you,' shouted Mum, who is starting to seem grateful for Moomin's intervention after her initial objections. She has pretty much had her phone in her hand or her pocket for the last five days and, since last night, she is developing a habit of double-checking it's switched on, set to its highest volume and not on silent.

After Moomin left for London, we collected Dannatt from the kennels. He seemed so happy to see us, nearly pulling the sturdy dog handler off her feet as she brought him out to us. He leapt into the boot without needing to be called and pressed his nose against the dog guard all the way home, smiling down at me, if dogs can smile. Home felt homier once he had scattered his dog hair over everything and snuggled into his bed.

This evening Mum's phone rang. Dannatt sloped out of the room when she answered and started making high-pitched noises. As soon as that call was over, she phoned Aunty Chloe.

'He arrived in Baghdad on Sunday,' Mum said. 'But he wasn't able to get in touch until today. They didn't issue him with any phone or internet credit until just now.'

It was time for my feed so she struggled out of her top and put the phone on speaker, before latching me on. We've sort of cracked the feeding thing at last.

'He's used all his credits up just now so we won't be able to chat again for a week unless he can buy some more.'

'At least you got to chat!' said Aunty Chloe.

'Yes, I s'pose so. It was a bit of a rubbish chat. There was a time delay so we just kept talking over one another. And he couldn't answer most of my question because he can't tell me anything about what he's doing. All I found out was that he had a burger for a dinner and he's been to the gym three times since he arrived.'

'Mark and I have had hundreds of those chats. It's not personal,' said Aunty Chloe. 'They just can't say much about.'

'Well, they don't need to say 'I'll speak to you laters, mate,' when they're saying good-bye, though, do they?'

'Is that what he said?'

'Yes.'

'Maybe there were people listening. There was often a queue when Mark called me. They don't have any privacy there.'

Mum didn't reply. Maybe she regretted not being nicer to Dad.

Saturday 20 October

A parcel arrived in the post for me today! Mum opened it. She looked puzzled as she pulled out a CD with a front cover showing a photo of me and Dad. She played it in the stereo and Dad's voice boomed out all around us on the surround sound.

'On Monday, Millie drank a whole bottle of Mum's lovingly pumped milk without spitting it out all over Dad's flying suit. But she was still hungry. On Tuesday, she breastfed for a whole ten minutes without regurgitating any of it down Dad's back. But she was still hungry.'

It took me a minute to work out that he was telling his own version of 'The Very Hungry Caterpillar.'

'He must have recorded it before left,' said Mum to Aunty Chloe on the phone tonight. 'There's an RAF charity that does it so kids can listen to their parents reading whilst they're away.'

At bedtime, Mum fed me in the rocking chair in my bedroom and we listened to Dad reading all of the Spot stories, only Spot was called Dannatt in his version. Much later, I woke up, still on my Mum's lap. I was cold and the CD had finished playing. I wished the real Dad was with us.

Monday 22 October

Mum is still fretting about her milk drying up. Only she could blame her low milk supply on the situation in Iraq but, according to her, it's all due to the stress of the past few weeks, worrying about Dad and looking after me by herself.

'It's dwindling to nothing, I'm sure of it,' Mum told the health visitor when we visited the drop-in session at the med centre today. She explained her theory.

'Stress and tiredness are undoubtedly part of it,' said the health visitor, 'but you only recently got the breastfeeding properly underway- it might be a case of too little too late. We need to boost your milk supply so I would suggest a 'bed day'.'

'I tried that. I didn't think it really helped.'

'Give it another go. At the very least, the rest will do you good.'

Mum didn't need any more encouragement to spend another day in bed. On the phone at lunchtime, Bunny suggested combining the bed day with eating dates.

'They're so healing, darling. I lived off dates when I was feeding mine. I could have fed the whole bloody village, I was positively bursting with milk. According to nursing mothers in ancient Egypt, dates have medicinal properties that encourage milk production.'

The station Spar shop didn't have any dates so Mum bought tinned prunes in syrup.

Tuesday 23 October

Having now done three of them, I wouldn't recommend a bed day, especially with no one to help. Mum was right when she told Dad it's harder than it looks. By late morning, she was full of wind from all the prunes she had gorged on. Unhappily aware of their effects, I also had a cricked neck from being wedged up against her bosoms. My colic kicked in much earlier than usual, probably from all the air I'd inhaled from the constant feeding and, before long, I was rigid with tummy pain and screaming non-stop. Mum abandoned the whole exercise and carried me downstairs.

She tried to settle me in front of CBeebies but I refused to watch Mr Tumble, screaming throughout bath and story time. Mum hadn't eaten anything all day except the prunes and her lozenges. When she started to make herself an omelette, she laid me in my papoose on the kitchen counter beside her, stroking my head and desperately singing nursery rhymes as she cracked the eggs one-handed. Then the phone rang. Dad has an uncanny knack of ringing when Mum has just started making or eating her dinner.

'Damn it, damn I, damn it, please don't hang up,' she said as she searched around for the handset. She can't ring him back so if she misses his call, she must wait for the next one.

She came back into the kitchen, holding the now lifeless handset, stared beyond me and then screamed. The corner of my papoose was near the hob and it had caught alight. She scooped me up and threw a glass of water at the empty papoose but most of it went into the pan, causing the hot oil to burst into flames that leapt almost up to the ceiling.

She hopped about the kitchen, looking in various cupboards, and found a blanket tied up with Velcro. With me in her arms, she couldn't get it undone so she opened the kitchen door and flung the papoose outside, quickly followed by the pan. Then she sank to the floor, still holding me. The phone started ringing and this time she made it.

'I nearly set Millie on fire,' she sobbed into the handset. I was glad it was Dad and not the health visitor, who was supposed to be ringing to check on the bed day. 'I'm so tired, I can't even make myself some dinner.'

Mum and Dad stayed on the phone a long time, then the line went dead. After waiting a while, she dropped the phone into her dressing gown pocket and carried me up to bed. As she was putting me in to my Babygro, it rang again.

'Sorry, my minutes ran out so I had to go and buy some more. But then queue for the phone was massive by the time I got back.'

Mum didn't seem to mind. 'What did you have for dinner?' she asked.

'I missed dinner. I was enjoying our chat so much,' he said as Mum zipped me into my sleeping bag.

She put me in my Moses basket and held the phone to my ear. Dad read me the live version of 'The Very Hungry Caterpillar' but I fell asleep before we got to Tuesday.

Friday 26 October

A letter from the hospital arrived this morning, offering Mum an appointment with a consultant gynaecologist in a couple of weeks' time. She seemed pleased but I'm not; I thought Dad might look after me for this particular medical appointment. I'm sure it can't be normal to have this amount of gynaecological knowledge aged 9 weeks.

Sunday 28 October

Mum and I went to church for the first time since Dad left. Padre Claire prayed for me, Mum and Dad during the prayers and, after the service, she came straight over to us.

'How are you getting on?' she asked.

'We're ok, thanks,' said Mum.

'And how's Will? Have you heard from him?'

'A bit but he can't tell me much when he phones. He seems to be flying a lot at night and sleeping during the day. That combined with the time difference means it tricky for him to ring when we're awake. I've had a couple of emails.'

'I imagine his time won't be his own- they'll be working him hard,' said Claire. 'Call me if you fancy some company. I'm on my own most nights too. Andy's just been posted to Lossiemouth so I'm only seeing him at weekends.'

Claire is married to Andy, an RAF engineer. Mum has a photo at home of her and Dad at their wedding.

'I didn't realise that, I'm sorry,' said Mum. 'I've been in my own little world recently.'

'That's understandable with a baby and a husband in Iraq!'

'I thought they had to post you to the same place if you were married.'

'No, it doesn't always work like that,' said Claire.

Colin, a retired padre who helps Claire with the services, came over to us. Dad says he served in the Second World War and did something important in the Battle of Britain.

'Morning,' he said, his face crinkling up as he greeted us. 'I am convinced this fine young lady gave me a smile during the blessing,' he said, smiling himself.

'I think that was wind,' Mum said, gathering up our things. 'I hope it was. I wanted Will to see her first smile,' she added sadly.

'He'll be back before she's laughing,' said Colin. 'I will pray for that.'

On our way home, Mum couldn't push my buggy up the hill (I'm sure Dad didn't assemble it properly). The wheels kept sending us towards the curb, like one of those errant supermarket trolleys. As she was giving one of the tyres a hearty kick, a military Land Rover pulled up alongside us and a uniformed man called out through the open window.

'Can I give you a lift, ma'am?' he asked.

'That's very kind,' said Mum, getting up from her confused attempts to remedy the issue. 'There seems to be something wrong with the buggy wheels.'

The man got out, gave me to Mum and put the buggy in the back of his vehicle.

'Hop in,' he said and he drove us home, with me on Mum's lap.

As he was helping us up the steps, he asked where we keep our toolbox. Mum pointed to the shed. Whilst she fed me by the window in our sitting room, I could hear him tinkering away out in the garden with Dad's spanners.

On our walk this afternoon, my buggy behaved perfectly. Dad's absence isn't generally a good thing but occasionally it is. People round here seem very keen to help us when we are by ourselves.

Wednesday 31 October

Mum doesn't celebrate Halloween but it seems to be an almost unavoidable celebration on the station. Lots of the houses have been decorated with skeletons and cobwebs for days now and hordes of children were already out in their costumes when we gave Dannatt his afternoon walk.

Christians don't seem to go in for witches and warlocks. Or Mum doesn't, anyway. To make sure no one bothers us with trick or treating, she's blu-tacked a sign to our front door, asking people not to disturb us for reasons of faith. She could have just said there's a baby at the property.

'I love your sign,' said Claire when she popped in for coffee. 'Rather like Martin Luther's 95 Theses nailed to the door of the Wittenberg Church.'

But no one else has paid any attention to Mum's request. We've had streams of children ringing the doorbell, making Dannatt bark, waking me up and asking for sweets, leaving her looking decidedly unchristian. She went through an entire strip of nicotine lozenges in about half an hour during the busiest spell.

After settling me back in my Moses basket for the fifth time, I heard her running a bath. From the long list of complaints about the bathroom that she submitted during the appraisal of our house, I know that the overflow pipe, in true S.H.I.T.-style, has not been connected to anything, meaning excess bathwater flows freely onto the doorstep below.

As more trick or treaters came to the door, ringing the bell and laughing at the sign, I heard her easing herself into the bathwater.

Thursday 1 November

Amy came over again today. Because of our trip to Germany, we haven't seen her for a month. After blowing into the smoking detector, Mum fessed up.

'I haven't actually been reducing my lozenges,' she said, looking at the carpet.

'OK', said Amy. 'How many are you averaging a day?'

'Thirty,' said Mum, still looking at the carpet.

Amy didn't say anything. She stroked Dannatt. Frown lines that I hadn't noticed before appeared on her forehead.

'The recommended maximum is fifteen a day,' she said slowly. 'It would probably be safer to smoke.'

Mum went the colour of a beetroot. Maybe she realised she'd hit an unchartered low when her smoking cessation counsellor was recommending a return to smoking.

'You were absorbing less nicotine into your blood stream when you were smoking a few cigarettes a day,' Amy explained. 'The nicotine from all those lozenges will be passing into your breast milk. We might need to think about you bottle feeding if you can't reduce your use.'

'I don't want to bottle feed after I've worked so hard to breastfeed.'

'You have to think about what's best for Millie.'

For a moment, it was like Amy was my advocate in this horrid world where Daddies go off to war and Mummies, even those wanting to do their best, struggle to be good parents. But even as Amy was advancing my right to drink nicotine-free milk, I felt sorry for Mum. She looked so ashamed. I know first-hand how much she relies on her lozenges in her efforts to keep everything ticking along on her own.

'How about you reduce your lozenges down to 15 by next week?' suggested Amy. 'We'll squeeze in an emergency meeting next Friday?'

Mum nodded. This afternoon we went to the shop and bought twenty packets of mints.

Friday 2 November

We were on a walk with Charlotte and Laura this morning, enjoying the autumn sunshine, when Mum suddenly swore, which she doesn't often do.

'What's the matter?' asked Charlotte.

'I've just remembered my first online food shop is coming between ten and twelve so I have to be back at home in... twelve minutes.'

She barely said good-bye as she yelled for Dannatt and started running back through the woods, bouncing me about like a sack of potatoes on her front.

At the car, she shoved me into my car seat, forgetting to strap me in, and then pushed Dannatt into the boot, dog lead and wellies flying everywhere, before flooring it back to the station.

Military stations have gates manned by guards with guns, guards who need to be satisfied that anyone passing through has a legitimate reason for entering. Breaking the 20mph speed limit on the approach to the station, Mum screeched into the entrance area and zoomed straight past the guards. Gunshot went off as the guards came racing after us, running almost as fast as we were travelling. I had an excellent view of it all from my rear-facing car seat.

Mum executed a last-minute emergency stop, throwing us all forward. As she wound her window down, a guard approached, demanding an explanation. More guards appeared until there was a wall of uniforms around the car.

'You could have been shot, Mrs Child,' he said, thankfully recognising us.

'I'm so sorry,' she said, over and over.

'You need to drive your vehicle over to the guard room,' said another guard. 'The Station Security Officer's will want to know what you were doing.'

In the guard room, the Station Security Officer demanded Mum's military ID and a full account of what had happened.

'What on earth were you doing? Do you know how serious this could have been? And with your child in the car too.'

'My husband is in Iraq' (Mum says this as a matter of course now whenever she is required to explain anything) 'and I have my first online delivery coming today and I forgot about it and now I may have missed it.'

'Hang on a minute, ma'am,' said the Station Security Officer, dialling a number into the phone on his desk.

'I'm so sorry, please don't-' said Mum. He held a hand up as if to silence her.

He replaced the handset. 'I've arranged for my men to locate your supermarket van if it's still on the patch. They'll request that it returns to your house. You've been very fortunate- this could have ended up with more than a missed supermarket shop,' he warned.

As we pulled up outside our house, we found two guards helping the supermarket van driver to unload our shopping. They carried it up the front steps and even brought the bags into the house.

'You happy with Tesco's own brand wipes?' asked one of the guards. 'The driver says they're out of Johnsons.'

Mum nodded. The other guard walked into the kitchen, gingerly holding a large cardboard box. 'Did you mean to order twelve dozen eggs?'

The supermarket driver followed behind, carrying a similar box. 'It's actually twenty-three dozen. Don't you have chickens?' he asked.

As if on cue, one of the hens scuttled in between his legs.

'They don't lay,' she said, looking overwhelmed.

'Still, that's a lot of eggs,' he said, shooing the hen back outside.

'And a lot of washing powder,' said the first guard returning, humping four sacks of Aerial through the doorway.

I saw Mum repeatedly clicking on the mouse when she did her order, grumping about the slow connection. Maybe she didn't want to own up to another mistake as she let them leave us a year's supply of various household items.

'So that's a total of £320,' said the driver.

After the supermarket man and guards had gone, Mum carried a table outside and laid it with her unwanted goods and a donation box. She didn't mention any of this to Dad when he rang her at bedtime.

Monday 5 November

This evening, as it was getting dark, Mum wrapped us both up in our hats and gloves and bundled me into my buggy for the station fireworks' display. In most respects the military is under-resourced but one thing it's not yet short of is explosives.

We joined a huge crowd of revellers heading towards the playing field. An enormous fire blazed in the distance. Given that every second family here has a Labrador, there was a distinct lack of them out tonight and I thought Charlotte, Laura and their husbands looked a bit concerned when we arrived with Dannatt.

'He's a gun dog,' Mum explained, 'it's good practise for him to be around loud bangs.'

Her theory was put to the test when an impressive collection of rockets went squealing off into the darkness and Dannatt shot away from her, dragging her to the floor. Although she scrambled to her feet and chased after him, he was impossible to locate amongst the huge gathering of people. Our friends split up and joined in the hunt for Dannatt, missing the rest of the display, but no one could find him and eventually we went home without him.

Much later on, as I was having my final feed, there was a knock at the door. It was the RAF Police Dog Handlers. They'd found Dannatt in the bin area behind the Officers' Mess. They handed him back with a warning about the effect of fireworks on pets. Mum took Dannatt off his lead and he slunk past her to hide again.

Mum found him under her bed. She fished out an old pair of ear defenders that Dad uses for shooting practice and covered his ears with them. I didn't think Dannatt looked particularly grateful.

Thursday 8 November

Amy was so pleased with Mum for reducing her lozenges down to fifteen that she threw her arms around her at today's appointment. Mum has achieved this by replacing every second lozenge with a peppermint, which are a similar shape and size. As far as I can tell, she's just swapped Amy's wrath for the dentist's but maybe that is progress of sorts.

Friday 9 November

We are never on time for anything but Mum had us ready here half an hour early for her gynaecology appointment. A female doctor welcomed us into the consultation room and asked Mum to undress. The nurse rocked me in her arms whilst the doctor examined her.

After a long silence, the doctor stood up. 'You can get dressed. I can't see that there's anything amiss,' she said.

'Really? I'm still a proper woman?'

'Yes, you look good to me. Maybe you just needed time to heal. I think you should go home and try again,' said the doctor.

'My husband's in Iraq. He won't be home for another month.'

'So's mine. Tiny world. What does he do?'

'He's in the RAF. Helicopter pilot.'

'Mine's Army. He's only just gone. I can't even let myself think about his return date- it's a six monther.'

'I'm sorry, that must be hard.'

'We've just got to keep busy, haven't we?' said the doctor. 'You must be busy with your little one. Enjoy hubby's homecoming and if there's still a problem, get back in touch.'

I had to listen to the same conversation again when we got home. Bunny rang to find out how the appointment had gone.

'I just wanted to get it sorted out before he comes home,' said Mum. 'I won't know for another month if I need anything doing.'

'Just have a go with a cucumber, darling. Then if there's a problem, you can ring them back tomorrow and get booked in for an operation.'

Mum didn't seem taken with this plan and I didn't have a clue what they were on about.

Wednesday 14 November

With Christmas on its way, Mum took us out present shopping. Since the fireworks debacle, Dannatt's chewing has gone from being a nuisance to an acute problem. He destroys stuff every day. Nothing is sacred apart from his chew toy. As it was sunny, we left him in the garden with a bone and a bowl of water.

We had quite a successful time at the shopping centre, if you exclude the incident on the escalators. Mum ignored the sign prohibiting the use of buggies. Maybe it wouldn't have been so bad if we'd been on an 'up' escalator but as we were going down, the result was more disastrous. Various people below us were knocked sideways, their shopping squashed flat, and one little boy lost his pretzel beneath my buggy wheels.

This was all small fry compared with the scene that greeted us when we got back home. After taking in the shopping bags, we went into the garden to check on Dannatt. It's hard to convey the transformation. It had been an idyllic scene when we left, insofar as you can ever describe anything in a military garden as idyllic. Happy dog, sunshine, clucky chickens.

Now it was a chicken graveyard. In the middle of the lawn, on a carpet of feathers, lay one of our hens, not looking too chipper, and behind it was our other hen, warbling and scraping away at the ground, deep in grief for its friend. Dannatt was bouncing around as he always does when we come home. Clean as a whistle. Not a feather on him. The picture of canine innocence.

Mum's not good with birds, alive or dead. I'm not sure why she bought chickens for Dad; they scare her if they get too close or flap their wings at her. I think her decision to buy them is testament to how much she didn't want a dog. Maybe, on some sub-conscious level, she planned this massacre. It will be interesting to see how long the remaining chicken lasts now.

Thursday 15 November

Today Mum didn't open any of the curtains with north-facing windows. The dead chicken is still out there, in need of a burial. I don't believe she would have done anything about it if Dad hadn't rung.

She ended up telling him the whole thing over speaker phone as she sat in our darkened sitting room, feeding me. The most obvious question hung in the air but he never asked it: 'Why did you leave a gun dog in the garden for the day with loose fowl?'

'Have you told anyone about it?' he asked instead.

'No, I thought they might wonder why I left a gun dog in the garden with the chickens.'

'I'm sure they'd understand,' he said, unconvincingly.

'Now he's a killer, we're going to need to get him rehomed. I can't have him here.'

'Where is he?' asked Dad.

'I've locked him in the spare room.'

'He's a pack animal,' Dad explained. 'We're his pack. You're his pack. He's not going to hurt you or Millie.'

Mum sounded unsure. 'Anyway, I can't deal with the chicken carcass.'

'I'll ring the squadron and get it sorted if you let Dannatt out of the spare room and keep the curtains shut.'

She stuck to half the bargain and kept the curtains shut.

Friday 16 November

We achieved a greater degree of normality today after the weirdness of the past few days. One of Dad's colleagues came over mid-morning to dispose of the chicken so we were able to introduce daylight back into the sitting rooms and bedrooms. It's strange to think that Dad sorted out the removal of a chicken carcass in our Oxfordshire garden from a tent in Baghdad.

In the afternoon, Fiona, who lives opposite us, came over for coffee with her toddler, Catherine. Whilst Catherine wobbled about between the furniture, practicing her walking, Mum kept her eyes trained on Dannatt.

'That awful terrier's been trying to get at our neighbours' rabbits again,' said Fiona. 'I wonder if it killed your chicken. Maybe it wasn't actually Dannatt? Whenever I see it, it's got something hanging out of its mouth.'

'What's that, a terrier?' asked Mum, momentarily distracted from her study of Dannatt.

'Yes, people are always complaining about it.'

As Fiona was gathering up her things to go, Catherine pulled herself up on my Moses basket and peeked her head over. The stand wobbled dangerously as she fell sideways, rocking me about until I nearly capsized.

Dannatt leapt to attention. He gave a low warning growl at Catherine, then padded across the room to me. He licked my face before taking up his station by my side. He wouldn't be persuaded to leave my basket after that, not even when Mum waved a dog treat at him.

'I'm so sorry, Fiona,' Mum said but she was smiling after they left.

'You do love us,' she said to Dannatt, stroking him.

She didn't put him in the spare room at bedtime.

Wednesday 21 November

Mum was feeding me in her bedroom this morning when the doorbell rang. It was early- the noisy pipes were quiet and the room was cold as she crept downstairs with me still latched on.

It was Claire. Already dressed in her dog collar, she looked very official.

'Don't be alarmed,' she said, looking at Mum, who had gone pale. 'I have news but not the worst kind.'

'What? What's happened?' asked Mum. 'Is he ok?'

'Let's go and sit down.'

'I can't bear it, Claire, please just say, whatever it is.'

'One of our helicopters crashed near Baghdad last night. It was being flown by a crew from Will's flight but we can't be sure who was onboard. We don't know if Will was on it. He may very well be safe and back at the camp.'

'What? How can they not know? Surely they must know who was flying and who wasn't.'

'They've shut down communications between the UK and Iraq to stop leaks. The reason for telling you now is that it will be on the news in a bit. We don't want families finding out about it that way.'

Mum started to cry.

'I realise it must be agony- to be told something massive and not know if you're directly affected.'

Claire put her arm around Mum and then reached in her handbag for a packet of tissues.

Blowing her nose, Mum moved over to the TV.

'It's better not to watch it,' said Claire. 'They have less information than us and what they do say may not be accurate.'

'They seem to know more than you,' said Mum. 'Three dead and six injured in Baghdad helicopter crash,' she read off the screen. 'Why are you telling me you don't know anything when the BBC does?'

'I'm so sorry. This is how it works. I haven't been given any more information to share other than what I have said. I know it's confusing.'

'It's not confusing, it doesn't make sense. Someone must know if Will was on board.'

'I'm really sorry, I know it's hard but I can't give you any more details.'

'The cause of the crash is not yet clear,' said the newsreader. 'There's speculation that it may have been shot down.'

'Shot down. How are they finding this stuff out? That may be my Will. I can't believe no one here knows anything but that sodding reporter does.'

'It's just speculation. They said so themselves. It would be best to switch it off, Anna.'

'When will you be able to tell me what's going on?'

'I don't know. Someone from the squadron will be over soon. They may know more. I asked if I could come and speak to you first.'

'Thank you,' said Mum.

'Would you like me to make you a cup of tea? Or I could start ringing round your family for you.'

'I can let them know,' said Mum, scrolling through the channels.

'I'll make you a tea,' said Claire.

Mum didn't reply. She was dialling a number into the phone when it started ringing in her hand.

'I was just dialling you,' Mum said. She started to cry again. 'They don't know if Will was onboard.'

Then Mum's mobile started to ring.

'Wait a second, Dad.'

Her mobile was in the next room. Claire came running in with it.

'Dad, I'm just going to answer my mobile.'

Mum took her mobile from Claire. 'Hello, Chloe? I'm just talking to Dad.'

Putting both calls on speaker phone, she spoke to Grandad and Aunty Chloe at the same time.

'I've got Claire here, the padre. She says they don't know if Will was involved.'

'How can they not know?' asked Grandad.

'I don't know- someone must know but they won't tell me. They won't even tell me when they will tell me.'

Mum cried again.

'Mum's just about to leave. She'll be with you soon,' said Grandad. 'I'm going to try and rearrange my operating list and then I'll be with you.'

'Darling, I will be there as soon as I can be,' said Moomin, coming on the line. She sounded wobbly, not her usual self.

'I'll start ringing round for you,' said Aunty Chloe. 'I'll do our side and then you can just focus on Will's.'

When they rang off, Mum cradled me in her arms.

'It's going to be alright. It's going to be fine. We're going to be fine. It's going to be ok. There's nothing to worry about,' she said, rocking me back and forth and kissing me.

Claire came and sat down next to us. 'I can take care of her whilst you ring round or vice versa,' she said.

'I'd better call people myself,' said Mum, handing me to Claire.

The phone rang again. It was the second in command from the squadron, or 2IC for short. It sounded much like Mum's chat with Claire.

'Can you really not tell me anymore?' asked Mum.

'I'm sorry, I know it must be hell but we simply don't know any more. It might be hours before we're in a position to release that information. Is the padre still with you?'

'Yes.'

'Good. I'll send someone over as soon as I can. In the meantime, try to keep calm and don't watch the news.'

Maybe he couldn't hear our TV blaring out.

Mum then rang Bunny. 'I'm sorry, have I woken you? I'm sorry to call so early.'

Mum started to cry. She made horrible noises that I had never heard her make before. Claire gently took the phone from her.

'This is Will's padre,' Claire said.

Mum took me upstairs as Claire explained what had happened. She changed my nappy and got me dressed, all the time crying.

When we went back downstairs, Mum put the TV back on and sat glued to it whilst Claire encouraged her to turn it off. There was lots of commentary on previous crashes but no new information. The phones seemed to take it in turns to ring and Claire answered them. Mum seemed to glaze over, as though she couldn't see anything apart from the TV.

'I'd better go down to the guard room to sign in Moomin and Bunny- they're both on their way,' she said from nowhere.

'I can do that,' said Claire.

'No, I need to get out,' said Mum.

'I'll drive you,' said Claire.

The entrance to the camp was swarming with journalists, photographers and the odd person walking their dog or out for a run who had stopped to watch the media circus of cameras and flashbulbs. It was a while before Claire was able to park. The queue at the guard room reception desk was the longest I have ever seen it. Claire pointed to me and one of the guards called us up ahead of the others. Once Mum had booked Moomin and Bunny in, Claire took us home.

Moomin's boy-racer driving meant she arrived much earlier than she probably should have done. She had picked up Bunny on her way. They exploded into the house, with bags of food, hugging everything, squashing me in their eagerness to help. Claire politely excused herself.

'Let's put the kettle on,' said Moomin. 'That's what we're supposed to do at a time like this, I think.'

As the kettle was boiling, Mum's mobile rang.

'Uncle Conal... That's so kind... You really don't need to do that,' said Mum, starting to cry again. Moomin took the phone from her.

'Who was that?' asked Bunny, putting her arm around Mum.

'Uncle Conal, my godfather. I think you met him at the wedding. He's a film director. He lives in LA at the moment but he's flying here in a bit so that he can be with us.'

'How did he know about the crash?'

'I think Chloe must have rung him when she was phoning round our side of the family. It's sweet that he would come all this way. You'll like him. He's a luvvie.'

'You should have sat me next to him at the wedding if he's a thespian, darling. I got sat next to some bloody boring person that wanted to tell me about his dry rot.'

Moomin and Bunny spent half the morning making an enormous lunch, which no one ate. When they had pushed their food around their plates for an hour or so, they threw themselves into clearing it all up. They were both strangely quiet. I didn't like it. Even one of Bunny's expletives would have been better than the silence.

The day passed more quickly than I imagined it would do. Every now and then, Mum, Moomin and Bunny got upset. Then they would put the kettle on again and make endless rounds of tea. Mum hates tea but they all seemed to have forgotten, even Mum, who took the odd sip. Claire popped back in the evening to see how we were doing. She still couldn't provide any more information. Instead, she said some prayers.

'Everyone at church is praying for you all,' she said.

As she was leaving, Grandad called with an update of his progress along the M40, asking who wanted what in the Indian takeaway he was going to collect on his way. Nobody seemed to know.

'I'll just get a good spread to share,' he said.

The doorbell rang. 'It can't be Dad- that's too quick,' said Mum, 'and it can't be Claire, she only just left.'

I felt like I was in the live version of 'The Tiger Who Came to Tea'. Mum hesitated as she went to open the door. It was Claire again.

'Oh no,' said Mum. 'Have you heard something.'

'No, no, don't worry. I found your godfather trapped outside the camp so I signed him in.'

A man dressed in a long black frock coat, surrounded by vintage leather trunks, was paying a taxi driver. He turned and waved at us. Claire ran to help him with his bags. It was Uncle Conal.

'Annie,' he said, approaching the front steps. 'Dear, sweet Annie. How are you bearing up?' He hugged her whilst Claire brought in the rest of his things. 'I brought you all Reese's Peanut Butter Cups. I didn't know else what to do- I've never experienced anything like this before.'

'Thank you, Uncle Conal,' said Mum, smiling for the first time all day.

'The worst is not so long as we can say 'This is the worst,' said Uncle Conal. 'Chin up, lovely.'

Mum introduced him to Bunny when curiosity drew her into the congested hallway. They instantly took a shine to one another, greeting one another like old friends.

'Meeting is such sweet sorrow,' said Uncle Conal, over Bunny's head, as Moomin joined the crush.

'It is,' she agreed, not at all phased by his strange way of talking. 'It truly is.'

Grandad seemed less comfortable when he arrived, laden down with takeaway bags, and Uncle Conal enveloped him in a lengthy embrace.

'Mine eyes smell onions; I shall weep anon,' he said, kissing Grandad on the cheek.

Much later on, surrounded by foil packets of half-eaten curry, Mum's mobile rang and the room fell silent as she answered.

She listened, staring at the floor. Then she cried. Everyone stared at the floor, apart from Moomin, who rushed to put her arm around her.

Mum broke the silence. 'It's him.'

There was a pause, as if the whole room wanted to yip 'Hurrah' but resisted the temptation just in time. Others had died. Other families must now be grieving loved ones who had made the ultimate sacrifice.

'The worst is not. For us, anyway,' said Uncle Conal.

Mum passed the phone to Bunny so she could hear Dad's voice and know for sure that he was safe. Everyone took their turn and relief flooded the room as the news sank in.

'I love you so much,' Mum said into the phone before she hung up.

Nobody spoke for several minutes. It was like the two-minute silence at church a couple of Sundays again, only without the poppies and flag.

Slowly, people started saying inane things and hugging but the relief didn't last. Nobody knew how the crash had happened. Dad couldn't or wouldn't say and there is almost another fortnight left of flying for him to do out there before he can come home.

'Stay safe,' Mum whispered into the phone before hanging up.

Thursday 22 November

Grandad went back to London to see his patients before the rest of us were even awake, taking Uncle Conal with him for his early morning flight. Moomin and Bunny offered to stay and look after us but Mum said she needed to get back to normal.

'Bye, sweetheart,' said Moomin, hugging Mum, not seeming to want to let go. As her car pulled away from the curb, I realised it was the first time I have ever seen Moomin drive slowly. She waved out of her window until they had disappeared around the corner.

Amy came over in the afternoon, full of praise.

'You could have so easily given in yesterday. I'm super proud of you for staying strong.'

After Amy left, the second in command of Dad's squadron came to the house to see Mum. He was in working dress, not the green flying suit I am used to seeing Dad wear. He looked very efficient in blue trousers and matching blue jumper with his wings velcroed to his chest.

'We're now in a position to share more information. As you know, the names of those involved in the crash were officially announced this morning. They were all soldiers, travelling as passengers in the aircraft. Being Army, none of them were from this station.'

Mum already knew this. She is an expert on the crash, or an expert on how it's being reported in the news anyway. It's strange that, after weeks of avoiding the news at all costs, Mum is now glued to all its many sources.

'I heard,' said Mum.

'I can't tell you what the helicopter was doing or why it crashed. That's still classified.'

'They're saying on the news that it was carrying troops on a covert mission but it wasn't shot down,' said Mum.

'As I say, I can't comment on that.'

'I don't understand why you couldn't tell me more when it all happened and why you are still being so cagey. The media tells us more than you do and you're supposed to be looking after us. You have a duty of care.'

I have never been in a war zone but this was starting to feel a bit hostile. Mum crossed her arms as she waited for a reply. The 2IC cleared his throat.

'We do have a duty of care, a much greater duty of care than any journalist has. I can see that the way we handle these situations may seem uncaring, though. You want information and you think it's callous of us not to share it. But imagine, in a tragedy like this one, if we reassured every spouse whose loved one was safe: what would the spouses think if they didn't get a call or a visit to say their loved one was ok?'

He paused. He suddenly looked exhausted.

'They would be sat at home joining up the dots for themselves,' he continued. 'In the absence of any reassurance, they might realise by themselves, with no support on hand, that their spouse was one of the unlucky ones. We cannot have people finding out that way. We must keep a blanket of silence over the whole thing until we can confirm to those affected that their loved one isn't coming home. The fallout is that there are families who are left in the dark for a time but that is the better way. Those families who have lost someone must be our priority but I am sorry for the additional suffering it causes. There are very few neat or happy solutions in war.'

'I'm sorry,' said Mum. The 2IC handed her a handkerchief. 'I didn't think of it like that.'

'You don't need to be sorry. You're entitled to an explanation.'

He looked weary and so sad.

'I shouldn't say this but some of this stuff could be handled better if there were more of us. We're feeling the cutbacks everywhere. I'm doing two people's job at the minute, just like Will was before he left. Like they say, one hand can't clap.'

When the 2IC left, Mum went back to watching the news' footage, showing the same helicopter flying around the desert, the same senior officer addressing the press with the names of those affected. She watched these snippets on loop, then trawled the net for news' articles.

After lunch, which Mum didn't really eat, Charlotte knocked at the front door.

'Coming for a walk?' she asked.

It was good to get out. Charlotte's husband, Matt, is due to leave for Iraq next week so despite her new fixation, Mum didn't talk about the crash whilst we were out.

Charlotte had spent the day buying Christmas presents for Matt to take with him as he will be away until January. She seemed quite calm, which was comforting, not at all how Mum was before Dad went.

When we got home, Mum didn't put the television or computer on again. Instead, we cuddled up on the sofa and watched three episodes of Peppa Pig, only turning it off when Miss Rabbit appeared in her helicopter.

Saturday 24 November

With all the events of the past week, Mum forgot that she had a long-standing arrangement to spend this weekend with Mary-Jane, one of her oldest friends. Just like Mum, Mary-Jane is one of the least military-type people you are ever likely to meet. Their friendship was cemented on a Duke of Edinburgh exercise they signed up for at school (a purely UCAS-based exercise aimed at getting them into university, even by their own admission). Their group failed its expedition to the Brecon Beacons when Mum set light to her hair on the camp stove and Mary-Jane lost vital parts of the tent after failing to zip up her rucksack.

The plan for the weekend was for Mary-Jane to catch the train from London to us on the Friday for a girly night of cava, face packs and midnight chats. It was always unlikely that on the Saturday, as a surprise for Dad's homecoming, they would put Mum's home improvement plan into action: namely, hire a white van, dispose of Mum and Dad's old bed and replace it with a new one from a knock-down furniture emporium in the next county.

Ever since they got married, Dad has been desperate to replace their pastel pink bed, one of Mum's contributions to the marital home when they pooled their furniture. Dad gets paid an extra chunk of money for being in Iraq; 'danger money', Mum calls it. She's decided to spend it, even though they haven't yet received it, which is very unlike her- she's usually the sort of person who keeps the family plastic in the freezer. Dad's absence seems to be doing strange things to her.

I'm not sure it's legal to rig a baby seat up in the front of a white van but that's what Mum and Mary-Jane did when we collected it from the rental depot earlier. Mum doesn't like leaving Dannatt at home alone after the chicken business so she crammed him into the foot well beneath me. It was quite a squash as we drove back home to get the old bed, which Mum and Mary-Jane dismantled this morning.

Back at the house, Mum and Mary-Jane persuaded the group of crewmen who share the quarter next to ours to load the old bed into the van for them. With everything going weirdly to plan, we drove to the recycling centre, launched the bed into an enormous skip, and then we were off, whizzing along country lanes in search of the bed shop. Taking corners too wide and forcing other cars onto the verge (Mum is a bad driver in her own car so she was never going to win any awards in a Ford Transit), Mary-Jane and Mum started singing 'Sisters Are Doin' It for Themselves' at the top of their voices. Midway through the chorus of the Pointer's Sisters 'Yes We Can Can', the engine lurched, before sputtering into an eerie silence, yet the van was still coasting along.

'The accelerator must have snapped,' Mum concluded when repeated pressing produced no power. The van drifted to a standstill in the middle of a small country lane, blocking most of the carriageway in both directions.

Mum and Mary-Jane embarked on a ridiculous conversation about how they might fix the van. Dannatt's weary expression suggested he thought they should learn to drive one first. And then, as if he'd been watching from his helicopter overhead, Dad chose this moment to ring Mum on her mobile.

'Have you checked the petrol gauge?'

'Oh no,' said Mum.

'What?'

'They said at the rental place we needed to to fill up. I forgot.'

'Where are you now?'

'I don't know.'

'How can you not know where you?'

'Well, we are somewhere between the station and the shops but I only know the way from memory, not road name.'

'Can you see a petrol station anywhere?'

'Just fields and sheep.'

'You're going to have to call the RAC.'

'I didn't renew our membership last month,' Mum said, her voice wobbling a bit.

'You're going to have to call and renew now then,' Dad said kindly 'Don't worry. I'll find the number for you.'

It was two hours before the fourth emergency service found us. £160 lighter (£90 for the emergency call out, £20 for the jerry can of petrol and £50 for the van hire), a little shamed-faced and bed-less, we returned the van to the rental depot. Mum and Mary-Jane tried to cheer themselves up with a takeaway and the X-Factor much later on but it was a grim-faced Mum who made herself up a camp bed on her bedroom floor with some of Dad's survival equipment.

Tuesday 27 November

Mum doesn't do camping so a £2,000 Tempura bed arrived today. Clearly all attempts at being frugal have been abandoned. The nice crewmen from next door assembled it for her. They didn't seem surprised when she explained that the original plan hadn't worked.

Thursday 29 November

We went over to Charlotte's house this morning to check if she was okay. Matt left for Iraq late last night and it was obvious from her puffy eyes that she had been crying. She didn't seem herself at all. Mum had brought a box of Charlotte's favourite cakes.

'I'm sorry, I just can't face them,' said Charlotte, looking as though she might gag.

Mum gave her a hug. 'I never feel hungry when I'm feeling low either,' she said.

Charlotte broke away and smiled, despite everything. 'I'm pregnant. I feel as sick as a dog.'

Instantly, the atmosphere lifted and Mum and Charlotte spent a happy couple of hours talking about babies. Mum let Charlotte change my nappy to get her into practice whilst Dannatt sneaked the uneaten cakes from the coffee table.

Friday 30 November

Dad just rang to say his flight home been confirmed and he will be arriving here on Tuesday.

'Matt and the others got here on Thursday and the handover's going well so we can come home as planned.'

'What?' Mum sounded startled.

Because she now refuses to believe anything the RAF has to say about dates and times, she has been telling people Dad is sure to be delayed. After consulting the Yellow Pages and making several frenzied calls, she established that the local beauty salons have no space to sort out the gorilla growth she is sporting on her legs and the hairdressers can only just squeeze her in for a cut if she agrees to dry her own hair.

Mum is learning the hard way that if you live on a military station, you need to book these things well in advance when there's a return of service husbands. We went straight out Boots to buy some Veet.

Sunday 2 December

Dad left Iraq today. He rang to confirm shortly before boarding his flight. Mum looked the happiest I have seen her look since Dad left.

Monday 3 December

Dad rang again today to say he has he had reached Cyprus, where military personnel returning from active service break their journey for twenty-hours to 'decompress'.

'Decompression' appears to mean sitting through lectures on how to cope with life back at home, followed by an evening unwinding with a voucher for two beers to encourage sensible celebrations. I imagine this is probably what most people need after a bad day at the office, rather than two months in a war zone, but at least the military is making efforts to support them.

'I reckon we'll be with you mid-afternoon tomorrow but I'll ring you when we land.'

Mum was applying the Veet as they chatted.

'I can't really stay,' she said, raising her leg in the air and trying to apply the cream to the back of her thigh. 'Right, I need to go.'

'What are you doing?' Dad asked, suspiciously.

'Just making myself beautiful for you,' she said. 'See you tomorrow!'

In raising her leg up, Mum had inadvertently smeared cream across an area of hair that I don't think she meant to defuzz. She looked like Eve in her fig leaf, except she had pink cream keeping her modest.

She scrambled into the shower to wash it off.

'Oh dear,' she said as the water washed everything away. 'I'm sure pilots like a landing strip.'

Tuesday 4 December

We are going to meet Dad off the coach later, down at the squadron hangars, with all the other families whose relatives have been on this deployment.

Mum has been up since 6am, making a 'Welcome Home' banner, blowing balloons and painting her nails. She looks manicured and exhausted, happy and nervous, all at the same time.

Wednesday 5 December

Mum squealed with delight when she saw Dad's mobile telephone number flashing up on the house phone yesterday afternoon. She didn't immediately answer, laughing nervously as she held the handset away from her. When she finally spoke, she sounded stilted. Just as she found her voice, Dad cut across her.

'I'm still in Cyprus,' his voice crackled down the line. 'Our plane went tits. I don't know when I'll be out of here'.

RAF planes and helicopters seem, in my limited experience, to go 'tits' on a fairly frequent basis. Part of the problem seems to be how old they are. The one Dad flies is nearly forty years old.

'Some of the aircraft are actually second-hand!' Mum explained to Bunny when she rang to update on Dad's journey this evening.

'Oh for F-', Mum put my hands over my ears, 'sake, darling. How is that even possible? That's crazy.'

'They sometimes buy aircraft from other countries when they are upgrading theirs for newer models.'

In normal circumstances, Mum and Bunny would support this sort of economy. They share a love of car boot sales, eBay bargains and charity shops.

'When it needs to stay in the bloody air, they should be buying new. The thought of Will having to fly about in someone else's cast off. I have never heard anything like it, it's a scandal.'

Like Mum, Bunny didn't receive the news that Dad was stuck in Cyprus due to a dodgy plane very well.

After they hung up, Mum took me out of the dress and matching tights ensemble she had bought in preparation for Dad's return, removed the bow she had attached to Dannatt's collar and swapped her new dress for her pyjamas. Then we all had a very early night.

Thursday 6 December

Dad rang several times today with updates that offered no useful information. The plane is still broken so he and his colleagues are kicking their heels whilst they wait for engineers to diagnose and fix the problem. Mum threw the phone at the wall.

Friday 7 December

More updates, no information.

Saturday 8 December

Dad should consider a career in politics. He is becoming extremely adept at delivering bulletins without saying anything.

Sunday 9 December

Only one bulletin today. I think Dad is starting to fear the response he will get when he calls to say nothing has changed.

Monday 10 December

At 5am this morning we were woken by the sound of Dannatt howling in the kitchen. Mum crept downstairs, holding me and Dad's cricket bat. Through the frosted glass in the back door, we could make out a figure carrying things from the side gate into the garden. Mum had me in a vice-like grip as Dannatt continued to bark, jumping up on his back legs and scrabbling at the door.

Then the person's full outline appeared in the window of the door, a key turned in the lock, the handle of the door moved and Dannatt went berserk.

A tanned, slightly gaunt Dad stepped into the kitchen, wearing his desert fatigues and an Iraqi shemagh. I found myself in a crush of arms and legs, tail-wagging, kisses, woofs, giggles and then raucous, celebratory belly-laughs as Mum and Dad hugged each other.

Their laughter was so infectiously happy that I laughed too.

'Has she done that before?' asked Dad, looking down at me and then at Mum, wide-eyed.

They laughed again and so did I.

'No, she must have been saving it up for you!'

Later on, over tea and toast, Dad explained how he had got home in the end.

'After five days of watching them trying to fix a plane without the correct parts, we heard the spares they had sent out to us were being held up in customs. That was when some of us decided to pay for a normal flight to Heathrow and share a taxi home.'

As the sun was rising, we got into Mum and Dad's new bed and snuggled down together. We slept most of the morning with me nestled in the middle. The rest of the day was almost dream-like, with everyone fuzzy from the sleep. Mum and Dad kept hugging one another, as though they couldn't quite believe they were finally back together and they needed to double-check it was true.

At bedtime, when we were settling down again, Mum put me in my nursery. I struggled to fall asleep. All I could hear was a lot of whispering and giggling.

'The best pilots don't need a landing strip,' said Dad.

2008

Thursday 1 May

Today is May Day, when tradition would have us dancing around maypoles and celebrating the arrival of spring, but there aren't many celebrations here. Dancing maybe; I'm sure Mum would tell you that she is being led a merry dance.

Dad is returning to Iraq for another eight-week deployment at the end of next month. His current posting is nearly over so, as soon as he gets back from the Middle East, he will move jobs, only nobody seems to know the location of the new posting. It could be Northern Ireland, Somerset, Cornwall, or possibly the other side of this station, if he switches over to the other helicopter type flown here. From a tent in Baghdad, he will try and determine where we are moving to and, from the study in our Oxfordshire military quarter, Mum will oversee the arrangements for a new house, hopefully in the same place. Maybe she would be coping better with all the exciting possibilities and changes that lie ahead if she wasn't due to have another baby in the middle of them all. The baby is due on 1 September, just 2 days after Dad is due home from Iraq.

The beautiful baby news was discovered when Mum's post-Christmas diet failed to reduce the spare tyre she was carrying around her midriff. The investigations into why she was continuing to gain weight once all the mince pies and stollen had been eaten up were woefully unceremonious. During a weekly shop in bleakest January, Mum chucked a pregnancy test into the trolley and, when we got home, whilst Dad unloaded the shopping from the car, she nipped off to the bathroom. As he struggled into the kitchen with another round of bags, she waved the pregnancy stick at him.

'Wouldn't it be a tick if you are pregnant and a cross if you aren't?' he asked.

'You know it doesn't work like that- it's not a piece of homework.'

After she had taken a second test to be doubly sure, they unpacked the baked beans and bananas in silence, both looking shell-shocked.

Mum is now five months pregnant with nesting instincts that have gone into overdrive. She constantly pesters Dad for updates on his new job but, despite his best efforts to get his posting officer to reveal what he's planning, they are still none the wiser. Knowing he may not make it home in time for the arrival of the new baby, his solution to the lack of domestic bliss in our house is to take us on holiday. We leave tomorrow morning.

A holiday is a good idea in theory but I'm not sure how helpful this particular holiday will be as a way of soothing a pregnant, grumpy, anxious Mum. If we were flying off somewhere hot, with childcare, catering, and a lounger by an infinity pool, Dad might have been onto something but the pennies wouldn't stretch that far. Instead, we are getting the ferry over to France for a week of self-catering. We're crossing from Poole to Cherbourg, which Grandad says is the route that involves the most amount of driving and the most amount of time on the ferry. I think one of Mum's money-off vouchers is responsible for this decision.

Once in France, we aren't taking the autoroutes, the fastest, most direct way of travelling. Instead, Mum plans to take us along the back roads, which are free (you have to pay a toll on the autoroutes), deluding herself that this will give us a more authentic, educational passage through France. And what is waiting for us at the other end? Not a hotel or a villa but a one-bedroom gite, which was worryingly still available online right before the holiday season. I may only be eight months old but I can hear a few alarm bells. The fact that:

a.) we need to leave home at 4am tomorrow to get the ferry

b.) our journey is thirteen hours long

c.) Mum's pregnancy means she needs the loo every twenty minutes

d.) she can't speak French

e.) she can't drive on the right side of the road at the best of times, let alone the wrong side

leads me to suspect that this is unlikely to be a relaxing experience for any of us.

Friday 2 May

If only Mum had agreed to let Dad buy the European maps for the Sat Nav. She insisted she would be able to get us to our gite with her map-reading skills but this is proving to be an ambitious claim. In his line of work, I expect Dad is accustomed to a better standard of navigation than what is currently on offer. I bet his navigator doesn't spill chai latte on the maps and make baby shower notes over the co-ordinates.

We have spent the past half an hour orbiting Rennes. Everyone is sick of the Irish lullaby CD that Mum has been playing since I started grizzling around Newbury. Dad has only been fed sporadically since leaving home so he's already tetchy, as am I, being well overdue a jar of baby food.

At least I am being spared Mum's selection of pulverised purees on this trip. Small mercies. A couple of months ago, in preparation for weaning me, she attended an organic baby food workshop run by the real nappy lady, who seems to be branching out into other baby-related industries. Real nappies and organic baby food just don't mix. How can you recommend putting orange and red purees of carrot and red pepper in one end of a baby, then suggest catching it in a cloth at the other end? The stains are horrendous. My real nappies look like they've been tie-died with vegetable juice.

To sum up, the atmosphere in our overcrowded BMW estate is tense. With the boot bursting at the seams, hemmed in by baby-related paraphernalia, it is beyond ridiculous that Mum originally planned to bring Dannatt with us. She had been at quite an advanced stage of acquiring a pet passport when she came up with an alternative plan- to get him rehomed.

To be fair, her affection for Dannatt had been seriously tested by the time she reached this decision. There was the constant chewing of her favourite things, which showed no signs of easing. There was his moodiness about my arrival, which improved temporarily, but grew worse again in March when I learned to crawl and he struggled to cope with another creature moving about his turf on all fours. And there were the walks where he disappeared off by himself and refused to rejoin us, which often ended with Mum calling on the RAF Dog Handling Unit to get him back.

The final straw came with the delivery of some new furniture last month. After two years of making do with a third hand set of sofas, Mum and Dad treated themselves to some new ones. Mum was so elated that our sitting room no longer looked like the waiting room in a used car showroom that she spent almost an entire day purring over them, plumping their cushions, going into the sitting room to admire them, even stroking them. To a dog still smarting from being dethroned by a baby, it was another new and unwelcome rival.

When Dad went downstairs to make breakfast the following morning, he found the ground floor of the house covered in feathers, a scene not dissimilar to the massacre of our chicken. Something had savaged the sofa cushions and there was no mysterious terrier to blame this time. Then Mum came downstairs, ever feverish about her morning fix of caffeine, and we held our breath as we awaited the explosion.

'Battersea' was all she said as she poured herself a coffee and returned upstairs without even a sideways glance at the mess.

After lengthy negotiations, Dad persuaded her to take things down a notch; the compromise was doggy borstal- a training establishment that promises to reform delinquent pets. At a cost of £800, this was not a cheap option. There was no money left to pay for it after the Easter Monday bank holiday sofa splurge so they returned the new suite to DFS for a partial refund (they were stuck with the matching armchair, which had taken the hit) and got their old suite back from their friends. A week later, we waved Dad off as he left for Hertfordshire to deliver Dannatt to his new trainers. Initially, four weeks of pet prison seemed unenviable but right now its possibly preferable to this disastrous trip.

Saturday 3 May

Last night, we broke our journey at a B&B in a tiny hamlet near Nantes. It was run by an elderly couple who had one guest room and not a word of English between them. As Mum can barely speak any French, dinner was hard work. We ate with our hosts, with Dad acting as interpreter because he was the only person able to speak a morsel of French.

'Ou est le jam-bon sand-witch?' asked Mum, pointing to the basket of sliced baguette.

Dad looked at Monsieur Chevrolet apologetically but he was staring silently at his plate of radishes and didn't appear to have heard. Dad passed Mum the bread.

'Ma femme est des ordures au francais,' Dad explained to Madam Chevrolet.

'What did you say?' asked Mum.

'I said you love French hors d'oeuvres.'

In the end, we only claimed one of the 'B's out of our B&B entitlement as no one could face the same awkward exchanges over breakfast. We left early and hungry.

After another two hours strapped in my rearward facing car seat, with nothing but a pile of fleece nappies and a travel cot for company, the strains of the same Irish melodies playing on loop over the car audio system, I began to object, volubly. Before arriving at the gite, Mum had thrown the CD out into the French countryside and started another map-related squabble with Dad.

Our gite is every bit as small as I imagined, although admittedly charming, with a wood burning stove, pretty furnishings and old beams. Peace reins in our household once again now that everyone is out of the car and digesting lunch in our tiny garden. Dad is ecstatic about the presence of a BBQ, as is Mum, as this means he will be usefully occupied in the evenings, making their dinner, leaving her free to sit outside with her book, catching the evening sunshine once I am tucked up in bed. Bliss.

Wednesday 7 May

There have been no BBQs because it hasn't stopped raining since we finished that first lunch in the garden. It's starting to look as though Mum needn't have brought sun tan lotion, sun hats, swimming costumes, beach towels- in fact, most of the things we carted six hundred miles with us.

There is virtually nothing to do here in the wet. Mum and Dad promised we would spend our time swimming at the pool we share with the main house, sitting in cafes or walking through the countryside. Instead, we have spent a large portion of the holiday at the local 'Ocean' supermarket, planning meals and buying food, and the rest of the time eating those meals.

It is now day four of this and we are all getting cabin fever. Dad thinks it might be fun to do a tour of one of the big brandy houses whilst we dodge the rain so we are off to Cognac later on.

'It's got nothing to do with the free Hennessy samples,' he said to Mum, unconvincingly, I thought.

Thursday 8 May

On arrival in Cognac, light drizzle quickly morphed into a torrential storm. I was cosy in my pram but Mum got soaked to the skin within seconds. Unlike Dad, who always packs for every conceivable climate, from blizzards through to droughts, she had nothing with her for anything except the perfect summer's day. Dad ran into a shop and came back with a plastic tourist poncho- basically, a giant polythene tent that she and her bump fill to capacity.

The tour was a distraction, if nothing else. Our guide took us on a little boat trip across the Charente to explore the huge cellars where the brandy is made and kept. Dad made friends with two RAF pilots, stranded in Cognac after flying here for an air show.

'Our plane went tits last night,' they explained. I am swiftly coming to the conclusion that it's actually more remarkable when a military aircraft attempts to get airborne and doesn't 'go tits.' The whole thing baffles me. Imagine if this same level of malfunction was experienced by holidaymakers when they booked their summer trip to Europe- if people heading for some August sunshine were stunned if their plane made it to Malaga or Crete without breaking down in a field in Kent on the way.

Unable to fly back, with engineers working around the clock to try and mend their aircraft, Dad's new friends were at a loose end, a bit like us. They must have sort of RAF radar or secret handshake; Dad can pick RAF officers out of a crowd at a thousand paces. Something to do with the immaculate haircut, beige chinos, the little horse symbol on their pink shirt and chunky aviator watch.

'You might as well have my tasting vouchers,' Mum said as we were led through to the tasting hall. 'I can hardly use them at the moment. I'll drive us back.'

Knowing they might have to fly home at a moment's notice, the pilots did the same, giving their vouchers to Dad. Within the space of thirty minutes, he had sampled eight different types of brandy and was suddenly finding everything hilarious. For the first time, I realised that he doesn't laugh very often. Maybe a life filled with impending pregnancies, tours of Iraq and house moves, with all their related uncertainties, can get a bit heavy at times.

It was good to see him discovering some bonhomie in his surroundings, or it was until his main source of amusement became the tour guide's use of English. The guide stared at us fiercely when Dad loudly recounted the Battle of Agincourt. As he started to manhandle a rare bottle of Hennessy XO, our pilot friends bade us farewell and went off in search of their broken plane.

We emerged from the gloom of the brandy cellars to find the storm had blown through and the sun was coming out from behind the clouds. We had an early tea at a café, sitting outside and warming ourselves in the afternoon rays.

'There's a lot of pressure on a holiday like this, isn't there?' Dad said, soaking up the cognac with some bread and cheese. Mum nodded. 'It's so hard to relax when we know there's another stretch of time apart on the horizon. I wanted this holiday to be perfect but it could never be because it's still life, just somewhere different, with the same worries. Like that plane going tits nearby, just like they do wherever we fly them.'

'I know,' she said, lacing her fingers through his and kissing him.

'I'm going to miss you,' he said.

'Me too.'

When Mum drove us back to the gite, minus her licence and with no idea of the route, Dad proved to be an even worse navigator than her but it didn't seem to matter; they both found it funny when the car got stuck down a muddy farm track and I liked listening to them giggling together as I nodded off to sleep in the back.

Saturday 10 May

Today is our last full day here. The rain returned so we spent it at 'Ocean'. Rather than feeling relaxed and tanned, Mum and Dad are leaving cranky, vitamin D deficient and each half a stone heavier.

Sunday 11 May

One of the few advantages of a road trip is the opportunity for long chats. During the journey home, Mum and Dad covered every topic they could think of, from baby names to their views on current foreign policy to Dad's next posting. All the things they didn't get the chance to talk about when Dad was off in Iraq.

Driving through the French countryside, now beautifully sunny, they decided that at work tomorrow Dad will accept the posting in Cornwall doing Search and Rescue.

'It's very rewarding work and, that way, I can be around whilst the baby's small as there are no tours in Iraq with that role.'

Instead of arguing about maps (we took the Autoroute), they spent the next thirteen hours swapping ideas about what their new Cornish life will look like, from clotted cream and Cornish pasties to trips out to Jamie Oliver's new restaurant in Newquay and walks along the Lizard Peninsula. It sounds idyllic-highly unlikely- but idyllic.

Friday 16 May

Dad rang home at lunch time with news about his job.

'It turns out there is no posting in Cornwall.'

'What? You mean someone else has been given it?'

'No, there was never a position for me to fill. Someone got their wires crossed.'

'What?' said Mum. 'I don't understand how that's possible. Either there's a job or there isn't.'

'There isn't.'

'But-.'

'Can we talk about this later?'

Mum always tries to get to the bottom of these confusions, failing to realise that they are the RAF equivalent of a black hole, from which nothing will ever escape, certainly not answers, information or logic.

In frustration, she rang Bunny.

'I'm glad, darling, to be honest. Cornwall's a bloody long way to visit. You might as well have been posted abroad. Couldn't he get a job in London?'

'Flying helicopters?'

'No, darling, as the Queen's equerry, something like that.'

'Don't they handle horses?'

'Oh, I don't know, darling, I just want to see a bit more of you all.'

'That was the reason for Cornwall,' Mum explained. 'Then he wouldn't have kept disappearing off to Iraq. I think we may end up in Somerset or Northern Ireland now.'

'Oh, for f-,' hands over my ears, 'sake, darling. Do they give you extra money for hardship tours?'

Later, during my bath time, Dad went over the options. 'We need to decide whether we want to move to Northern Ireland, where my posting officer's keen to send me,' he said, handing Mum my bunny rabbit towel. 'Or Somerset to do an exchange with the Navy.'

'What, become a sailor?'

'No, the Navy has an air corp. I'd be flying a Navy helicopter. We need quick decisions. I want this sorting before I go to Iraq and that's less than six weeks away now.'

Mum seemed completely thrown by the whole thing.

'I had a picture of the baby's nursery in our Cornish quarter by the coast. I was going to give Dannatt walks by the sea and teach the children to make sandcastles.'

I think that's the RAF definition of building castles in the sky.

Monday 19 May

After a weekend of agonising, deliberating and debating with Mum, Dad has decided to put himself forward for the Navy exchange. Mum has never been to Somerset but she likes the sound of the undulating countryside, cider and, most of all, the fact that Dad will have to convert to the different aircraft type flown by the Navy. That will take at least six months, during which time he can't be sent away...

Wednesday 21 May

Mum stood in the hallway this morning, gingerly opening an official-looking letter.

'You're a solicitor, you've hardly got form,' laughed Dad. 'Here, let me read it.'

It was from the Criminal Records' Bureau- the results of Mum's recent CRB application. She's decided to do some voluntary work with the chaplain at our local Young Offenders' Institution.

'Funnily enough, you don't have any convictions,' he said, passing Mum the letter. 'But I don't understand why you are doing this,' he said. 'You have enough going on looking after Millie and coping with all the changes that are coming up for us.'

I don't think Dad really wants Mum visiting potentially dangerous criminals in her spare time.

'I adore Millie but I just need something beyond these four walls, especially when there's so much coming up. It's all stuff I have barely any say over. If I stay at home just thinking about it all day long, I will go bananas.'

'Why don't you just go back to your old job? At least they pay you to hang around prisons.'

'We've been over this. I can't hold down a job that requires me to do out of hours work when I have Millie to look after and you're in Iraq. Anyway, we're moving in a few months' time. It would just be messing them round to go back for three months.'

'But you're pregnant. A prison's not a great environment for you to be in.'

'I worked until I was almost full term with Mille- I was always in and out of prisons back then. I want something for me. If not this, then something.'

Mum already knew from her workdays that we live almost next door to a YOI, home to young male offenders aged fifteen to eighteen. She got an address for the chaplaincy from the internet and wrote a letter, explaining her idea. A week later, she received a phone call from a man called Tom, the Church of England chaplain there, accepting her offer. It turns out prison visiting isn't a completely random idea dreamt up by Mum.

At lunchtime today, clutching her clean bill of health from the CRB, Mum telephoned Tom to see when she could begin helping. She had him on speaker phone whilst she tried to feed me a disgusting, homemade concoction of broccoli and alfalfa sprouts, a recipe dreamt up by the real nappy lady.

'Hang on a minute- it's these Catholics, always creating some drama,' Tom puffed, before dropping the handset. I spat green goo over Mum.

A few moments later, whilst Mum sponged her top, Tom was back on the line. 'Sorry about that, we're sharing an office at the moment and they're forever burning something.'

'Oh,' said Mum, sounding worried, forgetting she was holding another spoonful of mush. It slopped onto her slipper. 'The young offenders?'

'No, the Catholics. It's just some incense but the fire officer is annoyed with them for disabling our office smoke alarm. Anyway, come in next Wednesday at six and I'll collect you from reception. Bring your papers,' he barked before hanging up.

Mum hummed as she ran her slipper under the kitchen tap. Despite all of her complaining about how tough life was as a criminal solicitor, I think she must have liked it more than she lets on as she seems uncharacteristically excited about her new role. Abandoning her 'Sprouting Beans for Baby' recipe book and the mountain of aubergines ready to be liquidized, we drove to her favourite café, where she ordered a huge decaf cappuccino and a wedge of cheesecake. She spooned creamy deliciousness into our mouths until we were both in a dessert delirium; I will never ever eat another vegetable again.

Saturday 24 May

Dannatt, Mum and Dad's prodigal son, has returned. Having been through his time of rebellion, repentance and reform, we welcomed him back into the bosom of the family. The canine correction centre appears to have worked a minor miracle. He left a renegade and he has returned a genteel officer, with manners and etiquette. The fact that Mum had him stripped of his family jewels a few days before he went away may have contributed to this change. Whatever the case, even she seems to think the transformation was worth the cost of her new sitting room furniture.

Monday 26 May

Today provided Mum and Dad with an ugly reminder of their attempts last year to become property magnates. After watching one too many episodes of 'Property Ladder', they bought a rental property in Liverpool last year. Mum had seen someone on 'Homes Under the Hammer' say that Liverpool, the capital of culture for 2008, was bursting with property potential. On that basis, they called in for an afternoon and selected a flat. They appear to have put about as much thought into this as they do their Friday night takeaway or Blockbuster rental. Literally, the day after completion, the worldwide economy went into meltdown, shaving off a hefty slice of its value overnight.

Dad was briefly hopeful about their investment when he found an ancient Liverpool football shirt in the loft, signed by Kenny Dalglish. Mum asked if it would pay off the mortgage when he put it on eBay. I can't do the Maths but I think £167,000 minus £2.80 is still a lot of money.

Currently worth £40,000 less than they paid for it, miles from where we currently live, the rent failing to cover their interest-free mortgage, Mum and Dad can't afford to use managing agents. It can be excruciating when someone asks them if they own their own place, which they often do; it's a popular choice of conversation at patch dinner parties.

'Yes, we have a little investment, big enough for the three of us if we ever need to live there,' they say, trying to change the subject.

It all sounds very sensible until the person inevitably asks its location.

'Liverpool? Why there? That's a long way from you. It must be a nightmare to oversee. You must have agents managing it for you then?

'No, we do that ourselves.'

'At least it must be paying for itself,' they smile, before telling the rest of the table how much tax they owe on their property profits for the year.

When people ask them about the flat these days, Mum and Dad pretend they haven't heard. When things are really bad, they deny its existence even to one another, allowing any correspondence about it to sit on the hallway table for weeks.

The latest reminder of their property portfolio came in the form of a phone call. It was Spike, who runs the management company responsible for the communal aspects of the apartments. He collects ground rent and a monthly service charge from all the flat owners to cover cleaning, painting, electricity and general maintenance. The communal areas haven't been painted or cleaned since Mum and Dad bought the flat. Mum and Dad like to think the building is insured but they have never seen any evidence that it is, and their tenants frequently call them from the darkened hallways to complain that the electricity has been cut off.

There are rumours that Spike drives around Liverpool in a new Range Rover Sports with lowered suspension, blacked out windows and crocodile skin interior. I don't think we're talking mock croc. His company address changes every few months. In short, he's the epitome of all that is shady.

'Why the f***ing 'ell have I not had a cheque off of youse yet? I'm getting a right cob on, you posh twat.'

This was Spike's opener. It was relatively polite for him. The first time Mum spoke to him, she thought he was doing an impersonation of Harry Enfield's Scousers but she now thinks the Scousers do impersonations of Spike.

In the past, she has tried to be logical with Spike but he has no sense of reason. She has tried to be assertive but then he just gets vicious. Today she went straight for compliance, offering to send him the money immediately.

'I'm f***ing gonna suse youse,' he said. 'I'll see you in court, you f***ing southern scumbag.'

As Mum said to Dad later on, how do you deal with someone who threatens to sue you when you are actually offering them money? You would have thought she might know, as the lawyer amongst us.

Wednesday 28 May

Dad was night flying again this evening, something he is doing a lot at the moment. Apparently, it's safest to fly under cover of darkness when he's in Iraq so this is all part of his preparations for going back. It's now just over a month until he goes. As it doesn't get dark until after 9pm, he'll be out until at least midnight, buzzing about overhead, upsetting the locals. I quite like the noise of his helicopter; it's comforting to hear him patrolling the skies when I'm curled up in bed. Until he comes in, that is, and sets Dannatt off barking and disturbs us all.

Mum was due to do her first prison visit tonight so Charlotte came over to babysit me.

'You're so petite compared with me!' Mum said as she welcomed Charlotte in.

Charlotte is six months pregnant but Mum, who is a month behind her, looks considerably further along.

'I don't really want to advertise my bump- do you think this covers it?' Mum asked, dressed in Dad's enormous sweatshirt and a pair of tracksuit bottoms.

'You look great,' said Charlotte.

She didn't look great but I suppose she had successfully managed to make herself look fat rather than pregnant.

I didn't go to sleep for Charlotte; I was still awake when Mum returned, buzzing with her exploits.

'The boys were quite wary of me until Tom- he's the chaplain- explained I'm married to a helicopter pilot,' she said. 'I seemed to go up in their estimation then.'

'What did you spend the evening doing?' asked Charlotte.

'They'd just finished dinner when I arrived so Tom and I collected them from the dining area. We walked along endless corridors and through a million locked doors and gates to a quiet room away from the cells and noise. We sat in a circle and chatted as a group. Then Tom suggested we pray for each other. '

'Didn't that seem strange?'

'Not really. They were so open and honest. One boy asked us to pray for his Grandma's birthday tomorrow. There was another boy called Zachary who seemed so shy so I was surprised when he asked for prayer for his sentencing hearing, which is coming up soon. I didn't often get to see that sort of vulnerability when I was representing kids like them at court. We lit a candle each time we said a prayer.'

'Were you scared, letting them light candles?' asked Charlotte.

'I thought I might be but I wasn't. It was such a lovely group. I asked if someone would pray about Will going back to Iraq. They were so concerned they all prayed for him. They stayed quiet as we walked them back to their cells. It was beautiful, surreal and bizarrely peaceful.'

'That's remarkable. Well done, Anna. Will you go back?'

'I'm hoping to. When we were returning the boys, I managed to get locked in a cell. The gaolers weren't very happy with me.'

'How on earth did that happen?'

'I don't think my outfit helped.'

Once she mentioned it, it did seem a bit institutional.

'I'm sure it will be fine, I'll be here same time next week,' promised Charlotte.

As Mum laid me in my cot, we heard the whirring of blades just overhead and she smiled.

Friday 30 May

With all the preparations for Iraq and the ongoing saga of our mystery move, Dad forgot it was Mum's thirtieth birthday tomorrow. Months ago, he asked Aunty Chloe, Uncle Mark and Uncle Alex and his girlfriend Gemma to stay with us for the weekend but that's pretty much as far as the planning went.

Dad was on his mobile to Uncle Mark when he came home this evening, briefly kissing Mum as she blended parsnips and mung beans.

'Mate, you've not signed us in- we're stuck down here with this very friendly, super-helpful guard. NOT,' hissed Uncle Mark.

'Damn,' said Dad.

'You'd forgotten.'

'Not at all.'

'You'd forgotten you've got four people coming to stay for the weekend, which means you've forgotten it's Anna's birthday tomorrow.'

'Maybe a little bit,' Dad whispered.

'Good luck with that, matey.'

Mum stopped blending, leaving her baby food alchemy and appearing in the sitting room with grey mulch spread across her forehead. 'Can you come and feed Millie so I can get on with the goji berries?'

'I have a surprise for you, a birthday surprise,' Dad said, uncertainly. 'I have four surprise birthday guests waiting for you at the guard room. Ta-da.'

'Oh no, is this a wind up?' she said, spinning round to check behind her.

'No, it's a real-live treat.'

'What? Who?'

'Chloe, Mark, Alex and Gemma.'

'Bloodeeeeee hell. Is this a joke?' she said, wiping the mulch into her hair.

Dad shook his head. Mum's face fell. 'I wanted to watch Breaking Bad in my PJs and eat ice cream.'

'I'm so sorry but you need to pull yourself together and make up some beds whilst I collect them from the guard room.'

'This is why I hate surprises,' she yelled after him as he ran out of the house.

By the time they arrived at the house, she had managed to find an Alice band to cover the baby food and feed me but the house otherwise remained the same.

'Suuuurprise!' said Uncle Mark and Alex in unison, in a way that suggested they were loving watching Dad make such a monumental mess of his arrangements. Chloe and Gemma looked embarrassed.

'Sorry,' they said. They seemed to know how Mum was feeling. 'I expect you just wanted to watch Breaking Bad in your PJs, didn't you?'

Mum blushed. 'Not at all.'

'Well, we have champagne and chocolates,' said Uncle Mark 'so before long you won't care about the baby food in your hair and the four people you didn't want for the weekend camped out in various parts of your house. You will be positively embracing the thirties.'

'Mess?' asked Dad.

'Do you mean me?' asked Mum, her lip wobbling.

'No, THE Mess, for a birthday drinkie. You always look gorgeous to me, especially when you're coated in parsnip,' he said, pinching her bottom.

Mum didn't look as though the Mess was her preferred birthday venue but they were a bit short of options with no babysitter or reservation to allow them to go out and no solid food in the house.

The Mess has a bar and canteen and, as the name suggests, nights spent there can be a messy affair, with lots of uniformed, usually disciplined, men and women letting their hair down at the end of the day. Dad, Uncle Mark and Uncle Alex all love the Mess.

'It reminds them of their single days,' Mum told Gemma on the walk there, a little tactlessly maybe, given that Uncle Alex and Gemma were both single until they met on the Guardian website a few months ago. Yet Mum seemed to be right. An air of joyous abandon descended on the menfolk as they entered the bar and started ordering beers.

'They will forget us and possibly the way home,' she predicted, leaning across me to Gemma, whose crinkly brow suggested she already didn't like the Mess-effect.

This was Gemma's first visit to a military station. She seemed visibly shocked when someone called 'naked bar' and a group of men at the next table started to strip off, throwing flying boots and fire-retardant vests our way. She covered my eyes.

'Maybe we should get Millie home,' she said faintly.

It took a while to leave as Dad had started to give a very bad rendition of 'You've Lost That Loving Feeling' to Uncle Mark and Uncle Alex was aiming a champagne cork at the bar bell.

When we got back, Mum ordered Dad to make up some beds on the sofas for the uncles and aunties.

'What the hell is this?' said Dad, trying to disentangle himself from the spare sheets, duvets and nappies he had dragged out of the airing cupboard.

'I'm germinating some beans.'

'In the airing cupboard?'

'The real nappy lady said it's a great way to create organic baby food.'

'The real nappy lady reckons we should be growing Millie's food alongside her nappies? Let's hope the thirties deposits some wisdom in the night.'

Saturday 31 May

I think it's probably inhospitable to hoover under house guests and pack their belongings away when they are still asleep but this is what Mum started to do when she found her sitting room strewn with people and kebab detritus this morning.

'Oi!' shouted Uncle Alex, chucking a sofa cushion at her. Dannatt thought it was being thrown for him and started to savage it.

Dad had been to the Spar shop and was already frying bacon. He brought bacon sandwiches and coffee through to the sitting room, where my uncles and aunties were in various states of consciousness.

'Anyone ready to sing to the birthday girl?' Dad asked.

As people created a discordant dirge, he produced a velvet box and knelt down on one knee in front of Mum.

'For putting up with me and this way of life,' he said.

To say he hadn't planned this weekend, he had come up trumps with his gift. A diamond ring in the shape of a daisy.

'How did you afford it?' squealed Mum.

'You know when I said Spike needed paying extra for pest control? Well he did, or he said he did, but I inflated the price to you and used the money to buy this.'

'He bought your thirtieth birthday present with cockroach money,' Uncle Mark explained.

Mum didn't seem to hear; she was kissing Dad and breaking off to gaze at her present.

'Get a room,' said Uncle Alex.

'Why don't we give her our present?' said Aunty Chloe, nudging Gemma.

'Good idea. This is from the four of us,' said Gemma, producing a pink envelope from her bag.

'Pregnancy pilates!' said Mum, opening it.

'Yes, I got in touch with the real nappy lady you rate so highly; we wondered if she was running any courses and it turns out she's just trained in this.'

'Great,' said Dad. 'More chances to cross paths with the real nappy lady.'

Aunty Chloe didn't seem to pick up on Dad's ironic tone. 'She said on the phone that she's happy for you to attend with Anna. Apparently, at this stage, it can help to have an extra pair of hands to stop the pregnant person tipping sideways, that sort of thing.'

'I'd rather buy her another diamond ring.'

'It'll be fun,' smiled Mum. 'Thanks guys, it's so thoughtful of you to buy for both of us.'

'So what shall we do tonight?' asked Uncle Alex. 'Clubbing, pubbing?'

'Breaking Bad in our PJs!' said the girls. 'Boys can cook.'

The boys looked unimpressed.

'I am thirty, mother of a 9-month-old and pregnant again, 'said Mum. 'That's wild.'

Monday 2 June

Dad came home this evening with the news that he will be starting the Navy exchange in Somerset on 15 September. Mum seemed delighted to know where we'll be moving at last, although she was less happy about the timings. If the baby is overdue by a couple of weeks, it will be born during the move.

Wednesday 4 June

'Still smoke free!' said Mum.

We bumped into Amy as we were leaving our quarter to go to the med centre for the baby's 28-week check. Amy had parked her car outside a house a few doors down from us. There must be another pregnant lady on the patch trying to kick her habit.

'That's amazing, Anna! Good job. And how is this pregnancy going?' she asked, hugging Mum.

Amy knows all about this baby as it was Mum's morning sickness that finally forced her to give up the nicotine lozenges. By February, Mum couldn't stomach the sight of them, despite her cravings, and in less than a week, she was off them completely, bringing our sessions with Amy to an end.

'Really well, I think, only Will may be away for the birth.'

Amy looked concerned.

'We're actually on our way to see the midwife,' Mum explained. 'It will be fine, I'm sure,' she said breezily.

They said their good-byes and we hurried off, late as ever. Dad came across from his hangar to join us. As we sat together in the waiting room, I wished he hadn't been able to get away from work. We've had some tense times in doctors' surgeries these past few months.

The worst occasion was the booking-in appointment for this pregnancy. The three of us were assembled for what, I imagine, is often a special moment for a family- the official acknowledgement that a baby is on the way. It was all fine until the midwife got her due date wheel chart out.

'By my calculations, baby will be arriving on 1 September.'

Then she worked backwards to calculate the start of the pregnancy. 'So that means your pregnancy began on the 25 November,' she grinned.

Dad's jaw set.

'I was in Iraq then. I didn't get back until part way through December.'

There was an awkward pause. The midwife looked at the floor. Mum doesn't appear to have ever listened to anything her biology teachers taught her at school (here is a woman who has accidentally created life twice) so she didn't have the necessary knowledge to dig herself out of this hole.

'Oh,' was all she could say. 'But you are the father.'

More silence. I wasn't convinced the midwife had studied biology either. She didn't offer up any possible explanations. The whole thing became excruciating. It was only when the midwife failed to take Mum's blood and was forced to call the head midwife in to help her that we were offered a ray of light.

'It's possible that you're the father, chick,' the senior midwife said to Dad, stabbing Mum in the arm.

He didn't look chick-like to me. A bit more certainty would have helped.

'The start of the pregnancy is a technical thing- we say it begins two weeks before conception so baby could have been made up to a fortnight after the 21 November.'

The wheelie chart came out again and we all breathed a sigh of relief when two weeks on turned out to be the day Dad got back from Iraq.

At today's appointment, Dad wasn't won over by the arguments put forward by Mum, on the encouragement of the real nappy lady, and the midwife for having the baby at home.

'Look,' said Dad, 'the real nappy lady may think a home birth is the best possible start a baby can have but has she offered to come round and clear up the mess afterwards?'

'We provide plastic sheets, Mr Child, or you can use an old shower curtain,' the midwife explained.

Dad gagged. 'A shower curtain? I don't mean to be rude but what are you talking about? We live in a military quarter- we don't even have a shower. You are talking about my wife and baby doing the most primitive thing imaginable- giving birth- but what you don't understand is that our house is even more primitive than that.'

'Don't be silly,' said Mum. 'We can get a shower curtain from Homebase.'

"Silly'. You're calling me 'silly' when you want me to prepare for the arrival of our child by heading to a hardware shop? It's madness and you haven't even factored in S.H.I.T.'

'We have ways of managing if Mrs Child's bowels should open during the birth- it's very normal,' the midwife reassured them, nodding in Mum's direction. 'I have a poop-a-scoop I can bring and there'll be the shower curtain to protect your soft furnishings.'

'I am not talking about that sort of SHIT.' Dad looked outraged.

'Hopefully, that won't happen again,' said Mum, blushing.

'I am talking about the Service Housing Improvement Team. Howie-'

'Who's Howie- is this someone extra you want at the birth? It's useful to put these things in the notes,' said the midwife, her biro poised over Mum's pregnancy file.

'No, we do not want Howie at the birth. He's a pilot friend who used to live down the road from us. He spent weeks trying to clear up the carnage after his wife had their baby in their dining room. When they vacated the property, they still got billed £300 for a new carpet. The housing officer said he could detect the amniotic fluid stains, despite Howie's repeated efforts with a bar of Vanish.'

'Can you even guarantee that you are going to be at the birth?' asked Mum pointedly.

'You know I will do my best,' said Dad.

This is still a bit of a sore point between them. The RAF won't alter Dad's Iraq dates on account of the pregnancy, the rationale being that people might time their babies to get out of their deployments if they start doing this. I can see the logic but Mum can't.

'I'm sorry but, until you can guarantee that you will be at the birth, you don't get to have an opinion on the birthing arrangements,' said Mum.

Mum ordered 50 metres of builders' plastic sheeting from B&Q when we got home.

Friday 6 June

For days, the station's been buzzing with preparations for tonight's Officers' Summer Ball, an annual event held in the Mess and one of the highlights of the station's social calendar. Marquees and fairground rides went up yesterday. Overhead aircraft have been practicing display routines, with Chinook helicopters from a neighbouring base and our own Pumas and Merlins stopping local traffic with their stunts.

In our house, there have also been various preparations going on, the big decision being what Mum should wear now that nothing fits over her bump. The RAF has strict rules when it comes to the ladies' dress code for formal events. Dresses must be floor length and shoulders must be covered, further restricting Mum's current options.

'I don't think I need to worry too much,' se said. 'I am pregnant- they must make allowances.'

'You don't understand,' said Dad. 'People sometimes get sent home to change when they dress inappropriately.'

Mum finally dug out an old bridesmaid's dress that she wore to a cousin's wedding years ago.

'It fits if I don't do up the zip,' said Mum, twisting round to look in the mirror.

'You can't wear that,' said Dad, running the bath. 'My boss will be there. You'll be the talk of the night with your bra showing and half your back on display.'

'I could go without a bra.'

'No. They are like enormous melons again.'

'What? My boobs?' asked Mum, looking miserable.

'Beautiful melons. My melons,' said Dad hurriedly. 'Didn't you plan for this? We've known about the ball for ages.'

'When have I got time to go dress shopping in between midwife appointments, Annabel Karmel food prep and dog walks when I am weighed down by Millie and my bump? I thought something would still fit.'

She looked on the verge of tears.

'Why don't you wear it with a jacket over the top? Something like this?'

It barely fitted but it hid the unzipped bodice, even if it didn't match.

'I look ridiculous. No one wears a tweed jacket over a pastel pink dress,' she sobbed.

By comparison, Dad looked very dapper as he ran downstairs to answer the door. He was wearing the RAF variation of black tie, known as his Mess dress. Officially, it's known as number 5's (there are 14 different uniforms in the RAF for different occasions); unofficially, people refer to it as a 'drinking tracksuit.' It was set off by a cummerbund embroidered with his squadron's crest- a stag's head with the word 'Loyalty' written beneath.

'I'm sorry I'm late, darling,' said Bunny, squashing Dad in a hug. 'The traffic out of London was something else.'

'Why have you brought Pampers with you?'

Bunny was clutching a Family Value pack of nappies.

'We have nappies,' said Dad. 'Anna hates those ones.'

'For f-'

'Mum!'

'Look, I am as eco and veggie as the next actress but I am not using those cloths she favours. Anyway, forget that. You look stunning. What's this?' she asked, reaching for the medal pinned to his jacket.

'I got it after my tour of Iraq last year,' he said.

Bunny looked proud as she helped him put it straight.

Mum appeared on the stairs behind them, clutching the handrail in her tightly fitting bodice, wobbling in high heels that were squashing her swollen feet, giving her the appearance of Miss Piggy.

'Hello, darling. So you've tried to cobble something together. Well done,' she said, her eyebrows shooting up.

'What's the matter?' asked Mum.

'Nothing, it's a very 'avant-garde' look.'

Partially mollified, Mum clutched onto Dad as they shuffled down the hill towards the Mess. They made a rather sweet picture, as he carried her sparkly evening bag, struggling to slow down his pace to match hers in his eagerness to get to the drinks' reception.

'The Champagne and canapes never last very long,' we heard him saying as we stood waving them off.

Other couples were emerging from houses further down the road, an impressive collection of uniforms, the black tie worn by guests and a kaleidoscope of ball gowns in every colour. Bunny stood holding me on the doorstep long after Mum and Dad disappeared around the corner, admiring the train of guests all headed in the direction of the big marquee.

'The RAF scrubs up bloody well,' Bunny whispered to me.

It wasn't long before Mum and Dad were back, with Mum's bump now marked out like a giant bull's eye with a large orange stain. She looked tearful and Dad looked glum.

'Oh f**k, darling.'

'Mum!'

'Sorry, what the, what the poo happened?'

Dad explained that, whilst they were mingling outside at the drinks' reception waiting for the flypast, a group of chinooks had soared overhead so low and so loudly, seemingly from nowhere, that Mum had leapt a foot off the ground (quite a feat for one so pregnant) and knocked her neighbour's precious bubbles and Cathy Marie prawns down her front as she made her own crash landing.

'We didn't even make it into the dinner tent,' said Dad. 'I just got a glimpse of it. There were stalls set up everywhere- little carts offering Thai street food and pancake makers with every topping you could imagine and a Japanese chef juggling knives. I tried to sponge her down but it just spread the stain further and then I got ordered out of the ladies' Powder Room by the toilet attendant.'

Mum looked like she was in shock.

'Don't worry, darling, it wasn't a great outfit to start with, was it?' said Bunny. I think she was trying to comfort Mum. 'I didn't like to say it but you looked like one of those tragic figures on 'What Not to Wear'. Why don't we pop upstairs and find you something else?'

'The evening's a write-off. Nothing else fits her,' said Dad.

'Let's try, shall we? We know we can't make you look worse than you look now.'

Before long, Mum came back into the kitchen wearing a toga from a fancy-dress party she once went to in the Mess before I was born. It didn't cover her arms but it encompassed her bump and it was floor length.

'There we go,' said Bunny. 'You look beautiful, darling.'

Bunny was right; she did look rather lovely.

'We might make the duelling pianos if we hurry,' said Dad excitedly, grabbing Mum's arm.

They came in, hours later, crashing and banging around, giggling that it was one of the best parties they'd ever been to, even if some people thought Mum was part of the entertainment.

As they were getting undressed, Mum picked up Dad's jacket from the floor.

'I forget most of the time what a hero you are,' she said, looking at the medal. 'Do you remember when I decided I wanted to marry you?'

'When you saw me in my uniform for the first time?' Dad smiled.

'Yes.'

'Are you glad you did?'

'Always.'

'Even when I am irritating the hell out of you by leaving to go away?'

'Almost always,' she said, kissing him.

Monday 8 June

Something's happened to the television aerial. I hadn't realised what TV addicts Mum and Dad are until this weekend, when they had no access to it. I felt ashamed of them last night at dinner time when they were forced to eat at the table, rather than on the sofa, both scratching around for a shred of intelligent conversation, or any conversation really.

Mum rang the S.H.I.T. helpline as soon as its offices opened this morning, claiming to have an emergency. The lady she spoke to didn't seem impressed when she explained that the emergency was the likelihood of not being able to watch Big Brother tonight unless an engineer came out immediately. She laughed a big generous belly laugh, as though it was the funniest thing she'd ever heard.

'We've never got an engineer out to anyone immediately,' she chortled.

I admired her honesty. The television engineer is booked for Wednesday.

Wednesday 11 June

The TV aerial expert was booked to come between 8am and 6pm. At 6.01pm Mum rang the helpline to ask why no one has been out to us. She got the answer machine, which informed her that the offices shut at 5.30pm. I don't want to grow up cynical but I wonder if it's no coincidence that the offices have shut by the time you realise you've been seen off.

Thursday 12 June

The real nappy lady's Pregnancy Pilates began tonight at the local village hall. Claire offered to babysit me so I was spared the experience.

'I'm not going again,' said Dad as they let themselves in.

'How was it?' asked Claire.

'Horrendous. I was the only man there and it wasn't only Anna who required assistance.'

'Oh,' said Claire.

'There was one nearly full-term woman who couldn't maintain the cat position without support so I had to stand over her, holding her by the waist. Another woman got stuck sitting down cross-legged and needed a push up. The worst was a woman who ignored the advice not to lie on her back and got beached on the floor. I keep saying to Anna, 'I'm a pilot, not a Pilates assistant'.'

'How did you find it?' Claire asked Mum, who was looking unusually calm.

'Marvellous. It took a while to get into it but I feel so chilled now. The real nappy lady kept telling us to relax and breathe. Relax and breathe.'

'Which is hard to do when you're trying to stop a thirteen stone woman from slipping off her mat,' said Dad.

'I did seem to keep finding myself facing the opposite wall to all the other women or using the wrong leg,' said Mum. 'And just between us, I couldn't focus on my breathing very much because I was concentrating so hard on not breaking wind.'

'Others clearly weren't,' said Dad, raising his eyebrows, as though Claire might not understand his meaning.

'Oh dear,' said Claire, seeming to understand perfectly.

'Yep, I got that in the face several times when I was doing rear-end work.'

'I also couldn't find my pelvic floor,' confided Mum.

'Thankfully, no one asked me to help with that,' said Dad, pouring a beer.

'Same time next week?' asked Claire.

'No thanks- I will happily babysit next week,' said Dad, taking a big swig.

Friday 13 June

Since finding out we are moving to Somerset, Mum has been in planning mode. She doesn't get any say over the arrangements as the RAF decides when we move, who moves us and where we will live but she is strangely undeterred by this. This weekend we are off to Somerset to investigate potential quarters for us to live in.

Mum has had more free time lately to devote to her new moving-to-Somerset-project. This is because the real nappy lady recently went on to an international summit on weaning in Slough and has completely changed all her weaning advice. She is now promoting baby-led weaning.

BLW, as the real nappy lady and Mum call it, dispenses with all liquidisation and blending. Basically, the new approach is to load up the tray of the highchair with whatever you want and let the child fend for themselves. It creates the most almighty mess that Mum can't cope with. Bananas gets mulched, peas are scattered to the four corners of the kitchen, yogurt gets slathered over everything, Weetabix hardens like concrete to anything within reach. A full deep clean of my highchair and the surrounding environment is required after every meal and snack time.

'Can you make her lunch, please?' asked Mum when Dad walked in from work for a quick sandwich. 'I'm just finishing the packing for the weekend.'

'What should I give her?'

'There's some leftover beef in the fridge.'

'She's got three teeth. How's she going to chew through beef?'

'Just let her have a go. She can always have a banana and yogurt afterwards. If you promise to clear it up.'

'What is wrong with a jar of baby food, like our mums used to give us? Why are we feeding a child with no molars leathery meat? I haven't got time to tidy up the apocalyptic fallout this always leaves.'

But Mum had already hurried off.

Saturday 14 June

This morning, as Mum and Dad packed the car for our weekend away, storm clouds gathered overhead and seemed to follow us along the A303. Mum had talked of finding an Arthurian mound or cider orchard where we could stop to eat our lunch and walk Dannatt. To her disappointment, we didn't find any chivalric sites, only busy petrol stations.

As we pulled up in the Navy housing estate where we expect to be assigned our new home, the storm clouds finally unleashed themselves. I may be too young to fully understand pathetic fallacy but something felt ominous.

'Is this really it?' Mum asked. 'They are so grim, even for military properties.'

As you'd expect in a downpour, there was nobody about. Everywhere seemed empty and desolate. Even I could see that buildings this ugly weren't going to make a good first impression in sideways rain.

'They're not even behind the wire,' she said, miserably.

'But that's good,' said Dad. 'You're always complaining about having to plan visitors and getting caught out when your pass expires and you can't get on to camp. This is much more normal for everyone. It's part of a regular village.'

'Where's the base? Can you still cycle to work?'

'Yes, it's not that far away- down the road really. Why don't we jump out here and walk Dannatt?' said Dad, pointing to a disused lane that led away from the cul-de-sac where we had parked whilst we waited for the rain to ease.

Mum made no response. She just looked in the other direction, at a garage door flaking paint like dandruff. She sat in the passenger seat with her arms folded over her bump.

'Well, what do you think? It seems to be clearing,' said Dad.

She ignored the question.

'Are you ignoring me?' he asked.

'Nope, I was thinking,' she snapped.

'Thinking what?'

'How much I hate this place.'

Then she listed a catalogue of complaints based on everything she had observed so far, from the gloomy quarters to the weather to the lack of cider orchards.

'You're so inflexible' said Dad, banging the steering wheel.

Lesson number one from a ten-month-old to all military husbands everywhere: never ever call your wife inflexible, especially when you are on a trip to explore the new life your job is forcing on the rest of the family, and double-especially if your wife is pregnant and triple-especially if you are still an 'Undecided' for your invitation to the birth and the moving of houses.

Initially, I thought he had got away with it but like the storm clouds that followed us here from Oxfordshire, the emotional clouds of discontent had been brewing a while and they did not open immediately. Mum got out of the car in silence and assembled the buggy whilst Dad sorted out me and Dannatt.

'Watch out if you're planning to walk down the lane,' called a friendly voice from behind the car. 'Or Dog Shit Alley, as we call it. Sorry,' he said, seeing me.

The lane lived up to its name. It was like walking around an obstacle course of dog excrement. Someone had helpfully highlighted each pile by circling it with yellow spray paint.

'So I'm inflexible, am I?' said Mum under her breath. 'How dare you say that when I'm single-handedly going to arrange the move to this ghetto, whilst you fly around Iraq being a hero, and then spend my days here walking our children and dog back and forth along Dog Shit Alley.'

She carried on in this vein until we had walked the length of the road, which came to an abrupt dead end, disappearing inexplicably under a dual carriageway.

'This lane is like my life,' she declared, gesturing around her. She looked rather pitiful in her polythene poncho from our France trip. 'My life is Dog Shit Alley- all crappy and lonely, with somebody else's plans being driven across the top of it.'

Dad gave her a hug.

'I'm sorry,' he said.

We walked back up the lane in silence. At the car, whilst chatting with the friendly man who had advised us about the lane, we discovered there was another side to the estate, a privately funded initiative we had missed on the way in. Mum and Dad decided to drive over for a look before we went in search of our B&B.

Entering this new realm of housing was a bit like the scene in the Wizard of Oz where Dorothy's life goes from black and white to Technicolor. I wouldn't have been surprised if Glinda the Good Witch of the North had walked out of one of the quarters. Each one was individually styled and genuinely attractive, a housing first in the military where you normally get rows and rows of identical, hideous quarters.

The transformation in Mum was instantaneous.

'Let's drive around slowly so I can make notes,' she instructed, rummging about in her bag for her notepad.

We crawled around the estate, the car intermittently stalling and attracting suspicious stares from the people who had started to trickle outside with lawn mowers and shammy leathers to start on their Saturday chores. Whenever Mum identified an empty house, she made Dad take a photo of it on her camera whilst she recorded the address. If she wasn't sure whether a house was occupied or not, she made him to get out and press his face up against the windows to check, until he came face-to-face with a woman dusting her Feng Shui-styled sitting room.

'It's not our fault if she favours a minimalist look, it's confusing,' justified Mum as Dad angrily climbed back into the driver's seat.

Eventually, we had list of houses that Mum is willing to live in. When we get back home, she intends to use this list to persuade S.H.A.M (the Service Housing Allocation Management) to allocate us one of these quarters.

After a temporary lift in spirits, we spent a stressful night in the B&B. Even I could have predicted that if accommodation is cheap and dogs are welcome, it's going to resemble kennels. The room was so small there wasn't enough floor space for both my travel cot and Dannatt's bed, and since Mum and Dad wanted to keep the light on past my bedtime, I got shoved into the tiny en-suite. Mum spent the night sneezing (she has discovered since getting Dannatt that she's allergic to dog hair, of which there was plenty in our room) and going to the loo.

As I tried to go to sleep, I wondered whether Mum wished she hadn't arranged this trip as a way of investigating our new life. Perhaps the RAF deliberately cloaks its postings in mystery as an act of mercy; sometimes ignorance really is bliss.

Sunday 15 June

Judging from the fuss that other families at breakfast were making of the dads, I think today was Fathers' Day. We forgot. At the service station on the way home, Mum came back from the loos with a Snickers bar, a shammy leather and a map of the West Country. She tried to get me to give them to Dad but I was ashamed of her cobbled-together effort and threw the bag in the footwell.

'Thanks,' he said, not sounding grateful.

It seemed to sum up the weekend.

Monday 16 June

Dad was sent to work this morning with Mum's list of housing preferences, under strict instructions to assert himself when he calls S.H.A.M. After asserting himself, he returned with the news that he can't make an application for a quarter until he receives confirmation of his new posting in something called his Assignment Notice and he can't locate his posting officer to ask for it. There's a rumour that his posting officer has been posted to another posting so Dad's not sure who is managing his career. I don't want to be pessimistic but, if I were to hazard a guess, I would say no one.

In any event, we aren't eligible for four of the five houses selected by Mum as they are for officers in the rank above him. Mum has been getting above Dad's station. The only house we might be allowed from Mum's list is the one she has imaginatively christened, due to its red bricks and red front door, the 'Red House'. All hopes are pinned on it.

Tuesday 17 June

Dad was sent to work today under strict instructions to investigate the disappearance of his posting officer and demand an Assignment Notice immediately. Dad rang home shortly after getting into work.

'I've located my posting officer. He's doing a sponsored run along the Great Wall of China for the next nine days.'

'What?! Why? Forget it. Ask someone else.'

'I have. No one else has heard of the Navy exchange.'

'But you leave for Iraq in 13 days' time. You're going to struggle to get the housing application in before you go away at this rate. And someone else is bound to get allocated our house in the meantime.'

'It's not our house,' said Dad, testily. 'It's for S.H.A.M. to decide.'

Pick a side, Dad, I thought. It seems to me it's always best to pick a side and, in a military marriage, the safest one is invariably your spouse's.

'It had better be our house or I'm not coming,' Mum warned.

The tension in the house tonight was palpable. As a reformed character trying not to backslide, Dannatt has taken to grinding his teeth at times like this.

Wednesday 18 June

We waited in for the TV aerial technician again today. No one came. At 5pm, Mum rang the S.H.I.T helpline, anticipating that she had been seen off again.

Mum now minutes every phone call she has with them. This one was like two particularly stupid people trying to conduct their first telephone conversation. It went something like this:

Mum:	'I've waited in all day for a TV aerial person to mend my TV aerial and no one has attended and the exact same thing happened last week.'
	(Fifteen-minute wait for ancient decrepit computer system to bring up job details)
S.H.I.T:	'No one was ever due to attend your property.'
Mum:	'Pardon?'
S.H.I.T:	'No one was booked to come out to you today or last week.'
Mum:	'I don't understand?'
S.H.I.T:	'They were dummies.'
Mum:	'I don't know what you're talking about. Who were dummies?'

S.H.I.T:	'Your appointments.'
Mum:	'Are you being rude?'
S.H.I.T:	'No. I'm explaining they were FALSE appointments. We just say someone is coming out to you so we can pencil the job in and then we talk to the TV engineering people and find out when they can come out to you. They were busy today.'
Mum:	'WHAT! So no one was ever going to come out today or last week?'
S.H.I.T:	'THAT'S RIGHT. YOU'VE GOT IT.'
Mum:	'I'm not stupid, don't talk to me like that.'
S.H.I.T:	'Humph.'
Mum:	'So when are they coming out?'
S.H.I.T:	'I don't know. When they're free, I suppose. I don't have access to their diary.'
Mum:	'You don't have access to your own workforce's diary?'
S.H.I.T:	'No, they have a different system to ours. We just email them the dummy appointments and leave it to them to sort out.'
Mum:	'I feel like my head's going to explode. Can we approach this from another angle. Have you ever had problems with this fool-proof system?'
S.H.I.T:	'I wouldn't say it's fool-proof.'
Mum:	'Has it ever worked?'
S.H.I.T :	'No.'
Mum:	'What? So why don't you change the system then?'
S.H.I.T:	'That's the way we've always done it.'
Mum:	'So why don't you- oh FORGET IT.'

Mum hung up. Despite being nearly seven-months' pregnant, she got the ladder from the shed and disappeared into the loft. I think tottering about on the roof, risking her life, was preferable to having any more interaction with S.H.I.T.

To give Mum her dues, she got the TV working again. Whilst she spoon fed me some dinner in front of CBeebies later on (I think BLW would have pushed her over the edge tonight), there was a knock at the door. It was the TV engineer.

Friday 27 June

Today was Dad's last day at work before he heads off to Iraq on Monday and, miraculously, all our prayers were answered: the long-lost posting officer returned to work, Dad got a copy of his Assignment Notice, he was able to apply for a Navy quarter and he was informed that the Red House is still available.

S.H.A.M now has fifteen working days in which to allocate us a home of its choosing.

The bad news is that Dad's flight to Baghdad has been confirmed and he leaves, as planned, on Monday. Mum was remarkably relaxed when he started packing this evening. I was impressed until I heard her on the phone with Aunty Chloe:

'The sooner he goes, the sooner he can come back and the more chance he has of being with me when the baby's born.'

Sunday 29 June

Tom invited us to a church service he was conducting in a tiny, upmarket village near the camp tonight. The church currently doesn't have its own vicar so he was doing it as a favour whilst they look for a new one. Mum and I regularly walk past the church when we're out with Dannatt. It's a beautiful place, with a medieval tower and stained-glass windows.

When we arrived, the choir was sitting dignifiedly in its ancient choir stalls, immaculate in long white robes. Tom was dressed in his own vestments, which were pristine (possibly due to lack of wear), in contrast to his rakish hair. Mum and Dad sat down in a pew half-way back. Most of the pews were empty.

'Don't be Norman-no-mates down there by yourselves,' Tom bellowed at us from the front. 'Come and squash up with the choir- it's much better if we're all together. It creates a greater sense of family.'

The choir looked horrified. So did the tiny congregation. I got the impression not everyone wanted to be part of Tom's family; they can't have banked on his style when they asked him to fill in. To say he's a mainstream Church of England vicar, he's very unorthodox. However, good manners prevailed and those of us in the pews obediently shuffled forwards into the choir stalls.

'I don't go in for lofty, highfalutin stuff so I thought we'd try some more modern worship,' said Tom, seemingly oblivious to the effect he was having on his audience as he produced a CD player and some photocopied song sheets. 'No need for the pipes today,' he yelled back at the elderly lady hunched over the organ. She nearly jumped out of her skin.

The choir's indignation gave way to something resembling terror as they took the sheets Tom handed around. They made a show of trying to read the words, peering at them as though they were written in hieroglyphics, all the while hunting for spectacles and magnifying glasses. Tom cranked up the bass on his boombox and everyone stood to sing.

To be fair, the choir gave the Christian rock a good go. I even thought I caught sight of one elderly gentleman tapping his brogues under his robe during the last tune. Next came the sermon, a punchy piece about society's attitude to poverty.

One person seemed particularly challenged or scared, dropping his gold watch into the collection bag when it was passed around.

'I don't really like liturgy,' Tom said, tossing his order of service behind him, 'so instead of the usual intercessions, we're going to take it in turns to pray for one another.'

I think some people expect to get a bit of a cat nap during the intercessions, long prayers read out by the vicar or member of the congregation with the occasional collective 'Amen'. If this had come earlier in the service, people might have been more alarmed by the proposal but a weary sort of acceptance seemed to have descended.

'I want you all to write down what you want to pray about,' said Tom, marching up and down the stalls, handing out pens and bits of paper. 'Then we'll put your prayer topics on this plate,' he said, waving around a piece of precious-looking silverware from the altar, 'and take it in turns to pray out loud. Don't bother trying to sound holy or pompous. I want you to pray with passion, from your GUT,' he explained, jabbing Dad in the stomach. 'Right, I'll kick off. Lord God, we ask you to guide a new shepherd to this flock, someone of passion, with a heart on fire for Jesus, who wants to see you at the centre of this parish and this community.'

I think the person who put in the request for a new vicar may have regretted it. Some of the choir looked like they were doing their best to pray against Tom's vision of their new leader, their eyes screwed up in concentration, maybe praying instead for someone mild and well-versed in ecclesiastical protocol.

Once Tom had finished, we took it in turns to go around the stalls, with prayers being mumbled for someone's bad leg, the church bells and the summer fete. Then a lady stood up, leaning on her stick, and quietly prayed.

'I want to pray for someone here tonight who is scared about her husband leaving for Iraq tomorrow. I pray for the whole family and their unborn baby. Please bring this member of our Armed Forces home safely.'

At the end of the prayer, the lady left her choir stall and went over to Mum, whose massive tummy and tears gave her away as the person who had asked for the prayer. She enveloped Mum in a big hug, letting her cry over her starched robes.

Something in the church changed. I'm not saying the congregation now want Tom to become a regular fixture at the church- I think it may be a while before he's invited back- but the earlier embarrassment about his style evaporated. As he brought the service to a close, everyone flocked around us, full of support and concern.

Monday 30 June

'Text me when you're onboard. Promise?' said Mum as Dad tucked her up in their bed.

She was cosy in her pyjamas, he was dressed in his desert combats, pristinely ironed. She was sipping Horlicks to help her sleep whilst he gulped back coffee to wake himself up for the next twenty-four hours of travelling. Like the last time he went, he had arranged with a friend to catch a lift down to the coach to avoid us having to drop him off in the dark.

'Maybe we'll see you later if it's anything like last time,' said Mum. She didn't seem upset enough; it was all very odd.

Dad smiled, not quite meeting her eye.

'Try and stay in there until I come back,' he whispered as he kissed Mum's tummy.

Then he gave us each a quick final kiss before he left the room and I saw why he hadn't been looking at Mum properly. Tears were streaking his cheeks.

We listened to his footsteps receding as he walked down the stairs, things being banged around below, the front door slamming and then a silence, which was only broken by Dannatt whining. Mum suddenly picked me up and ran to wave from the window in the front bedroom but Dad was loading his bags into the car boot and didn't look up.

Part-way through the night, Mum's phone beeped and she started to cry, low muffled sobs. Then she dialled a number.

'Chloe. I'm sorry to call so late--- Yes, just now--- I thought I'd be ok---' She started to cry again. 'I think I was expecting there to be delay again--- I didn't really believe he would go--- I know, the sooner he goes, the sooner he comes back but I don't want him to go at all.'

Tuesday 1 July

This morning felt quiet and flat, waking up to silence with no alarm clock to wake us, no Dad tearing about, late for work, asking Mum to make him some lunch. Dannatt usually doubles up as an alarm clock, bursting into the bedroom, demanding breakfast, but we found him downstairs, lying by the front door.

We had no plans to distract us from Dad's departure. Mum had talked about going away, like we did last time, but that had caused such a drama that she thought it was best not to complicate things in case Dad's plans changed again.

As it turned out, Mum was kept busy for most of the day answering the phone and the door. Bunny and Moomin both rang to ask whether Dad had left and whether we were alright. Then Charlotte and Claire dropped in to check on us. Charlotte's baby is due in five weeks; Mum seemed touched that she'd struggled across the station to see us.

Around dinner time, the phone rang again.

'My name's Emma. I am from the Armed Forces Christian Union. I had an email from Will last week to say he was leaving for Iraq last night. I thought I'd ring to see how you are doing.'

Mum and Dad recently became members of the Armed Forces Christian union (AFCU), an organisation that supports Christians in the forces.

'That's really kind of you. We're ok, thanks.'

They chatted whilst I practised pulling myself up on the sofa next to where Mum was curled up.

'Stay in touch, Anna,' said Emma. 'You can ring the office or ping me an email. The whole team will be praying for Will and his colleagues. Is there anything specific that you would like us to pray about?'

Mum kept Emma on the phone another twenty minutes with her prayer requests. She must think Emma has no other work to do. I hope God hasn't got too much on, either.

Friday 4 July

Whilst I was crawling across Mum's bedroom floor this morning, heading for the laundry bin to sort through the dirty washing, I noticed some holes in the wall. We have them all over the house. I know you plug things into them but I am not sure how they work so I decided to investigate. Mum came into the room just as my fingers were poised over the holes.

'Stop!' she shouted.

I always do as she asks but I realised, for the first time, that this isn't obligatory. I fixed her with a stare and forced my thumb and index finger into the holes.

'Millie!' she screamed, throwing herself across the room and scooping me up in one motion, impressively agile for one so pregnant.

After silently admiring her footwork, I remembered my new defiance. I discovered that if I arch my back and go rigid, whilst screaming until the blood vessels in my head feel close to popping, I can register my annoyance very effectively. I kept this up for several minutes, until I felt Mum's grip weaken. She set me down on the floor, rather abruptly. We remained like this for a while, with her gazing down at me as though seeing me afresh, and me staring up at her, trying my hardest to look fierce.

'I'm sure this isn't meant to happen for at least another year,' she said wearily.

Later on, I found her trawling Mumsnet, reading about early tantrumming, looking very troubled. She rang Moomin whilst typing away to an anonymous mum called 'JohnnySplit.'

Moomin says Mum never tantrummed. 'You were very repressed. Alex was the same. Chloe made up for you both but I don't remember what I did. Have you tried talking to Millie about it?'

'She's 10 months old.'

'Research shows they understand so much before they speak. Like dogs.'

'Dogs don't speak.'

'Exactly. A really good heart-to-heart may be all that's needed. Work on annunciating your feelings to express them more effectively.'

Mum didn't even bother to try this. She rang Bunny instead.

'Have a bloody big tantrum back. Always worked a treat for me, darling.'

Mum returned to Mumsnet. 'JohnnySplit' had replied, advising Mum to lock herself in bathroom. I don't know if it was a genuine call of nature or not but that's where Mum went.

Saturday 5 July

Moomin and Grandad are with us this weekend. They're keeping us company whilst we get used to Dad being away, plus Grandad will be babysitting me this afternoon so Mum can attend a refresher ante-natal class with Moomin.

I imagine most mums who have had a baby as recently as Mum would skip more lessons in how to labour but Mum's current midwife was the same midwife who delivered me and she seems to think it's essential that Mum re-attends the course. I heard her saying something unfavourable about Mum's breathing technique at her last check-up. The other reason for going on the course is that Mum is convinced Dad won't make it home from Iraq in time for the birth so she wants Moomin to learn how to be an emergency birthing partner.

'I'll come to keep you company, sweetheart, but I do know how to birth. I have done it three times myself,' said Moomin.

They ended up being late leaving for the birthing centre, where the course is taking place, as Dad rang to say he has arrived in Baghdad. Mum had him on loud speaker so we could all hear him.

'When did you get there?' asked Mum.

'How's Millie?' asked Dad

'Did you find my note?'

'I've been here since Thursday.'

'She's fine. Have you done any flying yet?'

'Yes, I found your letter. Thanks.'

'HAVE YOU DONE ANY FLYING YET?'

'I can't answer that.'

'There seems to be a delay on the line. Damn it. Why haven't you rung before?' asked Mum.

'DON'T SHOUT AT ME.'

'I'm really sorry but Mum and I have to get to my ante-natal class- I'll pass you on to Dad.'

Mum passed the phone over to Grandad and hurried out of the front door with Moomin following behind. Grandad held the phone to his ear.

'There was another delay allocating phone and internet credits. I was so excited when I got them this morning. I've been missing you and your melons like crazy.'

'Steady on son, it's me, James.'

At least Grandad sounded cheerier than Mum had done.

'Anna's just left,' he explained as we stood on the doorstep together, waving at the Ferrari fumes and straining to hear Dad as they roared away.

At least we know Moomin will get Mum to the hospital in record time if she's called upon to act as her birthing partner.

Monday 7 July

'I'm having this baby alone, aren't I?' Mum prophesied as Grandad wrestled Moomin's suitcase out to the car. It was 7am; Moomin and Grandad both had work and were trying to beat the traffic into London.

'No, you won't be alone- even if Will doesn't get back, I will be there, guiding you through the pain and the trauma,' Moomin reassured her. 'It all came flooding back to me the minute we entered that birthing place. The noise, the smells, all so evocative.'

Grandad gave Moomin a look.

'It's going to be fine, better than fine,' Moomin continued. 'Men don't understand these things the way we do. It will be bonding for us to relive the birth experience together in a new way. I could video it if you like so we go can back over it afterwards. I've had clients who have found that helpful.'

'Don't worry,' said Grandad, dropping his voice, 'she can't work the TV, there's no way she'd know how to do that.'

Just as I was questioning Moomin's credentials as a therapist, she pulled Mum into a hug: 'Have a little faith, sweetheart. I am sure Will is going to be back at your side in time for the baby.'

Mum snuggled into Moomin as Grandad finished packing the car. 'We are all here for you.'

Once they left, Mum got us ready for Dannatt's walk. We headed for the neighbouring village, past the church where Tom invited us last Sunday, along some country lanes and then back across a cow field, where Mum usually lets Dannatt off the lead to give him a proper stretch of his legs. We tend to lose him for a bit as he disappears into the long grass to chase rabbits.

As we entered the field, Mum rang Uncle Alex. 'How are you? I wondered if you fancied coming to stay one weekend whilst Will's away.'

Uncle Alex is a teacher. I've heard him ask Mum not to ring him when he's at work but she often does. She seems to have figured out the school's break times.

'That will be a detention, Brad,' said Uncle Alex.

The field is vast and undulating and it's impossible to see the full length of it from the gate.

'So would you like to come down?' Mum asked as she bumped the buggy over the first hillock. She didn't seem to notice the herd of surly bullocks emerging on the other side.

On every other occasion that we have walked through this field, there has been a group of cows lazily munching the grass or lying in the shade, occasionally flicking the flies away with their tails, always indifferent to our presence. Today was different; we were of immediate interest to these bullocks. I could hear them snorting and scraping the ground with their hooves as Mum blithely pushed my three-wheeler towards them with one hand, her mobile pressed against her ear in the other.

'You could come this weekend if it's not too last minute. Bring Gemma if she's free,' she said.

The bullocks moved closer together, forming one entity as their shoulders touched and their heads lowered, their gaze fixing on us. And then it was as if someone had waved a matador's cape or yelled 'Charge'; the group leapt forwards and stampeded towards us.

'ARRRRRRGGGGGGGGGGGGGGGHHHHHHHHHHHHHHHH!!!!'

Finally, Mum realised the danger we were in. She let out a series of screams, which caused the herd to pause, but only momentarily. As she gasped for breath, it surged towards us again. She let out a second round of screams and the bullocks slowed down. And so a pattern emerged. Charge, scream, pause, charge, scream, pause.

'What's going on? Are you ok?' asked Uncle Alex.

'Dear God, please help us, please please please please please please PLLLLEEEEEEEEEEEEEEEEEEESSSSSSSSSSSS,' she screamed.

For several minutes, Mum kept the bullocks at arm's length with her screaming but it wasn't long before she was almost hoarse.

'We're going to DIE,' she panted into her mobile. 'Help, Alex. HELP US.' She screamed some more at the bullocks and then started shouting out prayers randomly.

'Jesus, please save us. SAVE US.'

The bullocks looked perplexed, possibly sensing, as Mum began circling Dannatt's lead around her head in the manner of a lasso, that their opponent was more dangerous than they had initially thought. Mum reversed my buggy back towards the gate we had come through. The bullocks stood still, allowing us to retreat.

Just as it looked as though we might escape, Dannatt appeared at our side and the bullocks forgot their caution. Their interest in running him through became apparent as their heads turned in his direction and their necks lowered in preparation for another stampede.

It was as though all Dannatt's Christmases had come at once. He threw himself into the role of guard dog with gusto, never having had anyone other than the postman to defend us from. He ran back and forth in front of my buggy, all the while barking furiously. It would have been touching if his performance wasn't putting our lives in peril. The bullocks ran at us again and this time Mum started throwing things at them from the shopping basket beneath my buggy.

First, a bicycle pump, which went miles wide of the mark, then a tin of baked beans (it must have rolled out of a shopping bag on one of our many trips to the station Spar), then her telescopic umbrella, which nearly took out Dannatt. Finally, my whole changing bag, which burst open in mid-air, showering the bullocks with packets of baby wipes and nappy sacs. The bullocks looked unimpressed but they did, at least, come to a halt.

Mum used the pause to launch a tennis ball over the bullocks' heads for Dannatt to chase. He went bounding off, a fair-weather protector, it would seem, easily distracted by the prospect of a game of fetch over saving his family. The bullocks tried, clumsily, to turn in pursuit of their preferred target and Mum swivelled the buggy in the direction of the gate and powered across the field, bumping and knocking me over rocks and cow pats until we reached safety.

Only when we were back outside the field did we turn to see Dannatt's fate. He was doing huge circles of the field, with the bullocks hot on his heels, looking as though he was having the time of his life. Mum yelled at him to come back until he headed in our direction, outrunning the herd before slipping beneath the gate to us.

As he stood panting by my buggy, she put him on the lead and we turned back the way we had come. Once we were some distance from the field, she sat down by the side of the road and phoned Uncle Alex back. He didn't answer.

Tuesday 8 July

Uncle Alex isn't speaking to Mum. He's furious with her for making him think we were being murdered yesterday. He spent a large chunk of the afternoon on the telephone to the police, first informing them that his pregnant sister and baby were under attack, then trying to explain how he had could have been mistaken about this. I am not sure he will be coming to visit us now. It may depend on whether the police drop the plan to charge him with wasting police time. Mum says she will represent him at court for free but there seemed to be a problem on the line and they got cut off.

She spent the rest of the day trying to identify which farmer is responsible for the field to tell him he must move the bullocks as they are a threat to the public on a public right of way. She didn't get very far. No one at the Highways Authority or the Health & Safety Executive was very interested in her killer cows.

When Dad rang this evening, he supplied the farmer's name straight away. Apparently, he's always ringing the Station Commander with complaints about Dad and his colleagues flying their helicopters too close to his cattle.

Charlotte's husband, Matt, was dispatched after work to go and retrieve Mum's belongings from the cow field.

'They've gone,' Matt said as he handed Mum her muddy things this evening,

'Really? That was quick work.'

Monday 13 July

The health visitor wasn't very pleased at my one-year check this morning when Mum couldn't find my red book. Mum searched the changing bag several times before she worked out where it probably was.

'It must be in the field,' said Mum, producing baby wipes, hand gel and some old raisins.

'In the field?' questioned the health visitor.

'Yes,' said Mum, looking into the distance. 'I think I remember throwing it at the cows.'

She seemed relieved to have worked out its whereabouts. The health visitor looked troubled.

'Have you been keeping in touch with your doctor, Mrs Child? I see you suffered a touch of post-natal depression.'

'I'm fine. It's a long story- nothing to worry about.'

The health visitor didn't seem convinced; scribbling furiously in her notepad, she didn't look up as we left.

After lunch, we returned to the field in search of the book. Mum scoured the horizon. Matt was right- there was no evidence of any livestock- but even so, we stuck to the fence line. Mum kept Dannatt on the lead, searching the field as she pushed me. A packet of baby wipes lay trampled in the grass but there was no sign of the book.

As we rounded a clump of trees and cleared the brow of a large hillock, the herd of bullocks rose up in the distance, as though waiting for our arrival. Either Matt had been mistaken or the farmer had moved them back. Now more than halfway across the field, it wasn't obvious whether it was best to advance or retreat.

Mum started to pray again, her default position, it would seem, when trapped in a field facing a stampede. She decided to push on and, as we advanced, our view of the area at the bottom of the hillock increased. In a gentle dip between us and the bullocks, a man was sitting cross-legged, with his back to us. He'd been hidden up until now in the folds of the field. Before they could reach us, the bullocks would need to trample him first. Not the cheeriest scenario but it emboldened Mum.

As we neared the end of the field, the herd remained where it was, paying no attention to us, and we slipped through the gate unnoticed.

Back at home (where we later found the red book in another bag), Mum rang Aunty Chloe to tell her about our second meeting with the bullocks. They share the same beliefs.

'That was an angel, Anna.'

Wednesday 15 July

Tom laughed at Mum when she told him about the angel in the field. They were packing away the candles after prayers with the boys.

'Piff,' he snorted.

Mum told Charlotte about it when she got home, whilst I was pretended to be asleep on Charlotte's tummy. I think Charlotte enjoys practising being a Mum now her baby is almost here.

'I told Tom my cow story and he said the man in the field was a tree hugger! John leapt to my defence- he was totally on board with my idea.'

'Who's John?'

'The Catholic chaplain. They have this pretend rivalry going on but I think it's an act. They've been friends since university.'

'What was John's view?'

'He believes in angels and asked Tom why he doesn't. Tom said he also believes in angels, just not ones who moonlight for Greenpeace on their days off.'

Charlotte laughed.

'Zachary- the boy who prays every week for us to get the 'Red House- he whispered to me that he believes in my angel.'

'I believe in your angel,' said Charlotte. 'I think they're all around us, whether we realise it or not.'

Thursday 17 July

I don't know why Mum chose to make life more complicated than it already is but, for reasons known only to herself, she invited the whole of her Pilates Pregnancy group and their offspring over for lunch today, perhaps for the company. The real nappy lady, who instructs the lessons, had to cancel at the last minute; her home sewage plant had sprung a leak and she was up to her knees in the contents of her real nappy washing service.

'Oh dear,' said Mum when the real nappy lady explained that the main victim of the leakage was the Pilates equipment. She didn't sound reassured when the real nappy lady said she hoped to get off the worst of the stains off with Ecover.

'Good luck,' Mum said, 'I'm not sure I can make tonight's class, I'll text you.'

Our kitchen is quite roomy but it was not designed for seven pregnant women and eight children, especially ones in need of highchairs. All the mums had brought highchair apparatus that needed strapping onto our dining chairs but once they all stood back to admire their handiwork, they realised there were no more seats left for themselves.

'It's fine, we can just eat off the kids' trays,' said one jolly-looking lady, bizarrely wearing Liquorice Allsorts tights in July.

'O-kay,' said Mum, looking forlorn as she distributed the artisan bread rolls and selection of cheese that she had bought from our local, bank-loans-needed-to-shop-there organic deli. My little friends refused the carrot and cucumber sticks, baby bels and bread and butter prepared for them. Instead, they stamped their fists into the mums' mini ciabattas and focaccias, rolled and squished the fontina and goats' cheese like playdough, then hurled it all on the floor for Dannatt. Mum had to put him outside when he started to retching, whilst the other mums tried to rescue a kid who got a Tuscan olive wedged in its nose.

'It's great for them to really get the feel of the food and understand different culinary textures, don't you think?' asked a lady whose child was spooning the fig chutney intended for the mums straight from the jar into its dribbly, toothless mouth.

Mum didn't reply. I saw her slide the red onion relish behind the microwave.

'Is Millie potty-trained yet? asked the liquorice lady.

'Er, no, she's 11 months old.'

'You're a bit behind the rest of us then,' said the fig chutney mum.

'Millie's barely done her first solid poo yet.'

'Buttercup is 9 months old,' said the liquorice lady, 'but she already does all her poos in a potty. Just working on the wees. I'll put her on for a sit now,' she said, producing a potty from inside a Mary Poppins style bag. 'I brought a few spares if others want to put theirs on,' she said, proffering it around.

It was like a cue- a well-rehearsed signal that everyone else seemed to recognise. Toilet rings and potties appeared from all around.

'But Mumsnet says to wait until they are between two and three,' said Mum, staring all about her as mums started undressing their children.

'That's probably a bit early, even we hadn't started by three months,' said the fig chutney lady.

'Years!' said Mum.

'MUMSNET,' guffawed another mum, catching on after getting entangled in her son's dungaree straps. 'I think you'll find we are a Mumsnet-free group. Surely, all hope has gone out the window when you find yourself resorting to Mumsnet?'

'You mean to other mum's tried and tested, real experience and advice?' asked Mum.

The group dispersed shortly after that. Dannatt helped clear up the floor but we all just looked on in confusion, even Dannatt, when we found brown bottom prints along the sitting room wall. I saw Mum wipe away a tear as she fetched a bucket and sponge.

Friday 18 July

Today was the deadline for S.H.A.M. to allocate us a property. Since Dad left for Iraq, Mum has fruitlessly phoned S.H.A.M. daily to ask for updates on the Red House. Every day, she is told the same thing- that no one knows anything and to wait for a mystical letter that will magically reveal all the things S.H.A.M. can't tell her. I wonder who writes their letters...

Before today's call, Mum went to check the post to see if the long-awaited letter had arrived. Dannatt's new bad habit, the only one so far since he was rebirthed at doggy Borstal, is to savage our mail every day. Wrestling envelopes out of his mouth, she sorted through the teeth-marked letters, then snatched up the phone and dialled; she knows the number for S.H.A.M. off by heart.

I imagine most nuisance callers incite hostility but no one at S.H.A.M. acts as though Mum's calls are anything out of the ordinary. This makes me suspect that she's not the only frustrated military wife putting in constant calls to their offices. There are possibly hundreds of similar scenarios being played out up and down the country. I wonder if someone has ever thought about setting up a support group for people who are in the process of applying for new quarters.

Mum had to go through various telephone selections, followed by a long period on hold. She put the call on loudspeaker so she could do some jobs around the house whilst she waited. She would literally lose whole days of her life if she didn't multi-task when she phones them.

By the time the unsuspecting housing officer answered, Mum was spoiling for a fight. The officer recognised her and pulled up our details on the system.

'We haven't been able to allocate a property in this instance because the Responsible Officer hasn't signed the Declaration in Part 6 of the Application.'

'Pardon? Can you repeat that?'

'The form hasn't been filled out in its entirety, Madam, so we haven't been able to process your application yet.'

'WHATTTTTTTTTTTTTTTT?' I've been on the telephone to you most days for the past three weeks and no one has ever mentioned this.'

'I can't comment on that but until this has been rectified, I can't move your application forward.'

'Forward. You've just moved the application backwards. Last time we spoke you were at the point of allocating us a property. Now you're saying the application form you've been using is incomplete.'

'There's nothing I can do until this form has been signed by the appropriate officer'.

'How long will that take?'

'I can't say. I will have to locate the appropriate officer and then return the forms to them.'

Mum hung up. She kicked the sitting room door several times and then went to the computer and started bashing away at the keyboard, presumably emailing Dad or S.H.A.M., maybe both.

Saturday 19 July

Dad sounded as upset as Mum when she told him about the housing debacle on the phone tonight. He has promised to contact S.H.A.M. himself on Monday to try and sort it out.

'We'll get an offer of a house before the baby arrives. I know you want to start nesting,' he said but, if anything, that just made her look even sadder.

Mum was folding some of the flannel Babygros I wore when I was born, which she fished out of the loft when she was up there fixing the TV aerial problem. They looked so tiny.

'But we don't have a nest, that's exactly the point,' she said, smoothing one out.

Mum's low mood seemed to be contagious. A general atmosphere of unhappiness filled the house. Even Dannatt looked morose. Mum barely seemed to notice me or him tonight; I found I couldn't resist another tantrum.

My specific gripe was the catering arrangements. Mum gave up on baby-led weaning as a result of the Pregnancy Pilates party so I am now back on pots of liquidised mush. This evening I decided to demonstrate what I think about her pulverised cheesy pasta. I spat out every mouthful she spooned into me. Then I grabbed the bowl and threw it at her head. It covered her in creamy goo.

Usually, if I muck about with my food, Mum gets cross but, on this occasion, she burst into tears and sat, covered in my dinner, not moving. It was all so odd that I cried as loud as I could, wishing Dad would come and help us. It was only when Dannatt came in and started to lick her clean that she seemed to remember that I was there.

Tuesday 22 July

Mum slipped in dog sick as she went downstairs to make breakfast. This isn't unusual. Dannatt's always had a sensitive tummy, made worse this summer by the windfall plums in the garden.

She put him outside whilst she cleared up the mess. He began to whine almost immediately and, when she opened the kitchen door to let him back inside, he padded over to his bowl for a drink, limping. She checked his paw.

'You big softie. It looks fine.'

We left him resting on his bed whilst we went to the med centre for the baby's 36-week check-up with the midwife. We weren't gone long as Mum had got her dates mixed up- the appointment is next week. It was strange how one minute we were singing Jack and Jill as Mum struggled to push the buggy back up the hill to our house, the next we were in the kitchen, staring at Dannatt, who had collapsed into his water bowl. He was lying face down, his legs splayed out, surrounded by water and broken bits of ceramic.

Mum dumped me in my highchair and hurried over to him. She tried to lift him up but she couldn't so she rang the vets, who told her to take him in immediately.

No one answered when Mum phoned around to see if anyone could help her move Dannatt out to the car. Eventually, she disappeared into the street and came back with a gardener who had been strimming hedges further down our road when we were on our way back from the med centre. He staggered as he carried Dannatt outside to the boot of our car.

Mum tucked an old blanket around Dannatt and the gardener offered him half a Rich Tea from his pocket. Dannatt showed no interest in it. It was then that I really started to worry.

'I think he's sprained his leg,' Mum said to the vet who came to meet us in the car park. A nurse came out to help move him inside.

In the examination room, the vet shook her head. 'Your dog's been poisoned. He's in a critical state. Haven't you noticed his drooling?'

A large pool of saliva had formed on the floor beneath the examination table where Dannatt lay. 'Look at his laboured breathing and glassy stare?'

It seemed to take Mum a while to catch up. 'Poisoned? By what?'

'Well, you tell me,' said the vet. She was a cold fish, not the sympathetic person you might hope for in an emergency. 'Has he eaten anything out of the ordinary?'

'Only plums, I think, but he's been eating those from the garden all summer. And he sometimes gets the odd bit out of our neighbours' bins when I walk him near our house'.

'Well, it's something highly toxic,' the vet replied.

'Can you give him an antidote?'

'Not without knowing the cause. We're going to need to run some tests.'

'Can we stay or would you prefer us to come back later?'

'He won't be going home today. One of us will need to monitor him here.'

'Will I be able to collect him in the morning?'

'I can't say. He may not survive the night.'

'Survive?'

'We have a very sick dog here,' said the vet. 'Ring us first thing in the morning for an update.'

Mum smothered Dannatt in kisses and cuddles, which he tried to reciprocate by wagging his tail and lifting his head, but he seemed to be getting worse, too feeble to do either very well.

'We'll come and get you in the morning.'.

Dannatt didn't look convinced. By then, the vet had made him a bed on the floor. He struggled to get up as we moved away, dragging his bottom off the bed, before collapsing back down. Mum gave him a final hug and then turned away from him, carrying me out of the room without looking back.

We sat in the vets' car park for a while. I turned in my seat to see why we weren't driving off. Mum had her head on the steering wheel.

Back at home, whilst I ate some banana sandwiches, obligingly for once, Mum phoned around the family, asking everyone to pray for Dannatt.

"Don't say anything to Will if you're in touch with him,' she said to Bunny before they rang off. 'I don't think we ought to distract whilst he's flying around out there.'

'No, of course not, darling. I'm an actress- I am marvellous at lying. I can think of a side drama to throw him off the scent if you need me to.'

'I think just not mentioning it will work fine.'

'Let me know, I can consult the Bard for plot lines if necessary.'

Later on, the phone rang repeatedly. Mum didn't answer. We have caller ID. It was Dad.

Wednesday 23 July

Mum rang the vets as soon as they opened.

'How is he?' She was using speaker phone whilst she changed my nappy. We are never up this early and we are certainly never dressed by this time. 'Can we come and get him?'

'I'm sorry to have to say this but he's deteriorated during the night. He's struggling to breathe and we just haven't got the facilities to look after him here. You'll need to take him to the Royal Veterinary College, on the outskirts of London. They have ventilators there to support his breathing and neurologists, who will have a much better idea of how to treat him. The next issue is funding. Once he's on ventilation, you're looking at costs of up to a thousand pounds a day. What's the limit on your insurance cover?'

Mum didn't know so she had to phone the insurers before we set off to the vets. It turns out Dannatt is covered up to £7,000 per illness. By my calculations, that gives him a week at the animal hospital.

As we were walking out of the house, Grandad called Mum on her mobile.

'I'm at the guard room- I thought you should have someone with you today.'

Grandad is never free on a weekday; he must have done some serious reshuffling to be here. We drove straight to the gates to meet him. As we approached the guard room, I saw Grandad's car, big and solid like him. He got out and hugged Mum.

'Let's go and get him,' he said. 'You lead the way.'

I could see Grandad through our rear windscreen. I waved at him from my seat but he didn't wave back. I don't think he could see me through the dog guard. It felt lonely without Dannatt panting through the grill at me, like he usually does on car journeys.

Hooked up to a drip, Dannatt was brought out to the car on a stretcher with the nurses at pains not to bump or drop him. He lay still but his tail moved weakly when he saw us. Everyone agreed he should travel in the boot of Grandad's car, which is bigger than ours. The nurses made him snug with blankets and pillows. Then we drove off in convoy.

The veterinary college seemed to pop up out of nowhere, new and sparkly in a huge campus in the middle of the countryside.

'This is the top place to be poorly,' Grandad told Dannatt as we waited for some help to move him inside.

We spent most of the day in a consultation room with a lovely vet called Sarah.

'I'll be taking care of Dannatt from now on,' she promised.

Sarah has friendly, open sort of face. She smiles a lot but not in the fake way adults sometimes do. She seems as worried for Dannatt as we are, a face full of empathy whenever Mum asks a question about his chance of recovery.

Sarah spent ages examining Dannatt and taking his history. All the while, I ransacked the place, emptying out boxes of bandages and rooting through drawers and cupboards. Nobody seemed to mind.

'It might take several days to get an accurate diagnosis but these are my initial thoughts. It might be botulism, caused by eating bad meat, or it could be Dannatt's own immune system attacking itself. Both things could correct themselves without treatment. The concern is what happens whilst his body is trying to fight the problem. The biggest issue is his breathing.'

'What is the likelihood of him making it through the night? The last vet said he might not survive.'.

'I can't make any promises but he will be monitored all the time, day and night, and we will put him on a ventilator if he deteriorates, even just a bit. I will ring you tonight with an update. Just try and get some rest. You have your daughter and your baby to take care of as well,' she said kindly.

It was 5pm by the time we left. Mum said she was too tired to drive us back to Oxfordshire. Instead, we drove to London to stay with Grandad and Moomin. The only positive thing that can be said about the last forty-eight hours is that she hasn't mentioned S.H.A.M. once.

Thursday 24 July

Grandad couldn't take another day off work so Moomin rearranged her appointments and came with us to see Dannatt. She led the way in her car, with Mum struggling to keep up as Moomin whizzed along back roads, expertly weaving between double-parked cars and around bollards like an F1 racer, only slowing for speed cameras. I don't suppose Mum had a chance to worry about Dannatt as she tried desperately not to lose her licence.

On arrival at the college, Sarah immediately reassured us that Dannatt was stable. His blood tests had all come back clear and his breathing was marginally better. The bad news is that he is now struggling to blink and swallow.

'He's too sick to be sedated so I haven't been able to carry out the main tests I need to run. It's now a waiting game to see if he improves enough for me to do them. Until then, I can't diagnose the problem, which means I can't start treating him.'

Sarah updated Mum as we walked over to the intensive care unit, where Dannatt was lying in a big cage with an open door, surrounded by a group of nurses, all clucking around him. He seemed to have become an instant favourite. We stayed to watch as he was given his first meal since we took him to the Oxfordshire vets on Tuesday. He was hand fed because of his difficulties swallowing.

We stayed most of the morning, chatting to the nurses and stroking Dannatt. Eventually, Moomin said she needed to get back for work and, as I was tired, Mum came away too. When we moved towards the door, Dannatt tried to get up again and Mum started crying as the nurses pushed his bottom down and stood in his way.

'I'll phone you this evening,' Sarah promised.

In the car park, Moomin looked at Mum, cupping her head in her hands. 'He's going to be all right, sweetheart. I know it- I'm not sure why, maybe my razor-sharp instincts,' she smiled, 'but he is so chin up.'

They said good-bye and set off in opposite directions. Mum ignored her phone when it rang on the way back. I expect it was Dad. He often phones around this time. It was annoying when, every few seconds, the ringing started up again but it was more unsettling when it stopped altogether and there was just silence.

Friday 25 July

Sarah rang first thing to say that Dannatt is the same as he was yesterday-stable but not well enough for the tests.

'We won't visit today,' said Mum. 'I am exhausted and I think Millie needs a change of scene and a rest from all the travelling.'

Almost as soon as she put the phone down, it rang again. Mum snatched it back up.

'Sarah?'

'No, it's me. Who's Sarah?'

It was Dad. He was so full of his own news that he didn't stop to hear about Sarah or ask why he had been unable to get hold of us for the past few days. He hurried to update Mum on the ongoing saga of our new home.

'The problem with the missing signature had been corrected. We are now back in the system,' he said triumphantly. 'Ready to rock and roll!'

Mum seemed to have forgotten all about the house in the high-drama Dannatt saga.

'Ta-da,' said Dad. 'I thought you'd be pleased.'

Mum slowly caught up. 'So they can offer us a house?' she asked.

'Not quite, they have another fifteen working days from yesterday to find us one.'

'What?'

Dad seemed to think he had performed a minor miracle in getting our application back on track; Mum was less than impressed.

'Did you ask if the Red House is still available?'

Dad had forgotten to check. I looked over at Dannatt's tartan bed. It looked so sad without him curled up inside it. Whilst Mum and Dad squabbled, I crawled over and curled up in it.

'So we are going to end up living in that concrete jungle on the other side, aren't we?'

Deflated and miserable, they rang off soon afterwards.

Saturday 26 July

We went back to the veterinary college today to see Dannatt. The change in him was remarkable. As Mum huffed and puffed her way down to the intensive care unit, carrying me around her bump, we found him hobbling about, playing with the staff and breathing normally.

'We'll be able to do the tests tomorrow if he stays like this,' beamed Sarah.

After a happy hour, we left with Mum looking more relaxed than she has done in days.

Sunday 27 July

'Did he ring you?' asked Bunny.

'No,' said Mum.

'What the hell does that mean?'

'I expect he's busy,' said Mum, uncertainly. 'Or he's run out of credit.'

Today is his birthday but he hasn't called anyone. Mum didn't seem convinced by her own hypotheses; I saw her checking all the news' websites this evening.

Monday 28 July

Dannatt was able to have the tests yesterday. Sarah phoned with the results.

'Every single one of them is clear. With no positive results showing any sort of illness, I can only conclude that Dannatt's own immune system was the culprit. The whole thing is a bit of a mystery. We think the most likely explanation is stress. When we took Dannatt's history, it was apparent that your family has been experiencing quite high levels of stress with your husband deploying.'

'Surely that's not enough to make him so unwell,' said Mum.

'I agree it's strange but it's certainly not unheard of, especially if the stress has been acute. Dannatt will have absorbed all of your anxieties and fears if you were worried about your husband going or if you have been struggling with him gone. It's deeply unsettling for a male dog to lose the alpha male from his pack and that's what has happened here. Your husband is the leader of your pack. With him gone, there is a big hole in Dannatt's life.'

Mum didn't answer.

'Anna, are you there?'

'Yes, yes I'm fine. Will he be ok then?'

'We very much hope so. That's the good news, the most important thing. An accurate diagnosis would have been nice but it's becoming more and more academic now. At a guess, you might be able to bring Dannatt home at the end of the week.'

Mum rang around the family to let everyone know.

'Thank f-,' said Bunny.

'Bunny!' yelled Mum.

'Well, sometimes it's the perfect word, darling. Sorry.'

'Fank f***,' I said, filling in the interruption.

'Did Mille just say something?'

'Yes, her first words. Marvellous.'

Thursday 31 July

With only four weeks left until the baby arrives, and with us moving to Somerset soon afterwards, Mum attended her final session at the YOI last night.

'Tom bought party food and a cake for me,' she told Charlotte. 'And instead of going around the group and praying for one another like we usually do, he asked the boys to pray for me. Zachary prayed again for us to get the house we want. He knelt down in the middle of the circle and didn't seem to care when some of the boys made fun of him.'

'That's so sweet,' said Charlotte.

'Tom bought birthday candles for the boys to stick in my cake rather than the tea lights we usually light. When I blew them out, they all relit themselves.'

'I got magic candles to demonstrate that our prayers for you won't go out,' Tom explained.

Saturday 2 August

'You can collect take Dannatt home tomorrow!' It was Sarah, working late on a Saturday night. I'm not sure when she eats or sleeps; perhaps she is another one of Mum's angels.

I have never seen the expression Mum pulled when she heard news. It was like happiness and relief were having a tug-of-war on her features, contorting them into a twist of emotions, wetted with tears.

Almost as soon as Sarah rang off, Dad called. Knowing Dannatt was finally out of danger, Mum shared the whole story with him. Dad managed to convey shock, delight and sadness by the time she had finished her explanation, quickly followed by guilt.

'You shouldn't have had to cope with all that alone, especially with Millie and the baby. I should have been there.'

'How could you be?'

'Do they know what caused it?'

'No, it's a mystery,' said Mum, not mentioning the Iraq-deployment-induced-stress theory.

'Hearing all this makes me feel even further away from you,' he said.

Sunday 3 August

Dad was right. He felt even further away from us than ever when we arrived at the veterinary college to bring Dannatt home. We were a man down, a flight without our commanding officer, a pack without its leader.

As Sarah tried to explain to Mum how to hand feed and how to administer eye drops for the blinking problem, Dannatt wagged his tail furiously, licking me whilst I sat and reorganised the vet's shelves. He was still a bit jelly-legged, stumbling over to Mum to nuzzle her, then lurching over to lick me, then back to nuzzle Mum.

Thankfully, it was impossible to feel sad whilst Dannatt was so deliriously happy. And home felt more like home when we arrived back there together.

Wednesday 6 August

In the past, I have heard Mum complain about the sort of person who hovers around a pregnant woman when they are full term, demanding hourly bulletins on their progress. None of that stopped Mum from driving us over to Charlotte's house this morning to check on her when she remembered that today is her due date.

Charlotte didn't seem to mind. She came to the door with a raspberry leaf tea in her hand, eating pineapple chunks directly from the tin. The nursery was ready and her hospital bag was by the door.

'Good,' said Mum, clocking these details as we walked through to the sitting room.

We hadn't seen Charlotte for more than a week because of Dannatt's illness and all our trips to Hertfordshire. Mum and Charlotte started swapping news as I nodded off for my nap on the sofa. The last thing I saw before I fell asleep was Mum teaching Charlotte a set of lunges.

'I read on Mumsnet that they bring on labour almost immediately,' she promised.

Charlotte looked like she was happy to stick with her raspberry leaf tea and pineapple but she obligingly joined in.

Monday 11 August

Mum sang nursery rhymes to me as we made our way over to the station post office this morning. We didn't have Dannatt with us; she has never taken him back there since the incident with the Station Commander. The purpose of our trip and the reason for Mum's ebullient mood was the parcel resting in the bottom of my pram- the final one we will send Dad for this deployment. With only a fortnight left until he comes home, nothing sent after today will reach him.

Mum seems to have run out of ideas for things to send him. She and Charlotte agree that there are only so many lads' mags and snacks they can buy so, this time, Mum filled the jiffy bag with baby manuals she's too tired to look at, with instructions for Dad to read and summarise them on the flight home so that the pair of them have a better idea of what to do this time.

Mum's midwife keeps giving her reading lists at her check-ups, like a tutor encouraging a student to cram for an exam, and this is a midwife who originally admitted she doesn't believe in parenting books. 'Birth is instinctive, your body shows you what to do,' she had advised.

Clearly, Mum has caused a complete revision of this woman's forty-year-old philosophy about birthing babies.

Wednesday 13 August

Mum drove us over to Charlotte's house to drop off some super-strength raspberry leaf pills. Charlotte seemed restless, her swollen tummy, looking ready to pop. Before we'd even got through the front door, she had swallowed a fistful of the pills with the raspberry leaf tea she was already drinking. She even suggested doing more of Mum's lunges.

As she stood on her sitting room rug, her left leg thrust forward and her right leg stretched back, wobbling slightly from side to side, with Mum instructing her to 'dig deeper', a strange thing happened. Water gushed out from beneath her, soaking her maternity leggings and leaving her suspended over a giant puddle.

'Bingo', yelled Mum, triumphantly.

Charlotte looked both shocked and proud.

'My waters,' she marvelled as she shuffled upstairs to change.

When she returned, she went to sit down on the sofa but Mum was having none of it.

'We need to keep the momentum going. Continue with the lunges,' she commanded, joining Charlotte in another round of them.

Before long, Charlotte started to bend over and hug her tummy, occasionally kneeling down on all fours. When she wasn't groaning, she called Matt's squadron to ask him to come home.

'He's where? When will he be back?'

Matt had apparently gone on a routine flying exercise, which shouldn't have taken him out of the local area, but whilst they were airborne another helicopter had broken down several counties away and Matt's helicopter had been sent to collect the stranded crew.

'He could be a couple of hours,' Charlotte said, her hand shaking as she put the phone back.

Mum tried to comfort her.

'Your labour could go on far longer than that. First babies usually take hours and hours to come, sometimes days,' she reassured Charlotte.

Mum made a cradle with her hands for Charlotte to put her foot in 'so we can really extend the lunge.'

Straddling the coffee table, Charlotte looked scared.

'He won't miss a thing', Mum promised, 'and I can drive you to the hospital if necessary.'

Neither of them seemed to twig that they now needed to slow the labour down, not rev it up. As Charlotte's groans grew deeper and longer, she rang the midwives and they told her to come straight in. Hurrying outside. Mum put my car seat in the front, before helping Charlotte climb into the back, shoving her hospital bag into the boot. Fortunately, we hadn't brought Dannatt with us.

Every few minutes, reminding me a lot of the bullocks, a sort of mooing noise would come from the back, where Charlotte had adopted a highly illegal position on all fours. I didn't quite understand what was going on. Maybe she thought it would be best to look like a cow if she was going to sound like one.

A few minutes into the trip, as she was half way through a groan, Mum started to make similar noises, only more quietly. At first, I thought she was just being sociable, maybe thinking Charlotte would feel less awkward about her mooing if others joined in. Then I thought it might be a copying reflex, similar to when Mum spoon feeds me, opening her mouth like a goldfish every time I take a bite.

'Are you ok?' panted Charlotte.

'Yes, fine thanks. Keep breathing,' Mum replied.

'I mean, why are you groaning?'

'Am I?' asked Mum.

'Yes,' said Charlotte, before letting out a low moan.

Mum joined in with the cow noise again.

'See!' said Charlotte.

'It must be Braxton Hicks. They're a bit uncomfortable but nothing to worry about.'

She clutched her tummy with her left hand and held the wheel with her right.

'Shiiiiiiiiiiiiiitttttttttttt,' she screamed.

Mum rarely swears. Suddenly, it all made sense. I was in the car with two labouring women, one of them, a poor driver at the best of times, responsible for getting us to the hospital in one piece.

By the time we pulled into the hospital car park, there was nothing controlled about the noises and breathing coming from Mum and Charlotte. It was like being in a dairy farm with a herd of unmilked cows. They were grunting and snorting and rocking back and forth and from side to side.

Mum skidded into an ambulance bay with her hazard warning lights on and did an emergency stop, throwing Charlotte off the back seat. She flashed her headlights on and off repeatedly and then sat on the horn as she turned to help Charlotte out of the foot well.

'HELP!' she shouted, opening her door.

Two paramedics came rushing over to us and Mum demanded wheelchairs for her and Charlotte, explaining that they were both in labour. A few moments later, Mum and Charlotte were being wheeled up to the labour ward whilst an elderly porter, who looked like he could have done with a wheelchair himself, struggled behind with Charlotte's bag and me in my car seat. I'm not sure what happened to our car. We just abandoned it in front of the hospital main entrance with the hazards still flashing.

Up in the labour suite, the midwives had only prepared one room for our arrival, knowing nothing of Mum's condition, so we were all put in there together. There was only one gas and air supply so Charlotte and Mum hung over it together, at first managing to wait politely for the other to finish. It wasn't long before there was an unchristian exchange of words. Mum's mobile started to ring inside her handbag and she answered it between contractions.

'Tom! Where are you?' she asked.

Loud mooing noise.

'I'm in labour,' she panted. 'Don't be so rude. If you've been at the magistrates' court does that mean you're in Oxford? Could you drive home via the John Radcliffe and take Millie back to camp for me? She's here with me on the labour ward'.

With Tom en-route to get me, Mum called Moomin to ask for her help. Then a midwife wheeled Mum into her own labour room, whilst her colleague carried me.

'Bye Charlotte,' Mum yelled behind us. 'Good luck!'

A few indecipherable noises came back in response.

Mum's midwives then set about constructing a makeshift play area for me with gym mats in one corner of the room, filling it with knitted toys from the charity gift shop that we had walked past on our way in.

In keeping with the cow theme, one of the midwives examined Mum in the most rudimentary way and told her she was seven centimetres dilated. Not long after, without warning, Tom barged into the room.

'I didn't expect to find myself in this scenario,' he said cheerfully. 'This really is a job for your old man, not your vicar, but given the circs, I've brought you some of my Christian CDs from the car. It'll be a lot more helpful than the whale music these madwives will try getting you to listen to,' he said, lowering his voice, but clearly not enough, given the furious look one of the midwives gave him.

'So you want me to take Millie?' he asked, going over to the CD machine. 'Would you like me to pray with you before I go? Or would you prefer me to stay? It can't be easy, doing this by yourself.'

The other midwife, who hadn't heard the 'madwife' comment, urged Mum to let Tom act as her birthing partner.

'You ought to have someone with you and we can manage Millie if your mum comes and gets her as soon as she can.'

What happened next is testament either to 1) how frightened Mum must have been feeling at the idea of giving birth alone, 2) the mind-altering powers of gas and air or 3) the amount of pain she was in, or perhaps all three. The upshot was that Tom became Mum's birthing partner. Through a mixture of Christian rock, lots of prayer and swearing, my little baby brother was delivered.

'Why were you ringing me before?' Mum later asked Tom as she tried to feed my wrinkly little sibling for the first time.

'I went to court with Zachary for his sentencing hearing. I thought you might like to hear the outcome.'

Mum looked up.

'Six months' Detention & Training Order'.

'Oh no,' said Mum.

'Not 'Oh no,'' said Tom. 'He gets three more months with me and the other chaplains. It's not a bad outcome.'

Mum smiled. 'I like the name Zachary,' she said, holding the baby's tiny hand in hers.

'It's a great name,' said Tom. 'Means 'God has remembered'.'

'Welcome to the world, Zachary,' said Mum, kissing the top of my baby brother's head.

'Great choice. God bless you, little man. May God's face shine on you always. And on your mum too,' he said, high-fiving Mum.

As Mum was wheeled onto the post-natal ward, Moomin and Grandad arrived and Tom left to give us some time by ourselves. Moomin and Grandad cuddled Zach, as he was already being called, and played with me, whilst Mum tried to contact the Joint Casualty and Compassionate Centre (the people you ring when you need to get in touch with someone deployed in a warzone) to get a message to Dad.

Dad had given Mum a card with a hotline number for JCCC when he went to Iraq the first time. It's been in her purse ever since. I expect she had hoped she would never need to use it.

After speaking to the JCCC staff, who reassured her several times that they would do their utmost to get Dad to call her, she rang around the rest of the family to tell them the news of Zach's arrival. She then called Claire to ask her if she could rescue Dannatt from our house. In all the commotion, no one had thought about him.

Because of the blood loss Mum had with me, the hospital advised her to stay in overnight for observation. At teatime, Moomin and Grandad went to try and find our car and get me home for bedtime. As we were leaving, another bed was wheeled onto the post-natal ward. It was Charlotte. Matt followed behind, pushing a little cot containing their new baby. He made it to the hospital just in time to see their little girl, Rachel, being born. We left them all chatting, the labour-related unfriendliness forgotten as they cooed over the babies.

Thursday 14 August

Moomin and I returned to the hospital this morning to find Mum sitting up in bed, feeding Zach. She said Dad had called her first thing. He was both delighted and devastated to hear about Zach's safe arrival without him.

'He kept apologising for not being here.'

'Will they get him home now?' Moomin asked.

'He's leaving Iraq in less than 10 days anyway so he probably won't get home any sooner than we expected him back. His boss is doing his best to bring his flight forward. We'll see.'

Dad had some news of his own. It sounds as though he has spent every non-flying minute he has had over the past few days plaguing the housing office with phone calls, demanding updates on our Somerset accommodation.

'He found out yesterday that we have been allocated the Red House! He accepted straight away.'

'That's fabulous, sweetheart.' said Moomin.

Mum looked serene. 'God has remembered,' she said, stroking Zach's head.

Friday 15 August

I wasn't sure I wanted a crying baby brother but I will take anything over Moomin's snoring. She set up my cot next to her last night and I didn't sleep a wink. I reckon her bedtime snorting is louder than the revving of her Ferrari.

Thankfully, Mum and Zach are now back at home with us. Moomin and I collected them from the hospital. As we pulled up outside our house, Mum saw the huge wooden stork and bunch of blue balloons that someone had secretly hung on our porch the previous night.

'You see what I was talking about?' said Moomin, pointing to it. 'It gave me the shock of my life when we left the house this morning. I thought I'd woken up in a Jurassic Park film.'

Mum laughed. 'That's Kerry's handiwork. She's a military mum who introduced the idea to the patch when she moved here a few months ago. As soon as she hears someone's had a baby, she sneaks over to their house and hangs the stork outside to show there's been a new arrival. '

As Moomin unlocked the front door, Mum saw that Zach's name has been added to the list of babies written on the stork's neck. She smiled as she carried him inside.

Saturday 16 August

Zach seems to be a very easy baby so far, not a crier at all. He barely makes any noise and sleeps whenever he's not feeding. Moomin is shopping and cooking whilst Mum looks after Zach and has some rest. She's a surprisingly good cook, producing coq au vin and souffles from memory, but she doesn't seem to do housework. The laundry basket has socks and trousers climbing out of it.

Grandad came up after work last night to join us for the weekend. Everyone is muddling along quite well but Mum keeps crying. Maybe she is missing Dad.

Tuesday 19 August

It seems there may have been a false dawn in my assessment of Zach as an 'easy baby'. We were all kept awake half the night by his crying and fussing. Mum was so tired today that she barely seemed to notice Bunny arriving to take over from Moomin and Grandad.

'You look terrible, darling,' Bunny announced. 'What the hell are you wearing?'

Mum was dressed in Dad's green fire-retardant long johns and roll neck, the ones he wears for flying.

'You must be boiling.'

'I've run out of clean clothes. Everything is covered in either milk or sick or both.'

Bunny hugged Mum, somehow managing to keep her at arms' length.

'Look in there,' said Bunny, holding out her suitcase, 'and I'll whack some washing on.'

Mum dug around in Bunny's packing and pulled out an artist-style smock. Then she dragged out some dungarees and a cheesecloth dress.

'I brought my old maternity clothes for you, I thought they might be handy.'

Mum reappeared, looking like something from a Vermeer painting.

'Darling, surely you aren't persisting with these?' said Bunny, waving the bucket of dirty real nappies around. 'Disposables liberated women. We burned our terry towelling with our bras.'

'I do it for the environment.'

'Okay, darling,' said Bunny, as though she was talking to a small child, 'let's help the environment when you feel better. You have two small children in nappies and you've got the baby blues. I'm going to drive to the shop and buy some disposables.'

Mum started to cry.

'Please get biodegradable, at least.'

'I'll try, darling, but I am not sure that tremendous Spar shop will have heard of them.'

Mum continued to cry whilst Bunny was gone.

'I don't think that shop sells anything of benefit to the environment,' said Bunny, rolling up her sleeves as she came back in. 'Let's get boiling.'

Mum wept on and off all afternoon. She didn't even seem interested when Dad rang to say that he is hoping to get on a flight home tomorrow instead of the weekend. If he does, he will be home on Thursday, which is my birthday. I hope Mum has remembered.

Thursday 21 August

What a difference a year and another baby make. When Dad came home from Iraq the first time, Mum had us all decked out in new clothes, the fridge full of Dad's favourite food, the house sparkling clean and decorated with banners and balloons. This time she spent the day in an old pair of maternity trousers, with me in an outfit that should have been retired with my last growth spurt, Zach in a pink Babygro (because he had been sick all over his own and Mum only had my old ones to dress him in) and very little in the fridge that wasn't past its sell-by date.

At least, Mum had remembered that it was my birthday. Dad was due to arrive late evening so his squadron had organised a driver to collect him from Brize Norton and bring him to the house. The grandparents had suggested coming up to help us celebrate my birthday and the homecoming but Mum declined their offer. I heard her telling Bunny that she wanted our reunion to be just the four of us when Dad hasn't met Zach yet.

Mum and I spent quite a fun morning together opening my presents in between Zach's feeds and bouts of crying. There were lots of presents from friends and family. When we had unwrapped them all, and the downstairs was strewn with wrapping paper, Mum went off and reappeared with a little ride-on car from her and Dad. It wasn't wrapped and there was no card but I didn't care. She lifted me onto my new wheels and I drove around until I fell off sideways whilst she had her back to me, trying to comfort Zach, who was grizzling. I tried to cry louder than him.

I wondered if Mum was regretting not taking the grandparents up on their offer as she sat on some bubble wrap, baby sick down her top, Zach now screaming and me crawling off towards Dannatt's water bowl, which I like to upend so I can spread the water around with my hands.

As Mum started to make us some lunch, there was a knock at the door. She went to answer it, dirty muslin slung over her shoulder, dirty nappy in her hand, and found Dad on the front step, holding a huge birthday cake, a bunch of flowers and a Teddy bear.

'You're early. This has never, ever happened before,' she squealed. They both dropped everything and Dad swung her into his arms.

'I've missed you.'

I wanted to join in the fun but Mum had left me in the sitting room so I pulled myself up on my new car and stumbled a few steps into the hallway.

'You didn't tell me the birthday girl could walk,' said Dad, striding over towards me with his arms wide open.

'I didn't know she could,' laughed Mum.

Dad looked strange to me and so I ignored him, dropping to my knees and crawling away as fast as I could. Zach started crying in his Moses basket as Dad came after me.

'Do you want to show me your new baby brother?' he asked.

Bending down to me, he tried to pick me up. I started to cry too.

Dad looked a bit helpless. He turned around, leaving me on the carpet, and reached inside the Moses basket but Zach just screamed even harder. Dad passed him to Mum and he stopped crying almost immediately.

'You and I need to get to know one another,' Dad said to Zach as he nestled the teddy bear into the crook of Mum's arm. Then he looked over at me. I threw my head back and screeched as loud as I could.

'And so do we,' he said, standing in the middle of the room, not seeming to know what to do. 'Where's Dannatt?'

'On his bed,' said Mum, pointing to the other side of the room.

Dad went over to stroke him. Dannatt lay completely still, not even twitching his tail. Dad looked so sad.

'He's ignoring you because he missed you,' said Mum. 'Come and sit with us.'

She shuffled up to make room on the sofa where she had sat to feed Zach. I crawled off to clean the kitchen floor some more.

I preferred it when it was just me and Mum in charge of Zach and Dannatt.

Monday 24 August

The past few days have been quite strange. I still don't feel comfortable with Dad so I won't let him help me with anything. I know this is hard on Mum because she is also doing the lion's share of the work with Zach, who similarly doesn't want to be held or helped by Dad. Dad's been a bit of a spare part, a guest in his own home, politely deferring to Mum on most things as he tries to work out where he fits in. Mum looks a wreck.

The housing officer came this afternoon to do the pre-march out, which didn't help anyone's stress levels. The pre-march out is a visit made by a housing officer, who assesses the state of the quarter and advises on what needs to be done for it to pass the march-out. The march-out is the final check carried out by the housing officer to ensure that the quarter is in an acceptable state before it is formally handed back. If you fail the march out, you can be fined and ordered to put right whatever caused it to fail.

The housing officer was a slight man, with a tight little smile and the clip board all housing officers seem to clutch. Initially, he seemed quite friendly, handing Mum and Dad a DVD.

'I recommend you watch this together before you attempt to tackle anything. It's a comprehensive explanation of the standard of cleanliness and state of repair we expect when the quarter is handed back. It's amazing what little nooks and crannies catch people out. The inside of windows frames is always a guaranteed fail,' he smiled.

'The inside of the windows,' whispered Mum to Dad, 'I didn't know anyone cleaned there.'

'Now, let's take a look around so I can highlight areas of concern.'

As they walked from room to room, Mum carrying me, the man started to tell us about other march-outs he had done, dripping bits of information into the conversation like a slow leaking tap, at first barely perceptible:

'The Smiths failed their march-out last month because of the oven- maybe they didn't know you could pull it away from the wall.'

Until the insults were gushing forth: 'The Johnsons were a filthy lot.'

Mum knew some of the people the housing officer was talking about. 'I think you've helped us enough and we have the DVD so you can go now- we don't want to keep you,' she said, moving towards the front door.

The man didn't take kindly to being dismissed. He dropped the small talk and opened a nearby window, grimacing as he inspected the inside of the frame.

'Well, my advice to you is to get in professional cleaners,' he said stiffly. 'I will be the one assessing the property and I can't see it passing without an industrial clean.'

'Excuse me?' said Mum. 'Are you saying my house is dirty?'

'That's your choice of words.'

'I have been diagnosed with OCD, albeit mildly. No one has ever accused me of having a dirty house.'

'It must be very mild.'

After being an observer in our house for nearly a week, Dad's new role seemed to occur to him in a flash.

'My wife's very tired. New baby, house move, I've only just got back from operations, it's all been very stressful,' he said, opening the front door and shaking the man's hand. 'You have probably seen it before in your line of work. Professional cleaners seem advisable. Thanks for your invaluable assistance. Top job. I look forward to seeing you at the march-out.'

Somewhat placated, the man turned to leave whilst Mum glowered in the background.

'You can't get these people's backs ups,' said Dad, putting an arm around her once the door was shut and the housing officer was driving away. 'He could make our lives very difficult if we get on the wrong side of him.'

Within half an hour, Dad had negotiated a price with some professional cleaners over the phone, poured himself a beer and ordered a takeaway after a fruitless forage in the fridge. The leader of our pack was back.

Wednesday 26 August

Mum and Dad forgot that today is their third wedding anniversary- déjà vu from last year. They only remembered when the postman delivered a card from Moomin and Grandad. Mum seemed cross with Dad after that. They don't seem to be slotting back together very well.

Friday 29 August

A letter from S.H.A.M. dropped onto the mat this morning, advising us that we can march into the Red House on Tuesday 9 September. The military uses the most archaic language, or at least I hope it's archaic; I can't imagine what we will wear if they really expect us to do a quick march over the threshold, nor can I picture how Zach and Dannatt will fit into that scenario.

Mum rang the removal company to book the dates for the move. At such short notice, they can only deliver our belongings the day after the march-in. Mum rang S.H.A.M. back to change the march-in date.

'Sorry, the Navy only does march-ins on Tuesdays.'

Another call to the removal firm.

'This is the only day we can move you this month.'

Another call to S.H.A.M.

'The Navy only does march-ins on Tuesdays.'

This has apparently been the case for hundreds of years. No one has ever questioned it. The Navy only does march-ins on Tuesdays.

We are expected to move into our new home with none of our stuff and leave the removal men in our old house to pack up without us.

'Can't we just not go to the march-in?' asked Mum. 'Maybe they could leave the keys under the mat.'

'You can't get the keys until you have been marched-in,' Dad explained. 'They won't release the keys until then.'

'Can't someone else do it for us?'

'Yes, but they have to be military personnel and I don't know anyone in the Navy who lives on that patch who can help us.'

'Great,' muttered Mum.

Tuesday 2 September

Dad has found a solution to the march-in problem. The Armed Forces Christin Union have put him in touch with some of our new neighbours. The have offered to do the march-in for us. Mum and Dad already love these people.

Wednesday 3 September

With most aspects of the move now resolved, Mum and Dad are sorting through various jobs around the quarter. The paintwork inside the house must be made good, with all picture hook holes filled in and scuffs covered over. As Mum didn't do anything green-fingered whilst Dad was in Iraq, the jungle that is our garden needs re-landscaping. Plus they need to work out how to transport a dog and a chicken in the same car down to the West Country. It's like that riddle about getting grain, a chicken and a fox across a river without something being eaten.

Thursday 4 September

Dad thinks we should release the chicken into the field behind the house so that it can become truly free-range. Mum says it will be savaged and prefers the idea of roast chicken as our final meal before we leave. It would certainly be preferable to the endless stream of fish fingers and peas I'm being given. Mum is trying to clear the freezer.

Saturday 6 September

Our remaining chicken obligingly died in the night. To quote Mum, 'everything is coming together.'

Tuesday 9 September

After a difficult day, requiring Dad to fill in the crater left by the chicken run in the centre of the garden, reconnect the 1970's electric death-trap heater he removed from the sitting room when they moved in and cover up all evidence of the failed DIY job he attempted with shelving in the kitchen, we are ready to leave.

Zach and I are wedged in by boxes containing all the items Mum doesn't trust the packers with (jewellery, bank statements, passports etc), and Dannatt is wedged in by all the items the packers refused to take (cans of petrol, BBQ lighter fluid, paint and alcohol). If we crash on our way to the West Country, we should die instantaneously.

Charlotte, Matt, Rachel, Claire and some of the neighbours gathered around the car to wave us off. There were lots of promises to visit and jokes about Dad becoming a sailor and then we were off, driving past the station church, the officers' mess, the Spar shop and the guard on the gates with machine guns, leaving it all behind for the Red House and two years with the Navy.

'I'll miss the RAF,' said Mum as we drove away from the camp.

'What?' asked Dad, turning to stare at her.

'I will,' insisted Mum.

'You have never shown even an iota of affection for the RAF,' he said, looking confused.

'I am sure I have,' she said.

'No,' said Dad.

Mum didn't reply. 'I'm sorry in that case. I must never say it.'

'Say what?'

'How proud I am of you. Of the person you are. You and your colleagues. I struggle with military life but I still believe in you and what you do.'

We drove to Somerset in silence. In the rear-view mirror, I caught sight of Dad smiling.

2009

Monday 3 September

We have been living with our sailor friends for a year now but life with the Navy has been far from plain sailing. Our current struggles began a couple of months ago, when Mum fractured her kneecap on a rare child-free night out with Dad to celebrate his birthday. Her downfall was a manhole that that her unfamiliar heels failed to navigate in central Yeovil; she's been trussed up in a leg brace ever since, wishing she hadn't deviated from her trusty Uggs.

After narrowly avoiding an operation, the doctors decided to incarcerate her knee in some plastic scaffolding that reaches from her thigh down to her ankle, before sending her away with a pair of crutches. She's been like this ever since, partially immobilised and completely frustrated.

'Who was I trying to impress?' she frequently laments.

'Me, I hope,' says Dad.

Discovering early on that crutches are not a good mix with a one and two-year old, with Dad warning we would all end up in body casts unless she got rid of them, she now goes about with her brace-encased leg dragging behind her, cruising round the furniture at home like Zach and using our buggy as a Zimmer frame when we go out.

If every cloud has a silver lining, then this was Mum's immediate notoriety. After ten months in Somerset, we were still the outsiders on the patch, the RAF newcomers amongst a sea of Navy families, but Mum's predicament put us firmly on the map. People who didn't know her soon started referring to her as 'The Bionic Mum.' Dad had already been christened 'The Crab' by his new colleagues. Even the Navy can't remember why it calls members of the RAF 'crabs' so Mum googled it and discovered the cream used for the treatment of pubic crabs in the second World War was the same colour as the RAF uniform. Nice. It casts military attire in a whole new light.

With 'The Crab' and 'Robocop' for parents, you'd think we would be the oddballs on the patch but the Navy are an odd lot themselves. Their basic problem is that they all think we are living on a ship, even though we are twenty miles inland. If they talk about their bedroom, they will refer to their 'cabin', if they have a night out, they are on a 'run ashore', if they lose something, it's gone 'adrift'. This is called Jack speak and it takes some getting used to. Even Dad doesn't know what they are talking about half the time unless it's 'scran' (food) or 'duff' (pudding). Mum says he now knows how she feels as a military wife, trying to decipher his RAF jargon.

Today we had a family outing to Yeovil District Hospital for Mum to see the orthopaedic surgeon. Since the accident, she hasn't been able to drive so Dad ferries us around. The surgeon said that her leg is healing well and she could be out of the brace within the month. The downside to her recovery is the fact that she will be back behind the wheel again. It's lovely being virtually housebound with lots of time in front of CBeebies and no supermarket shops. Mum has had to embrace online shopping again. The only time we regularly leave the house is to walk Dannatt down Dog Shit Alley. I think this is great but I don't think Mum is enjoying it.

Sunday 6 September

We went to church this morning. It's a very different sort of church to our old one. When we moved to Somerset, Dad was keen for us to try out the Navy church so that we could pick up where we left off with the traditional style of worship favoured by the military, but the Christians who came to our rescue when we needed someone to collect our house keys for the march-in had other ideas.

On our first night here, when we were standing in our hallway surrounded by packing boxes, unable to locate the kettle and Super Noodles that Mum had packed separately for supper, a strange lady let herself in.

'Alright, me luvvers,' she said in a West Country accent, throwing her arms around Mum. 'Welcome! Look at you- you're not at all what I'd pictured,' she said, assuming her mother tongue, which is Northern, possibly Yorkshire. 'I'm Cathy. I did your march-in.'

Maybe Cathy was expecting cheery new neighbours. Mum didn't look at all cheery. She just stared at the keys in Cathy's hand.

'You obviously found your keys then,' smiled Cathy, 'the ones I left under the mat for you. These ones are mine,' she said, swirling the keys she'd just used to let herself in around her index finger. 'I got myself a set cut so I can keep some safe for you.'

'That's very kind,' said Dad, filling the silence left by Mum.

'So you're coming over to ours for tea then? I've left Paul opening some of his home brew so we can toast your arrival and I've done a beetroot bourguignon. And I've got some soup and messy craft for you,' she said, swinging me up on to her hip. 'You don't want to listen to the boring grown-ups, do you?'

My initial appraisal is that Cathy is Upsy-Daisy, Nanny McPhee and Peter Pan all rolled into one. Zany, crazily fun but still competent, definitely a bit magical, with her feet just a little bit off the ground.

'Come on, then, folks. Let's go and celebrate. Between you and me,' she said to Mum, giving her a wink and dropping her voice, 'Paul's home brew tastes like wee so I got us a bottle of Cava to share.'

Mum stopped hunting for the kettle.

By the end of the evening, Mum, Dad, Cathy and Paul were acting like old friends, weaving their way back to our house. Cathy and Mum paired up to do my bedtime whilst Dad and Paul unpacked our boxes. We did the same thing every night for a week and, on Sunday morning, Cathy and Paul called for us to take us to their church, which quickly became ours too.

Our new church is Pentecostal. In fact, it doesn't look like a church at all. It's a modern building so crammed full of people that latecomers usually have to sit on the floor. We couldn't tell who was in charge when we arrived because there was a band playing on the stage at the front and there was no sign of any vicar.

'The pastor's the one on the drums,' Cathy explained.

I noticed Dad studying the location of the fire exits.

'I may have to go if work needs me,' he said, toying with his mobile. Mum wasn't listening. Her foot was tapping to the music. She looked as though she had arrived back at the mother ship.

'I love it here,' she whispered to no one in particular.

And so we are now Pentecostals, even Dad. Or, to quote Mum, 'We are just Christians, currently worshipping at a Pentecostal church. Let's stop pigeon-holing ourselves with labels when we encounter God in very different churches.' I think Dad was actually very happy in his C of E pigeonhole, where there was no room for electric guitars and clapping.

At this morning's service, we were sitting by the stage after Mum won the weekly seat squabble (like a naughty schoolboy, Dad tries to sit at the back but Mum, the classroom swat, always powers to the front, even with her leg brace to contend with). Pastor Tim was leading the church in a new song. You might assume from my references to him playing the drums and singing that he is musical but he can't sing a note and I think it's fair to say that he's tone deaf. He's just devoted to his flock. If the guitarist is ill or the coffee rota's missing a volunteer, he's first to fill the gap so that the church gets its worship or refreshments or whatever it needs. I like him.

Every week, during the worship, before we disappear off to Kids' Church, the children are allowed to stand on the stage either side of the band and bash percussion instruments or wave brightly coloured flags but I've discovered that it's far more fun to join in the main act in the middle of the stage. I like to get my triangle and smack it down on the electric keyboard or use the end of my flag to help the drummer. Mum usually manages to intercept me as I make my way centre stage but the leg brace gives me a few seconds advantage at the moment.

I didn't need it today. Zach and I hatched a plan in the car on the way to church. I described the effect I was after and Zach masterminded how best to achieve it. Whilst Mum was pursuing me on all fours towards the stage steps (I was the decoy), and Dad was hovering around the back of church looking busy on his phone (where we had banked on him being), Zach quietly crawled ahead and made for the back of the stage.

Zach has often warned me of the fire risk posed by the church's electrical set up, with amps, guitars, the drums, keyboard and mics all trailing off one socket using a collection of extension leads and adaptors. With one quick tug on an electric cable, Zach was able to halt the entire church's enjoyment of a favourite song.

Around the building, people stood with arms extended and mouths open, initially from singing but now simply agog. The recently noisy hall lay in silence as people strained to see what had happened. The determined pianist kept striking his keyboard but to no avail. The drummer stared at his drumsticks in bemusement. The guitarist looked peeved whilst the backing singers used the opportunity to pray. Pastor Tim was the only person who seemed amused.

'Was that the hand of God, young Zach, or was it yours?'

Zach stared at him briefly before crawling furiously away with Mum hot on his little heels. Maybe there was an emergency at work; Dad was nowhere to be seen.

Wednesday 9 September

Today Cathy gave us a lift into Yeovil. We were there to buy sun cream and insect repellent for our summer holidays whilst Cathy stocked up on supplies at the local health food shop. Just the smell of that place gets her excited. She used to live in a commune and loves anything that reminds her of a simpler way of life, be it organic food, recycling or campaigning. I have no idea how she came to be a Navy wife, with all its traditions and protocols. Maybe she is a secret mutineer, with a plan to topple the Rear Admiral and his sailors.

Whatever the case, Cathy hurried off with her wicker basket and we went in search of summer holiday essentials. I say summer holiday but it will be more of an autumn break as Mum and Dad refuse to pay school holiday prices. Almost as soon as we get back from our holibobs, Dad goes to Morocco for a month to practice his desert flying in preparation for Afghanistan, where he is deploying in November for four months. So there is a lot of pressure on this holiday...

As Mum pushed us to the chemist in our three-wheeler buggy, a jerky shunt-drag-shunt-drag journey, we passed a trestle table covered with leaflets, manned by a couple of bored-looking men in shiny suits. I grabbed one of the leaflets when Mum swerved the buggy dangerously close to the table, knocking it slightly and alerting the men to our presence.

The leaflet showed a jolly-looking lady in a wheelchair holding up one end of an enormous cheque. An elderly man in a neck collar, clutching a set of crutches in one hand, was trying to hold up the other end. I didn't understand it so I passed it to forward to Zach. He leaned round to the back of the buggy- I was sitting behind him- and rolled his eyes, motioning to the suited men, who no longer looked bored but positively animated, fizzing with energy and legal jargon. The shunt-drag motion quickened; Mum had noticed the same thing. As she was about to discover, it's hard to deny you've been injured in a trip or fall when your leg's in a brace.

'Have you considered taking legal action for your injury, madam?' yelled one of the men, catching up with us.

He had a tiny goatee and too much aftershave. Mum tried the tack she employs with Jehovah's Witnesses, which is to explain they are preaching to the converted.

'I am a lawyer too,' she declared pompously.

I don't know why she thought this would help. Stating 'I am a Christian' has never had the desired effect with the Jehovah's Witnesses either. Reference to her legal training sent the men into a frenzy.

'In that case, you'll already know that you could be entitled to compensation.'

Mum has been taking me and Zach to baby sign lessons since we moved to Somerset and we are now quite skilled at signing.

'That looks nasty,' said the other suit, moving alongside the buggy, very agile despite his long pointy shoes, like something Rumpelstiltskin might wear.

Zach swivelled round in his seat and translated in sign-language to me: 'We could make a fortune here.'

'We'd really like to assist you in making a claim,' Rumpelstiltskin continued.

'Our billing for this month is rubbish and we need your case,' signed Zach.

'We'd be very interested in representing you.'

Zach: 'We'd like to suck your blood and bleed your bank account dry.'

The bearded, perfumed man got out a calculator. 'This is a conservative estimate but I imagine we'd get you this sort of figure,' he said, thrusting his Casio into Mum's face.

Zach leant forward and grabbed the front wheel of our three-wheeler buggy, causing the whole thing to veer into the man and knock him off the curb. Mum started peg-legging away. I looked around the side of the buggy and saw that Rumpelstiltskin had stopped, presumably to help his colleague out of the road, or maybe to save the calculator, which was about to go under a bus but instead, he got out his camera and started photographing his friend, the curb and then his friend's neck.

'Can we sue a baby?' I heard him ask his friend, who was still lying on his back.

'No, but we'll nail the mum. Vicarious liability,' the goatee man croaked back, sitting up and rotating his head, conducting his own little physio session in the gutter.

Apart from muttering something about buggy chasers, Mum stayed very quiet for the rest of the day, not even feigning excitement for Cathy when she presented us with her five-for- the-price-of-one-organic protein balls.

But that figure on the Casio must have been playing on Mum's mind, despite the surrounding upset. When Dad was giving me a late drink of milk downstairs, a personal injury advert came on the T.V. and I saw her copying down the number for the claims' hotline.

Friday 18 September

We are supposed to be driving to Bunny's house tonight so that we can wake up in London, near the airport, ready to fly to Lazio (or as Dad calls it 'the poor man's Tuscany'). None of that is looking likely now, given that it is 10pm and we are still in Somerset.

No one could have foreseen this situation. Despite her bad leg, Mum had us nicely packed up by lunchtime, weirdly early for her. With time to fill before Dad got home from work, Mum gratefully accepted an invitation to Marina's house for an impromptu playdate, probably thinking it would keep us out of mischief for a few hours.

Marina lives in the house opposite ours, which is bigger than ours as her husband is a rank above Dad. She's a cosy woman, who always hugs me when we go over and never lets me leave without a treat or a toy. She has four children, five-year-old triplet girls and a two-year-old boy.

There was a huge red velvet cake set out on the table as Marina beckoned us through the side gate into the garden. Her little boy, Benjy, had stuck his fist in the centre and was hollowing it out.

Marina laughed. 'Benjy's serving up.'

She took over, cutting portions of the half-mangled cake for us. I treat little boy hands with suspicion so I slunk away without eating mine. I decided to investigate the giant lump of plastic at the end of the garden- the triplets' Wendy house. There was a Fisher Price tool kit on the floor, as though Benjy had been doing some DIY jobs for his sisters.

As the triplets are very territorial about their Wendy house, they followed me in almost immediately. Benjy then appeared to reclaim his tools. Zach doesn't like role play so he stayed with the mums, reading the newspaper spread out on the grass where Marina had perhaps hoped to get a minute to herself.

The triplets wouldn't let me join in their game of Disney princesses so I decided to wind up Benjy by hiding his tool kit, piece by piece. I kept the plastic hammer so I could hit him periodically. Eventually, he toddled off and I thought I'd won the game but a few minutes later, he came staggering back into the Wendy house, dragging another hammer behind him. It was a real one made of metal. His face was a mixture of strain and triumph as he held it above his head and brought it down on mine. I couldn't see for the blood running into my eyes as I fled from the Wendy house, screaming.

Marina drove us to Yeovil's A&E department immediately, apologising all the way there, only breaking off to shout at Benjy, who was throwing pieces of red velvet cake at the rest of us from his booster seat in the boot. She stayed with us in the waiting area, making us a party of two frazzled mums and six children, with me still screaming and Benjy intermittently finding more weapons (a fire extinguisher, an abandoned wheelchair) so he could launch another attack, seemingly not satisfied with his first taste of blood. I saw people with quite serious injuries (a man with his head wrapped in a blood-soaked tea towel, a woman with her hands superglued together) come through the A&E revolving doors, see us and turn back the way they had come.

I had a nasty gash to my temple that needed stitches- nine steri strips which I can't get wet for the next five days. I could see Mum's heart sinking as she pictured the pool at our holiday villa and a week of trying to keep me out of it. By the time we got home, Mum decided it was too late, and we were too exhausted, to set off for London. As Bunny was meant to be dog sitting Dannatt, Marina agreed to have him so that we can drive straight to the airport tomorrow. I hope he survives a week with Benjy and his tools.

One of the worst and best things about patch life is that everyone knows your business, whether you want them to or not. When Marina dropped us home, there was a collection of gifts on the doorstep- a lollipop for me, a lasagne for supper and a half-used bottle of Calpol. The incident was all over the Navy WAGSs page on Facebook, with lots of well wishes for me and a few derogatory comments about irresponsible dads not locking up their sheds. When she tucked me up in bed, I sensed Mum won't mind swapping the Navy limelight for a bit of Italian sunshine.

Saturday 19 September

We nearly missed our flight due to a traffic jam near Stonehenge that meant we moved past the ancient monuments more slowly, I suspect, than the speed at which they were dragged there. I am only two years old but even I could tell our local Town & Country Planning Department that SOMEONE NEEDS TO WIDEN THE A303.

The check-in lady only just allowed us through but the panic was all for nothing in the end. One Mr and Mrs Let's-Get-Boozed-Up-In-The-Lounge didn't hear the call for final boarding so we had to wait ages whilst their luggage was removed from the plane. They eventually staggered into the departure lounge, angrily swinging their duty-free bags around, refusing to believe their holiday was already over.

I was so bored I thought it would be interesting to see how many Capuchin Friars I could knock over with my Trunki. Seven, it would seem. Mum was still shouting at me as we boarded the flight. She thought I deliberately attached myself to a chair as we were trying to find our seats but I didn't intend to delay take-off; my dress genuinely got caught on another passenger's loose seat belt.

We arrived in the dark, in a storm, with no food or drink except a few bullet-hard vacuum-packed bread rolls Mum swiped from the flight; everywhere in Italy had shut by the time we landed.

Sunday 20 September

Mum's list of complaints about the holiday villa to jog Dad's memory when he rings the letting agents' emergency helpline:

1. Why did the builders leave before finishing the place?

2. Why is the bath water green?

3. Why does the green bath water not empty from the bath?

4. Why does the walk to the shared pool, described in the villa particulars as being a short stroll away, require hiking boots and trekking poles? We brought Crocs.

5. Why do the electric lights outside the children's bedroom smoke?

6. Why is there no hand rail for the fifteen foot high concrete staircase leading to the upstairs of the villa? We are a party comprising a one and two-year old and a woman in a leg brace.

Mum looked deathly pale when she came into our room to get us up this morning. She told Dad that she hadn't slept a wink last night for fear of us burning in our beds, drowning in the stagnant bathwater or falling down the death-trap staircase.

Dad got nowhere when he rang the agents. The office is shut until tomorrow so he left four messages (because that's how many attempts it took to satisfy Mum that he had covered every topic fully. Why doesn't she ring them?!). Then she insisted on some family prayer time. Dad suggested God might have bigger problems on his plate than our holiday (maybe he didn't get much sleep either) but Mum said God wants to hear all our troubles, be they Italian plumbing, misrepresentations by travel agents or unhelpful husbands. Dad kicked off with a prayer, asking God to help Mum with her bad temper, which may have been a counter-productive request.

During lunch, which we were eating in the postage stamp-sized yard (not the luxurious giardino we had expected), someone we took to be a gardener/caretaker appeared by the shed. He clearly had no intention of coming over to us but Mum wasn't going to let him get away. The man saw her, maybe noticed the glint in her eye, and beat a hasty retreat.

She had already spotted his moped and was hobbling over to it, blocking his way. She launched into a beautifully crafted legal argument with case law (undoubtedly made-up) and frequent references to the Sale of Goods Act 1979 (the only bit of legislation that seemed to stick at law school, possibly because it allowed her to take things back to shops) for why we need immediately rehousing, refunding and compensating for trauma.

'Che cosa?' he said blankly, jangling his spanners.

Mum looked nonplussed, as though he had no right to speak Italian at her.

'No Inglese,' said the man, looking longingly at his moped.

Mum approached the communication obstacles from a number of different angles. To start with, she tried baby sign language (it didn't help her develop her argument very far as her main vocab is 'peekaboo', 'dirty bottom' and 'I need a wee'.) There was some Latin (she studied it for A 'Level) but 'Caecilius est in horto' didn't get her much further. Then she tried the universal language of tears.

The man looked alarmed when she started to cry but then a light bulb moment seemed to come over him and he dialled a number on his mobile phone, before offering it to Mum. It was the owner of the villa on the other end. She spoke English and perhaps she is also a lawyer as she accepted Mum's legal arguments without objection.

This afternoon, we moved into the owner's countryside residence (the owner is holidaying in her beach residence). Our new accommodation is just up the road from where we were, an enormous palazzo-style place with electric gates, a terrace so large the gorge below appears to have been placed there entirely for our benefit, servants (the caretaker and his wife) and a cellar of very good Italian wine. Mum and Dad are suddenly very happy.

Monday 21 September

I knocked over a vase today (Zach said he saw a similar one on the Antiques Road Show) in one of the many hallways here. Mum says we won't be getting our deposit back now. As a result, she has banned us from the house. We are only allowed inside at bedtime so we spend all our time bothering the caretaker, following him around the immense garden, tracking him to the vineyards and along the driveway lined with Cypress trees.

He speaks perfect English. I heard him ask his wife, 'When are those English brats leaving?'

Sunday 27 September

We are back in the West Country again, having swapped paradise for military quarter-cum-laundrette. Dad is due to go to Morocco tomorrow (the exercise was brought forward whilst we were away) so Mum is frantically washing the contents of his case so he has enough pants.

Dannatt started pacing along the upstairs hallway when Dad brought his heavy-duty luggage down from the attic. He began to drool when Dad returned from the garage with his helmet and desert fatigues.

'It's happening again,' shrieked Mum, hiding dog tranquilisers inside spoonfuls of peanut butter and administering them to Dannatt.

'You'd better see if Cathy will have him,' said Dad, appearing from the garage again with his body armour.

Mum and I drove the three hundred yards to Cathy's house with Dannatt, his bed and all of his toys. Cathy wasn't impressed with the use of Valium. She made up his bed in front of the T.V. and found 'Strictly Come Dancing.'

'That'll take his mind off it,' she said. 'It's the results tonight. I'll give him a massage whilst we watch them together.'

Mum scooped dog biscuits into a bowl for Dannatt's dinner and put it on the floor. Cathy emptied an entire bottle of Rescue Remedy into it.

'We don't want any more of your pills,' she said to Mum, waving away the tranquilisers.

We left Dannatt caught in the cross fire between conventional medicine and alternative therapies. This is bound to mean a trip to the vets.

Monday 28 September

Dannatt survived the night but the rest of us are struggling after a tearful round of good-byes with Dad this morning. He's only gone for three weeks but Mum seems as upset as if he had just left for Afghanistan.

'Are you ok?' asked Cathy when we went over to collect Dannatt.

'Not really. It feels like this is it now until March when he comes back from Afghanistan. He will be only at home for a week in between the two trips and I expect that will just be a week of washing and squabbling. I know it sounds harsh but part of me wishes he wasn't coming back. Then we could just get on with the separation and not have another lot of good-byes hanging over us.'

Cathy gave Mum a hug. I don't know why. Mum is so horrid.

Tuesday 29 September

Mum would have been wise not to go on the Navy WAGs page this morning. There were photos of some of the people on the Morocco trip, sharing hubbly bubblies on a night out.

'Looks like they're having a terrible time,' one of the wives had written beneath a photo of Dad and his colleagues being served drinks by a beautiful lady dressed like Princess Jasmine from 'Aladdin', only with bigger boobies.

Mum checked the online banking. Zach says Dad has spent a lot of money in a place called 'Palais Marrakesh.' I don't know why Mum is so upset but it seems to be Princess Jasmine's fault.

Wednesday 30 September

I hate Dad. I know it's his job to go away but why doesn't he get another job? Maybe he likes having a break from us. Perhaps if we weren't so badly behaved, he wouldn't keep leaving.

Thursday 1 October

I'm worried about Dad. I don't even know where Morocco is. I hate Mum. If she was nicer to Dad, maybe he wouldn't want to go away. She needs to stop nagging him and wear prettier clothes, like she used to before Zach was born. She doesn't seem to notice that her leggings have orange bleach stains on them from cleaning the loos and that she's still wearing nursing bras. She should dress like Princess Jasmine. Zach thinks she should also get the hairdresser to cover up the wiry grey hairs she's started sprouting recently.

Friday 2 October

I hate the Navy. I can't work out whose fault it is that life is so miserable but I think may they are the reason.

Monday 5 October

Cathy drove us into Yeovil today for Mum to see the orthopaedic surgeon. The rest of us stayed in the hospital car park whilst Mum had her appointment. After an hour of sitting in Cathy's Citroen Dyane, our extremities turning blue, eating banana chips and shrivelled up apple, Mum emerged through the automatic doors carrying her brace. She waved it over her head excitedly when she saw us. It's the first time I have seen her smile in weeks.

Tuesday 6 October

Uncle Mark has decided to leave the Army. Aunty Chloe is four months' pregnant, tired and still struggling with morning sickness. They are due to move to Scotland in a week's time for Uncle Mark to start a new job but dates and logistics mean they are still in Germany, packing up their quarter and getting ready for the march-out inspection.

I could hear Aunty Chloe shrieking down the phone at tea-time, even though Mum had her mobile pressed against her ear. Things must be bad.

'I have a roll of bubble wrap next to a mop bucket so that when I'm not vomiting, I can wrap the breakables,' said Aunty Chloe before making retching sounds.

I wonder if you need to be pregnant or have a new-born baby in order to do a military move. I have never heard of a military wife moving house without being in the early stages of child-rearing. Perhaps it is a box you must tick on the march out paperwork.

After a while, Mum seemed to disengage from the conversation. I don't think she likes hearing about Uncle Mark and Aunty Chloe leaving the military. She made sympathetic noises every now and then but her attention was on the leak she discovered this morning. We noticed it when water started dripping on us as we read stories in bed together. Mum called S.H.I.T straight away but she got their answerphone and no one has returned her message. She has now got various vessels scattered across her duvet to catch the drips. She checked the water levels whilst Aunty Chloe chatted away.

When they rang off, Mum telephoned S.H.I.T again.

'Is it an emergency?'

'I wouldn't say so yet but it's certainly inconvenient when it's over my bed,' said Mum.

Wrong move- always say it's an emergency.

They've arranged for someone to come around in a week's time. Mum spent the evening trying to move her bed. Eventually, she admitted defeat and slept in the spare room.

Thursday 8 October

The small brown stain on Mum and Dad's bedroom ceiling is now elephant sized. The repair people say this is not an emergency. They are calling it a 'cosmetic' issue.

'Look, a cosmetic issue is when my daughter redecorates my bedroom with the contents of my make-up bag whilst my back is turned for thirty seconds. A burst pipe in the loft is NOT A COSMETIC ISSUE.'

'If you or your daughter have defaced the property with make-up you will need to pay privately for that or risk a fine at march-out.'

The ceiling repair job is still booked for next week.

Monday 12 October

Mum and Dad's bedroom ceiling has now become bulbous. The repair team say it's not an emergency unless there is a visible flow of water. Zach says Mum ought to go into the loft herself to check what's going on but we don't have a ladder and I am pretty sure she knows, with a dodgy knee and two small children, that this might not end well.

Tuesday 13 October

Cathy drove us into Yeovil today for Mum's first physiotherapy appointment. Whilst Mum tottered off for her session at the hospital, Cathy took us to the library. We sat on the mini sofas in the children's section with picture books scattered all around us. Cathy read us 'Five Minutes Peace' six times whilst offering us handfuls of trail mix from her basket. She kept encouraging me not to pick at the scab on my temple where Benjy hit me with the hammer. It's taking a while to heal over. I was snuggled into her chest at the time, sucking my thumb. I didn't realise I was doing it.

'Beautiful, leave it alone. Have some more trail mix.'

I kept forgetting and then she would tell me again.

'You must stop doing that, beautiful,' she said, taking my hand in hers. She sounded worried.

In the car on the way back, I heard her telling Mum about it. Mum looked sad when we got home. She held my hand during our bedtime story tonight and spent longer than usual tucking me up.

I couldn't wait for her to say good night to us so I could pick at my head some more.

Thursday 15 October

A plumber came to investigate our loft today. He said there was a major leak up there, which he was able to fix straight away, but the bedroom ceiling is more of an issue. He concluded that half of the ceiling boards are now saturated and will need replacing.

'When can you start?' asked Mum.

'No one'll touch this job until you've had an asbestos survey carried out.'

Mum didn't even bother to ask how long that would take. Zach says if there is risk of exposure to asbestos that we should be rehoused. I laughed my first cynical laugh.

Friday 16 October

Mum and Dad's bedroom ceiling collapsed this afternoon. Fortunately, Mum wasn't in the room when the plasterboard caved in. The ceiling now needs to be replaced in its entirety. Zach says it was a false economy, on the part of the housing repair people, not to pay the emergency call out fee a fortnight ago. Mum didn't say anything when she saw her bed covered in rubble. She moved some of her things into the spare room and shut the door.

Monday 19 October

Mum's physiotherapist has told her she can drive again when she feels ready so Mum has been practicing around the housing estate. Cathy bravely sat in the passenger seat next to her whilst Zach and I watched from the back. I'm not sure her attempt at an emergency stop would have passed any tests but other than that, it was a good, if rather wobbly, effort.

This afternoon, Mum drove us into to Yeovil by herself, even though we had no real need to go. The hospital won't take her crutches or leg brace back so she tried to donate them to one of the charity shops on the high street but, for health and safety reasons, no one would take them.

She pushed us back to the car in our buggy, the crutches hanging off her shopping bag hooks, the brace slung across the hood. I noticed we went the long way around and not the obvious route, which would have taken us past the personal injury firm.

Zach reckons they would love to get their hands on those sorts of props.

When we got home, Zach and I were tired and hungry but instead of starting tea, Mum spent an hour on the phone, calling various charities to see if they would take her crutches and leg brace. She came off the phone crying. I don't think anyone wants them.

By then, I was crying too. Zach kept telling me not to pick at my scab. Mum wasn't watching what we were doing so I ignored him and pulled the entire thing off.

It made Mum cry even more when she saw it bleeding in the bath.

Tuesday 20 October

Mum came into our room to get us up this morning, dressed in messy clothes. I almost tripped on the tool box lying in the middle of the upstairs hallway on our way downstairs for our Weetabix. After breakfast, we played in our pyjamas whilst she took down all the pictures along the wall outside our room. She got out her tape measure and pencil and started measuring up.

When we first moved into this quarter last year, Dad was given the task of putting all the pictures up. He did it remarkably quickly and seemed very pleased with himself until Mum pointed out that everything was at different heights and various light switches were now hidden beneath mirrors and clip frames. I'm sure she would have liked to redo them all at the time but the explosive argument that ensued meant the subject was never brought up again.

She measured and hammered away all morning. When it was way beyond lunch time, Zach and I started to whine with hunger. Eventually, we found some fig rolls in a cupboard in the kitchen and I managed to get a jam jar open. We ate the whole packet of biscuits, dunking them in the jam, until Zach was a little bit sick.

Mum came into the kitchen, smiling until she saw us sitting in a corner of the kitchen, covered in red goop. Then she went berserk; I don't think I've ever seen her so angry before.

Thankfully, my hair was so full of jam she couldn't see that my forehead was bleeding again.

Thursday 22 October

Dad's training exercise went according to plan. He came home today, no delays. He looked slimmer after a bout of food poisoning helped him shed his holiday pounds. He asked Mum where she has put hers. I suppose she has lost a bit of weight recently.

With a week to fill before he leaves again, Dad has been told he can take a few days leave. No one was sure if the training exercise might overrun so Mum and Dad hadn't booked anything. Cathy and Paul have offered us their holiday house in Devon for a few days so that we can get away together before Dad goes to Afghanistan.

Mum spent the evening washing and packing so that we can set off early tomorrow morning. Zach and I don't think she seems very pleased to see Dad. She is talking to him but it's all very stilted. I know I'm not imagining it as Dannatt slunk away to his basket soon after Dad got back. I don't understand it. Zach thinks it's got something to do with the beautiful lady in the photos. I think he may be right. Tonight, I heard Dad shouting downstairs.

'She was a waitress. Our plane went tits-'

'So you thought you'd go and see some!'

'So we went out for lunch. That's where I got sick. I spent the afternoon throwing up.'

'That doesn't explain the money you spent at 'Palais Marrakesh.'

'Sue me for buying you something for Christmas. I know you hate surprises so you should be pleased because now you're not getting one.'

Tuesday 27 October

We got back late from Devon last night. It's hard to say whether it was a successful trip or not. Mum and Dad would be smooching one minute, grossing us out, and then having a blazing row the next. The best moments were when no one was talking- when we were eating or cuddled up together watching T.V. Or when Zach and I were being naughty. Mum and Dad seemed to agree with one another whenever there was a common opponent.

I prefer being in trouble with them to listening to them row so once we had worked this out, we kept up a steady flow of bad behaviour. One of my favourite tricks was to steal something when we went into a shop or restaurant. I would ram my mouth full of pick and mix, steal a Matchbox car for Zach, or stuff my pockets full of sugar cubes or teaspoons. Small things that made them furious with me and supportive of one another.

We pulled out all the stops on a trip to Paignton. Mooching along the sea front, we found a Punch and Judy show in full swing. I have no idea what the puppeteer was doing there in October but he had managed to attract a small crowd. There was a group of elderly people already watching when we arrived, some of them with walking frames and wheelchairs. We sat down on a nearby bench to watch.

Whilst everyone was distracted by a sea gull that kept dive bombing Mum's head, I sneaked over to the crowd and picked up an old lady's walking stick. When Punch started beating the policeman with a truncheon, screeching 'That's the way to do it,' I pummelled the Punch and Judy booth with the walking stick until the harassed puppeteer, with a mess of wild hair and a face as red as Punch's, emerged from around the back to see what was happening.

After careful inspection, the puppeteer discovered Punch had a chip to his nose. Looking defeated by life, he started to pack up his show, despite Dad's repeated apologies and offers to pay for the damage. The older crowd scowled at us when they realised the show was over. Dad went in search of a cash point to pay the puppeteer and, probably, to get away from all the humiliation. When Mum located the elderly lady who was minus a walking stick, her carer grabbed Mum by the arm.

'Have you thought of taking your little girl to see a psychiatrist?' she asked. 'That's a lot of rage she's carrying.'

Mum looked alarmed.

After that, she and Dad were especially nice to one another.

Thursday 29 October

This afternoon the bathroom light broke. After an hour spent teetering on a stool with a screwdriver, Mum concluded that the casing has been deliberately designed to prevent occupants from replacing the bulbs themselves. This was confirmed when she called the repair team.

'It's standard practice. We just send out an electrician when your bathroom bulb needs changing.'

'That seems a terrible waste of resources.'

'That's how we do it. I will instruct an electrician to carry out the work and post out the appointment time.'

'But I need to bath the children. I can't bath them in the dark,' Mum protested.

'Can't you bath them in the morning? Or light some candles?'

Zach says we are now officially living in the Dark Ages.

Friday 30 October

Dad is best man tomorrow for his Navy friend Pete. They went through university and officer training together so they go back a long way. I am not sure how much Dad has prepared for the role with all the time he's spent away lately and with his mind now on Afghanistan. I am assuming that's where his mind is as it's not really on us. He is very distracted.

Bunny is coming to stay with us tonight so that Mum and Dad can head off first thing to Oxfordshire, where the wedding is being held. Zach and I weren't invited, or that's what we've been told anyway. The last wedding we went to may have put them off taking us to another one for a while. I don't think the bride liked it when I climbed into the pulpit during the vows and we all agreed that the cake had looked better upright.

Bunny says this trip will give Mum and Dad some special time together before he leaves for Afghanistan on Monday.

'You just need a lovely, romantic night in a country hotel by yourselves, darling,' she told Dad when she arrived.

She's clearly clueless. Time alone just before a major separation means major rows but at least we won't be subjected to them.

At 9am, whilst we were still covering ourselves in Weetabix, Dad ran through his checklist of things to take: speech, rings, uniform, port, port glasses.

'Why are you taking port glasses to a wedding? Am I missing something?' asked Bunny.

'I'm in charge of the sword party,' Dad explained.

'What's that?'

'We had one at our wedding. The sword party is made up of guests in uniform who form an arch with their swords for the bride and groom to walk under.'

'What has port got to do with that?' she asked.

'It's traditional for the sword party to have a glass of port together before the wedding.'

'Like people do before a hunt. Are animals going to be harmed at this wedding?'

'No, of course not, Mum, why would we be hunting?' said Dad.

'I don't know, darling, I'm not the one going to a wedding armed with a sword.'

Fair point.

'It's all bloody odd, if you ask me, but have FUN. Enjoy yourselves.'

Mum and Dad said their good-byes. We waved to them as they drove away.

'Right, what mischief can we make whilst they're gone?' asked Bunny, laughing.

We were half-way through making some fairy cakes when her mobile rang in the pocket of her pinny. Zach was licking the spoon and I had my head in the bowl. She answered with a hand covered in batter.

'Yes?' she said. 'OK.'

She was only on the phone for a moment. Without explanation, she scooped us up and bundled us into the back of her car. Then she ran inside the house and came charging out, brandishing Dad's sword, which she threw onto the passenger seat beside her before manoeuvring us off the housing estate in a manner that even Moomin would have admired.

Her phone rang again and she answered.

'I'm on the A303. I'll meet you on the A34. Surely this is going to make you miss the wedding?'

I can only imagine the row that broke out when Dad realised he'd forgotten his sword. Apparently, he noticed its absence when he looked in the boot of the car at some services to check on his port glasses. Mum then rang every military friend they have between Somerset and Oxfordshire to see if anyone had a spare sword they might lend Dad. It was a pointless exercise as even military folk don't have swords knocking around their garage. They cost thousands of pounds and military weddings seem to be the only occasions when they're needed. It's hardly an essential part of the kit these days.

We met up with Dad and Mum in a lay-by, where a ruddy looking woman was selling strawberries from the boot of her car. Barely looking up from her book, she didn't seem the least bit bothered by the exchange of weaponry going on a few feet away from her.

'Beautiful straws if you want some- two punnets for a fiver?' she said lazily.

'Hurry, darling,' urged Bunny as she handed him the sword.

When Mum rang later on to say good night to us, she told Bunny that they had arrived after the bride, when the service was well under way.

'I had to change into my dress on the verge outside the church. Will had to wee behind a hedge. I think the chauffeur waiting to drive them away saw the whole thing. And when it all came out at the reception, Pete said Will could have borrowed his sword.'

'I think Pete might have preferred the wedding rings,' said Bunny, who found them in the hallway when we got home. 'Well, did they at least drink the bloody port, darling?'

'No.'

'Oh for f-. Sorry, darling.'

Military planning. Need I say more.

Monday 2 November

The drama of repeatedly waving Dad off to war seems to have exhausted and drained our family of a normal response to such a monumental event. This is the third time we have done this and apart from a few tears, life continued in the usual way. As Dad headed out to Kandahar, we headed to Cathy's to collect Dannatt.

'No wobbles from him this time,' she said as Dannatt came bounding round her to lick us all. He was wearing an amber bracelet around one of his legs.

'Always works a treat,' smiled Cathy when she saw Mum looking at the bracelet. 'Now how are you beautiful peeps doing?'

She waved a plate of home-grown courgette flower fritters at us but on one took one. Even Dannatt didn't try and swipe one.

'How about Mums and Tots?' Cathy asked.

I could tell Mum didn't want to go but Cathy insisted. It's held at the community centre, just a five-minute walk from our house. They have something on there most mornings- Coffee Shop, a craft group, breastfeeding support. Mum's got a bit lazy about taking us. She used to have a lot more get-up-and-go than she does these days.

'I'll get my coat and off we toddle. We can pop Dannatt back at yours on the way,' said Cathy.

As we walked through the housing estate, a car pulled up just ahead of us and a woman in naval uniform opened the driver's side window.

'Hi. I thought I'd introduce myself,' she said to Mum. 'I'm Rebecca, Ed's wife.'

'Ed?'

'Your husband's boss. I thought with the boys heading out there together, it would be nice to meet up.'

'Sorry, yes of course, I'd like that,' said Mum.

'I'm also in the Navy so I'm a good point of contact if you need to get in touch with Will. Do you fancy a glass of wine tonight? I could come to you if that's easier as I don't have kids.'

Dad had suggested that Mum might call on Rebecca whilst he's away. I'm not sure Mum would have gone over by herself, although military people often do that sort of thing, turning up on a new neighbour's doorstep with a bottle of wine, offering to mow a person's lawn when their husband's deployed, stuff like that. Mum and Rebecca swapped numbers before they said good-bye.

'That's nice,' said Cathy. 'I can let you have some of my chickpea nibbles for it- make it more of an occasion.'

Tuesday 3 November

Zach wonders if the military housing repair service is deliberately abysmal in order to create a common enemy within the housing system. Regardless of rank, differing deployments and workloads, everyone has to deal with the same S.H.I.T.

Today Mum received the following letter from S.H.I.T about the bathroom light:

Dear Customer

Thank you for calling us to report your fault. Please find below details of the problem you reported, along with the job number and your appointment slot:

Job No: 3096354577786540752444-2009

Brief Description: Broken bulb

Work Raised: PLumber

Appointment Date: [Insert Date]

Appointment Time: [Insert Time]

The above appointment time is the period during which our engineer will arrive to carry out the work and it is not an indication of how long the works will actually take.

So that was worth the postage.

We had another interesting bath time tonight conducted by torchlight.

Thursday 5 November

When most people were bundling up in hats and gloves to go to the Navy fireworks' display, we stood in the garden waving sparklers. I made a hole in Mum's coat with mine, which upset her, but she deserved it when she wouldn't let us go to the big display with the others. The reason we couldn't go is a pottery course she starts tonight in a nearby village. She signed up for it when Dad was preparing to leave for Afghanistan.

'Why are you becoming a potter?' Dad had asked. 'I don't get it.'

'To stretch myself and explore my creativity. I am a very creative person. You remember how I used to like to paint before we had children? And to write you poetry in your birthday cards? You were so proud, you framed them.'

'Yes,' he said, looking away.

'It was so sad that the removal men lost that box of our packing. I still don't understand it.'

'Mmm. Maybe we could re-enact 'Ghost' when I get back,' he said, steering the conversation.

'Cheeky,' she said, throwing a cushion at him.

When we went back into the house, Mum's coat was still smouldering. She sent me to the naughty step whilst she grabbed the hall phone. It was Aunty Chloe.

'I feel a bit nervous about going now,' said Mum, whacking her coat sleeve with her shoe. 'I won't know anyone.'

'Yes but you soon will and it's great that you're doing this- you should have something for yourself whilst Will's away, otherwise you'll just have a functional existence, caring for the kids and doing nothing for yourself.'

Aunty Chloe always tries something new when Uncle Mark goes away. During his deployments, she has been to Nepal to teach and South Africa to care for lions. Pottery lessons aren't in quite the same league as international travel but I suppose Mum's adventures into the unknown need to fit around us.

It was very late when I heard her park the car on the driveway below our bedroom window. She came in to kiss us good night on her way to bed, her teeth chattering, her hands icy cold. I hadn't been asleep. I don't like it when she goes out, especially at nighttime. Pastor Tim and his wife, Jill, babysat for us. They were lovely- they weren't the problem. I just worry, when Dad is away and Mum leaves us too, that something might happen to them and we'll be left alone forever. As I lay awake in the dark, I wished I hadn't singed her new padded jacket with my sparkler.

Mum seemed to have forgotten all about it.

'I made something called a coil pot in a freezing cold shed in the potter's garden.'

She hates being cold. 'The potter says perishing conditions are best for working with clay,' she said softly, twiddling my hair.

I wanted to sit up to hug her but my forehead was stuck to the pillow.

Friday 6 November

The pottery must be acting as a tonic. Mum was full of good cheer this morning when she came into our room. Her bonhomie wasn't even dented when she saw the enormous mountain we had constructed from all of our books, toys and clothing. She hummed to herself as she made us pancakes for breakfast and laughed when we got honey in our hair.

We were in the car on our way to a soft play centre to meet Marina when Mum's new-found peace was shattered by an incoming call on the car's audio system.

'What da f*ck are yer f*cking tenants doin' up dare?' (No 'Hello' or 'How are you?')

'I have my children in the car. Could you tone your language down please?'

'Not until you answer me f*cking question, ya t*sspot. Wha' da hell iz going on up dare?'

'I don't know what you mean by 'up dare'? What's the problem?'

'Da problem, ya f*ckwit (his vocab is really quite limited) izzda water pouring from your apartment intooz mine.' (Spike doesn't just manage the flats, he also owns the apartment beneath Mum and Dad's.)

'I didn't know there was a leak.'

'Iz not a leak, ya posh knob biscuit, izza f*cking tsunami. Izza flood, a Noah anda Ark type situation, but I don't seeze any rainbows, ya get me? No doves an dry land round here, ya gobshite.'

Spike seems to know his Bible.

'I'll ring our tenants and find out what's going on.'

'No, you're gonna call a plumber ana builder to sort dis out anden I'm-'

'Going to sue me?'

'Don't you get f*cking arsey with me, divvy.'

Mum hung up and called the tenants. They were at work but they said one of them would pop back as soon as they could. They called her back when we were in the car again, on our way home from soft play. The tenant described what she had found in the bathroom:

'The tap end of the bath has disappeared through the floorboards.'

I imagine that must be on a top ten list somewhere of things landlords don't want to hear from their tenants.

If our family believed in yin and yang or karma, I would say this is the universe getting Mum back for all the times she has moaned about military housing. We may have had front doors positioned so they nearly rip off the hallway light every time you come home, giant dog wees and leaking radiators to greet us on march-ins, even the odd ceiling collapsing, but to give the military its due, their baths have never tried to move floors.

Monday 9 November

Mum was fielding and dodging calls from Spike all weekend. Because the flat isn't managed, there's no one she can call to help her sort out the problem with the bath and Dad hasn't rung since Spike told her about the leak so she can't ask him for advice. She did some research on Google yesterday and instructed the tenants in how to turn the main water supply off to stop the leak but they have consequently had to move in with friends as they can't exist without water. They aren't happy and want compensating.

Mum has tried ringing various plumbers but either they don't return her calls or they haven't sounded professional enough to her. I'm thinking she's not really in a position to be picky here.

There was another fruity exchange with Spike during breakfast:

'Yer doin' me 'ed in. Wha exackelly 'av yooze done since yesterday?'

'I've stopped the leak and I'm in the process of instructing a plumber to repair the damage.'

'Oh, I'm made up. Well chuffed. Well yer can swerve on it, d'yer hear? If yuz don't get dis fixed proper by da end of termorrer, I'm gunna brick up yer front door.'

It was clear that Mum didn't know what to do. She looked downcast as she got us ready for a new tots group that is starting at church this morning. Judging by the number of people who honked at us on the journey there, she must be very distracted. When we arrived at church, we found Pastor Tim laying out toys in the community room. Mum started to cry.

'Would you like a chat with me in my office,' he asked, beckoning one of the group leaders over to look after me and Zach.

Not long afterwards, he emerged from his office, carrying an enormous tool box.

'There's a bit of an emergency that I need to deal with so I'll be gone for the rest of the day,' he told the group. 'Nothing to worry about. Please could you tidy the things away for me when you're done?'

It turns out that Pastor Tim used to be a plumber before entering ministry. He didn't think the situation with the flat could be resolved from a distance so he elected to drive up there himself and deal with the tsunami and Spike. Mum looked more grateful than I think I have ever seen her.

At bedtime, Pastor Tim rang Mum. He was only just leaving Liverpool. He'd patched things up, turned the water supply back on again and instructed a local builder to rectify the remaining damage. The tenants can move back in tomorrow as long as they don't mind not using the bath.

Spike got Pastor Tim in a headlock when he saw him coming out of Mum and Dad's flat. Mum didn't laugh when Pastor Tim joked that he might need the number of Mum's personal injury lawyers.

Wednesday 11 November

'Is Pastor Tim there?' Mum was phoning church whilst we had our morning snack, clutching a copy of the notices from Sunday's service.

'Morning, Anna. Are you ok? Everything alright at the flat?'

'Yes, all thanks to you. I can't tell you how grateful I am. I've been wondering how I can return the favour.'

'It doesn't work like that! There's nothing to repay.'

'Well, I want to thank you somehow and an idea just came to me. I saw, in the notices, that you need help organising this year's nativity. My godfather's a film director and I am sure he would help. I could ask him.'

'Anna, that's a really kind offer but it's very low-key. We can manage. It's just a shout out for an extra pair of hands. You have more than enough going on.'

'Please let me ask him. I would love to do something to help. He's so gifted- this would be easy for him.'

Mum didn't seem to notice how reluctantly Pastor Tim agreed.

'I'll email you the script,' he said, 'but tell him there's really no need.'

Mum rang Uncle Conal straight away.

'Darling, I would be delighted to help. As you know, I'm in the U.K, guest-directing 'Twelfth Night' at the National. Viola's a prima donna extraordinare. Hell is empty- all the devils seem to be in my production- but I can squeeze in a little nativity. No problem. Just send me the script so I can cast my eye over it.'

Thursday 12 November

Mum returned to the potter's shed tonight for her second lesson. She was wearing Dad's flying thermals and three of his coats, one of them a specialist cold weather jacket he was given for a survival course in Norway when it was -25C. I couldn't imagine how she was going to drive to the course, let alone fashion anything out of clay, with her arms restricted by all the layers of clothing.

Perhaps this proved to be the problem. She returned after only an hour, not saying very much, but her appearance spoke volumes. She was covered, from head to toe, in a powdery grey film.

'Is it better not to ask?' asked Cathy, who was babysitting.

'I slipped in the slip bucket.'

'That sounds like the correct thing to do. Isn't it?'

'No, the slip is a type of slurry you dip your pottery in. But my whole class looked like this as after my fall. The potter said he's sure I am gifted at other things.'

'Well, I know that's true- you are,' said Cathy. 'To be honest, I never saw you as a potter.'

'What do you see me as?'

'I think the God's the potter, you're the clay, quite literally now.'

They laughed.

'I made you this,' said Mum.

She handed Cathy a wonky lump.

'Thank you. What is it?'

'A bowl for your chickpea dip.'

'I will treasure it always.'

Monday 16 November

The builder instructed by Pastor Tim phoned Mum about the sunken bath. He'd been over to the flat to assess the damage. It wasn't good news. He said the seal around the bath had perished, possibly months ago, and water has been leaking through ever since to the floorboards below, turning them to mulch.

'Your boards are like shredded wheat that's been sat in the milk too long. The bathroom wall's not much better.'

You could almost hear him shaking his head in disapproval as his voice boomed over the loud speaker. Mum was changing my nappy at the time and she had her mobile propped up on the bin whilst she tried to get my tights back on. The phone fell down behind my bookshelf just as the builder was giving his quote.

'Sorry, I dropped the phone. How much?'

'You're looking at £3K, I'm afraid. Plus VAT'

'Three thousand pounds?'

'Yep. And I'm doing you a deal cos your friend Tim was in the trade. Someone else might charge you four.'

'Oh. Right. When can you start?'

'We've had a job fall through so I could get one of my boys on it tomorrow but I'll need you to transfer part of the money tonight for materials. I'd normally ask for half but I'll take a grand now, balance on completion of the work. OK?'

When we went to the shop by the community centre this afternoon for milk, Mum bought five lottery tickets. It was Zach's turn to shake his head. He disapproves of gambling. So does Mum.

Tuesday 17 November

'Darling, I've been over your 'Little Donkey' script. It's sweet but it lacks theatrical depth so as soon as I've made some amendments, I'll email it back.'

I hope Mum has explained the average age of the cast is three years old. I don't think Uncle Conal's Yeovil youth theatre will know what 'theatrical depth' is. Pastor Tim's main aim last year seemed to be to stop them falling off the stage and dribbling into the mic.

Wednesday 18 November

Mum discovered me playing with Dad's wedding ring today. I had found it in the drawer of his bedside table.

'What's that?' she said, snatching it out of my hand.

I tried to hide it behind my back when I saw how cross she looked but she pulled my hand towards her and uncurled my fingers. She looked so sad when she saw it.

Thursday 19 November

Mum received a letter today from the personal injury lawyers she saw on the TV. One wet afternoon in September, after trawling endless websites looking at luxury hotels with kids' clubs, she instructed them to make a claim for compensation for her fractured knee cap. I imagine, as she opened the envelope, she was hoping the compensation might help pay for Bathgate instead. But it was bad news again. As far as I can tell, her legal team's skills are only marginally more honed than her own and they have been trying to sue the wrong people for the past six weeks.

Friday 20 November

Is it normal to recommend counselling as a treatment for thrush? This was the GP's suggestion to Mum when we went to the surgery today. He said it's uncommon to get it as often as she does so he thinks it may be an indication of how rundown she is.

'You're very isolated- you've no family nearby, you have two little ones and no husband around to help you a lot of the time. Your body's exhausted so it's struggling to regulate the thrush spores that we all have all the time- which normally don't cause problems.'

Mum laughed. 'I haven't got time for counselling. Who's going to look after the children for me every week?'

I could think of lots of people who would help. Cathy, Pastor Tim, Marina.

On the way home, we went to the chemist to buy some Canesten. Talk about papering over the cracks. I think Mum and S.H.I.T. have more in common than she realises.

Saturday 21 November

Newly-weds Pete and Liz invited to us to visit them in Portsmouth whilst Dad is in Afghanistan 'to give Mum a rest'. They thought it would be fun if we drove over for the Navy Families' Day, which was being held onboard Pete's ship this weekend. We've been to something similar before with the RAF; every military camp has an annual Families' Day, where treats are laid on to thank the families of military personnel. People take spouses, children, grandmas and granddads, uncles and aunts.

It's quite a long journey to Portsmouth so Mum let us bring some toys in the car to keep us quiet. I brought my dolly buggy, a stuffed elephant called 'Elepants' and a few chewed board books and Zach brought a compass and a map of Europe (he doesn't trust sailors since he read Swiss Family Robinson). Mum wanted me to leave the buggy behind but she gave up the fight after ten minutes of me thrashing around on the front lawn with it.

As we were driving along, I secretly got Zach to erect it for me, omitting to explain that I planned on using it to beat him around the head. He hadn't really done anything; I was just bored. Mum used to sing songs and play car games with us on journeys but lately she turns up her 'Back to Bedlam' CD and seems to forget we are in the back.

Bedlam broke out in the car when Mum noticed what was happening behind her. She started thrusting her left arm between the seats, trying to arrest the violence, whilst steering the car with her other hand.

'Stop it! Stop doing that! NOW! I'm going to crash if you keep this up!'

I didn't stop. I cracked the buggy down as hard as I could, narrowly missing Zach's head as he ducked inside his car seat.

The car swerved, periodically, towards the oncoming traffic as Mum tried to collapse the buggy single-handedly. When it eventually folded flat, it trapped her hand inside its metal frame. Because the buggy is wider than the space between the front seats, her hand became stuck in the back of the car with us, which had a noticeable impact on her ability to drive. The strangulated noises she uttered from time to time suggested it was a painful arrangement.

Mum's solution was to slow the car to a crawl whilst she looked for somewhere to stop, only there was nowhere to stop as we were driving through a mess of road works and cones. Before long, we had half the West Country behind us, headlights flashing and horns honking behind us. I knew it was bad when we topped Radio Gosport's traffic news, delivered by Chopper Charlie, who referred to Mum as 'that joker.'

When we piled out of the car at Pete and Liz's Navy quarter, Mum described the whole thing as though it was a comic anecdote but none of it felt very funny and I wished I had left the buggy behind. I saw Mum's hand was red and swollen, covered with blood blisters. I wanted to kiss it better for her but, even though she was being light-hearted with Liz, I knew she was still cross with me.

'Golly gosh, have you seen the time? Let's start walking over,' said Pete, 'we don't want to miss out on the fun.'

Pete is the archetypal military officer. Like his ship, he is steady and strong, made of old-fashioned things like duty and manners. He makes me feel safe, like Dad does when he's around, and like Mum used to.

'There she is,' said Pete proudly as his ship came into view. There was no denying H.M.S Jubilant looked jubilant, festooned with balloons and bunting. She was surrounded by other huge ships and I felt very small, despite being high up on Pete's shoulders. Inside the ship, I felt less small as everything was so cramped. I didn't really like it. The corridors were narrow, the ceilings were low and I couldn't imagine how a crew of two hundred could ever fit in the tiny Wardroom where we ate lunch.

There was lots to do; the Navy seems to know how to show its guests a good time. I got my face painted as a mermaid, there was a magician who foolishly invited Zach to help him with a trick, not realising Zach had worked out where he was hiding his rabbit, and a guided tour, where we all took turns to pretend we were driving the ship.

Later, we gathered on deck to watch some of the uniformed officers firing a cannon. Every other little boy and girl there seemed to be with their Mum and their Dad. As the crowd concentrated on the display, I noticed the magician slipping away, carrying his big trunk of tricks. I decided to follow him. In his show, he used a box that he said could send you anywhere in the world. He told us that he had gone to the moon in it. I wanted to ask him if it could magic me to Afghanistan. As the magician left the ship, he didn't close the gate across the gang plank behind him. I walked along it and down onto the dock. Then he seemed to vanish. Maybe he magicked himself home.

I searched for the magician and his magical box until my legs felt heavy with tiredness. I sat down and realised I was in a fairground. Mum says I'm not allowed to go on rides by myself so I walked back over to the seafront. Waves were breaking over the wall, making big splashy puddles on the promenade.

It was cold and getting dark. I wanted to see the sea better so I pulled myself up onto the wall and lay across it on my tummy, my head hanging down over the side. An extra big wave crashed over me, soaking through my clothes to my skin, and I felt myself tipping forwards. I tried to feel for the ground with my feet but they were waving in the air and my head felt heavier than the rest of me. As I slipped further over the edge, I wondered what it would feel like to swim in the water. Would mermaids catch me?

Then something grabbed my ankles and I didn't get to find out.

The grabby things held me so tightly they hurt. Then they were around my waist and I was being lifted down from the wall. My top had risen up and the skin on my tummy grazed the stone. Whatever was holding me lifted me up, turned me away from the seafront and carried me towards a bench beyond the waves' reach. Carefully, I was lowered to the ground. As I twisted around, I found myself staring into the face of a policewoman.

She said nice things to me and then stern things into a radio attached to her shoulder. A wail of police sirens in the distance grew closer and louder and then three police cars pulled up on the road beside us. The policewoman put me in the back of one of them, tucking a blanket around me, all the time saying soothing things. By then, it was pitch black.

Not long afterwards, Mum appeared in the darkness as if from nowhere, drenched, with her hair plastered to her forehead, her face intermittently blue from the flashing lights. There were lots of naval officers with her, looking as wet and dishevelled as her. They smiled when they saw me. Mum cried. The policewoman spoke to her in a serious voice, using words like 'neglect' and 'Social Services'. She wrote things in her pad whenever Mum spoke.

Then Pete arrived in his car. I don't know where Liz and Zach were. He spent a long time speaking with the policewoman. Eventually, when I was shivering uncontrollably beneath my blanket, she decided not to take action against Mum 'this time'.

'Let this fright be a lesson to you,' she warned Mum.

We weren't meant to be spending the night in Portsmouth but Liz had already made up beds for us on their sitting room floor by the time we got back. I fell asleep soon afterwards with Mum curled up next to me.

Sunday 22 November

We ended up spending the whole day in Portsmouth at Pete and Liz's house, only driving home after teatime. We hadn't back long when Mum's mobile started ringing. It was Dad. Mum quickly sounded defensive.

'You haven't got a clue what it's like dealing with everything on my own,' she said. 'And whilst you're on, why did you leave your wedding ring behind? You have never ever done that before.'

'I was worried about losing-'

She hung up, cutting Dad off mid-sentence, omitting to tell him that Zach started walking today.

Monday 23 November

Moomin mysteriously 'dropped in' on us today. Even I know that no one with a full-time job in London 'drops in' to Somerset. Mum seemed as suspicious as me when she opened the front door and found Moomin standing there with a bunch of flowers and a bag of groceries.

'Why are you here?' she asked, rudely.

Moomin can't keep a secret. Before she had even hung up her coat, she confessed that Dad had asked her to come down and check on us.

'I'm sorry, sweetheart, but we are all a bit worried about you. Your friend Pete called Will yesterday.'

Although Mum can't call Dad when he's deployed, military friends like Pete seem to have ways of locating colleagues, even when they are in Afghanistan.

'Will called me. I thought I should just see how you are doing. We are all concerned about you, Dad and I, not just Will,' she said. 'You're so thin and so pale. And the house...'

Mum still manages to keep everything at right angles- she follows me and Zach around half the day, readjusting anything we move out of place- but she doesn't seem to notice the layer of dust everywhere, the black outline of dog hair around Dannatt's bed and the cobwebs in the corners of the rooms. I have never seen Moomin risk her manicure or designer clothes with anything domestic. When she found the mop and started cleaning the kitchen floor, I realised how worried she must be.

After some housework, Mum started telling Moomin about some of the things that have been happening recently. As she opened up, Moomin made Mum lie on the sofa with her eyes shut, 'free-associating.' I imagine you're supposed to use a technique like this in a relaxed environment, in a quiet room with the lights low, not with Peppa Pig playing in the background, in full view of the road outside and the neighbours opposite. The exercise was brought to halt when Mum's mobile phone started ringing.

'I'm not getting that,' said Mum, looking at the screen. 'It's Spike'.

'Give it to me,' said Moomin, reaching for the handset, now armed with all the facts about the bathroom debacle.

'No, this is her mother,' she said. 'There's no need to use that sort of language with me, Mr Spike. I want to sort this out. Right now. I don't want any more nonsense from you, do you hear?'

She put her hand over the phone. 'I'm only understanding one in every five words,' she said to Mum. 'What a monstrous individual.'

Resuming her conversation with Spike: 'Now look here. My daughter has instructed builders to repair the damage. She is doing everything she can. You're supposed to be in charge of the building so you must have details of the building insurance. We need a copy straight away so that we can make a claim for the repair work.'

Moomin winked at Mum. There was a pause whilst Spike told Moomin what he thought about this.

'Have you ever considered seeing a therapist for rage?' asked Moomin. 'You may think you're upset about the bath coming through the ceiling but I don't think that's really the cause. There must another root to your deep-seated anger. Talking as a professional, I suspect you're projecting your feelings onto the bath. These rage attacks are probably connected to a troubled relationship, perhaps some sort of trauma.'

There was another long gap before Moomin spoke again.

'I really think you need to seek help, Mr Spike. You sound terribly conflicted. It must be hard managing this degree of fury.'

One of Moomin's gel nails touched the speaker phone button.

'Yer snot-nosed southern w*nker, f***ing rich b*tch.'

'I've had enough of this. I have my grandchildren here and I would appreciate it if you would wash your foul mouth out, you odious, obnoxious, rude, ignoramus,' said Moomin, the therapist mask finally slipping. 'I was trying to be nice but if you want to do this your way, then yes, I am a rich B-I-T-C-H,' she spelt out, dropping her voice and looking apologetically towards Mum. 'I have the means to investigate you and your dodgy dealings. I imagine I could gather enough evidence to have you arrested several times over. Now if you want to keep this simple, post my daughter a copy of the insurance immediately.'

The line went dead and Moomin gave Mum a high five. Mum smiled; it was like the sun coming out after a very long winter.

Tuesday 24 November

Mum rang Uncle Conal to ask about the script. 'The performance is on Sunday 20 December- I really ought to get it out to people so they can start practising their lines.'

'Of course, darling. I'm so sorry. I've been a bit distracted. Viola and Olivia have fallen out- I'm in the middle of a full-on cat fight here. They're both in love with Sebastian and Sebastian's in love with Malvolio, who is being played by a very large opera diva, who I thought would add a comic touch but who is just plain terrifying and who, to make things even more dangerous, also seems to be falling for Sebastian. It's going to be a three-way skirmish, a brawl amidst Furies crown'd with snakes.'

Uncle Conal is working under the delusion that 'Little Donkey' is going to be less complicated than this.

Wednesday 25 November

A dog-eared, coffee-spattered copy of the building insurance for the flat arrived by special delivery today. Amazingly, the building is insured. Mum did a little dance around the kitchen when she opened the letter, waving it around as we ate our Weetabix.

After breakfast, she rang the insurers.

'We can consider a claim, Mrs Child, provided you can demonstrate that, as a landlord, you have made regular visits to the flat to check for wear and tear. In the absence of evidence to this effect, the policy will not cover the damage.'

Mum and Dad last visited the flat in 2007 when they first looked around it with the estate agent. So that's the end of that. If I were Mum, I would ask Moomin to lend me the money to pay the builders.

Mum bought another lottery ticket this afternoon.

Thursday 26 November

Mum must be doubtful about her chances of winning the lottery as we spent this morning exploring option number 2) in the 'how to raise £3000?' conundrum: apply for a bank loan.

We arrived in Yeovil so early that we had to wait on the pavement until the bank opened its doors. Once inside, Mum announced that she wanted to apply for a personal loan. Zach was not impressed. He says over-borrowing caused the crash that put Mum and Dad's flat into negative equity.

I was bored, sitting in the front seat of the pushchair, whilst Mum divulged all the family finances to a man who seemed even more bored than me. As he yawned and rubbed his eyes, I wondered why he had five biros in the top pocket of his suit. It seemed excessive until I saw Mum walking off with one of them at the end of the meeting.

Mum told the man she needed to borrow three thousand pounds. There were roughly three thousand questions on the application form for the money. The man glazed over as he listened to the answers but somehow managed to type them into his computer as I tried to wriggle out of my pushchair straps.

'I'll print this information off and then get you to sign it,' he said, his voice a dull monotone. 'You never know, you might get it.'

He made it sound like bank loans are also a form of lottery.

As I watched the man walk away to the printer, his computer screen went blank. All around the room, bank staff sitting at similar desks started to complain that their computer screens had gone off too.

'Dean,' shouted one of them helplessly.

It turned out Dean was the techy guy called on to sort out computer problem. He was completely stumped.

After a long wait, with Mum torn between getting her loan or a parking ticket, we left Dean scratching his head, fielding questions from various angry customers. Downcast, Mum pushed us out of the bank without completing the paperwork.

As we passed the bank window, I saw Dean lean under the desk where Mum had answered the bank loan questionnaire. He flipped a switch right by where Zach had sat in the pushchair. People started slapping Dean on the back and smiling. Mum quickened her pace.

Friday 27 November

We usually drink our bedtime milk in front of 'In the Night Garden' before Mum takes us upstairs to tuck us up with a story. As she searched for Iggle Piggle and Makka Pakka, she accidentally flipped onto the evening news, the top headline blasting out uninvited: 'Death toll this month for British troops in Afghanistan rises to eleven.'

She quickly turned the television off.

'Hurry up with your milk,' she said.

We wanted to stay down so we drank extra slowly.

Just as Mum was getting cross with us, the doorbell rang. Dannatt barked furiously, as he has taken to doing since Dad left. The postman hates Dannatt. He leave our post in the garage these days and chucks dog biscuits over his shoulder whilst running for his van if we happen to be out when he is.

We sneaked into the hallway to see who was at the door. It was Rebecca, the wife of Dad's boss.

'I tried to phone you but I couldn't get through,' said Rebecca.

Mum stared at her uniform. It started to seem rude.

'Why are you here?'

'Pardon, oh, well, I was wondering,'

'They send someone in uniform when there's bad news, don't they?' said Mum, holding the door frame.

'Yes, but that's-'

'So why are you here?' Mum's voice cracked.

'I, I wondered if you wanted to come to the Christmas Draw with me since we're both on our own.'

The Christmas Draw is a ball, named Draw because one of the highlights of the evening is a huge Christmas raffle, with genuinely good prizes. Not a bottle of Grappa that has appeared in raffles for the last three years or a Body

Shop basket of bubble bath that someone received in 1999. We are talking cars and skiing holidays.

'The Christmas Draw?'

'Did you think I had bad news? Oh no, I'm so sorry. I shouldn't have worn my uniform. I just thought I'd pop in on my way home from work.'

Rebecca gave Mum a hug, knocking her in the face with the brim of her big Navy hat.

'Let me help you get the children to bed,' she said, 'then maybe we could have a drink together?'

When Rebecca eventually left, Mum spent the rest of the evening trying on ball dresses. We wanted to see them so we made noises from time to time to get her to come into our room and shush us. We got a glimpse of them as she settled us back down. They all seemed a bit big for her.

Saturday 28 November

The bill for the building work on the flat arrived in the post today. Dannatt savaged it as a new postman unsuspectingly pushed it through the flap. By the time Mum had prised it from his jaws, it had several teeth mark in it; maybe Dannatt knew what it contained.

Mum left it out on the kitchen table. £2997.32. It looks worse in black and white. I didn't know numbers could look so unfriendly.

Sunday 29 November

'Any news on the script,' asked Pastor Tim over coffee at church this morning. 'I'm sorry to ask, it's just that the performance is only three weeks away. If it's an issue, we can cobble something together ourselves.'

Actual beads of sweat were forming on Pastor Tim's brow.

'No, no, it's all in hand. Uncle Conal is all over it,' said Mum, offering reassurance.

Pastor Tim didn't look reassured.

Monday 30 November

We've been living hand-to-mouth this week, eating weird combinations of pasta with baked beans and fish finger stir fry. Mum usually gets the food delivered to the house to spare herself the supermarket-cum-toddler experience but she's not doing very well at planning ahead lately so this afternoon we went to Tescos in person.

We did the usual thirty-minute hunt for the only trolley with twin seats, which has almost always been abandoned at the furthest point of the car park from the supermarket entrance. Once she had wrestled us into it, Mum hung our nappy bag over the handle. We hadn't even got to the third aisle when she ran out of the snacks she's packed to placate us on the way around. She grabbed a packet of rice cakes from one of the shelves, opened it and started belt feeding us them. She had a list and a calculator with her so I knew she was trying to economise. The calculator always comes out when she's worried about money.

I assume she's still worrying about the builder's bill, plus there's the car rear bumper to repair now too. She ripped it off yesterday when she got into a fight with a post box whilst doing a three-point turn to try and hide the fact she had gone the wrong way down a one-way street. Only she couldn't because she had an audience of oncoming traffic angrily watching her, plus Zach and I were screaming lots in the back, trying to warn her that she was about to hit the post box, but in retrospect, that may have distracted her.

I knew Mum was being careful about money before we even left the house and I saw her writing her shopping list with Delia's 'Frugal Food' cookery book. My suspicions were confirmed when we went down the wine aisle and she didn't buy herself her usual bottle of Chardonnay. I know stealing is wrong but I thought it might cheer her up if she found some of her favourite things in the nappy bag when we got home. So I started slipping the odd thing in when Mum and Zach weren't looking. A bar of Green & Blacks, a pair of shiny tights, a lipstick, some posh coffee, a mini bottle of Champagne.

When we go to the checkout, the fear set in. What if the cashier could tell I had a bag of unpaid swag? I decided the best thing to do was wiggle out of my seat straps, stand up in the trolley and throw my clothes at the horrified couple buying cat food behind us, whilst screaming at the top of my voice. For good measure, I ripped off my nappy and did a moonie at the cashier. I screamed so loudly I hurt my throat and ears.

Mum tried wrestling with me, apologising to the cashier and anyone else who was watching. 'I'm so sorry about this, she's very tired. Her Dad's in Afghanistan and she's very distressed,' she explained.

I am not sure it helped. It seemed to me that this vignette into our lives created more questions than it answered. The cat people looked positively alarmed and started a panicked discussion about whether the cat could make do with a tin of tuna they had at home.

All the while, Mum tried to get some purchase on me but she was impotent to do very much as I alternated between what I call 'the ironing board' and 'the hump back bridge'. Eventually, I calmed down and Mum hurriedly tried to redress me and pay for the shopping.

Mum has a hot flush whenever she gets embarrassed or hassled. By the time she pushed us towards the exit, her cheeks were burning red. She peeled off her coat and hung it over the trolley, even though we were about to step out into a November dusk.

Only we didn't get to step very far outside the shop. The alarms around the exit went into overdrive as we passed through them, lights flashing, sirens wailing. A man and a woman dressed in ordinary clothes appeared at our side.

'Step away from the trolley please, Madam,' said the man.

'Pardon?' said Mum, turning towards him.

The woman slid between Mum and the trolley, seizing the nappy bag.

'We'll take that, thank you very much.'

'I don't think we've caused this,' said Mum, gesturing towards the flashing lights.

'We can talk about that once we're back inside. Come with us,' said the woman, taking charge of the trolley and taking us back the way we had just come.

There was a door marked 'Private' near the entrance. The woman punched in a code on the pad beside it and pushed us and the trolley through as Mum scuttled along behind us, firing off questions.

'What is it I'm meant to have done? Where are we going?'

Neither the man nor the woman seemed interested in explaining anything until we were all assembled in a small, stuffy office with hard strip lighting that made everyone look weary. There was a set of monitors on a desk surrounded by piles of papers and a few half-drunk cups of tea.

'Sit down, please,' said the man, pointing to a plastic chair in the corner.

'To start off with, can you give us your name and address?' asked the woman.

'No. I'm a criminal solicitor and I would like you to tell me what this is all about first,' said Mum.

The man looked at her in a manner that suggested she wasn't the first solicitor they'd had to deal with.

'OK, if it gets you to co-operate, we have reason to believe-'

'Actually, evidence proving,' said the woman, pointing to one of the monitors.

'Evidence proving that inside this bag you have items stolen from this shop.'

'No, I don't,' said Mum. 'You're welcome to check the bag. Take my receipt too if you want,' she said, holding it out. 'But you'll be wearing egg on your face if you do.'

'Like this egg,' said the woman, removing a Cadbury's cream egg from the outer pocket of the changing bag. Mum loves them so I got her three. 'Do you normally pack your changing bag with Champagne, hold ups and Illy coffee?'

Mum looked baffled. 'But I didn't put them in there.'

'We know you didn't but you coached your little girl to,' said the man. 'We've been following you round the shop on the cameras.'

'What?'

'You came to our store today with a child prepped to steal for you. You got her to throw the worst tantrum we have ever witnessed at the tills. And that's saying something, we work in a supermarket after all. This was a decoy, a ruse to distract the cashier. You even thought to bring a foil-lined bag in the hope of getting the items out of the shop without triggering the alarms.'

'Foil-lined bag? What are you talking about?'

The man opened the bottle compartment of the changing bag, which is lined with silvery material to keep our milk warm. It was currently stuffed with packets of chocolate buttons. A little treat for me.

'Preparing for acts of theft in this manner is called going equipped and it's very serious.'

'I know what going equipped is,' exploded Mum.

'We know you do,' said the man, starting to sound a bit smug.

'This is ridiculous.'

'I'm going to add to my notes that your face is tomato red- a proven sign of stress and some might say guilt. And I will also be noting that you hung your coat over the trolley on your way out of the shop, when most people would put their coat on upon exiting the store, in a bid to hide your stash. Finally, I would like to note that we have witnessed your daughter stealing from this store previously.'

'What are you talking about?' Mum shouted. 'This is preposterous.'

'Like I said, that child bit the head off a chocolate bunny at Easter and she licked one of our toffee apples around Halloween. We let it go. We just thought it was a bit of naughtiness, we didn't realise you were tutoring her.'

'And I will be adding to my notes,' said the woman, 'that you have a half-eaten packet of rice cakes that we saw you take on your way round the shop, and which do not appear on your receipt, sticking out of your coat pocket. There are still bits of rice cake around your son's mouth.'

Zach went red like Mum. He hates having a messy face.

'The police are on their way,' said the man. 'Is there anyone who can take your kids home for you as you may be some time at the station.'

At that point Mum threw the worst tantrum I have ever seen- it certainly rivalled mine. She kicked the plastic chair and screamed and sobbed.

'My husband's in Afghanistan, I have the naughtiest children EVER, I can't control them, I'm exhausted, I have no one to help me, my family lives miles away, I'm exhausted and MY HUSBAND'S IN AFGHANISTAN.'

There was a long silence broken only by the odd sob from Mum. Then the woman started to cry.

'My son's out there too,' she said, handing Mum a tissue from a little packet in her nylon uniform. 'Helmand. Grenadier Guards.' She blew her nose. 'We've seen you've got your hands full with these two,' she said, patting my head. 'We often notice you when you're in. There's usually some drama, isn't there?' She smiled at Mum. 'Shall we let this one go, Bob?'

Bob's eyes were wet. 'If Sheila wants to let this go, that's fine by me,' he said to Mum, dabbing at his eyes. 'You've gotten so thin. Hasn't she, Sheila?' he said, blowing his nose. 'We thought it was drugs. Keep the cream eggs. You need fattening up.'

Having thought Mum was going to spend the night in a police cell, we actually made it home in time for tea. She couldn't be bothered to unpack the shopping when we got in so we ate cold fish finger stir fry. I've been trying not to pick my scab recently but I couldn't help myself at bedtime. I don't want her to get cross about the mess so I am hiding the bits in the tea pot in my toy kitchen.

Tuesday 1 December

Mum found a card from the Armed Forces Christian Union in the garage this morning. The old postman must be back on duty. The note inside was written by Emma. It said they would be praying for us on Friday and Mum could ring or email with any prayer requests.

Mum called Emma straight away.

'I don't know where to start really,' she said, before launching into all her many problems. 'There's psycho Spike, that deviant bath, the builders' eye-watering bill, the impending church nativity missing a script, Tesco security guards and, to top it all off, I'm going to a Christmas ball on Friday and I have nothing to wear.'

Mum spent almost an hour unpacking this list to Emma so that it made more sense. When she finally came off the phone, she stuck the card up on the fridge. I looked at it as I ate my Weetabix. It showed a picture of a helicopter, the same helicopter Dad flies, taking off in a swirl of sand. Beneath it was a Bible verse, "Draw near to God and He will draw near to you' (James 4:8).

Thursday 3 December

It's the Christmas Draw tomorrow and Mum's only option is still an ancient collection of dresses that hang off her. Cathy came around and tried to pin her into the smallest one. Years ago, when she lived in the commune, Cathy used to take in sewing to earn money for the collective pot so she's a bit of whizz on the sewing machine. The problem is that all Mum's dresses are from her university years and, even in the hands of a master seamstress, they look a bit dated.

Mum described the dress she would really like. Basically, she wants to look like Heidi Klum at this year's Oscars. I saw her admiring the Oscar dresses in a celebrity magazine the last time we were waiting in the doctors' surgery.

'You'll have to get on the blower to your fairy godmother if you want something like that,' laughed Cathy. 'I could do something for you with a set of net curtains I took down to wash this week. They're good ones. Lacy, not polyester.'

Maybe Cathy had Bjork's 2001 Oscar dress in mind. I saw a picture of it in the celebrity magazine under 'All-Time Oscar Lows.'

I think Mum would prefer to wear an actual dead swan than let Cathy dress her.

Friday 4 December

Despite all the money troubles, Mum took us on an emergency trip into Yeovil and dragged us around Monsoon and Denners to find a dress that hasn't been crocheted or woven by Cathy. She found several but they were all over £100. Slowly, she pushed us back to the car, empty-handed. And then there it was. As we passed Cineworld, there appeared on the horizon in the window of the St Margaret's Hospice shop a red silk taffeta gown with asymmetric neckline and side split.

Mum crammed us into the tiny fitting room and tried to hide her modesty with the shower-cubicle-style curtain but it wouldn't stretch around the buggy, the gap allowing a man perusing the board games an eye-full of her bra. She didn't seem to care. The dress fitted her perfectly and cost a mere £15. I'm not sure if Heidi's been in town lately but she may as well have been.

When Rebecca called in a taxi, Mum hurried downstairs, looking truly beautiful. Cathy had straightened her hair and Marina had popped across with some huge gold statement earrings. I felt sad that Dad wasn't there to see her swap her ratty old leggings for a bit of red-carpet glamour.

Saturday 5 December

Mum treated us to a morning at soft play and lunch afterwards at a nearby café. She ordered a creamy coffee for herself, milkshakes for us and three cream teas. Zach and I painted ourselves in jam and cream and she didn't seem to mind.

Mum was singing nursery rhymes to us when Dad rang as we were driving home.

'I need to see a gynaecologist asap,' Mum said.

You know the romance has gone out of a relationship when this is the opening line of your long-distance telephone call. Dad didn't answer immediately.

'When is it due?' he asked. The line wasn't good; he suddenly sounded very far away.

'Pardon?'

'The baby, when's it due and how did this happen? This is insane. We've now managed to make three babies without meaning to and we are both educated people who ought to know how to prevent this. I thought you had the birth control side of things in hand?'

'The children can hear you,' said Mum. 'And that's not what I meant. I am hardly going to tell you about a third pregnancy whilst pulling onto the driveway.'

'Why not? You told me about Zach when I was unpacking the Tesco shop.'

'All I meant was that my pelvic floor isn't what it used to be? Marina describes hers as being like a wizard's sleeve since having the triplets.'

'Why is it ok for you to tell me that EVER? Doesn't that fall into a category of things you don't need to share with me?'

'What?! It was through bearing your children that this has happened to me.'

'Look, I'm sorry. I'm just processing the fact you're not pregnant. And I have a queue of big burly American soldiers behind me. This area of life is best dealt with by email.'

'Fine,' she said. 'I'd better go, don't want to hold you up.'

'Don't be like that. Tell me your gyne woes if you must.'

'I just wanted to tell you about the Christmas Draw last night. My name got called out after the speeches because- wait for it- I won the top prize!'

'Which was?'

'£3,000!'

'Wow! That's awesome news!! The best thing I've heard since the pregnancy muddle,' he laughed. 'Post-Afghan holiday here we come! Well done! Maybe we could fly off somewhere for a cheeky bit of winter sun when I get back.'

'Sorry, no we can't.'

Mum explained about the bath.

Dad sounded like someone had just weed on his birthday cake. 'What does any of this have to do with your pelvic floor?' he asked wearily.

'By the time they called my name I was desperate for the loo. I had to go up cross-legged because they hadn't given us a comfort break. I looked like a penguin waddling up there. People were commenting.'

Generally, at formal dinners in the military, guests aren't allowed to leave the table until the port is passed around at the end of the meal.

'That rule clearly needs revising when there are women present who've had children,' she said.

But I don't think she really minded. We can pay the builders! Dad sounded less than ecstatic when they rang off.

Sunday 6 December

'Any news from your Uncle Conal?' asked Pastor Tim at the end of church this morning.

'He's currently caught in the middle of an operatic love triangle at The National but he's almost finished.'

'We could easily do a simple carol service if it's all too much,' he offered.

'No, no, I really want to help,' said Mum.

Pastor Tim looked as though he'd prefer it if she didn't.

Monday 7 December

Mum was late making our tea tonight so we were still eating our spaghetti hoops when the doorbell rang. It was Rebecca, this time in her ordinary clothes. She had come to have a drink with Mum.

'I'm sorry I'm late, I was trying to make the post office before it shut,' said Rebecca. 'And then I had to pop home to change. Didn't want to repeat that gaffe again. I brought chocolate.' She waved a bar of Dairy Milk.

'Tea or wine?' asked Mum, holding a mug and a wine glass up.

'Tea would be great.'

'Did you make the Post Office in time?' asked Mum, boiling the kettle.

'Yes, I did thanks. Today was the last day for posting things to Japan and I just made it as they were about to lock the doors.'

'Japan?'

'My sister's there on her GAP year- she won't be back for Christmas so I wanted to get her present in the post. I only just remembered the Afghan one last week. My memory's been hopeless lately.'

'So has mine. It's probably the stress of husbands being away.'

Mum started to make the tea. 'What do you mean- the Afghan one?' she asked.

'You know, having to get our Christmas things in the post by last Monday to get them there in time.'

Mum's hand went up to her mouth. She has spent a large chunk of the last five weeks making Dad's Christmas present- a scrap book stuffed full of

Christmas messages from almost everyone he knows. She emailed all our family and friends the day he went; cards and messages have been pouring in ever since for her to stick inside the book.

This morning, she made some Christmas Anzac biscuits (her own concoction so I'm not sure they'll be edible) for Dad to share with his friends and she's been gathering various stocking fillers- an 'It's A Wonderful Life' DVD, some reindeer antlers, party poppers, a Terry's chocolate orange, a yard of Toblerone, some new Bible notes and a pair of red knickers trimmed with white fur (they didn't look like they would fit him).

It is all laid out on the floor of the spare room ready to parcel up.

'Oh no,' said Rebecca. 'You forgot.'

Mum welled up, nodding her head.

'I'm sure the dates are overly cautious. If you take your parcel down first thing tomorrow, it may well get there. Don't worry. Let's get these little ones to bed. It's going to be fine,' she said, hugging Mum.

Mum didn't look like it was going to be fine.

Tuesday 8 December

We couldn't get to the post office first thing like Rebecca suggested because, during breakfast, Mum remembered that she had agreed to provide the snack for our Mum & Tots group this morning. She phoned Cathy.

'I have nothing remotely healthy in the house and it's my turn to do snack time at tots- I don't suppose you have anything?'

Cathy brought over some raw beetroot sticks and mashed avocado. It looked more like the Mum & Tots' craft than the snack and it made more mess. The other mums looked furious with Mum when they led their children home covered in purple and green stains that everyone knew would never come out.

It wasn't until the afternoon that we made our way into the post office with Dad's parcel.

'Are you related to the recipient of this parcel?' the postmaster asked when Mum explained where it was headed.

'Yes,' she said. 'Why?'

'We don't want random people bunging up the postal system, delaying relatives' mail from getting through to their loved ones.'

'You mean kind, well-meaning strangers sending things out to our forces to bring them some Christmas cheer? I don't have a problem with my mail being delayed by that sort of generosity.'

I know this isn't completely true. She wouldn't have said a prayer over the parcel before we left the house if she didn't mind it arriving late.

'Well, this is going to be delayed anyway, it's all a bit academic. You're a week late. It won't get there in time now,' said the man. 'Have you filled in the contents label? No, I see you haven't.' He sighed. 'What's in there?'

There was a postman behind the glass by the cashier, filling his sack with parcels. He smiled at Mum as she listed the contents of the parcel. She didn't mention the knickers.

'Put it on the scales.'

Mum did. Her hands were shaking.

'Right, you're over the weight allowance. You're going to have to split it into two parcels. I can't be holding up the queue while you sort this out. Go over there, repackage it all and come back when you're done.'

Mum looked at the queue, which was going out through the door by now, and pushed us over to the stationary section where the man had pointed. She picked up some new jiffy bags and Sellotape and tore open her carefully-constructed packet. I was bored so I grabbed a roll of wrapping paper and hit Zach over the head with it. It bent in two. It was so enjoyable I got another one and did it again.

'Oi!' shouted the postmaster. 'You'll have to pay for those.'

In retrospect, the commotion may have distracted Mum, who dropped her packet. Half the things fell onto the floor, her biscuits in the Chinese takeaway plastic box smashing into oaty crumbs. The knickers landed on top of the yard of chocolate.

She knelt and started scraping up the crumbs as the cashier audibly tutted in our direction. The nice postman stopped to help.

'Don't worry. I am sure it will get there,' he said, handing Mum the Bible notes back. 'I've prayed that it will.'

He gave her his handkerchief and repackaged everything for her.

Wednesday 9 December

There is some rule somewhere in a military archive or bunker that says the repair people have to come out within twenty-four hours if your boiler breaks when there are young children in a married quarter. Our boiler broke today but I'm not holding my breath (which, by the way, I can see inside the house.)

After forty-five minutes on hold to S.H.I.T, with only a S.H.I.T. pre-recorded message to offer assistance, Mum decided we should go and choose a Christmas tree.

'It's actually warmer out here than it is in the house,' she said, bundling us into the car.

We won't be at our house for Christmas as Aunty Chloe and Uncle Mark have invited us to go and spend it in Scotland with her, Uncle Mark, Moomin and Grandad. It's a generous offer, given they only moved house just over a month ago and their baby is due in less than three months.

'I don't want to be travelling the length of the country to see you all so this suits us,' Aunty Chloe explained when Mum protested that it was too much for them to host us all.

We won't get to enjoy the tree on the actual day but Dad made Mum promise she would buy one to cheer us all up.

'I don't want them missing out just because I'm stuck here,' he said.

Dad's favourite bit of Christmas is getting wrapped up in hats and scarves and going to choose the Christmas tree and mistletoe together. It was odd doing it without him. Maybe Mum felt the same way; she certainly wasn't in a very festive mood on the way into town. She turned 'Do They Know It's Christmas?' off when it came on the radio and put on 'A Long December' from her Counting Crows CD.

At the garden centre, she lined up three potential Christmas trees by the netting machine whilst she puzzled over which had the prettiest shape but she made the fatal error of turning her back on them (when I dropped the wreath I was supposed to be looking after). Another friendly-looking family came walking past, smiling and wishing us 'Merry Christmas' and, as we responded in surprise, deftly plucked our Norwegian Spruce, then sauntered off with it.

'Outrageous!' Mum spluttered and instantly decided the stolen tree that was the one she most wanted. She made us follow 'The Thieves', as she quickly christened them, until they stopped near the check-out to pick out a glittery gnome.

'No taste,' spat Mum as we hovered nearby for a chance to reclaim their quarry but they expertly kept hold of the tree's trunk, like seasoned Christmas tree rustlers.

As we stood with our teeth chattering, our tummies rumbling now that it was well past lunchtime, I wished we could just go home. None of this felt Christmassy, despite the carols playing overhead and the smell of fir cones. I started to feel concerned when Mum looked ready to trip the other mother up with a Christmas tree stand.

Thankfully, just as I noticed a dangerous glint in her eye, the boiler man called her to say he was on his way out to us. Forced to abandon her silent feud in order to hurry home, Mum grabbed a random tree on the way out. It looked very long.

Maybe it was the rush that made her forget to buy mistletoe.

The boiler man had been waiting for us for an hour by the time we arrived back at home. Getting an eight-foot tree into our estate car was never going to be a quick job and removing it proved to be no mean feat either. When Mum dragged it out onto the kerbside, there seemed to be more needles in the car than on the tree. The boiler man carried what was left of it inside for her.

'It can't be fixed today,' he said after inspecting the boiler. 'It needs a new part. I should have it by tomorrow. I can leave you with some fan heaters overnight, then I'll be off.'

After he left, Mum tried to erect the tree in the sitting room. As the room is only six and half feet high, she had to saw top of the tree off first. That turned out to be the easy part. Trying to get the tree to stand up straight when she had no one to hold it or to tell her how it looked whilst she was lying beneath it proved trickier. When the tree eventually collapsed on her, as I could have told her it would, pinning her beneath it, I rushed to get help. As I let myself out through the patio door to get Cathy, Dannatt escaped, disappearing through the garden gate ahead of me.

Dannatt nearly became Christmas mincemeat as he ran in front of a white van in the road outside our house. The van screeched to a standstill, just inches from Dannatt. It was the boiler man again. He leapt out and grabbed Dannatt by the collar.

I led him by the hand into our house to where Mum's feet were poking out from under the tree. Within minutes, the man, whom we later came to know as Steve, had the tree and Mum standing upright again.

'Why did you come back?' asked Mum, handing him a cup of tea.

'Left my mobile,' Steve said, dunking a biscuit. 'But, if I'm honest, I did wonder how you were going to manage. I was more worried about leaving you with that tree than the dodgy boiler.'

Thursday 10 December

The post brought with it Uncle Conal's long-awaited rewrite of 'Little Donkey,' handwritten in his inky scrawl.

'You've got to come over now,' said Mum. I knew she was calling Cathy because she can't type anyone else's phone number that fast.

'What is it?' asked Cathy.

'An Elizabethan retelling of the first Christmas, in no way, shape or from suitable for a kids' nativity. I don't even understand it.'

'Right you are, lovely,' said Cathy, not sounding surprised.

Mum got out her Bible, cross referencing Uncle Conal's version with the original until Cathy arrived.

'What do you think?' asked Mum as Cathy read through it. 'It's quite cleverly done, I think. But not always true to scripture,' she added.

'What language is it written in?' said Cathy. 'I feel like I recognise bits. 'Come, let's away to Bethlehem, we three alone will search the night skies.' I'm sure I've heard that before.'

'I think it's been tweaked from King Lear. Uncle Conal's note says he's woven together lines from Shakespeare's plays to tell the story.'

'So, let me get this right, he's expecting your wisemen, who are five years old, to remember 'To sleep; perchance to dream'?'

'I may have been a bit vague about the age of the children.'

'Oh-kaaay. These are the options as I see it. Number 1: sack it off.'

'What? I can't- I would be failing Pastor Tim.'

'Believe me, I am certain he won't mind if this is the alternative.'

'And I would be messing around Uncle Conal, who's given up his time to help me.' Mum's voice cracked.

'OK, I know this is important to you,' said Cathy. 'Number 2: we use subtitles. I'll make some banners and write out a translation.'

'But we don't know what most of it means so how can we translate it? Plus, the kids aren't going to be able to say any of this stuff for us to translate and Uncle Conal may be hurt if we admit no one understands his script.'

'Ok. Then it's got to be option 3: the adults take on the main roles and by that, I mean you, me, whoever we can drag in. I'll be the lead shepherd. I used to look after the animals in our smallholding back in the day so I know my way around a sheep and I already have an outfit.'

'R-iiiight.'

'I'll take charge of the little shepherds. You can be the lead wise man and control the other wise men, my Paul will be Joseph, maybe Marina could be Mary.'

'She doesn't even go to church.'

'She owes me big time.'

'But she'll bring Benjy.'

'True. Scrap that. Bunny can be Mary. She's an actress, right?'

'Yes.'

'Moomin can be Herod and Grandad can be the angel Gabriel. Sorted. Give me their email addresses and I'll tell them what's happening.'

Mum's teeth were chattering as Cathy left. I don't know if it's anxiety or the Baltic conditions in our unheated quarter.

Friday 11 December

The heating is back on again, which is good as the temperature has plummeted and it is now perishing outside. The media is calling it the 'The Big Freeze'. We were initially excited by the flurry of snowflakes yesterday. It made everything look so pretty, creating an instant winter wonderland.

This morning, I looked out of my window and checked to see if the snowy carpet was still there. It was. Just beyond our front garden, children were pulling each other along on sledges and throwing snowballs. Mum looked out of her bedroom window into the back garden. She saw footprints in the snow. Hundreds of them. Tiny. Leaving a well-trodden path between the chicken coop and the nearby hedge.

'Rats!' she screamed down the phone.

The rat man came out immediately. He didn't have a spare slot so he squeezed us into his coffee break. You could tell this was a man on a mission, someone with a calling. Strangely, he looked like a rat himself. He had a black woolly hat on, small beady eyes, a moustache and a nose that moved independently of everything else. I don't think he really wanted Mum to show him the tracks. I think he would have liked to sniff them out himself.

Roland, the name on his Pest Control badge, stood in the garden, examining the coop and the rat run, whilst Mum hung out of her bedroom window, asking him questions.

'You've had them for months. They're going for the chicken feed. Have you found any broken eggs?'

'Yes, they're often broken,' Mum called down.

'Right, they're eating your eggs. They'll be attacking the chickens next. '

'What do you mean?'

'Nibbling their legs, that sort of thing,' said the man, scouting around, wrinkling his nose. 'I'll lay traps. Big traps. Everywhere. Load them up with the good stuff.'

'Good stuff?'

'Poison. Lots of it. But it means you're going to have to keep the dog and kids out of the garden for a while. And you'll have to bring the chicken food in every night and lock the chickens in the coop to keep them safe.'

Keeping us inside won't be the problem but I know there's no way Mum is going to set foot out there again now. The chickens are more likely to die from starvation than a rat attack.

'Would you come and do it for me?' she yelled down.

The man wrinkled his nose. I think he is more of a rat killer than a chicken charmer.

'Pest control doesn't offer that service, I'm afraid.'

Mum reached for her phone and rang Cathy, perhaps recalling that she was responsible for vermin at the commune, apparently a full-time job when you have a small holding, compost heaps and a reed bed sewage system. Cathy came straight round with her oven gloves and a giant net.

Sunday 13 December

'I don't want to pester you,' said Pastor Tim over coffee at the end of church, 'but how's the play coming along? Just a week to go.'

He sounded hysterical.

'It's perfect. We are having a dress rehearsal on Saturday, ready for Sunday morning. It's all under control.'

Tuesday 15 December

'It's all too much, it's all too much, it's all TOO MUCH,' shrieked Mum.

Cathy was dressed in a camel hair coat she acquired years ago when she lived on a kibbutz, which she had teamed with a tea cloth headdress. She threw a glass of water over Mum. It did the trick. Mum seemed to rejoin us.

'Anna, let's just cancel this. No one will mind.'

'I don't want to.'

'OK, then focus. You and I can't remember our lines and we're more than quadruple the age of most of the cast. We have four days to fix this. If I had got us into this mess, what would you advise?'

'I don't know. Ring my Aunty Christine? She's usually away on business but it could be worth a shot.'

'Just so we don't make this situation worse, and please don't take this the wrong way: why would involving more of your family help us?'

'She's a fixer. A director for a massive company who multi-tasks and organises, an all-round problem solver.'

'Ring the woman.'

Wednesday 16 December

'We've done six weeks!' It was Dad, sounding unusually cheerful. 'We're over a third of the way there.'

'I miss you,' said Mum.

'You've not said that lately.'

'I know, I don't say it enough, but I do.'

'Are you ok?' asked Dad.

'I'm fine.'

She didn't mention the nativity.

Friday 18 December

Aunty Christine is Grandad's younger sister. When she drew up outside our house in a black limo, armed with Champagne, a box of tissues and a laptop, I remembered how similar she and Grandad are. Not just in appearance but their air of calm and order.

'This is to drink when we have nailed this,' Aunty Christine said, pointing to the Veuve Clicquot, 'these are to mop up the tears along the way because, from the way you have described this, there will be bucket loads.' She waved the Kleenex at Mum, who took one. 'And this is how we are going to turn this mess around,' she added, putting her laptop onto charge.

'I love you, Aunty Christine.'

'I love you too,' she said, hugging Mum. 'Now enough of that. I've got sound and lighting arriving tomorrow. We'll get mics for the actors who warrant them. Those who can't remember their lines won't be miked up or allowed the spotlight. There's a lot we can mask just with the technical side of things.'

Mum started to cry.

'No tears, this is going to be fab! LA's coming to Yeovil. We'll knock their socks off.'

Saturday 19 December

'Where are they all going to sleep?' whimpered Mum, looking in the airing cupboard for bedding.

'I've booked your parents and Bunny into a local hotel. They are all en route to the church as we speak, with an ETA of 10:00 for the rehearsal. Cathy is already there sorting the costumes. It's going to be fine.'

I wanted to believe Aunty Christine's powers of control and organisation were sufficient for the task in hand but this was unfamiliar territory, even for her, and I feared she had underestimated her protagonists.

The grandparents all knew their lines at least, impressively so, in fact. Bunny was word-perfect but she kept ad lobbing with expletives.

'Cut! Cut! Darling, this is a church. You can't use that kind of language,' bellowed Uncle Conal from the director's seat that Aunty Christine had rustled up from somewhere.

'The bard's as bawdy as they come,' said Bunny. 'Just adding a bit of realism and grit.'

'Right, she's not getting a mic,' whispered Aunty Christine to the sound engineer.

Cathy's sub-team of shepherds thought it was funny to make fart sounds whenever she spoke, either genuine ones or with their arm pits, it wasn't always clear.

'Don't give her a mic either. We can't add volume to that toilet humour.'

Mum kept getting tongue-tied and saying her words back-to-front.

'Melchior,' she said, poking the little boy next to her, 'the conditions above us govern our stars.'

'No!' said the little boy, stamping his foot. 'It's 'The stars above us govern our conditions.' Get it right for once.'

'Neither of those statements is biblically correct,' Mum sniffed. 'The order makes no difference.'

'Better not give her a mic either.'

I was an angel. Zach wanted to be one as well but Bunny had scuppered that dream for him. She was insisting on having a real baby Jesus and, whilst far too big for the role, as the youngest member of the cast, she had selected him. He looked so miserable, trying to extricate himself from his swaddling, which Cathy had fashioned out of some loo rolls made from recycled coffee cups that she bulk buys.

'We can't have the baby Jesus climbing out of the manger and undressing like a Mum returning to life. He's going to freak people out,' yelled Uncle Conal, sounding even more emotional than normal.

I don't know what suppressed anger Moomin was channelling but she was positively ferocious as Herod, with a maniacal laugh and glittering stares, swiping her orb at the wisemen with such energy that the youngest ran off to the toilets and had to be collected by his mum. Zach was happy as he was demoted from the role of Jesus to replace him as the third wiseman and Bunny was given a rubber doll from the Mums and Tots box.

Grandad and Paul were the only unproblematic members of the cast.

'We can't just mic up the Angel Gabriel and Joseph. It'll look odd,' said Aunty Christine. 'Where's Uncle Conal?'

It took a while to locate him; he was at the back of the church, praying.

Sunday 20 December

'Is there any way you can remove my name from the programme?' asked Uncle Conal as people began to arrive in church for the nativity, a stream of bobbing antlers and Santa hats finding their seats.

'Uncle Conal, get a grip,' said Aunty Christine. 'It's going to be fine. Just sit in your seat and leave the rest to me.'

Turning to the cast, she whispered: 'Do what you did yesterday and I'll magic up the rest.'

A supremely nervous Pastor Tim climbed onto the stage to welcome the audience. 'We have an extraordinary performance for you,' he said, leaving it at that and sitting down quickly.

As the audience fell quiet, music filled the church from every corner of the building. 'Little Donkey' played in surround-sound, covering over the noisiest sweetie-wrapper-rustler, all of Bunny's blue language, the armpit farting and Mum's muddled lines. A spotlight picked out Mary and Joseph as they journeyed to Bethlehem, the shepherds in the fields, the angels in the night sky and the wisemen travelling to Herod and, finally, the stable and the baby Jesus. It all became one beautiful, starlit mime.

'Bravo!' said Pastor Tim at the end. 'Bravo!'

He held off asking for an encore, leaving things safely where they were.

Even Uncle Conal seemed happy. 'You can be my assistant director any day,' he said to Aunty Christine when we waved them all off.

As Mum stood on the driveway, motionless, you wouldn't have guessed it had gone so well; she looked destroyed.

Monday 21 December

I'm so excited. I feel all Christmassy at last. We are now packed up for Hogmanay in Scotland! Roland came to check on his traps and Mum roped him into putting the roof box on the car for her. He was quite amenable as the traps are working (Mum studiously avoided asking him how he knew). He kept humming a little ditty to himself as he positioned the roof box on the roof rack.

'There's a rat in mi kitchen, wha' Roland gonna do, Rolly catch dat rat, dat what Roland do, Rolly splat that rat...'

Mum asked him to stop. She's not been in the kitchen since then.

When Roland finally scuttled off to his next job, she loaded up the car with suitcases, cots, the buggy, backpacks, wellies. I don't know where we're going to sit as she's left the boot empty for Dannatt and the roof box empty for no apparent reason whatsoever. Basically, everything is packed around our seats and in the passenger foot well.

After bedtime, I got back out of bed to put another scab in my teapot and I heard Mum on the driveway outside. I stood on a chair and peeped through the curtains. There she was, teetering on the side of the car, throwing packages up into the roof box. Some of them shone in the moonlight and some had bows on them. I could only see outlines but one of them looked like a trike.

Tuesday 22 December

At 5.30am, whilst it was still dark outside, I lay in bed listening to Mum creeping around the house, showering and getting dressed. Within the hour, we were driving away from the Red House, making tracks in the next layer of freshly fallen snow, bound for Liverpool, where we are breaking the journey to Aunty Chloe's. We're not delivering a Christmas card to Spike or a landlord's annual check on the flat. We're breaking the journey at the half-way point with Mum's friend, Donna.

Donna used to live across the road from us until her husband got a new posting a few months ago and they moved away. They have three children. A girl and two boys. Donna is expecting another baby so she will soon have four children under the age of five, a prospect that leaves Mum baffled and admiring in equal measure. She thinks Donna makes having three children look easy and memorizes anything Donna offers in the way of parenting advice.

I don't like Donna. She introduced the naughty step to our house, which is where I now seem to spend a large chunk of every day. To be fair, Donna said Mum should only put me on the step for the same number of minutes as my age but lately, Mum's converted the minutes into hours. Yesterday, I had to sit there for nearly two hours after I tried to trick Zach into eating some rat poison.

We arrived at Donna's house around mid-afternoon. Coming out to greet us on the driveway, Donna's enthusiasm was less pronounced than her initial excitement when she extended the invitation for us to stay a few months ago. She looked heavy with child and heavy of heart and perhaps the prospect of looking after five children and a dog with only Mum to assist (Donna's husband is at sea) wasn't appealing. Mum must have sensed Donna's flagging spirits. After squash and biscuits, she offered to take us all for a play on the trampoline to give Donna a break. She climbed on with us, suggesting we play musical bumps, which she might as well have called 'Who wants to go to casualty first?' Minutes later, she landed on Zach.

Zach is usually quite brave but he cried for a very long time. Repeated attempts to get him back on his feet with the promise of Smarties and Magic Stars proved futile. He hasn't been walking a month yet and Mum has reduced him to crawling again. Donna came out of the house, holding out her phone to Mum. She must have been watching through the kitchen window.

'It's my GP surgery- they might see him as a visitor.'

Before long, Zach, Mum and I were back in the car on the way to the GP's. Mum was so hassled on the way in, trying to hold my hand and carry Zach, that she nearly dropped him. She managed to save him by hoiking him back on to her hip but, in the process, she inadvertently head butted him and gave him a bloody nose. I suggested to Zach in the waiting room that he should contact Mum's personal injury lawyers when we get home but he didn't find that funny. By the time we were called through to see the doctor, Zach looked more than a bit damaged.

The doctor examined Zach and asked Mum lots of questions. Mum looked terrified, hugging Zach to her. I expect she was wondering whether the doctor was going to let her leave with us. He asked why we are in Liverpool and Mum explained. She looked exhausted.

'Where is your Dad?' the doctor asked Zach. He held up a stuffed lion from his desk and tickled Zach with its mane.

'Ganstan,' said Zach, breaking off from his whimpering.

'Afghanistan?' the doctor asked, looking at Mum.

'Yes, that's right,' nodded Mum. 'I can't believe it. He's never said anything before- that was his first word.'

'I see,' said the doctor. 'I understand. Coming back to your son's leg, I am pretty certain that it's sprained, not broken. But if Zach's still not walking by tomorrow, we will need to get him to A&E. And you, Mum, I am sensing you're overwrought and in need of rest but you're a military mum and I don't suppose you're likely to get any until a certain person gets back from Ganstan.'

He stood up and lifted Zach off Mum's lap. She looked terrified.

'Where are you going? Please don't take him from me. It was an accident. It really was.'

She started to cry. So did Zach.

'I'm taking him to your car, where you are going to sit with your children and have a little break whilst I queue up in Boots for this prescription,' he said, waving a green bit of paper at her. 'And if you're lucky, I'll get you a coffee to drink whilst you wait.'

As we walked out through the surgery, the doctor carrying Zach, Zach and Mum tearstained, me trailing behind with the lion, I wished Dad could come home right away and look after us, like the nice doctor was doing.

Wednesday 23 December

It doesn't take a rocket scientist to guess where we spent this morning. Zach still couldn't walk when we came to say our farewells to Donna so we set off in search of the hospital. I helped Mum push Zach around the wards in a wheelchair that we were offered in triage. After a trip to the X-ray department, the doctors confirmed Zach's leg is only sprained. They wrapped it up in bandages and sent us on our way with a bucket of Calpol.

As we were pulling out of the hospital car park, Aunty Chloe rang.

'We've had another three feet of snow in the night. We're officially cut off- they've closed the roads surrounding our village and they say they might have to start shutting some of the main roads too.'

'Oh no,' said Mum.

'The whole of Scotland is one massive weather warning. Mum's not sure they're going to get through on the sleeper. I don't want to say this but I don't think you should try to drive up here.'

Another call came in.

'Chloe, I'll ring you back.'

It was Cathy.

'I've been worried sick,' she said. 'Are you in Scotland yet?'

Mum explained where we were.

'There's no way you're going to make it up to Aberdeen now. Come and join us. It'll be fab!'

Mum was trapped. Cathy now knew we were homeless at Christmas. We would have to accept her invitation.

'Are you at the commune yet?' asked Mum. Cathy and Paul were spending Christmas there, staying with their old friends.

'Yes and it's just a hop, skip and a jump from where you are.'

'In Stockport?'

'Yes, that's us, come on over!'

Cathy gave Mum the postcode and she punched it into the Sat Nav. Her face in the rear-view mirror looked strained.

Maybe she was worrying about the same things as me- namely, (1) Will Santa know where we are going to be if we change our plans at the last minute? (2) Will we have to share our Christmas presents with the other children there? and (3) Will there be rats and only cold water at the commune? Cathy's communal living seems to have made her adept at managing with both but if that is the case, I would prefer to go home to our own rats and our own cold water.

Friday 25 December

Santa did know where to find us, there is hot water here and I have not yet met a rat. We do have to share our presents with the other children, though, but they all clearly identifiable as ours as someone has tipexed each one with our full name. Weirdly, every present looked like it had been ripped open and rewrapped. Maybe Santa had been at the sherry when he did his wrapping this year.

Mum's Christmas package to Dad arrived in time. Dad sounded pretend-happy on the phone when he rang earlier. He said everything that can be done to make it Christmassy out there has been done. They even had turkey and stuffing for lunch, which is more than can be said for us. We had stuffed tofu. So we are all having an uncomfortable Christmas, camping out somewhere we'd prefer not be, a bit like Mary, Joseph and Jesus. However, I imagine Mum would say that that's where any similarities between us and the holy family end.

After thanking Mum for his presents, Dad described looking down from his helicopter last night as he flew over the desert.

'The moon was so large and bright. I saw a group of Afghan nomads making their way across the countryside with all their possessions strapped to their camels' backs, just like a scene from the Bible. It was as if I was watching the wise men following the star that very first Christmas. For a few minutes, it was possible to imagine that there was no war, no terrorists. But when we flew back into Camp Bastion, over the 30-foot fences and miles of razor wire, watch towers and tanks, it was as though I'd imagined it all.'

Dad must have realised he was being less than festive, and possibly divulging more than he's allowed to. He tried to tell us a joke after that but as he was delivering the punch line, the connection failed. The call went dead. Maybe there was a security issue. He didn't ring us back.

2010

Dear Dad

This is what I would write to you if I could write but I can't yet so you'll probably won't ever hear this.

You must know that Mum isn't well, at least. Grandad called the emergency number you told us to call if we ever needed you urgently whilst you are deployed. I assumed, when I heard you explain how it works, that if we rang it, you would instantly come back from Afghanistan to rescue us, maybe on a magic carpet or in a rocket. But that doesn't seem to be how it works.

Maybe they didn't tell you how ill she has been. Maybe if they had done, you would have tried to come back. I heard Aunty Chloe whispering down the phone to Uncle Mark that Mum has had a breakdown. I don't like that word. I don't want Mum to be broken but I suppose she is.

She stays in bed a lot and almost everything makes her cry, even nice things, like hugs. When our car breaks down, we call a breakdown service but there doesn't seem to be an equivalent for Mum. There are people who try to help, like the psychiatrist Moomin arranged for her to see when all of this happened. And her GP, who gives her pills to take and who has put her on a waiting list for some counselling. And there are the kind people from church, who offer to pray and bring lasagne over for us to warm up. But there's no one who can give her a jump start, something to get her going again.

I think people had been worrying about Mum for a while. The tears and the mood swings were a bit of a giveaway. Things got better in February when you came home from your Christmas deployment. Mum definitely seemed brighter. Perhaps you thought people were exaggerating when they told you how hard she had found it, with Spike and the bath, the rats and the aborted trip to Scotland.

I think Mum properly started to unravel whilst she was preparing for this current period of separation. As you packed your trunks again, and she busied herself arranging a joint birthday party for me and Zach, knowing you wouldn't be there to celebrate with us or to help her, I saw a look of panic in her eyes, like the look Dannatt had when we found him collapsed in his water bowl, helpless and scared.

She started to look like that more and more after you went. There were several occasions when she just stood motionless in the kitchen, surrounded by things she needed to sort out- me and Zach crying at the table because she hadn't got tea ready in time and we were hungry, the baked beans boiling furiously on the stove, welding themselves to the bottom of the pan, Dannatt looking forlornly at his empty bowl, the phone ringing. She always used to have an action plan, the best way of maximising her time so that things get ticked off her list, but she started to struggle with even the basics.

If someone tells you later how bad things got, you'll still never truly know. It's rare that someone can use words to transport you accurately back in time to something you weren't a part of. You'll never understand what it felt like to have Mum's face in mine, red with rage, screaming at me to stop crying, to eat my supper, to stop stressing her out, to stop being naughty.

You probably wouldn't believe me if I told you that she tipped the burnt baked beans I refused to eat all over the floor and jumped up and down in them, explaining that she would show me what a real tantrum looked like.

I'm sure you won't believe that the person who has always made me feel the most secure and loved made me feel more terrified and alone than I have ever felt. Zach and I barely recognised her whilst this was going on and yet she managed to look just normal enough when we went out for other people not to get involved. They might have looked concerned that she appeared so tired and thin but not overly concerned. They offered to help but Mum rarely took them up on their offers.

You might wonder why she didn't let them give her a hand. I think maybe it's the language people use. They say things like 'Give us a shout if you need anything' or 'We're only at the end of the phone'. It's too vague. You're not sure if people mean it. It's a bit like when people say 'We must get together', then never make an arrangement. Do these people really want to be called out at 8pm when they're sitting down to dinner because our bedtimes gone wrong- everyone's tired and in tears, we've run out of nappies, there's poo on the carpet, a mountain of washing to be done if any of us are to have clean clothes the next day, no bread or milk left for the morning?

The other problem with accepting people's offers of help is that sometimes the amount of preparation needed to take them up on it (explaining where the nappies are kept, the times for lunch and naps, moving car seats around etc) sometimes makes doing it yourself seem easier.

One of the only people who offered any real help was Cathy. She would turn up on our doorstep, having already got our buggy from our garage, and say she was taking us to the park. Or she would order a Chinese to be delivered to our house if she'd been round earlier for a coffee and seen we had nothing decent in the fridge for dinner. Cathy doesn't mess around making polite overtures.

We were staying with Moomin and Grandad when Mum finally broke. Moomin and Grandad had been at the birthday party Mum organised for me and Zach and they saw firsthand that she was struggling. She got angry with the other children during the party games when they were being silly (having fun), she was overly anxious when Grandad opened 'too many' chocolate fingers for the tea party (can you have too many?) and she had a row with the man who came to collect the bouncy castle when he complained about the jelly in the fan blower (the man had a point).

Moomin and Grandad asked us to spend the last week in August with them in London to give Mum a rest. Moomin offered to treat Mum to dinner out on the last night. Grandad stayed at home with us to babysit. They came home after an hour, mascara streaking down Mum's freshly made up face, a strained look on Moomin's. Whilst they were looking at the menus, Mum had started to cry. Then, more embarrassingly, she'd reverted to laughing uncontrollably. She veered between histrionics and hysteria until Moomin suggested they leave. As they got ready to go, Mum became jelly-legged and couldn't walk. The waiting staff had to carry her out to a taxi, which Mum thought was hilarious, until she started weeping at how undignified she must seem. I heard all of this because I was still up with Grandad having a story when they came back.

The next morning Moomin made an appointment for Mum to see a psychiatrist contact of hers. Mum said she wasn't mad but Moomin insisted on taking her anyway. They had a big row and Mum cried a lot.

'I think you will need medication, sweetheart- we need to get you better for Millie's sake as well as yours. This is the right thing to do.'

Mum eventually ran out of tears and Moomin helped her to get dressed. I went with them to some very smart rooms in Sloane Square. The reason they took me was that Moomin had noticed me picking my skin. She told Mum this was due to anxiety. She said I needed professional help too. Perhaps if Mum hadn't been so distracted, she would have done something herself earlier.

Mum saw the psychiatrist first, a beautiful, tidy-looking lady with shiny swishy hair like a My Little Pony, older than Mum but younger than Moomin. I sat in the plush waiting room with Moomin until it was my turn. Mum was in there for ages. Moomin was restless, picking up glossy magazines and putting them down again without looking at them, checking her watch and pacing the thick carpet. I could tell she wanted to go in too. She had looked cross when the psychiatrist asked her to watch me in the waiting room instead. Maybe Moomin wanted to offer her own theories, or just make sure Mum told the lady everything.

After a while, the beautiful lady came and invited us to join her and Mum.

'My name's Tamzen,' she said, smiling at me. Tamzen asked me lots of questions. She was very kind. She told Mum I have something called Excoriation Disorder. She said it's related to Obsessive Compulsive Disorder so maybe I caught it from Mum. She told me that I need to go and speak to someone when I get back to Somerset about the things that worry me. I'm not sure how that will work as I can't say how I feel very easily. Tamzen said she would write to my doctor to ask him to arrange this.

In the car on the way home, Mum told Moomin about her appointment. She said Tamzen had been cold and unsympathetic. I found this almost impossible to believe. She said she'd told her she treats lots of military wives, which Mum doubts.

'How many military families can afford £300 per appointment?' she asked.

Moomin paid for today's session.

Tamzen said that anxiety and depression for military folk, both personnel and dependants, are far more commonplace than most people realise. Mum thought this was code for: suck it up. I'm sure it wasn't. I don't think Tamzen would ever use those words. Maybe Mum saw somebody else- this can't have been the lady I saw.

Mum was given a prescription for some anti-anxiety pills called Citalopram. Moomin pulled over at the first sight of a chemist to get it made up. She came running out with a bottle of mineral water so Mum could take one of the pills straight away. Like me, Mum is going to have some counselling when we get home.

We stayed with Moomin and Grandad for the bank holiday weekend. Moomin wanted us to stay longer but she also thought we needed to get home to set up the counselling. She drove us back to Somerset and stayed with us for a week to make sure we were alright. She took us to the GP to tell him all about what's been going on.

At the end of the week, Aunty Chloe arrived to take over. She brought baby Sara with her so she had her hands full with all of us It was lovely to see Sara again. I don't suppose you've seen her yet? You were away on a training exercise when we flew up to meet him at Easter shortly after she was born. I wished we lived all nearer to one another.

Mum seemed stronger when Aunty Chloe left. She was getting dressed everyday and spending less time in bed. She was doing some jobs around the house and even drove us to the supermarket to do the weekly shop. Now that we are by ourselves again, Cathy comes in twice a day to check on us and she often ends up staying most of the day. And Pastor Tim now knows everything after a phone call from Moomin so there is a daily dinner rota, with different people from church popping by with something for us to eat.

My main worry is that Mum will break again. She still looks very breakable. Zach and I spend a lot of time tidying things up around the house to keep her calm. We sorted out the recycling for her in the sitting room last week; that seemed to upset her, though. I cleaned the toilets with our face cloths yesterday and I tried to do some polishing today but I sprayed Zach in the eye and he woke Mum up with his screaming. I don't think she appreciated my efforts.

It's hard to know how we can help. I wish someone would tell you how much we need you to come home. They've probably been very British about the whole thing, not telling you when Mum was in a tailspin because they believed it would all be alright, not telling you when she crashed for fear of worrying you, playing down the aftermath because it's all a bit embarrassing and she's on the mend now anyway, we hope.

We aren't just separated by 3,000 miles. We're separated by our experiences, which are poles apart. We'll never understand what you go through when you're away, flying your helicopter around the Afghan skies, living under canvas with hundreds of other people. The only thing I can picture when I hear about Afghanistan is the Afghan Hound in my book about dogs. I have no other pictures in my mind to help me imagine where you are. Are there any Afghan Hounds in your camp? Do they sit round the campfire with you?

Even when you tell Mum over a takeaway one night when you are home (and I sneak down claiming ear ache just so I can check you are still with us and haven't gone away again), even when you tell her what it's like to have a terrorist in the back of your helicopter, or when you describe being shot at whilst you wait for injured colleagues to be loaded through the cargo door, unable to take off until they are safe- she won't really know what that was like and neither will I. It will sound like a fantasy, something too far removed from our small Somerset lives for us to comprehend.

In other ways, our experiences aren't so different. You're in a war zone and, in a sense, so are we. It's hard to know who the victims in our battle are, though. Mum? Me and Zach? Dannatt? You? Moomin and Grandad? Aunty Chloe, Uncle Mark and baby Sara? Cathy? Pastor Tim?

I don't fully understand why you do this job. I know you love flying. I know you love your colleagues and you want to serve your country. And we are so proud of you for that. We still salute the picture of you in your uniform outside the bathroom every morning on our way down to breakfast.

But on a bad day, like today, we wish you could just protect our family unit, our little squadron. I wish you could join the Home Guard instead, like in the reruns of Dad's Army- protect those of us back here. But maybe that's what you are doing and I just don't understand.

All I know is that we miss you. Things don't work around here when you're away. I cry sometimes when I go to bed. Everything feels scarier then and I worry about Mum downstairs alone. Sometimes I hear Zach crying. Even Dannett whines by the front door when he senses our unhappiness.

I really hope you make it home for Christmas. Please fly your helicopter carefully. Please keep safe.

I love you.

All my hugs,

Millie Tori Child x

2011

Friday 3 June

I think Dad must have got my imaginary letter somehow. Maybe he's like God and knows what you are thinking and wanting without you having to say anything. Whatever way it happened, he made it home from Afghanistan in time for Christmas. Happily, for us, he's been in the UK ever since.

We enjoyed a quiet Christmas with minimum fuss and maximum input from Dad to ensure Mum's recovery wasn't put in jeopardy. The medication prescribed by the doctors had started to take effect by then and she was slowly re-emerging as the Mum of old. Our GP had put me and Mum on the waiting list for some counselling. By the time Dad got back in December, we had both started to have weekly sessions with a psychotherapist and things were generally, gradually improving.

It was probably just as well that Mum had this safety net around her when the news came that we would need to move again and leave the life we had settled into here. It felt as though we had only just got the Christmas decorations back up into the loft when Dad's career manager got in touch to say Dad would be posted back to an RAF station in Hampshire eight weeks later. With no quarter on the new station for us to move into at such short notice, the only real option was for Dad to live in the Mess in Hampshire during the weeks and visit us in Somerset at weekends.

This is how we come to be in the throes of another housing battle. Dad says it sometimes feels like the most long-standing threat to military personnel is the Service Housing Allocation Management. Or S.H.A.M. for short.

Living apart immediately raised the question of transport for Dad. In the past, he had always cycled to work but he couldn't continue to do that once he had a 170-mile round trip. There wasn't much money available for a car that they hadn't planned on buying so one wet weekend in March, Dad chose an old rust bucket from the forecourt of a local second-hand car dealership. Then he packed his bags and drove away, leaving us standing in a cloud of exhaust fumes, waving him off from the driveway.

That was three months ago. Zach says this short-term arrangement to tide us over whilst the housing people find us a quarter is a false economy; he estimates the housing situation will outlast the car. He wants to be an actuary when he grows up. Applying actuarial science to the situation, he gives the housing debacle six months and the car half that.

The only advantage of having Dad's new job sprung on us in January was that it allowed Mum to withdraw her application to Somerset County Council for my school place. With only three days until the school admissions' deadline, she submitted a new application to Hampshire County Council for a school there.

Instead of the guided tours of prospective schools, with careful deliberations and long discussions about which one to select, Mum and Dad missed Property Ladder to spend an evening in front of the computer looking at school websites, selecting their top three without ever having seen any of them in person. Without a home address in Hampshire, they had to use the address of the camp where Dad now works for the application.

'Tell me again why you have picked these ones,' said Dad.

'Choice number one is a Christian school so that's easy. Choice number two has good parking and I like the uniform of our third option.'

Sorted. She spends longer choosing broccoli.

S.H.A.M did offer us a house within a month of Dad starting his new job but it wasn't a tempting offer. It wasn't on the camp where Dad is stationed but in an old barracks, near a creepy wood, by a building site, too far away for us to go to the school and pre-school Mum had chosen for us and the school application deadline had passed by then.

'We'll feel so isolated if we're miles from all the other RAF families,' she reasoned. 'And you won't be able to sell your old tin-can-on-wheels if we live that far away. You'll have to drive to work in it every day.'

She knows that there are lots of single pilots on Dad's squadron with enough disposable income to drive BMW coupes and Porsches. Dad refers to this fact every Friday night when he walks in after his three-hour journey home being bumped around on seventeen-year-old suspension. Zach has calculated that, on average, he mentions other people's smart wheels within 2 minutes 37 seconds of returning home, usually before he has greeted any of us. But I guess it must be tough for him to park his Lada next to his colleagues new, shinier models. And it must have been even tougher to contemplate living in a quarter that would require him to keep doing so.

'Let's look at it at least,' he said, 'It may be better than you think.'

The following weekend, we went up to stay with Dad in the Mess, all of us squashed into his tiny bedroom, so that we could go and view the house. We didn't have keys to the property so when we drove over, we had to make do with peering through the dirty windows to see inside. There were dustbin bags of rubbish strewn about the otherwise empty rooms, nothing appeared to have been cleaned and the garden was an over-grown postage stamp with a broken fence.

'It doesn't look like anyone did a march out,' said Mum.

'What?' shouted Dad.

There were lorries rumbling past the house, spraying gravel around as they trundled up to a half-built housing estate. It was too noisy to hold a proper conversation.

After a little cry, Mum tried to be positive.

'Building work is a good sign,' she sniffed. 'It means growth, new opportunities.'

She researched the area on her phone as we drove back to the Mess.

'It was used as a location for a James Bond film,' she said hopefully. Possible encounters with Daniel Craig seemed to lift her spirits until she discovered that it had served as the demilitarised zone between North and South Korea in 'Die Another Day'.

We turned the house down.

During the same trip, we went to look around the primary school where Mum and Dad have applied for me to start in September. It's a small village school set in the middle of the countryside. The school sports' field is a meadow, near some stables that are home to a Shire horse and a Shetland pony. The headmistress is a fierce-looking lady but she must be warm-hearted because she came and met us on a Saturday just to give us a guided tour of the school, showing me the classrooms, the lunch hall, the miniature loos and the playground.

She held my hand as we walked around.

'I hope you will be able to join us here, Millie,' she said.

I caught Mum smiling at the multi-coloured cross hanging in reception when we said our good-byes.

'This is the school,' Mum said to Dad afterwards. 'I'm praying she gets in.'

'Pray for a house; it's not much good if she gets in and you're still living in Somerset.'

Six weeks ago, we got a letter confirming my place at the first-choice school. Mum let out a whoop when she read it, swinging me into the air and taking us out for ice-cream. A couple of weeks later, S.H.A.M. offered us another house but it was in the same demilitarised wasteland again. This time Mum and Dad had to accept the property as S.H.A.M isn't obliged to offer a third property.

That is how things stand for now. We will have to move to the building site, Dad will have to keep his car and we will have to reject my school place or spend hours every day on the school run. To make things worse, we could now be evicted from the Red House as we are only entitled to stay here three months from the start of Dad's new job and he's been in in his new post for almost four months.

Some of our military friends have encouraged us to stay put, suggesting we become squatters.

'You could sit out on your front lawn, get the kids to wave protest banners around,' laughed Marina's husband, Stuart. 'They wouldn't touch you. Go on hunger strike, invite the local press. It wouldn't pass the Daily Mail test, that's for sure.'

'I don't read the Daily Mail,' said Mum, not laughing back. 'I don't know about their quizzes.'

'It's not a quiz,' said Stuart, 'it's one of the ways the military judges whether a course of action is advisable- they consider whether it would it look damning on the front page of the Daily Mail?'

'I don't want to be on the front of the Daily Mail,' said Mum, looking horrified, totally missing the point. Zach rolled his eyes.

Our new neighbour, Andria, came out of her house to where we were all standing awkwardly, studying our lawn, wondering how it would look on the cover of the tabloids.

'It won't come to that! I've been briefing Anna, she knows what to do. Hi, I'm Andria,' she said, introducing herself to Stuart. 'My husband and I are both in the military and we know the housing loopholes like the back of our hand. We've literally spent years trying to get our postings to marry up and houses in the right place together. Have you put my plan into action?' she asked, turning to Mum.

Mum looked even more awkward. She hasn't updated Andria yet about what happened when she followed her advice. After consulting over the garden fence with Andria a few days ago, just as Dad was about to accept the second offer of a quarter, Mum came up with an alternative plan: he would go in person to the housing allocation offices, armed with a generous supply of biscuits for the housing officers, and strike a deal. According to Andria, the biscuit ploy has never failed. Ever. Fortuitously, S.H.A.M.'s offices are in Hampshire, not too far from where Dad now works.

Dad went on his push bike during his lunch break with a big selection box of Family Circle to the housing allocation office block. On arrival, distracted by someone telling him he wasn't authorised to be there, he smashed into a housing officer's personal plant pot and left with a bill for £27.93 and no housing deal. Mum called Dad for a progress report and he was forced to admit total defeat.

'You'll have to try again tomorrow,' she insisted.

Maybe that seemed easier than the inevitable row that would follow if he refused because he agreed to try again. The next time they wouldn't even let him onsite.

'The biscuits didn't work,' said Mum.

'What?' said Andria, looking shocked. 'What brand did he get?'

'I don't think that was the issue. He smashed into someone's tomato plant on arrival. They were growing it for their local village fete. The damage was terminal and the tomatoes had to be composted, along with our deal.'

'I'll think of something else,' said Andria but she looked stumped. 'That never fails,' she muttered as she went inside.

Dad came in tonight, looking exhausted from his weekly drive home down the A303, stuck behind weekenders heading to the coast.

'Johnny's off to choose a Z3 this weekend,' he said.

'Hello to you too,' said Mum.

He gave her a quick kiss and then showed her a letter he received at work today. It was a notice for us to vacate the Red House.

Mum threw the letter in the bin.

'Andria's just been over. She's come up with a new plan.'

'Can I get a beer before I hear this plan that undoubtedly involves me doing something humiliating.'

'No, it's me that's taking the hit this time,' said Mum. 'Andria says we should make a welfare case based on my mental health. If it's successful, S.H.A.M. will have to give us a house on the camp. It's a good ruse.'

Mum calls the new strategy 'a ruse' as though she is doing something frightfully cunning, forgetting that this argument for housing us in our community would actually be based on fact. I don't think Dad knew whether to be pleased or alarmed as he carried his bags upstairs. He plumped for wary. Although he also wants a better house, I doubt he wants to advertise at work what happened with Mum last year.

Sunday 5 June

Dad headed back to Hampshire this afternoon, as he does every Sunday now that he works such a long way away. He went extra early, straight after lunch, as he wanted to go into work to sort out the paperwork he will need to submit for the welfare case he has agreed to make.

Sundays have become a miserable affair. We go to church in the morning, with tensions on the rise as the impending good-byes draw nearer. There is often an argument on the way there about why Dad has no clean flying socks to take back to Hampshire or why he didn't get the chicken out of the freezer in time to defrost for lunch. Rubbish arguments, really. After church, we come home, eat the roast chicken (if it's a week when it has been defrosted in time) and then we clock-watch until Dad goes, maybe squeezing in a walk down Dog Shit Alley if there's time. Sometimes it's a relief when he drives off and it's just us again and we can get on with the week. But it always feels empty, knowing it will be another five sleeps until he can come back.

Today I thought it was Dad who looked relieved as he wound down the window of his jalopy to give us one last wave before he drove off. Perhaps he was feeling hassled by Mum's continual reminders to get the housing application in. It is certainly wearing to listen to her constantly quoting Andria: 'Andria says you must...' and 'Andria thinks it's important to mention...'

It's obvious that Mum doesn't trust Dad since the plant pot episode. It wasn't just the pot he broke. She seems to have lost all faith in his ability to sort the housing situation out.

Monday 6 June

I think Zach must be missing Dad. He didn't say so but this morning he calculated how much time we have spent apart from him since we were born. I am now almost four years old and Zach is nearly three years old. By Zach's calculations, if we include the two tours of Iraq, the training in Morocco, the two tours of Afghanistan and the time living apart now (and we don't include all the short training exercises and one-off nights away):

I have spent one year, five weeks and six days without Dad

Zach has spent forty-three weeks and two days without Dad

Zach says that we have, so far, spent over a quarter of our lives without Dad. He estimates that by the time we are eighteen years old we will have spent more than four and a half years missing him. I felt pretty glum by the end of his presentation.

I tried to remember all of this to tell my therapist, Hayley, when I see her later but I know I won't be able to. I've been seeing Hayley most Mondays since last November, when a space became available for me to start my counselling. She comes to our house for my sessions and Mum and Zach leave us alone, usually playing upstairs or in the garden.

Hayley looks like Mum, with the same chestnut hair and dimples, bit that's where the similarity ends. Unlike Mum, Hayley is very calm and considered. Sometimes, Hayley plays games with me but the thing I most enjoy doing with her is drawing pictures. She loves my pictures and always says nice things about them. My own Mum is usually too distracted to look at my art and, occasionally, puts fistfuls of my work in the recycling when she thinks I'm not looking.

Mum was offered some counselling last December, a few weeks after I started mine. She has to go to Yeovil to see her therapist, a lady called Val. We've never met Val but Mum seems to like her. Every week, once I've finished my session with Hayley, Cathy comes over to our house to look after me and Zach and Mum drives off by herself, often looking quite relieved as she hunts for her car keys, especially if Cathy tells her not to hurry back.

Wednesday 8 June

Dad rang last night to say he needs a report from Mum's GP, giving her medical history and outlining her breakdown, her current mental health and why, if it all, the doctor thinks that living in the house we have been offered will adversely affect her.

'We have to demonstrate that there are exceptional personal reasons for refusing the second offer of a quarter, otherwise we will be forced to take it,' he explained.

As soon as the surgery opened this morning, whilst she was sweeping up Cheerio's from under the kitchen table, Mum telephoned our GP practice and begged the receptionist to squeeze us in this afternoon.

Zach and I realised whilst we were sitting in the surgery waiting room that we were going to need to give Mum a helping hand when we got in there. We agreed we had to make her life look really hard so that the doctor would feel sorry for her and write a sympathetic report. As Mum wheeled us into the doctor's room, I reached out from the back seat of the buggy and dragged the full-size model skeleton that hangs in the corner over onto the filing cabinet.

'Millie!' Mum scolded.

I noticed the doctor was looking less than perky. He's a wiry middle-aged man with a weary sort of face but I'm starting to wonder if that's the effect we have on him. Maybe we are like a Ready Brek antidote for him, making him cold and miserable, when ordinarily he would be break-dancing through life, wearing an orange glow.

As Mum brought the buggy to a halt, she unwittingly positioned the front of it, and therefore Zach, next to a drawer of hypodermic needles and syringes. Within minutes, he had showered them all over the floor. The doctor listened to Mum whilst he simultaneously tried to repair his office, scrabbling round on the floor, picking up artificial limbs and blood vials. With our work complete, I realised there was never a question about whether he would write the report and make out the welfare case for Mum. The quicker we get rehoused in another county, the happier her GP will be. It's not just a welfare case that benefits her but various people in Somerset, our GP included. As we left, he promised to have it in the last post.

Friday 10 June

Mum's medical report arrived today. The doctor has certainly come up with the goods, describing her as 'vulnerable', 'unstable' and 'prone to anxiety'. He recommends, in the circumstances, that she is 'in need of strong community ties, especially in the absence of support from the wider family, who live some distance away'. He concludes that we should be housed with the other RAF families from Dad's squadron in order to give Mum the stability she needs to prevent her depression from worsening.

Mum seemed delighted. She took the report next door as soon as Andria came back from work for lunch. Andria hugged her after she read it. Mum went a bit red; maybe she realised that the doctor isn't actually allowed to make this stuff up.

Monday 13 June

Dad rang at lunchtime to say he has submitted the welfare case to the housing people, which means we can't be evicted from this house whilst the application is being considered.

'When will we hear back from them?' asked Mum.

'I've no idea; I've never had to do this before.'

Tuesday 14 June

My new school is starting a course of settling-in sessions. They are being held every Tuesday for the rest of the summer term. Never having met any of the other parents or children, and desperate for me to make some friends before I start, Mum was determined to get us there. After breakfast, she packed us, Dannatt and various overnight bags into the car. I imagine most other children in my class have a ten-minute drive to the school. Ours is a two-hour journey, provided we don't hit traffic.

Today's session was billed as a teddy bears' picnic so Mum had various snacks on paper plates, wrapped in cling film, on the passenger seat next to her. In the back, Zach and I clutched our favourite cuddly toys. Mine is my dirty elephant, 'Elepants', and Zach's is a tiger named 'Sumatra' (it was called 'Tigger' but he renamed it). Dad said he would come across from work if he got back from his flying sortie in time.

As was inevitable, we arrived late. I don't know if it was Mum's fault or the Sat Nav's. I think they would blame one another. Mum says the Sat Nav changes its mind all the time and lets her know about exits when we have almost passed them. I think our Tom Tom has achieved the virtually impossible and made Mum's driving even more dangerous than it would be if she were left to her own devices. With it at the helm, we regularly screech across all three lanes on the motorway to make the slip road and cut people up on roundabouts.

Our nerves were definitely a little frayed by the time we passed the 'Welcome to Hampshire' sign. When we eventually found the school, there was nowhere for us to park. The pretty country lane nearby was filled with huge four by fours, 'Chelsea Tractors' as Mum calls them, big and shiny with personalised plates. It reminded me of when Moomin and Grandad once took us for lunch at Cliveden. On arrival, Dad was forced to park our dirty estate in amongst the vintage Bentleys and Bugattis lined up on the pristine gravel driveway. Even the hotel shuttle bus had looked smarter than our car.

Mum parked miles away from the school and attempted to chivvy us back down the lane but I didn't want to meet the new children so I kept dropping Elepants in the nearby ditch to slow us down. Nobody has asked me where I want to go to school. If they had, I would have told them that I want to stay in Somerset and go to the school where my best friend, Jen, and all my other pre-school friends are going.

Every Monday morning, they are taken across to the nearby infant school where they all have places. They spend the morning there in order to get used to it before they start going full-time. As they form a crocodile in the pre-school hallway and disappear through the door en masse, and I am left behind, the only one my age not to be included in their trip, I feel angry and left out. If I admitted any of this to Hayley, she would probably say that this is why I've started bullying the little ones. I pull their hair and knock over their paints and drop rolling pins on their feet whilst I join in with their art or cookery sessions, wishing I was doing grown-up learning with my friends. The staff usually make me do time out and then I feel even more angry and left out.

Today, as we were walking down the lane to the teddy bears' picnic, I still felt angry and left out because I know I am not part of this group either. And, even worse, I felt scared.

Maybe Mum felt scared too. She was ratty as she concentrated on keeping us walking in the same direction as her (she eventually picked Zach and Sumatra up), all the while trying not to drop her paper plates. It started to rain. By the time we arrived, we were soggy and bedraggled.

In the reception area, the school secretary showed us through to the hall. The picnic was taking place inside due to the rain. Everyone was sitting on cushions in a circle around a checked rug, which was covered with china plates laden with food. Not frozen sausage rolls and a few Cheetos like we were expecting but brioche-encased mini burgers, homemade parmesan straws, spelt bread sandwiches, a cheese platter and beautiful cupcakes with perfect glittery frosting. Mum had been forced on the journey here to feed me and Zach from her picnic supplies- the only way she could find to keep us from maiming one another. She looked a bit embarrassed as she added our half-eaten contribution of Wotsits and slightly browned chopped apples and bananas to the smorgasbord laid out in front of us.

The receptionist introduced us and explained that we were late because of our long journey. I think this was kindly meant but it instantly put Mum in the firing line for all sorts of questions.

'You've come from SOMERSET?! My best friend couldn't get her little one in and she's IN CATCHMENT!'

'Wow, you have done well- what a wheeze'.

Through the hall window, I saw Dad pull up outside the school in his decrepit car, look at the other cars and drive away. I noticed Mum saw him too. He might have got away undetected if his car hadn't backfired.

Mum's intention had been to make friends and blend in. She had said as much to Dad on the phone last night.

'How on earth did you manage to get your daughter in? My neighbour will be livid,' yelled another mum.

Mum starting playing with the cross on her necklace. I could see she was hating this as much as me.

'We're practising Christians,' she mumbled.

'Pardon, darling- what was that?'

'PRACTISING CHRISTIANS.'

Mum's volume control could sometimes do with a bit of readjustment. The way she shouted this out, you'd have thought the woman quizzing her had been holding an ear trumpet. The room fell silent. Mum could have said so many other things. Mentioned the military covenant, talked about the difficulties of school entry for a forces' family living between counties.

But I was happy things weren't going well. I decided to walk through the picnic. Big, heavy, stamping footsteps through the princess cupcakes, a hearty kick for the artisan cheese straws and then I broke wind, loudly, before swiping Elepants through the brioche.

Wednesday 14 June

Cathy called in this afternoon to see how we got on in Hampshire. Mum described the trip- the teddy bears' picnic and the monumental row she and Dad had afterwards- in great detail over tea and Jaffa cakes. Dad hadn't got a leg to stand on. He shouldn't have driven off from the school and he knew it. But that just seemed to make him extra angry. Hayley would probably have said he was employing anger as a defence mechanism to deflect Mum's accusations that he had been proud and cowardly.

I didn't hear Mum repeating the 'proud-cowardly' bit to Cathy, maybe because she knew it wasn't just mean but also hypocritical. Like Dad, Mum hadn't wanted anyone to see our car either. We parked in a farmer's field, behind some tall hedges. I suspect this was done to hide it from the other mums. An angry farmer then had to help push us out of the ditch Mum had wedged us in before he could spray his crops and we could leave. We had planned to spend the night in Hampshire but when Mum and Dad still weren't speaking after dinner, she packed up our bags and drove home without saying good-bye.

When Cathy was getting ready to leave, she suggested Mum ring Dad.

'Give him a bell. He'll want to make up as much as you do,' she said.

Mum didn't seem to hear. She just smiled and thanked her for coming over.

Thursday 15 June

Most Thursday afternoons since Easter I have been going to ballet lessons in the village hall just down the road from us. Lots of the little girls from my pre-school also go. Mum sits outside in the draughty hallway whilst my friends and I dance. Zach stands with his nose pressed up against the glass in the door to watch. It's been obvious for several weeks that he wants to join in. My suspicions were confirmed after last week's lesson when Mum and I discovered him in the bathroom with my ballet case, trying to put on my ballet outfit. His legs and arms were tangled up in the leotard but he had managed to pull the satin slippers on.

Before today's lesson started, Mum drew the teacher, Mrs Clutterbuck, to one side and whispered something to her. When Mrs Clutterbuck put her finger up to her lips to shush us and then motioned for Zach to come up to the front.

'Zach is going to be joining us today,' she said. 'Let's all give Zach a welcome curtsy.'

Mum left the hall, assuming Zach's usual position outside the door, with her nose pressed up against the glass pane. It became apparent, almost immediately, that Zach is better than the rest of us. At the end, he got a star for his interpretation of Swan Lake, which Mrs Clutterbuck says could rival Matthew Bourne's.

Friday 16 June

When Dad came home tonight, grumpy from another long journey, complaining that the driver's door is now slightly loose and rattles when he goes over 50mph (which can't be often- Zach says the car's top speed is 55mph), Mum would have been wise to delay dishing up the ballet news. I think it's fair to describe Dad as a modern man. He likes to put on an apron every now and then and bake a cake, leaf through Mum's celebrity magazines, make the odd origami napkin when they have friends over for dinner but even so, he was never going to take this particular development well. I wondered if Mum told Dad to upset him deliberately.

'I thought I'd treat him to a leotard so he fits in with the girls.'

'But they wear pink.'

'Yes,' said Mum.

That was gratuitous; I heard the teacher say Zach can wear tracksuit bottoms for now.

If this wasn't the right moment for the ballet update, then it definitely wasn't the right moment for Dad to share his news. But perhaps he felt provoked. Earlier in the week, he completed his training on the aircraft he will fly in Hampshire for his new job. That should have been a cause for celebration (I later saw Dad unpack some champagne from his luggage) but on the back of this news came the news that he will be going to Afghanistan for three and a half months at the end of the summer.

'I'm due to leave on 7 September.'

'That's the day Millie starts school.'

'Yes.'

We still have no idea where we will be living by then. There was a distinct lack of housing news.

'I should come home from Afghanistan on 22 December.'

'So too close to Christmas to guarantee you'll be back in time?'

'Yes.'

I heard Mum come up to bed early. Much later on, I heard Dad go into the spare room.

Monday 20 June

Dad went back to Hampshire last night. I'm pleased. It's much calmer here now. Or it was, anyway, until Mum announced that she is going to tackle potty training with Zach this week. Zach knew this was coming. He has had a well-laid plan prepared for weeks. He already knows how to use the loo but he learnt, when I was potty training, that it is a potential goldmine.

When Mum potty trained me, she started off by rewarding me with raisins when I weed in the potty. After two weeks of puddles and full changes of clothes, she was offering me Barbie's beach house and the Sylvanian Family Country House Hotel. Hopefully, Zach will achieve his aim and get the night vision goggles and metal detector he wants.

Today Zach implemented stage one of the plan and weed everywhere other than the potty. By the time Cathy came over to watch us so that Mum could go to her therapy appointment, Zach had already been through five sets of 'big boy' pants.

Cathy definitely shouldn't have taken us to the corner shop to get more kitchen roll. She had to pay the angry shop lady a lot of money to restock the comic stand and she ended up using the entire kitchen roll she had just bought trying to sort out the mess. By the time Mum returned, Cathy's usual aura of tranquillity had evaporated. She had ditched Mum's raisin-based reward scheme for Celebrations and, as soon as she heard Mum's key in the door, she hurried off home with barely a good-bye.

The plan is working.

Wednesday 22 June

Mum is now offering Hot Wheels cars for every poo Zach does in the potty. He's constipated at the moment so he's getting me to do them for him when Mum isn't looking. In return, he gives me the chocolate buttons he gets for his wees.

Thursday 23 June

The housing people have written to Dad to say that they are not obliged to make a third offer of a quarter, regardless of any welfare issues, as he should have put forward his case earlier in the process. This means Dad's only option now is to involve his boss, whom Dad thinks may refer the whole thing onto the Station Commander. So basically, if they do ever get the quarter they want, half the station will know Mum's problems before we even arrive.

Sometimes, I think it's helpful that Dad doesn't live with us. Judging by Mum and Dad's phone call tonight, it wouldn't be a very happy house if he was here right now. Zach says this is an erroneous point since, if we were all living together, we wouldn't be in this mess in the first place and Mum and Dad would be happy.

Friday 24 June

Dad came home tonight carrying part of his car's gear stick. He says it came off in his hand near Andover. Strangely, he didn't seem upset. In fact, he was unusually cheery, not at all how he tends to be after his Friday commute.

Within minutes of his return, he was parading around the house with a poster that he's been working on in the evenings this week. It shows a toddler standing by a football under the heading 'Toddler Dribble- Football Lessons for the Under 5s.'

Mum looked askance when she saw it. 'When are you planning on doing this?' she asked.

'Saturday mornings,' said Dad, pointing to the part of the poster that said '10am-11am Saturdays'.

'Who will you get to coach them?'

Dad has apparently appointed himself to this role. Mum is to make the half-time milk and snacks.

'Can you really not cope with your son doing ballet?' Mum asked, a little spitefully I thought.

'Nothing to do with that,' replied Dad, hunting through his man box for a whistle and a notepad. 'It's something I've always wanted to do.'

'Right.'

She might as well have said, 'As if.'

Just before story time, Dad fished two presents out of his holdall. Zach and I tore them open. They were the first treats this week which didn't require us to produce a wee or poo. Mine was a nurse's outfit and Zach's was a mini-RAF pilot's flying suit.

'No gender stereotyping in this house, then,' whispered Zach.

Mum laughed a nasty laugh when she saw them.

Saturday 25 June

Football coaching starts next Saturday so we spent this afternoon doing a leaflet drop to advertise the sessions. Dad looked perplexed when Zach insisted on doing a demi-plie in front of every house before posting each of his leaflets. Zach's worked out that this is another potential source of presents. If he makes Dad think he's about to join the Royal Ballet, he'll be in line for more gifts, albeit macho/military related ones.

Sunday 26 June

Whilst Dad was repacking to go back to Hampshire, I overheard Mum saying that he needs to chase up his appointment with the snake tamer. Moomin and Grandad took me and Zach to the circus earlier in the year and we loved it (Zach wants to be a sword thrower if he can juggle this with his plan to help Carol Vorderman on Countdown). I was hoping Mum meant we could all go to the circus, maybe get ringside seats again, but it turns out that we are excluded from the trip to see the snake tamer. In hushed tones, Dad told Mum that his appointment is next Friday in Glastonbury.

'You'll need to get someone to have the kids,' he said.

'I can look after the kids whilst you're getting it done,' she replied.

'No, you'll need to drive me home afterwards- I'll be whoosy and SORE,' he said with meaning, although I had no idea what his meaning was.

Thursday 30 June

Dad has tomorrow off so that he can see the snake person. Without the Friday night traffic to battle through, he got home early enough to come with us to ballet. Whilst we were practising with Mrs Clutterbuck, Mum and Dad waited for us in the hallway with some of the other mums. Dad gave a cursory look at us through the glass pane and, I suspect, only then at Mum's insistence.

When Zach came pirouetting out of the class, wafting violet silk scarves around his head to represent the dance of the dragonfly, Dad rugby tackled him to the ground and tried to give him a high five, only Zach couldn't get up to join in as Dad was sitting on his skirt (Mum let him borrow a fairy costume from the fancy dress box).

Mum and Dad slept in separate rooms again tonight.

Friday 1 July

From the moment he came into our room to get us dressed this morning, Dad looked distracted. Mum looked serene and happy.

During breakfast, I overheard her say to Dad, 'It's for the best. I can't cope if you go away again and I have three children to look after by myself.'

'I know,' said Dad, 'you have said that before.'

'We just can't afford any surprises. It'll tip me over the edge.'

'I know, so you've said.'

When Mum was packing up our little rucksacks to get us ready for a day at Cathy's (we were being sent there whilst Mum and Dad went off on their jolly), Cathy rang.

'All night? Poor you... How awful... Yes, I totally understand... Not to worry... Just get better,' Mum said.

Cathy ate a dodgy curry last night so plan B quickly kicked in: we would all go with Dad. You might have thought Dad would be pleased by the prospect of a bonus day out with us (Zach and I were elated at the idea of meeting the snake tamer) but as he crammed us, our rucksacks and Dannatt into the back of the car, he just looked anguished.

Tensions appeared to be running high as we drove around Glastonbury in circles, looking for a place to park. All the car parks seemed to be either full or pay-and-display. As Mum had spent all the pay-and-display money from the driver's cubby hole (she didn't admit she'd used it to buy a Costa the other day), they had to resort to street parking, of which there was even less. They started to get crabby with one another as time ticked away and Dad's appointment crept closer. It didn't help when Dad came across the Costa receipt whilst searching the cubby hole again, in vain, for change.

Eventually, Mum spied a car further up the road that appeared to be about to move off. She leapt out and ran ahead. The car in front of ours went to drive into it but Mum blocked its way, shaking her head.

'Disabled,' she mouthed at the driver. 'Disabled,' she said again, gesticulating at our car.

When Dad had parked in the spot himself, he looked ready to explode. He just kept shaking his head and throwing Mum dark looks until finally he erupted.

'I thought we aspired to telling the TRUTH,' he said incredulously. 'Disabled?'

'Well, it will be when you come out.'

I couldn't tell if this was a very bad joke or just plain cruel but she might as well have poked an angry Rottweiler with a massive stick and stuck her tongue out at it.

'Don't you even think of coming with me,' Dad spat out, strapping me into the buggy.

'Of course we're coming with you, you can't go through this alone,' said Mum, wheeling out the compassion too late.

'I'm doing this by myself. You can amuse yourself in whatever way you like but you're not coming with me.'

He strapped Zach into the back of the buggy and walked off.

Dad has very long legs. He was half-way down the road by the time Mum was ready to push off with us but she wouldn't be thwarted. She broke into a sprint, achieving impressive, if somewhat dangerous, speeds for someone in charge of a buggy.

'Leave me alone,' said Dad, not even looking round at us.

'I'm really sorry. I shouldn't have said that. Let us come with you.'

'I'm stressed enough as it is,' he said, working up to a jog as he hurried away again.

Dad couldn't find wherever it was he needed to be. He kept stopping to use the map app on his phone, which gave Mum time to catch up with him. Then he would run off again, with us chasing after him. Quickly a pattern was established: walk-jog-sprint-bit of yelling from Mum- lots of hissing from Dad-walk-jog-sprint-bit of yelling from Mum- lots of hissing from Dad. We probably looked like some sort of badly rehearsed circus act ourselves but this is Glastonbury- we didn't stick out too much.

As we all waited for Dad's map app to reload again, we were spotted by a man sitting outside a cafe dressed as goblin, with a long pointy hat drooped over his shoulder. The goblin man must have realised there was marital strife in his midst. He came running over to us, entreating Dad to forgive Mum.

'You just need to let it go, man. Life's too short. Just forgive and live. I have a crystal I could sell you. It'll centre you, balance your energy.'

He held out a lump of pink quartz. Zach was in the front of the buggy. He turned to me, looking amused.

'I'm sure you mean well but we're Christian,' said Mum, eyeing the crystal warily, 'and my husband's under a lot of pressure right now. He's due to be snipped.'

You'd have thought Mum was brandishing a pair of scissors herself from the goblin's reaction. Clearly his faith in the crystal was limited as he started to back away.

'Don't do it, mate,' he muttered to Dad as he retreated back to the hessian sack he'd left by his cappuccino. 'I don't think there's a crystal that's gonna help with that,' he said, before disappearing up a nearby alley.

'Right, now you've told all of Glastonbury about it, I'm not going to get it done,' said Dad.

We walked miserably back to the car, only we couldn't find it. No one had noted the name of the road where we had parked it and we had walked miles and miles since leaving it. I saw hope flicker in Dad's eyes. I don't know if he was more excited by the prospect of losing the car, mentally spending the insurance money on an X5, or the fact he had escaped the snake tamer.

But then Mum saw a sign bearing the name of the road we had originally been looking for, the road where the snake tamer lives. Unable to drive home, they reverted to the original plan, maybe because it seemed easier than trying to tackle the lost car problem.

'At least I'll be sedated for a bit this way,' said Dad.

'Not fully,' said Mum.

We walked along the road until we came to a building that looked like a house, not the Big Top I had been expecting.

'Here we go,' said Mum brightly.

The receptionist barred entry to everyone except Dad. 'You can't come in. No children, I'm afraid. Come back in twenty minutes,' she instructed us.

Mum gave Dad a quick squeeze as he stepped inside.

Whilst we were waiting, Mum found the car and texted Dad to tell him where we were. Shortly afterwards, he came hobbling up the road, slightly bent over.

On the way home, Zach and I pondered what the snake tamer had done to Dad. We think he must have been teaching him a new walk, something resembling Quasimodo or a footballer trying to earn a penalty kick. Either that or the snake bit him somewhere unfortunate.

Saturday 2 July

It seems ill-advised to see the snake tamer the day before you start your second career as a football coach. At 9.45am, when we made our way over to the park near our house, the venue for our first football lesson, Dad was still struggling to walk.

'You're going to have coach them,' he said to Mum, passing her his whistle.

'Me?'

'I've got it all written down,' he said, handing her a laminated sheet.

'It was only a snip,' she said, 'hardly forceps or a head. I was doing the weekly shop the day after Zach.'

By the time we had set out the cones and unpacked the balls (Mum had borrowed some kit from the Navy Sports' Hall), we had three customers. There was Benjy, the boy who hit me with the hammer. He was still in killer mode and quickly discovered he could use the cones as missiles. There was Liesel, a timid little girl from our ballet lessons, who showed no interest in football (she screamed every time the ball came near her) and finally, Rhett, a nine year old whose parents seemed to want some free childcare (the boy sat on the park bench and played football on his DS).

Mum made a valiant attempt at teaching something she knows nothing about. She even tackled the ballet girl's father, who was the only other parent to stay and take part; we soon realised they were here for his benefit. He fouled anyone who got in his way of the ball, even his own daughter.

Dad limped over to us at half time with squash and donuts. The first half of the match had been warm up and practise. The second half was the match. The David Beckham-wannabe dad captained a team comprising me and his daughter. I was put in goal. Mum captained the other team and acted as referee, which gave her an unfair advantage, as David Beckham kept pointing out. On her side there was Benjy, Rhett and Zach. Benjy didn't really count. He just stood by the park bin, retrieving bottles and smashing them on the floor until Dad called Marina to come and collect him. Zach and Liesel disappeared under the climbing frame to work on their arabesque. Rhett wouldn't go in goal so Dad was forced to. At least he could remain pretty much stationary there.

The match, therefore, was basically between Mum and Beckham. After just five minutes of play, it ended abruptly with Mum scoring an own goal, the ball ricocheting off Dad's nether regions into the net.

Beckham had to carry Dad home.

Monday 4 July

I had my final therapy session with Hayley today. There's no sign that Mum is ready to conclude her therapy anytime soon, although I suppose she will have to if we ever move.

Everyone seems so happy that I am better that I daren't tell them that I feel sad again. I don't know why I feel sad but I would really like to pick my forehead.

But I didn't tell Hayley this. I just drew her a picture of my family as I would like it to be, which made her even happier. I drew me, Zach and Dannatt. To either side of us stood Dad and Hayley, holding our hands.

Hayley left it for Mum to look at when she came home. Mum beamed when she saw it.

'That's so sweet, you've drawn me very well.'

I didn't have the heart to tell her it was Hayley.

Tuesday 5 July

Over coffee in Cathy's garden, Mum told Cathy that she and Dad are not getting on very well at the moment.

'You need a date night,' winked Cathy. 'I'd babysit for you but we're away this weekend.'

She was quiet for a minute.

'I know, you could do date night at home. Send an email inviting him to have dinner with you. Get some champagne and tell him to dress up. I'll help you write it if you want.'

Coffee turned into cocktails as Mum and Cathy composed the email. Dad is invited to:

A Night of Fine Dining, Wine & Romance

8pm Saturday

Dress Code: One Piece of Clothing Only!

'Is it all working again?' asked Cathy.

'I think so,' said Mum. 'Only one way to find out.'

You'd think they were comedians; they find each other so funny.

Wednesday 6 July

My first tooth fell out tonight! I was brushing my teeth in the upstairs bathroom before bedtime when I brushed it right out of my mouth and down the plug hole in the sink. Mum spent the next half an hour on You Tube, trying to figure out how you remove the u-bend. It was a gross business. Grey gunk slid all over the bathroom floor when she finally managed to wrestle the pipework off. In amongst the gunk was my tooth. I put it under my pillow and tried to go to sleep extra fast so that morning would come quicker and I could see what the tooth fairy had brought me.

Thursday 7 July

Mum says the tooth fairy had lots of children to visit last night, which is why she didn't visit me.

'WHO WAS SHE VISITING?'I shouted.

'Mmm, I don't know their names but I'm SURE she'll come tonight.'

Humph.

Friday 8 July

Stupid tooth fairy.

Saturday 9 July

I got woken up by Dad in the middle of the night. He came in and said he missed me so much, he needed an extra cuddle.

I found a euro under my pillow this morning. Maybe that's why the tooth fairy took three nights to come. She must live abroad. Dad swapped it for a ten pound note when I showed him.

'That's a great precedent to set,' snapped Mum.

'I couldn't find any change,' he said, 'now or in the middle of the night. Maybe if the tooth fairy had planned ahead a bit better...'

I can't even be bothered to recount football coaching today but it was a NIGHTMARE. I'm sure the trip to A&E with Benjy was not part of the scheduled programme.

Sunday 10 July

We are having a weekend of broken sleep. Last night Zach and I were both awoken by the fire alarm and the smell of burning. Mum came running into our room, wearing only a pinny, her bottom cheeks jiggling about, to reassure us that it wasn't a real fire, they had just got distracted whilst making dinner. Dad came up a few minutes later, waving a lever arch file of flying notes under the smoke sensor (the only time I've ever seen him use them). He was wearing a bow tie and nothing else. And it wasn't around his neck.

Cathy's date night idea, as weird as it turned out, seemed to work a treat. This morning and all day long Mum and Dad kept holding hands and hugging, right up until the point when Dad started packing to go back to Hampshire.

'You're packing more than usual,' said Mum.

Dad looked sheepish. 'I know. I'm off to the US tomorrow.'

'Pardon?'

'The course they want me to do- you remember I told you about it. Well, someone's pulled out so there's a space for me to go tomorrow. It's only for two or three weeks.'

'What? Why are you telling me this now?'

'I only found out on Friday.'

'So, you've had the weekend to tell me.'

'Well things got in the way.'

'What things?'

'Football coaching, A&E, date night, willycopters,' he said, lowering his voice.

'We were together for all of those things.'

'I didn't want to spoil the weekend when things were going so well.' (Good point) 'I knew you'd be like this.' (Should have kept that one in his head)

'Like WHAT? Upset? Upset that my husband, who currently doesn't live with us, is going off again whilst I'm up to my eyeballs on medication and therapy, whilst trying to bring up two kids by myself, whilst trying not to get us evicted and settle our daughter in a school twenty counties away (Mum's not good at Geography), a school she's probably not going to be able to go to because we haven't got a HOUSE! And at some point in this whole nightmare, you're going to disappear off to Afghanistan. Well you can willycopter off. I mean it. I can't cope with all the arguing and being left and arguing and being left. I don't want to argue again. Just go and don't come back. I mean it. DON'T COME BACK.'

Dad zipped up his bag and left.

Monday 11 July

Mum didn't seem to know what to do after breakfast this morning. She was uncharacteristically aimless, picking things up and putting them down, walking into a room, then walking out again.

In a way, it was nice. Usually, she is too busy to play with us. I asked her to come for a pretend tea party in my bedroom. It was fun to start with. I offered her a plastic cake with pieces that Velcro together.

'Delicious!' she said. 'Did you make it, Millie'

'Yes,' I smiled.

'I think the tea needs a stir,' she said, picking up a plastic teaspoon.

She lifted the lid off the teapot. Then I remembered that it was full of my scabs. I tried to put the lid back on but she held my hand away and looked more closely inside the pot. Then she started to cry.

'We'll bury these in the garden,' she said, hugging me. 'And we'll say a prayer that God takes all these sadnesses away forever.'

That would be great if she hadn't just created a whole new tea set full of sadnesses.

Dad didn't ring us and Mum didn't ring him either. Instead, she rang Hayley to tell her about the teapot.

And then she rang Jane, an old law school friend, who knows about divorce. Or I'm assuming she does. Mum's first question was 'How do I get a divorce?'

Jane said she is going to email Mum some advice and then speak to her again in a week or so.

I didn't know what a divorce is so Zach looked it up in one of Mum's old law books.

'It's the termination of a marriage,' he read out. 'Usually involving a tonne of misery,' he added as he put the book back. 'That bit's not in the book, just my guess.'

Thursday 14 July

At 10am this morning (that's what time my GroClock said it was), Zach and I were still playing in our bedroom. Mum hadn't got up. The phone had rung several times but she hadn't answered it. It just rang and rang and rang.

At 10.41am, someone knocked on the front door, then pressed the bell. Mum still didn't get up. We heard the door being unlocked and pushed open.

'Coo-ee, just me,' Cathy called up.

We ran out of our bedroom to greet her. Mum's door remained shut.

'Hello,' Cathy said, hugging us on the stairs. 'Where's Mum, I wonder?'

When Cathy saw that her bedroom door was closed, she told us to go and tidy our room. I pretended to do what she said but secretly peeked out to watch. Cathy quietly opened the door and tiptoed in. We followed on tiptoe.

'Coo-eee, are you ok?'

Mum's head emerged from the covers, her hair a birds' nest. 'Cathy?'

'I've been worrying about you. Are you alright? You've not been answering my texts, you missed coffee this morning and you weren't answering the phone earlier,' she said, opening the curtains.

'I'm sorry. I've not been sleeping and then stupidly, at 4am, I took two Nytol out of desperation.'

'Silly Mum,' said Cathy, smiling at us. 'Go and get dressed you two.'

I pretended to go to our room again but I stayed and listened outside the door.

'Now what's going on?' said Cathy, sitting on the bed.

'We had a major bust up at the weekend and I told him to leave and not come back. We've not spoken since and I'm seeing a divorce lawyer friend when she can fit me in.'

It's not easy to shock Cathy but she looked shocked now.

'Divorce?'

'Yes, it's been building up for months. You know it has. I can't keep doing this.'

'You've kicked him out?'

'Yes, I suppose so, sort of, but he's in America now so he wouldn't be home for a few weeks anyway. That was the final straw.'

'Why, has he gone on holiday?'

'No, it's work.'

'So, he didn't have a choice?'

'No, but I can't cope with all the uncertainty and the coming and the going.'

'Yes, but you married someone in the forces. Sorry. I don't want to sound harsh but you did.'

'The point is I'm not strong enough to deal with all of this.'

'No, the point is you have two small children, a lovely husband and you can't break up your family like this.'

'I don't want to hear this right now.'

'I know you don't but this is dangerous territory you're moving into. You can't do this. You made promises. You said 'for better, for worse.' This is the 'worse' bit. You promised to stay with him.'

'I can't.'

'I'm your best friend and I'm telling you, out of love, that you can and you must.'

'I don't want to.'

'That's different. I don't always want to be married either. I bet no one does all the time. But this is bigger than what you want. What about those beautiful children? Come on. Get dressed and come downstairs. I'll make us a brew.'

Cathy handed Mum her dressing gown from the back of the door. Mum stayed in bed.

'Before I put the kettle on, I'm going to make you a promise of my own,' said Cathy. 'I will be over here every day until you have put this right.'

Friday 15 July

'As promised,' said Cathy when Mum opened the door to her this morning. 'I'm a woman on a mission. Now have you spoken to him?'

'No.'

'You need to sort this out. I'll be back again tomorrow.'

Saturday 16 July

We met Cathy coming up our path as we were heading out to football.

'Not now Cathy, I have a football class to run,' said Mum.

'I know- I'm bringing the snack, remember?' said Cathy, holding up a string bag with a thermos sticking out of the top. 'Sugar-free hot chocolate and caraway bars.'

Yuck.

When we arrived for the lesson, we were, literally, swamped by toddlers and mud. After a week of rain, with kids trapped inside driving their parents mad, Mum was handed a whole division of little people to occupy in the quagmire that was currently the park. Cathy had planned to go shopping but she stayed, acting as jailer when various errant toddlers tried to sneak off through the park gate, providing crowd control when they collectively decided to run at Mum and later fight over the caraway bars (that stopped once they tried them), as well as standing in as referee and first aider.

We were all coated in a thick film of dirt by the time we walked home. Cathy even had it in her hair.

'So have you rung him?'

'No.'

'Are you going to?'

'No.'

'Then I'll be back round tomorrow.'

Sunday 17 July

Jane came for lunch today. We had no idea Mum had arranged for her to visit; she just appeared on our doorstep whilst Mum was warming up some soup.

Jane is lovely. Pretty and tidy, with polished shoes and a twin set. She doesn't look like someone who helps to break up families. I didn't know what to make of her.

Cathy did. When she came to the door for her daily check-up, she instantly seemed to know who Jane was.

'So you didn't make it to church then?' asked Cathy, after she'd been introduced to Jane.

'I wasn't feeling well,' said Mum.

'But you're well enough to get a D-I-V-O-R-C-E?'

Jane looked at her patent ballet shoes. Mum went red.

'Jane's a friend.'

'Whatever. Shame she left her Family Law book on the dashboard of her Merc.'

'Cathy, don't be rude.'

'This is not good- this is not YOU,' she said to Mum, before walking out.

I wanted to go with Cathy.

'Do you think we could run away?' I asked Zach when Mum and Jane were having a quiet chat in the next room.

'I don't think that's a good plan,' he replied. 'Who would look after Mum if we went too?'

He looked utterly miserable. His definition of divorces seems fairly accurate so far.

Monday 18 July

'You missed a great talk at church yesterday,' said Cathy as she walked past Mum into the kitchen this morning. 'Pastor Tim was on fire.'

'Please, Cathy. Don't.'

'It was about Jesus telling his disciples to take a boat across Lake Galilee whilst he stayed behind on land to pray. The disciples did what he said but whilst they were in the boat, a storm blew up. You know it already. Their boat was knocked around by the wind and waves and they were terrified. They thought Jesus had abandoned them but he hadn't. He came out to find them in the storm and told them to have courage and then he helped them. That's what you need to do.'

'What does that even mean?'

'It means you're also in a storm right now and you're frightened but instead of taking courage and leaning on your faith, you're trying to sort this mess out by yourself. And all you're doing is making an even bigger mess. Divorce is messy.'

'No, my current life is a mess. Once I'm by myself, just me and the kids, away from the RAF, things will be easier.'

'Your therapist's explained your OCD to you, right? That you do things to soothe yourself when life feels out of control. You order things and you tidy. That's what you're doing now. You have no say in a lot of the big stuff: the military tells you where you have to live, which house you have to have, when you can move, when you can see your husband. So you're trying to exert control in order to soothe yourself. Why do you think so many people in the military love order?'

Mum didn't answer.

'Because they're trying to do the same thing. Mowing their lawns to within an inch of their life every Saturday, polishing their cars every week til they can see their face in the paint. It's all about control. You're in a storm and you can't control it.'

'Well, I'm fed up of being in a storm. We always seem to be in one.'

'I know, lovely. Having a faith doesn't make the storm go away but it does mean God's got your back. You're going to be alright.'

'How has he got my back?'

'Well, you've got me to start with. You've been fairly unlovable lately but I still love you anyway. Plus I've had an idea. I went to see the Navy Family Liaison Officer about you today. I didn't mention your name, I said I have 'a friend' with marriage problems so now they all think I have marriage problems.'

Mum smiled a watery smile.

'They told me, as military personnel and dependants, we're entitled to at least six free sessions with a marriage guidance counsellor. You just have to call this number to arrange it,' Cathy said, handing Mum a leaflet. 'I'm going to leave it on your fridge so you can have a think about it.'

I wish we were like other people- other people have the weekly shopping list on their fridge or magnetic letters.

Tuesday 19 July

Mum was packing up the car for today's trip up to my new school for the next settling in session when Cathy called round. She followed Mum into the kitchen when Mum went back in to get our picnic lunch. The leaflet was still on the fridge.

'Have you called them?'

'No,' said Mum.

Cathy saw a pile of papers on the kitchen table from Mum's solicitor. She shook her head as she walked back out.

Today's trip to Hampshire was easier than the last. We didn't get lost and we weren't late. As we drove past the RAF camp where Dad works, Mum looked straight ahead but I stared as hard as I could, hoping to see Dad. I thought I caught sight of his skip but I know I can't have done as he's still in America. We haven't seen him now for nine days.

This settling-in session was the penultimate one before the school breaks up for the summer holidays. With life being so chaotic, we've missed the last four sessions. I think it took a lot of courage for Mum to face this crowd of mums again after last time.

Everyone was surprisingly welcoming when we arrived. Our new form teacher had arranged a mini-sports' day for us and the weather was sunny so we had our races outside on the sports' field. Whilst I took part in the three-legged race with a polite little girl called Marina, who kept stopping to help me pull my socks up every time they fell down (we came in last), I saw Mum chatting to the lady she'd yelled 'Practising Christians' at. They seemed to be getting on well, with Mum laughing away and the other lady putting Mum's number into her mobile phone.

I fell asleep in the car on the way home. I dreamt we were living with Dad again. I felt sad when Mum carried me inside the house to bed and I saw another envelope on the doormat from Mum's solicitors.

Saturday 23 July

Today was Families' Day here in Somerset. It's a similar event to the one on Uncle Pete's ship, only this one was at the airfield where Dad used to work before he moved to Hampshire. The Navy pilots put on a helicopter display for family and friends to watch, with other aircraft flying in from stations across the UK, joined by overseas flying teams, over here for the air show season. Beneath the aerobatics, fairground attractions and food stalls jostle for space: an enormous Ferris wheel, dodgems, spinning teacups, burger vans, candy floss stalls and coconut shies, creating a playground of fun.

We would normally have gone to something like that but Dad didn't get us tickets because he and Mum aren't in touch and I don't suppose Mum would have wanted to go without him. Cathy tried to persuade Mum to join her and Paul.

'Paul could talk us all past the ticket checkpoint and it would be a break for you and epic for the kids.'

But Mum wouldn't relent.

Zach and I spent the morning on the sofa looking out of our front room window, watching the other Mummies and Daddies leaving their houses, holding their children's hands as they made their way over to the airfield. Zach ran off after a while and came back wearing his pilot's uniform. He didn't move off the sofa after that, just sat sucking his thumb, watching the different aircraft fly over our house as they came in to do their displays.

He didn't seem excited when the Red Arrows tore up the sky in a blaze of red and blue smoke but I saw a tear dribble down his cheek when Dad's old helicopter did a fly past to mark the end of the day. As it disappeared off into the distance, he stood up on the sofa and made a salute like Dad taught him to do when he first got his mini uniform. Then he wet himself.

As the families started to make their way back to their homes much later on, I saw Mum reading Cathy's leaflet.

Sunday 24 July

'Darling, I've not heard from you in an age. How are you? How are you feeling mentally?'

Bunny doesn't do much of a lead-in when she rings.

'I'm good,' said Mum. That's not what she said when she rang Cathy to tell her we couldn't go to church. She told Cathy she felt poorly.

'Are the pills working, darling? Are you still taking them?'

'Yes.'

'How's Will doing? I haven't heard from him much either.'

'Busy, you know.'

'How's the housing nightmare?'

'Still no news.'

'Are you alright, darling? You sound like a fu-' Mum muted the phone, '-ing lawyer, all tight-lipped, not your usual self.'

'Sorry, Bunny, I'm just a bit tired.'

Zach says Mum is going to need to get good at being tight-lipped with the in-laws if she's going ahead with this divorce.

Monday 25 July

The leaflet was back on the fridge today. Mum's bundle of legal papers lay on the kitchen table in a pre-paid envelope, ready to send back to Jane.

At lunchtime, the Tesco delivery arrived. As the driver brought the crates of food into the kitchen, he saw the leaflet.

'Probably not my place to say but they saved us,' he said to Mum.

I thought that might encourage her to call the number on the leaflet but this afternoon's dog walk was to the post box to post the legal bundle.

Tuesday 26 July

Today is Dad's birthday. We haven't seen him now in over two weeks. I wanted to ring him to sing 'Happy Birthday' but I didn't ask Mum if we could. I'm not sure that's what you do when you are getting a D-I-V-O-R-C-E.

Wednesday 27 July

Today Mum went through Dad's things. She removed all of his clothes from their wardrobe and his chest of drawers and packed them into his military luggage bags. Then she went through his bedside table. She barely looked at the things she found, stuffing it all into the side pockets of the bags, but she did stop when she pulled a pile of papers from the bottom drawer. I sat on the landing, watching through the open door as she perched on the edge of the bed and leafed through them.

There was the first Father's Day card I ever made, a Valentines' from Mum and an envelope addressed to 'Annie'. Mum turned it over a few times. It was dog-eared and a bit stained. She tore it open and yanked out the letter.

She stayed there for a long time reading it. Tears trickled silently down her cheeks.

October 2007

Dearest Annie,

This is the hardest thing I think I've ever had to do. My boss sent me home early today so I could write a letter to you to leave behind when I go to Iraq next week. That way there'll be a good-bye for you should the worst happen. This is my sixth attempt at this. Everything I write sounds trite so I will keep it brief.

You are my soul mate, the missing part that completes me. I love and adore you and I always will. Even death can't change that.

The worst part of having to imagine this is the feeling that I will be failing you if I die- leaving you to bring up Millie alone. I've made financial arrangements to take care of you both if anything happens to me but that's not really what I mean. Just know that I would never ever choose to be apart from you.

If I don't come back, you must try and find someone else to be happy with. Your happiness is the most important thing to me. As I said, this is the most horrible thing I have ever had to imagine and I just hope you never have to read this.

I will do my very best to come home so I can do the most important jobs I've been given: being your husband and Millie's Dad.

All my love forever

Will x

Mum sobbed quietly, twisting her wedding ring around on her finger. I didn't know what to do so I hurried downstairs to the kitchen and got Cathy's leaflet. I took it back upstairs and put it in Mum's hand. She gave me a hug, pressing me into her until my neck hurt, and then she asked me to get the phone. I ran around to her side of the bed and brought it back to her. She dialled a number and then I heard Dad's voice.

'I'm sorry,' she said.

Thursday 28 July

Dad drove down to see us at lunchtime. He said he had a quiet day and no one would miss him if he sneaked back for a reunion sandwich with us. After almost three weeks apart, there was lots to catch up on. It turns out Dad never went to America. The original person went as planned so he has been in Hampshire all this time. I think it must have been his car I saw when we went up for the school sports' day. He said he hid in the bushes by the school both Tuesdays after Mum asked him to leave in the hope of seeing us. He saw me win the egg and spoon race.

Mum asked Dad about his birthday. She was visibly upset when he admitted he went to the drive-thru McDonalds after work that day and took a Big Mac back to his room. He'd been too embarrassed to tell anyone he was by himself.

Mum sneaked off and covered a half-eaten Malt Loaf with candles so that we could sing a belated 'Happy Birthday' to him.

Later in the afternoon, when we were getting ready to go to ballet, Dad called Zach downstairs to give him a present.

'Thought you might like this for your dance practice,' Dad said, holding out a plastic bag he'd sellotaped down. 'Sorry, no. wrapping paper in my little bedsit.'

Zach carefully unwrapped it.

'It's called a unitard. All the professional male dancers wear them.'

'Thank you, Dad,' said Zach. He ran off and came back wearing his mini pilot's uniform.

'I like this one best.'

Zach refused to change out of it so the unitard remained on the kitchen table, still in its packet; Dad didn't seem to mind.

When we got back from our lesson, Dad took Cathy's leaflet and the phone and disappeared into the study.

'I've booked us in for next Friday,' he said when he came back.

Friday 29 July

Dad had to go back to Hampshire first this morning for work. As he kissed us all good-bye on the doorstep several times (he had to prise Zach, who was still wearing the pilot's uniform, from his leg), he promised Mum he would chase up the welfare case with the housing allocation people.

It didn't seem long before he was back again for the weekend. I have missed him coming in shouting about the car these past few Fridays but he didn't do that tonight. Instead, Mum hurried outside as soon as she heard the rust bucket pulling up and they stood hugging in the driveway.

Dad's big news when they eventually came in: S.H.A.M lost our welfare case papers six weeks ago. Nothing has happened during that time. They located our papers whilst they were on the phone with Dad today; they had archived them.

In summary, things have not moved on since mid-June. My school term starts in less than five weeks. Currently, a round trip to my school takes four hours. Mum won't be able to do that twice a day.

When Dad took me up for my bath, I saw Mum looking on Rightmove for houses to rent in Hampshire.

Saturday 30 July

Dad told us over breakfast that Bunny's birthday present to him this year was family membership to National Heritage.

'Why don't we use it this afternoon? Go on a family trip out?' Mum suggested.

Dad seemed pleased with the idea. With his mouth still full of croissant, he found his guidebook, looked up an historic house nearby and started making a picnic.

It turns out Mum and Dad used to be National Heritage members before we were born but gave up their membership when leaving the house with us in tow became a day out in itself. On the journey, Mum warned Dad not to fall out with any volunteers working at the house.

'I know you think it hasn't been a proper trip unless you upset a decent cohort but it's not nice behaviour,' she said.

Even before we got out of the car, Dad ignored Mum's plea for civility by parking too close to some ancient apple trees when he could see he was being directed away from them. A man wearing a deer stalker came straight towards us and did some miming that I think meant 'Open your window.' Dad took his time and then opened his car door into the man's Gandalf-style staff.

'These trees have been here for centuries, probably before King Henry VIII hunted around these woods with his court, so we don't want them destroyed by a tourist who can't be bothered to respect National Heritage parking laws.'

'Laws!' laughed Dad.

'Will, just move it,' said Mum.

'Kindly park over there,' said the man.

'Are you sure that bush won't mind?' asked Dad.

When we had parked again and got out, we found the same man peering into the boot at Dannatt.

'Have you got dog waste bags?' he asked Dad. 'I can't allow you to take the dog out of the boot unless you do. No stick and flick methods here.'

Dad glared, waving a handful of bags at him.

I'm puzzled by Dad's attitude towards National Heritage. His whole working life is governed by rules and protocol but perhaps that's the problem. Maybe he just wants a break from that sort of thing at the weekend.

We had a token look around the house, leaving Dannatt tied up outside, but we weren't really dressed correctly to be walking amidst antique furniture and vintage soft furnishings. 'Toddler Dribble' had delayed our departure so much so that Dad just shoved us all in the car covered in mud, still wearing shin pads and football boots.

'I don't know if you've heard the terrible news yet,' said the National Heritage tour guide, taking in our footwear. He handed plastic bags and elastic bands to Dad, indicating that we needed to wear them over our shoes. Dad made loud huffing noises as he knelt down to make improvised footwear for us.

'No,' said Mum, looking concerned, but I think she was more anxious about Dad than anything the guide had to say.

'It's hard to talk about. We're all so devastated,' said the guide. He started to well up.

'I'm so sorry,' said Mum. 'Don't upset yourself.'

'Thank you, dear. Earlier in the year, without any notice or warning,' said the man, blinking a lot, 'we lost the roof'.

There was a hard laugh from Dad's end of the hall.

'Did you find it?' asked Dad, pinging an elastic band at Zach.

'How terrible,' said Mum gently, eye-balling Dad. 'I'm so sorry.'

I'm not sure if she was sorry about the roof or Dad.

The man patted Mum's hand but gave Dad a stony stare.

'I'm afraid we can't allow football boots in the house. Or mud,' said the man, twitching his nose as he looked down at me and Zach and the hopeless plastic boots Dad had tried to make. 'You'll have to take their footwear off altogether if you want to look around.'

'Of course,' said Mum.

Dad can't bear any state of undress so, as we moved into the next room, he followed at a distance, not associating himself with the barefoot children.

I really wanted to run into the cordoned off sections of the house and bounce on the Tudor bed and climb in the bath with its little feet but I sensed that it might cause an argument between Mum and Dad if I did. So I held Mum's hand until we were back outside again.

'I'm starving. Let's have the picnic,' said Dad.

We followed him to a stripy lawn by a lake, with ducks waddling around the water's edge and people in deckchairs lazily watching them. Dad found a group of empty deckchairs, plonked himself down in one and started spreading out the food. Mum brought up the rear with Dannatt. There was nothing to tie him to so she looped his lead under the foot of a deckchair and sat down in it.

'There was no need to be so rude to that nice guide,' said Mum. She was wearing a dreadful scowl.

'He was an old fuss pot,' said Dad, taking a huge bite of pork pie.

'Well, it was idiotic of you to have the kids stamping around in there in football studs,' she said.

And they were off. Just like that. Zach looked at Mum's face and then at Dad's and then he put his hands over his ears and started crying. As Mum tried to comfort him, we each got a whiff of something that wasn't coming from the picnic.

'Oh no,' whispered Mum as she checked Zach's pants. 'Did you bring a change of clothes for him?' she asked Dad.

'No, I was on picnic duty, you were sorting the kids.'

Mum looked at him in disgust. He was right so that was the best she had. She spied a family on the other side of the stripy lawn with children a similar age to us and headed over in their direction. I'm not sure how she thought they could help. Zach decided he didn't like sitting in his dirty pants so he stood up and started to peel them off. The poo bomb exploded.

A National Heritage lady, wearing a bum bag rattling with coins, came over to tell us off for not paying for the deckchairs. Zach sat down bare bottomed in one of the chairs just as Dad started handing over money to the bum bag lady. The price leapt from £8 to £58 to cover the cost of a new deckchair.

With everyone distracted, Dannatt decided to launch himself into the lake after a terrified duck.

'That'll be another £50, sir,' said the bum bag lady as the deckchair Dannatt had been tied to disappeared into the water. Zach got up and ran across the lawn towards Mum, screaming.

Sunday 31 July

Cathy didn't hide her delight when she saw all of us coming into church together this morning.

'What happened?' she asked Mum when they were having coffee after the service.

'You were right, I was wrong,' said Mum, not meeting Cathy's gaze.

Cathy didn't say anything.

After a long pause, Mum continued: 'I realised his reasons for leaving us are much better than my reasons for making him leave us.'

'I don't think you ever really wanted him to leave. You were just registering your upset.'

'Maybe. But none of this means things are suddenly okay between us.' Mum described yesterday's trip out.

'That's why you're going for the counselling. I can babysit for you on Friday, by the way. Why don't you plan something fun to do afterwards? A film or a meal? Fully clothed.'

I silently seconded the last suggestion.

Wednesday 3 August

Zach went a whole day yesterday without wetting or spoiling his pants. We headed to Argos this afternoon to buy him a metal detector. According to Zach, our house is near a Roman settlement that now lies several feet beneath the ground. He intends to start an archaeological excavation of our garden as soon as Mum is distracted.

Friday 5 August

Dad got delayed coming home tonight. He was still on the A303 when Cathy arrived to babysit. Mum looked really pretty. She had done her make-up and she was wearing a dress I hadn't seen before.

'I'm going to have to meet him there,' she said, hunting around for her car keys. 'He'd better not miss it. Tonight's the assessment to see if we qualify for the sessions.'

It wasn't long before she was back. Her make-up had spread, giving her giant Panda eyes.

'What happened?' asked Cathy, giving her a hug and letting her smear black marks across her t-shirt.

'The good news is we definitely qualify for the help,' sobbed Mum. 'The bad news is I feel as though I've just done ten rounds in a boxing ring. He drove straight back to Hampshire when we came out.'

'Sometimes things have to get worse before they get better,' said Cathy, still cuddling Mum. 'Tonight was still a move in the right direction. How about I call for a take away while you go and sort out your face?'

Before she left, Cathy offered to do the football coaching for tomorrow's lesson. That woman deserves a medal.

Saturday 6 August

Dad pulled up alongside the park in his auto-be-scrapped-mobile (Zach's new name for it) just before kick-off at 'Toddler Dribble'. Cathy was wearing her old beekeeper suit from her commune days as she tried to call us to order. The gauze mask was creating problems for her whistle. I'm not sure what she thought we were going to do to her. She looked relieved when she saw Dad (I think anyway- it was hard to see her face properly).

Dad waved a white handkerchief as he approached Mum. She allowed him to give her a kiss whilst she handed out the football bibs. I wouldn't say they are back to normal yet but there seems to be a polite cease fire in place.

Tuesday 8 August

A letter arrived in the post this morning from the council, banning 'Toddler Dribble' from meeting in its park with immediate effect. Apparently, it's a good idea to have insurance if you are offering sports lessons to small children, especially near a road. It's also desirable for the coach to hold some sort of qualification and it's mandatory to have permission to hold the classes from those in charge of the premises. I thought Mum was a lawyer.

Wednesday 10 August

I am supposed to start school in Hampshire in four weeks. Zach has offered to home school me if S.H.A.M. doesn't get its act together soon.

Friday 12 August

Andria babysat us tonight so that Mum and Dad could go back to the boxing ring. I'm not sure Dad wants everyone to know about these sessions but Mum seems incapable of discretion so Andria knows everything. So do half the wives on the patch.

'It'll be on the Wives Facebook page before we know it,' Dad muttered as they were leaving.

'There's no shame in it,' Mum bellowed back.

Andria is not very good at keeping us in bed so Zach and I were up when Mum and Dad came in. Dad was very quiet.

'How did it go?' mouthed Andria when Dad's back was turned.

'I thought it was great but he's totally uncomfortable with the whole thing,' said Mum, as though Dad wasn't a foot away from her. 'We learnt that we talk in different love languages so that's one of the reasons we don't communicate well. I said we might communicate better if we lived together.'

I think things feel more loving when they don't communicate. Plus it was Mum who kicked Dad out!

Saturday 13 August

Zach turned three today. Dad missed the day of his birth and he missed his birthday last year so this is only the second time he's been around to celebrate. He made up for it, arriving back from Hampshire late last night with a boot full of presents. We watched from our bedroom window as he brought them into the house under the cover of darkness. I couldn't see anything but Zach mentally ticked off everything he was hoping for. He'd had another day of clean pants and was wearing his night vision goggles.

This morning, after breakfast and presents, Mum and Dad loaded us into the car with a picnic basket, buckets and spades, wind shield and sun cream. We all know Zach's ambition in life is to find a fossil. Our destination was Lyme Regis.

By lunchtime, we were well-established on the sea front with all of our kit, hunting for ammonites and belemnites. As Zach and I tried to smash a large boulder between us to see if there was a fossil hiding inside, I saw Mum throwing something at Dad further up the beach. It was only small and it disappeared instantly.

We didn't find any fossils. Zach was very disappointed but, on the way back, Mum passed him a shark's tooth that I think she slipped off to buy when we were packing up. It was a peaceful journey home, with Mum staying unusually quiet.

Sunday 14 August

We returned to Lyme Regis today. It turns out Mum dropped her wedding ring on the beach yesterday. We took both cars so that Dad could drive straight to Hampshire afterwards. This time we took Zach's metal detector with us. Unbelievably, within half an hour of us arriving, Zach found the ring. Dad dusted off the grit and put it back on Mum's finger, kissing her as he did. Then we all searched again for fossils.

Zach made Dad drag three rocks back to the cars, claiming they contain dinosaur remnants. Dad looked as though he regretted encouraging this new interest as he heaved the stone slabs into the boot of the estate.

Monday 15 August

Dad rang Mum this morning with the news that we have formally been offered a house on the camp where he works, exactly where we want to be! Hurray! Dad allowed Mum a few minutes to enjoy the news.

It turns out this was the silver lining. The big storm cloud is that we can't move into the quarter until mid-September, after I start school and after Dad goes to Afghanistan. Mum will have to oversee the move on her own. And because mid-September takes us six months and one week past the start of Dad's new job, we aren't entitled to a removal service. S.H.A.M's rules state you must move within six months of the start of the new job to qualify for professional packers. We will have to pack and move the contents of our house ourselves, or rather Mum will.

As soon as Dad rang off, Mum called the doctors for an emergency appointment. Then she rang Cathy, who came straight over with a paper bag for Mum to breathe into and a bottle of Rescue Remedy. When Mum had sufficiently calmed down, they prayed together.

Cathy never shuts her eyes or puts her hands together when she prays. She just calls things out like: 'Come on Father- you need to help us here.' It always makes Mum laugh, even today.

Cathy looked after us when Mum went to see the doctor, returning with a higher dose of her anti-anxiety medication.

'Why don't you put these stronger ones in a drawer as a plan B and I will be plan A: you can call me whenever you feel anxious and we'll chat it through. And if that doesn't help, you've got these as back-up.'

Mum reluctantly put the box of tablets in the medicine box.

At bedtime, Dad texted Mum a photograph of our new house. It's not very pretty to look at- the usual rubbish porch, some PVC cladding around the bottom half of the house and a garage door that doesn't shut but the address is 1 Love Lane, which at least sounds pretty. Dad must have taken the photo during a rain shower as there was a rainbow arched over the house.

Beneath the picture, he had written 'The calm after the storm.'

Tuesday 16 August

Despite the assurances of rainbows, Mum is beyond distracted by the housing saga at the moment. It was precisely for this reason that Zach chose today to start his archaeological dig of our back garden. He crept out when it was just getting light, whilst Mum was still sleeping, unlocked the side door into the garage, retrieved a spade and set to work with his metal detector.

It looked like a lot of work so I decided to help him. When the metal detector buzzed with excitement over the centre of the lawn, we attempted to dig down but we abandoned this plan after a while as all we were managing to do was rip up the turf, not bury as deep as we needed to go. After that we focused on the flower beds, digging up various plants and small shrubs. My hope was that we would find something valuable enough to pay for some removal men.

I don't think Mum understood my generous intentions when she opened her curtains.

'MILLIE! ZACH!' she roared. 'Stop that RIGHT NOW.'

By the time she dragged us inside, we'd found the bunch of keys that I lost last summer. I handed them over to her but they are not much good to us now as we had the locks replaced on the front door and on the car so the keys don't work anymore. Mum says the outside areas of the house must be pristine when we give the house back next month so as well as packing up the house she now also needs to re-landscape the back garden.

Wednesday 17 August

It is at times like this that you realise most people are decent and kind. Today Dad sent out a Facebook plea to everyone we know, asking for help moving the contents of our house to Hampshire. Almost instantly, we had twenty-three people with cars offering to drive our things to our new place. As most of Mum and Dad's friends now have two or more children, and since children's car seats require these people to drive MPVs, four by fours or buses, this is actually a lot of space. Uncle Pete has an HGV licence so he is going to hire something bigger. We may just do it.

Thursday 18 August

Mum showed Cathy the picture of our new house when she came over for coffee this morning.

'That's a lovely message,' Cathy said. 'Talking of storms, have you had any of the stronger medication?'

'No. I nearly have a few times but I've held off so far.'

'That's amazing! I was reading yesterday about what it's like to be in the eye of a storm. People say it's perfectly still. The surrounding winds can't reach the centre. I'm praying that whilst you're in this storm, you remain perfectly still and peaceful.'

I'm going to miss Cathy.

Saturday 20 August

Finally, it seems as though love is in the air in our house! Gross! Maybe this is the prelude to living in Love Lane. But it's got to be preferable to the fights, punctuated by long silences, which were fast becoming commonplace around here.

Dad is trying to speak Mum's love language (kind acts), bringing her breakfast in bed this morning and unloading the dishwasher without being asked. Mum is doing the same thing (only Dad likes to be spoken to with gifts. Don't we all?! That will be my language if I ever marry). She ordered his favourite food in the online order that came this morning and she keeps leaving little packages under his pillow and in his coat pockets.

They remained cheerful even when the postman delivered the packing boxes Mum ordered this week. Dad assembled them and Mum loaded them up with our books and china. You would never have guessed from their behaviour that our domestic life has been in shreds recently.

Things normalised around late afternoon when they tried to re-hang the military curtains Mum replaced with her own ones as soon as we arrived here two years ago. Thinking they were old rags (I can see how the confusion arose- they are a crime against soft furnishings), Dad let Marina's husband use them to protect his motorcycle when he was refurbishing it.

The fights punctuated by long silences resumed.

Sunday 21 August

Today was my birthday so everybody had to be nice- a useful house rule in times such as these. As a surprise, Mum had invited all of our closest friends over to celebrate with a BBQ in front of our house.

Cathy and Paul arrived first. Their gift to me was a tie-dye kit wrapped in recycled paper (by that I mean it had been used previously to wrap someone else's Christmas present, judging by the Santa design). Marina looked hassled when she arrived late with her children. Her husband is away again so she was by herself, trying to herd four kids whilst carrying a huge Upsy Daisy doll and large bowl of jelly.

I hate In the Night Garden now; I think it's babyish so I didn't mind when Benjy upended the jelly on her head. Marina didn't stay long.

Andria and her husband came after she went. They speak my language- they put cash in my birthday card. I wonder how many Smarties you can buy with £10.

Within minutes of the party starting, the British summer decided to shut us down. Following a pre-move purge, our garage is almost empty so we relocated the party in there, installing a CD player and 'Now That's What I Call Disney' in the corner so that we could dance around, eating burgers and playing musical bumps until we all felt sick.

I hadn't realised this was also a good-bye party. At the end, as people were making noises about going home, Mum made Dad, me and Zach get up to accompany her in 'So long, farewell' from the Sound of Music. Zach lost all powers of speech at that point. I mumbled a bit of the chorus. I thought it was awful but all the adults seemed to enjoy it and we had a group hug before saying good-night to one another.

If S.H.A.M. has anything to do with it, there will be hundreds more of these farewells before we're really waving good-bye.

Monday 22 August

Now that we have said our official good-byes, we are existing in a strange limbo. It feels as though we should be leaving but there is almost another month until we are due to move into the new place. This is partly Mum's fault for taking a BOGOF approach to my birthday party- she shouldn't have combined it with our farewells. But I can see that she didn't want to be organising another party just before the move when she's pretty much single-handedly packing up our house. That's all she does at the moment: assemble and fill boxes. We can no longer use the sitting room- it is a labyrinth of cardboard.

It's getting to us all. Zach keeps stepping out in to the back garden to get away from it. He thinks this is a test. Sometimes the military sends Dad on survival exercises, where they starve him, chuck buckets of water at him and make terrible threats to test his nerve. Zach reckons this is S.H.A.M's survival exercise for the whole family. They want to make us think we're going to be homeless to see what we're made of, to test our metal. Maybe that's true. I'm willing to believe anything right now.

Wednesday 24 August

When I got up this morning, Zach's bed was empty, which is unusual as I'm normally the first of us to wake up. I crept downstairs in my onesie to find him whirling around the downstairs rooms of the house, like a tornado destroying all in its wake, brandishing a permanent black marker pen, marking everything that had not yet been packed. The kitchen units, dishwasher, microwave, oven, walls- all of it had been graffitied with black scrawls.

I didn't care why he was doing it. I just wanted to join in. I couldn't find another pen and Zach looked weary so I made us some peanut butter sandwiches. When he had finally finished, he sank to the floor at the bottom of the stairs and we shared our breakfast.

'Why did you do that?' I asked.

'If I destroy this house, they might have to give us a new one. But I don't suppose it works like that, does it?' he said sadly.

Mum confirmed when she came downstairs that it definitely does not work like that. Then she rang Cathy, who came straight round.

'Shit,' she said as she took in all of the damage. 'Sorry, little ears. Have you taken any of those pills?'

Mum held up the box. 'Nearly,' she said.

'Right, give them to me. Let's keep perspective. It's just stuff, isn't it? Just stuff. And some of the graffiti is quite cool, very urban, a sort of resistance to social and cultural norms,' she added, unconvincingly. Then, when she turned and saw the defaced pastel-blue SMEG fridge, she put her hand over her mouth. 'Look, I can't sugar-coat this, this is a disaster of epic proportions. We need God and your house insurers. I'll pray if you phone them. Come on God, help us with this,' she called out to the ceiling.

After an hour-long telephonic interrogation, during which Cathy intermittently rubbed Badger Balm into Mum's temples, the insurers agreed to send over a team of industrial cleaners, the sort of people that visit trauma sites. This is all starting to feel a bit traumatic. Maybe we are a trauma site.

Friday 26 August

The insurers rang to say the special cleaning people are coming on Monday. I have noticed that Mum has started to walk around staring at the floor- one of the few places Zach didn't deface with his pen. Just looking at the mess seems to stress her. To be fair to her, even Andria took a sharp intake of breath when she came to babysit and she saw Zach's handiwork.

Her efforts to get us to bed had been as successful as usual and we were still awake when Mum and Dad came in from their marriage counselling. It seems to be helping; they were holding hands and, for the first time ever, they had remembered their wedding anniversary, which was today. They've now been married six years.

'What has Dad bought you for your anniwersee?' I asked Mum as she tucked me up.

'He says he's got me a surprise,' said Mum, kissing my nose 'so I'll tell you tomorrow.'

Saturday 28 August

When we went downstairs for breakfast this morning, every last trace of black pen had disappeared. Over muffins and crumpets, Mum said he magicked it all away for her anniversary.

Later on, I heard her telling Andria how Dad had made her sit with her eyes shut whilst he got his wedding anniversary present ready. She had been made to sit like that for half an hour. When she opened them, he had removed all of the pen marks. When he flies his helicopter, he writes notes to himself in black marker pen on plastic boards inserted into the legs of his flying suit and, when he lands, he cleans it off with nail varnish remover and cotton pads. He tried the same trick on the house.

Mum was delighted. Dad is definitely learning to speak her love language. Sadly, the insurance company is not. The annual premium has doubled, even though Mum and Dad didn't make a claim.

'Mrs Child, your son has revealed he is a risk factor, an underwriter's nightmare, akin to timber cladding or a trampoline,' the insurance representative explained.

'When will you reduce it back down?'

'When he moves out.'

'He's two.'

'So in a long time then.'

Monday 29 August

After lengthy negotiations, involving blood, sweat, tears and chocolate Hob Nobs, Dad has got S.H.A.M to let us have the keys to the new house on 6 September, the day before I start school. This means Dad will still be here to help with the move. And as this change of date brings us within S.H.A.M's six-month rule, we are now entitled to professional packers. Professional packers and a filthy house. That was the deal; move in early and they will not ensure its cleanliness.

The promise of not having to move alone quietened any misgivings Mum might have about moving into a tip. She spent the day calling friends and family to cancel the home-spun removal service they were going to provide.

Thursday 30 August

A removal firm came to the house today to assess the size of van they will need. They seemed pleased, given the short notice they have had, that at least half the house is already in boxes. They will finish the packing on Monday and deliver our belongings to our new house on Tuesday.

Friday 2 September

Mum decided to pay to have the house professionally cleaned for the march out. The cleaners came over to give an estimate. They wanted £300 for the general clean, £100 for the carpets and £80 for the oven. Mum was appalled. She said she will do the oven herself. Sadly, her OCD has never extended to the inside of the oven. I suspect this saving might be a false economy for someone who hasn't cleaned their cooker in three years...

Tonight was Mum and Dad's last counselling session. Their homework last week was to buy each other a gift. They exchanged their presents tonight in front of their counsellor. Mum came home sparkling- Dad's present to her was a pair of daisy-shaped pearl and diamond earrings to match her eternity ring. Mum had made a collage of photographs for Dad, which she had put in a heart-shaped frame, showing every year that they have been together, the first one taken when they were teenagers. I think Mum came off better in this exercise.

They had also made cards for one another. Mum's card was an apology for making Dad leave us. She had signed it Ruth 1:16, which is a Bible verse she had inscribed in his wedding ring before they got married. The front of Dad's card simply said 'I adore you.' The words had been written in the sky by a plane.

Monday 5 September

Zach, Dannatt and I spent the weekend with Cathy whilst Mum and Dad prepped the house for the move, filling in picture holes and the crater Zach and I made in the lawn. This morning, when we pulled open our curtains, there was an enormous removal truck outside the house surrounded by our boxes. The packers surged in around us as we finished our breakfast, removing the furniture almost from beneath us. You would put something down and moments later discover it had been packed. It wasn't long before Mum sent the men back onto the truck to search for Elepants, the television and her handbag.

As soon as she was dressed, she put me and Zach in front of CBeebies and got out her oven cleaning kit. She hadn't wanted to clean it any earlier in case it got messed up again. On the fifth attempt, when the oven was still oozing brown froth from every orifice, she sent Dad around to the shop for more cans of Mr Muscle. Eventually, admitting defeat, she allowed him to have a go and the upshot was that vital parts of the oven were boxed up by the movers. Dad only discovered this when the men were closing the back door of the truck and starting up the engine to drive off; there was nothing for it but to accept that half of our West Country oven would wake up in Hampshire. Not an easy situation to explain to those sympathetic housing officers during their final checks but apart from that, we moved without a hitch.

Tuesday 6 September

We left Somerset much later than planned yesterday. Mum didn't want to say good-bye to Cathy. A quick farewell cup of coffee at Cathy's house before we left became three cups of coffee and then supper. Mum and Cathy eventually had to agree not to say good-bye but to pretend they were seeing one another the next day and just wave when we drove away.

As we set off down the road, Cathy and Paul growing smaller and smaller in the rear windscreen, Mum made Dad reverse back to their house. She leapt out of the car and threw her arms around Cathy and they stood in the road crying until the men prised them apart.

We spent the night in a dog-friendly hotel in Hampshire, just a few miles from our new house. As soon as we checked out of the hotel this morning, we went to meet the removal truck in Love Lane. There was a lady housing officer waiting for us by the front door with the keys. As she went to let us in, Dad scooped Mum up in his arms and, to everyone's embarrassment, carried her over the threshold. I was secretly happy to see them so happy.

'I've missed living with you guys,' said Dad, giving us all a big hug.

The rest of the day passed in an exhausting blur. Zach and I made a fort out of the boxes that Mum discarded in the garden after emptying them of our things. We fell asleep hidden beneath several layers of cardboard, waking when it was cold to find Mum calling us inside for beans on toast. She had been very organised with the packing and labelled all of the boxes we needed for tonight and tomorrow so we knew where to find things.

The essentials were: kettle, toaster, coffee and tea, school uniform and Dad's military bags. It was hard to imagine, as I sat on a box eating my dinner, that tomorrow I will be at my new school and Dad will be on his way back to Afghanistan.

Wednesday 7 September

It felt a bit like my birthday this morning when Mum and Dad came into my new bedroom with breakfast and a pile of parcels. I opened some cards and various presents in between bites of toast. Aunty Chloe had sent me a set of hair accessories to match my uniform, Zach had helped Mum choose a pencil case full of pastel-coloured rubbers that smell of strawberry milkshake (and a trigonometry kit he insists I will need) and Cathy had bought me a packed lunch box and matching flask (she has made Mum promise never to let me eat school dinners until the government implements her campaign for them to be organic).

Mum helped me put on my new uniform and plaited my hair before we all assembled in front of the house for photographs. A man in uniform, who was cycling past in the direction of the airfield, pulled over and offered to take a picture of us all together. To say we are a family practised in the art of being late, I was impressed that we arrived at school before they had even opened the gates.

You could instantly pick out the children from my class. They were the ones with either immaculate uniforms or teary mothers, some with both. I felt frightened when I saw my classmates chatting to one another. Everyone else seemed to have a friend. I couldn't remember any of their names.

My new teacher opened a gate by our classroom and beckoned to us.

'I'm Mrs Shepherd. You can come in this way for the next few weeks, whilst you settle.'

I was glad I didn't have to go in through the main gates with the big children. Mum, Dad and Zach followed me in to my classroom. Zach found my peg. It had a label with my name on it and a picture of a rainbow.

'Look at this,' Mum said and I knew that she was taking comfort from it.

Then Dad knelt down in front of me. 'You know that I have to go away again today. I don't want to leave you. I hope you realise that. You, Zach, Mum and Dannatt are the most precious things in my life...'

I thought his voice had broken as he didn't finish his sentence.

'You're Millie, aren't you?' said Mrs Shepherd, coming over to us. 'I knew that because of your Dad's uniform.'

Dad was wearing his desert fatigues, in preparation for his trip. 'We're going to have to be brave little soldiers today, aren't we? Your Dad is going away and so is my husband. In fact, I think they will probably be on the same plane out of Brize. Your Mum wrote to me during the holidays and told me all about it. You and I are going to help one another, aren't we?'

She smiled at me and I smiled back. I liked her.

'There is a little girl called Ruth who I thought you could sit with today.'

She beckoned to a tiny girl with pigtails. Ruth came over, feeling in her pockets for something as she walked towards us.

'My Mum told me about you,' said Ruth. 'I made you a friendship bracelet over the summer.'

She handed it to me. Mum tied it round my wrist.

'Time for good-byes now,' said Mrs Shepherd.

Dad had been looking at something in the book corner. His eyes looked sore when he came over to me.

'Good-bye, beautiful girl. I can't wait to hear all the things you have learnt when I get back.'

I didn't know what to say so I just hugged him. He pulled away from me after a while and then Mum gave me a quick squeeze and Zach waved at me as he packed away some Maths puzzles he'd been doing.

'Come and sit down for the register,' said Mrs Shepherd.

Once I was sitting cross legged on the carpet with the other children, I turned around to wave to Dad one last time but all of the parents had left. A tear rolled down my cheek as Mrs Shepherd called out our names.

'This morning I'm going to tell you all about our topic for the term,' said Mrs Shepherd, closing the register. 'I thought it would be fun to learn about Noah and the Ark because it's something we probably all know something about already. It might be good to start by reading it,' she said, holding up a book.

When she had finished the story, she said: 'When I was getting your coat pegs ready for today, I put a picture from the story by each of your names. If you noticed what yours is, put up your hand.'

Most of us put our hands in the air.

'Roger, what do you have by your peg?'

'A fire extinguisher,' said Roger proudly.

'No, that's an actual fire extinguisher in case we have a fire but it's a good try. Katie, what about you?'

'I need a wee.'

'Off you go then.'

'Millie, how about you?'

'I have a rainbow.'

'Well done. And do you know what rainbows make me think of?'

'No,' I said.

'God's peace. God put the rainbow in the sky as a promise to Noah. Rainbows remind me that God is watching over the whole earth.'

'Does that one there make you think of God?' asked a girl called Miriam, pointing out of the window.

On the horizon there was a rainbow, the biggest and brightest one I had ever seen.

'God's promise of peace to the whole world,' whispered Mrs Shepherd, kneeling down beside me.

Then there was a noise overhead.

'Thunder, Mrs Shepherd,' screeched Roger, diving under a table.

'No, that's a chinook,' said Mrs Shepherd.

The sort of helicopter that Dad now flies came into view, huge and noisy with its twin rotor blades spinning furiously. It flew past our school in the direction of the rainbow.

'What's that you're holding?' Mrs Shepherd asked me.

I was clutching the badge Dad that velcros onto his flying suit every day. I sneaked it into my rucksack this morning.

'That's your Dad's squadron badge, isn't it? The same squadron my husband is on. I bet you don't know what those words mean,' she said. 'Animo et fide.'

I had no idea.

'Courage and faith,' she said quietly, answering her own question.

We all watched through the window, some of us waving, until the helicopter was too small to see and the rainbow had dissolved.

Author's Note

Some of you will know, and many may guess, that I am Anna, only more flawed! Not everything in the book has really happened to me or my family but some of Anna's struggles are based upon my own.

I offer my story in the hope that it brings comfort, maybe some giggles, but mostly a sense of solidarity for anyone who identifies with Anna's difficulties.

Marriage, parenting, mental health issues and military life, when mixed in part, or all together, can create a storm. But a storm, when mixed with sunshine, always creates a rainbow.

As a woman of faith, God is my sun but there have certainly been times when I couldn't feel His rays and He has reached me through others. This is my little list of sunshine for anyone in a storm, a list to help you find your own rainbow:

Marriage Counselling:

Seeking help is healthy in every sphere of life and it should be the same for marriage. Every branch of the military offers free access to counselling sessions to couples in need of support.

General information on marriage counselling can be sought by anyone through the Relate website.

www.relate.org.uk

The Marriage and Parenting Courses:

Whether your marriage is rocking or is on the rocks, whether you feel you are winning or losing at parenting, these courses are a one size fits all way to strengthen relationships. Check out the website to see if there's a course near you. These courses are run internationally, meaning wherever you are in the world, you may be able to find one nearby.

themarriagecourse.org

The Marriage Foundation

An organisation that champions marriage in a variety of ways, from offering information and research about marriage and relationships to providing links to help couples access help.

www.themarriagefoundation.org

DisrespectNoBody

As much as I champion marriage, I would never want anything I have written to suggest people should remain within a physically, mentally or emotionally abusive relationship. This is a government website sign-posting the different organisations that will support those in abusive relationships to get help and advice.

www.disrespectnobody.co.uk

Care for the Family

An international UK charity that provides support to promote strong family life and help to those facing family difficulties.

www.careforthefamily.org.uk

Your GP

If you or any of your family members needs help with depression, anxiety or any other mental health issues, start with a visit to your GP and keep pushing on the doors of the professionals until you get the help you deserve.

Mind

A charity providing information and support to anyone seeking help with a mental health issue- their website is a great place to navigate the resources and different types of help available.

www.mind.org.uk

CYPMHS (formerly CAMHS)

This stands for Children & Young People's Mental Health Service, which is a term used for all NHS services that work with children and young people. It is organised regionally so you need to find the one for your local area, which ought to have its own website. If it's not clear who to contact, your local GP practice should be able to point you in the right direction. Referrals can be made by a GP but it's worth noting that parents and young people of a certain age can also self-refer.

Military Padres

An awesome group of men and women who serve military personnel and their families on and off the battlefield. Quite literally, they are the glue that has held some of us together. Not only do they offer support themselves, they are practical, well-connected and can put you in touch with organisations and individuals who might be able to help you if that's needed/wanted. Whilst my husband was away for a long stretch and I was finding parenting hard alone, my padre arranged, in a matter of days, for a parent support adviser to visit me at home to give me a hand, which was invaluable.

For those outside the military, vicars, chaplains and pastors offer support to those with or without a faith or belief system.

The Armed Forces' Christian Union (AFCU)

A military organisation that supports all members of the UK Armed Forces in a range of ways, both spiritually and practically. One of the most precious aspects of my journey as a military wife has been my involvement with this exceptional group of people, many of whom I now call my friends.

www.afcu.org.uk

For more of my writing, you can find me at my website:

www.eagletswings.com

Acknowledgements

Thank you to everyone who has helped me along the way in turning what started life as a Christmas card Round Robin into an actual book!

Thank you to my dear friend (and super talented children's author), Donna David, who waded through my first draft and who has been such a kind and supportive writing buddy ever since.

Thank you, Liesel and Marina, for tirelessly proof-reading my penultimate draft and making such helpful and encouraging suggestions.

Thank you, Joe, Charlotte and Romain, for touting my work around and nudging me towards publication with your generous help.

Thank you, Chrissy, for reading my final draft and buoying me up with expletive-filled praise!

Thank you, Mike, for letting me harangue you with a million tech-related questions and for helping me with the soul-destroying publishing process.

Thank you to my mum, Mopsy, for painstakingly weeding out my bad grammar and spelling with a zeal not seen since Michael Gove was Education Secretary. And for making her friends promise to buy a copy!

Thank you to my amazing sister, Amy Dyas, beautiful blogger and artist, who always champions my work with boundless love and enthusiasm.

Thank you to our amazing children, for being so supportive, loving and kind about Mum trying to be an author!

And thank you to my husband, Jack, who comforted me through the rejections, secretly sent my book out to help me get it published, designed the prettiest cover when he should have been writing his dissertation and who has, as ever, been my best friend throughout.

Printed in Great Britain
by Amazon

76404359R00173

Perhaps like other military children, I was conceived before I was planned. My father is an RAF pilot and I sometimes wonder if this is true of all military operations. Or maybe it's just my family's unique way of operating...

And so begins the life of Millie, newly born to newly-weds Will and Anna. Everything is new to baby Millie; almost the same is true of Anna. Switching from career girl to military wife in the time it took to say 'I do', Anna is totally out of her depth on the battlefield that is military life in modern Britain. Juggling Millie and a wayward puppy, she lurches from one ridiculous disaster to another. As Iraq and Afghanistan call Will away with increasing regularity, the scrapes start to become less funny. With Anna and Millie's world beginning to unravel, will anyone notice their invisible wounds? Will someone patch them up? And can Anna's marriage survive?

Katie is a military wife, mother of 3 and recent puppy owner whose day-job is in charity work, but who also daydreams of being a writer. She moves where her husband's job calls from the Middle East to Oxfordshire where they now live in their 8th family home. Katie hopes this book blesses anyone struggling to create order and find meaning in the chaos of family life, relationships, marriage and work.

All proceeds of this book will be donated to the Afghanistan Crisis Appeal of the British Red Cross, and the RAF Benevolent Fund. Thank you for your generous support.

ISBN 9798796903629

90000

9 798796 903629